ABOUT THE AUTHORS

AMY WALLACE is the author of fifteen books, including (with her family) the number-one *New York Times* bestselling *Book of Lists*, which has sold over eight million copies worldwide. Over the years, these were followed by four more bestselling *Book of Lists* editions. She also wrote *The Psychic Healing Book*, with Bill Henkin, now in print for thirty years. Family collaborations include *The Intimate Sex Lives of Famous People* (recently re-released in an updated edition by Feral House), *Significa* (based on a long-running *Parade* magazine column), and *The Book of Predictions*. She coauthored a biography, *The Two: The Story of the Original Siamese Twins*, with her father, the world-famous novelist Irving Wallace. Her second biography was *The Prodigy: A Biography of William James Sidis, the World's Greatest Child Prodigy*. She also wrote an acclaimed erotic novel, *Desire*. Among her most recent works are the controversial memoir *Sorcerer's Apprentice: My Life with Carlos Castaneda* and *The Official Punk Rock Book of Lists* (with Handsome Dick Manitoba). Amy shares her birthday, July 3, with Franz Kafka and Mississippi John Hurt. She lives in Los Angeles with two cats, Hank and Bella, who serve as her editors by lying across the keyboard at critical moments.

SCOTT BRADLEY was born on July 25, 1972, in Springfield, Missouri, the birthplace of serial killer Francis Dolarhyde in *Red Dragon* by Thomas Harris. Scott considers himself generally better-adjusted than Mr. Dolarhyde, however, and even earned a bachelor's degree in English from the University of Missouri–Kansas City. He has worked a variety of jobs, including fast food cook, security guard, office temp, Hollywood talent agency assistant, and video store clerk. His criticism and journalism have appeared in *Film Quarterly*, *The Kansas City Star*, *Creative Screenwriting*, and other publications, as well as on the podcast Pod of Horror. He originally joined *The Book of Lists* series as a staff writer/researcher in 2004. He is at work on a novel and (with Jason Aaron) on the literary biography of the legendary Vietnam War author Gustav Hasford. Scott lives in Los Angeles, across the street from Amy Wallace, and suggests you visit www.myspace.com/ScottBradley007 for more information on his exploits, past and present.

DEL HOWISON, with his wife, Sue, created America's only all-horror book and gift store, Dark Delicacies, as fans and for fans, and they remain among horror's biggest aficionados. They, and the store, have been featured on many television documentaries concerning horror and the nature of evil. A former photojournalist, Del has also written articles for a variety of publications, including *Rue Morgue* and *Gauntlet* magazines, along with a foreword for the Wildside Press edition of *Varney the Vampyre*. His short stories have appeared in a variety of anthologies, and he coedited, with Jeff Gelb, the Bram Stoker Award–winning anthology *Dark Delicacies: Original Tales of Horror and the Macabre*, and its follow-up, *Dark Delicacies 2: Fear*.

THE
BOOK OF LISTS
HORROR

THE
BOOK OF LISTS
HORROR

**An All-New Collection Featuring
Stephen King, Eli Roth, Ray Bradbury, and More,
with an Introduction by Gahan Wilson**

AMY WALLACE, SCOTT BRADLEY, AND DEL HOWISON

HARPER

NEW YORK • LONDON • TORONTO • SYDNEY

HARPER

HarperCollins books may be purchased for educational, business, or sales promotional use. For information please write: Special Markets Department, HarperCollins Publishers, 10 East 53rd Street, New York, NY 10022.

FIRST EDITION

Designed by Laura Kaeppel

Library of Congress Cataloging-in-Publication Data is available upon request.

ISBN 978-0-06-153726-4

08 09 10 11 12 OV/RRD 10 9 8 7 6 5 4 3 2 1

To my soul brother, Ned Claflin. "In the middle of the journey of our life I came to myself in a dark wood where the straight way was lost." Thanks for the flashlight, Ned. I love you.

—A.W.

For my mother, Linda Bradley (1942–2006), and my father, Scott G. Bradley, Ph.D. As all other words fail, I can only say: "I love you and thank you for everything." And in loving memory of my grandparents: Sherman and Gladys Bradley, and James "Jiggs" Brake.

—S.B.

To the group at Champs. May this instigate a bunch of drunken arguments.

—D.H.

"Horror, at least in its artistic presentations, can be a comfort. And, like any agent of enlightenment, it may even confer—if briefly—a sense of power, wisdom, and transcendence, especially if the conferee is a willing one with a true feeling for ancient mysteries and a true fear of the skullduggery which a willing heart usually senses in the unknown."

—Thomas Ligotti, "The Consolations of Horror"

"'The horror! The horror!'"

—Joseph Conrad, *Heart of Darkness*

CONTENTS

ACKNOWLEDGMENTS

The authors would like to collectively thank the following individuals: our agent, Wendy Schmalz, who made the deal; at Harper-Collins: our editor, Rakesh Satyal, for his patience and guidance; Rob Crawford, always on top of things; and Kolt Beringer and Patricia Fernandez for genius copyediting; Gahan Wilson, for his wonderful introduction; and John Skipp, the "Fifth Beatle" of *The Book of Lists: Horror*, for his boundless wisdom and amazing contributions to this endeavor.

Amy Wallace's Acknowledgments

Thanks to the tireless Scott Bradley, who is almost solely responsible for steering this book into the light (or should I say dark?), and to Del Howison, who generously called on friends and acquaintances, and brought in wonderful contributions. To the inimitable Wendy Schmalz, my favorite agent ever, who as usual made a perfect marriage. Of friends, associates, and helpers, there are too many to name. Emily Bradley and Kevin Kelly, who brought energy and peace when each was needed; to Master John Skipp, who got his hands dirty at the crucial stages, *and* cooked a killer shepherd's pie, thus dirtying them again. Richard Stanley, who inspired me to watch all with my third eye; Scarlett Amaris, instant new friend. Sophie Duriez, always happy for me; Susan Rosner Pierson, always loving and cheering; Don Cushman, ever dear; Adam Parfrey and Jodi Wille, there are no words; all my friends at Skylight Books, too many to name; Mes Amis, Chip and Laurence, with gratitude; Irene Miracle, muse, beautiful artist, and sublime friend; F. X. Feeney, a wonderful writer whose continuous friendship and support has been a blessing; Joseph of the Best Fish Taco in Ensenada (www.best fishtacoinensenada.com); Linda Ramone and John Cafiero, Satan's Little Helpers, for their boundless generosity; Will, off in Romania but here in spirit; inspirational Ted and Erik; Tom and Nancy; Charles Black; Danny Fields, generous never to a fault; Michael, Michelle, and Luca, the Perfect Neighbors for a Writer. William Dailey, an angel always, especially at the eleventh hour. Lisa Tuttle, long-lost friend discovered, who inspires me in every way and knows what's *creepy*. T. E. D. Klein, one of the coolest guys ever—he is splendid and he answers the phone sounding like Alfred Hitchcock. My cousin Danny, I love you! My brother, who I knew would write a perfect list, all while he said, "I don't know anything about it!"—I love you. To the spirit of Robert Aickman, who opened my heart and soul to whatever that thing is they call horror, or "strange stories." Finally, to the peerless Hank and Bella, who slept on my computer and notebooks at the most inopportune times—I love you.

Scott Bradley's Acknowledgments

First and foremost thanks go to my coauthors, Amy Wallace and Del Howison, as well as our esteemed contributors, for helping unleash

The Book of Lists: Horror on the world. And deepest gratitude for aiding and abetting far beyond the call of duty goes to: Hank and Bella, the two greatest cats in the world (and their savior, Shelly Tidoni); my sisters, Sherri Cervantes (and her family) and Tammy Walker; my grandmother, Shirley Brake; my beloved mentor Yale Udoff and his fabulous wife, Shula; John Skipp and Mitch Brian, the big brothers I never had 'til I met them; Jason Aaron (Semper Gus); Melina Neet (I'm waiting to be thanked in *your* book!); "Wild" Bill Edwards (for adventures in Los Feliz and Romania); David Wallechinsky and the memory of Irving Wallace (for creating *The Book of Lists* series—an extraordinary legacy to live up to); the Video Hut boys, past and present—Ozzie, Andrew, Levon, Michael Bancroft, Derrek Everette, and Davey Johnson (Weeeeeeee!); Eric Press (for crab cakes and for turning me on to *Family Portraits: A Trilogy of America*); Richard Stanley (for magic, mystery, and the M.A.R.K.–13) and Miss Scarlett Amaris (who reads even more than *I* do!); Don D'Auria of Leisure Books; Franz Rodenkirchen; Irene Miracle; F. X. Feeney; Tom O'Connor; Jörg Buttgereit and Charlie Podrebarac (for generosity with images); Charles Black; Mark Savage, Stephen Volk, and Mikita Brottman (for taking the plunge with early lists); Tim Sullivan; James Gunn; Misssssssster Tom Gauer; Peter Avellino; Deb Wilborn (the only good writing teacher I ever had in school); Dallas Mayr, Ramsey Campbell, and Joe Hill (for answering trivia inquiries); everyone at Skylight Books (and to the memory of Lucy the Cat); Tony Timpone; Mark Justice, David T. Wilbanks, Pod of Horror, and its listeners; Mark Valentine; Toni Aloy; Ken Bussanmas; Eric John; Leo Thompson; David Kerekes; Joseph Cordova; Tim Lucas; the Flying Maciste Brothers; Kevin Kelly (healer of sick computers) and Emily (no relation) Bradley (formatting queen); Joe Straughan and his mother, Liz (for helping me remember that there *were* some "good old days"). Extra thanks to the Internet, without which this would have been a much thinner book. Finally, enormous thanks to _____ (I *know* I'm going to forget someone, so insert your name there).

Del Howison's Acknowledgments

First, and most importantly, to Amy and Scott. They brought me in with a lot of dreams and desire and I hope I didn't let them down. I am proud to be a part of this. To Sue, for putting up with the cave-dwelling writer who speaks in grunts and probably leaves her life at all the wrong times to go write. To Shelley Cherwinski, who was the muse on my first published story and who occasionally has to slap me into the correct state of mind. Fill up another glass of muse, please! To all the people who stepped up and gave us a list, and all of those who tried but couldn't due to time and industry constraints. We'll get you next time around. Finally, to John Skipp, who kept his head and made things fun again when they may have been slipping away. Thank you to all of the above.

INTRODUCTION

Trying to prod a thing as elusive, sneaky, and totally out-of-bounds as horror into an informative and highly usable book of lists would seem to be pretty much impossible.

Nevertheless, Amy Wallace (who cowrote the first *Book of Lists* in 1977 with her father, Irving Wallace, and brother David Wallechinsky), Scott Bradley, and Del Howison took it into their heads for some strange reason to inspire and/or gather up lists created by some of the world's most obsessed and knowledgeable specialists in and creators of horror, living and dead (trust a horror writer to contribute to a book after he or she is dead!), and they seem to have no serious problems whatsoever in successfully and neatly arranging them all in a tidy and accessible fashion, so that the book's a fortunate guide to anyone interested in the subject, ranging from total tyros to dedicated, lifelong aficionados.

The book will also educate and stimulate fans in a wide variety of ways, from revealing delightfully odd and surprising facets of the field and its varied practitioners, which should entertain the most blasé, to using the list format as a teaching device, which wonderfully, and sometimes downright awesomely, will open their eyes—as they certainly did mine—to aspects of horror rarely considered and new ways of looking at it, which will refresh and delight and downright surprise its most sophisticated fans.

The lists of best horror works are written by such towering figures as Stephen King, Robert Bloch, and Karl Edward Wagner, and, if put to use, would doubtless make an addict out of the most determined horror hater (there actually are such people). Guides to very special favorite horror fields are not neglected. Thomas Ligotti presents ten classics of horror poetry, and S. P. Somtow's opera list includes *Götterdämmerung* and *Don Giovanni*, which I think qualify fully by featuring, respectively, the end of the world and a living statue dragging singing victims off to hell.

There are a number of very funny lists, such as editor Anthony Timpone's rueful "Ten Movies I Wish I'd Never Put on the Cover of *Fangoria*"; T. E. D. Klein's "Twenty-Five Most Familiar Horror Plots" (of which my favorite is "Hey, I'm Really Dead!") and C. Courtney Joyner's well-observed "Ten Top Horror Movie Surgical Blunders." Perhaps the funniest title of the funny lists is Vince Churchill's "Wow, the Black Guy Lived!"

Maybe most interesting of all the categories are lists of widely varied horror works which will—I guarantee it—make you see legendary works of horror, or horror itself, in an entirely new light. I'll only cite two of them and let the rest come clawing at you out of the darkness: Caitlín R. Kiernan's sly "Thirteen of the Top Ten Lovecraftian Films Not Actually Based (or Only Loosely Based) on the Works of H. P. Lovecraft," which has forever and permanently, profoundly altered my opinion of the origin of one of my very absolutely favorite monsters, and may do the same for you; and the really brilliant "Ten Horror Films that Aren't Horror Films" by *Video Watchdog* editor Tim Lucas, which I think I can guarantee will remarkably, and healthily, widen your definition of horror itself.

Have a good time.

—Gahan Wilson

Gahan Wilson is the legendary and internationally famous cartoonist of the macabre, whose work appears regularly in Playboy *and* The New Yorker *and is available in numerous collections. He is also a well known and popular horror and mystery author. His many books include* Eddie Deco's Last Caper, Everybody's Favorite Duck, *and* Gravedigger's Party.

THE BOOK OF LISTS: HORROR
WRITING STAFF

ABBREVIATIONS

A.W.	Amy Wallace
D.H.	Del Howison
J.S.	John Skipp
L.M.	Lisa Morton
M.B.	Mitch Brian
R.P.	Rick Pickman
S.B.	Scott Bradley

A NOTE ON SPOILERS

precedes list entries that feature potential spoilers, as well as entire lists with numerous possible spoilers. While the authors have made every attempt to identify spoilers, one reader's spoiler could be another's old news, so we apologize for any we didn't catch.

CHAPTER 1

"Keep Repeating . . .
'It's Only a Movie . . . !'"

FEAR ON THE SILVER SCREEN

THE TOP SIX GROSSING HORROR FILMS OF ALL TIME IN THE UNITED STATES (ADJUSTED FOR INFLATION*)

Title	Adjusted Gross	Unadjusted Gross	Year
1. Jaws	$842,758,600	$260,000,000	1975
2. The Exorcist	$727,541,800	$232,671,011	1973
3. Jurassic Park	$567,234,400	$357,067,947	1993
4. The Sixth Sense	$378,870,700	$293,506,292	1999
5. The Rocky Horror Picture Show	$362,356,800	$112,892,319	1975
6. Ghost	$338,641,200	$217,631,306	1990

*Adjusted to the 2007 average ticket price of $6.58.
Source: www.boxofficemojo.com

SIX STARS WHO TURNED DOWN
FAMOUS HORROR MOVIE ROLES

1. **Bela Lugosi as the Monster in *Frankenstein* (1931):** Coming off the title role in the hit 1931 film version of *Dracula*, Bela Lugosi seemed like the natural choice to star as the creature in *Frankenstein*. While make-up tests with Lugosi were indeed conducted and shot, ultimately he did not play the role, although accounts differ as to why. Lugosi claimed that he "read the script and didn't like it. So I asked to be withdrawn from the picture." However, Jack Pierce, the film's makeup designer, was quoted as saying that the star "had too many ideas of his own that didn't correspond with those of the producer, Carl Laemmle. Lugosi thought his ideas were better than everybody's." Whatever the case, the part went to a forty-four-year-old character actor named Boris Karloff, and the rest is horror history.

2. **Shirley MacLaine as Chris MacNeil in *The Exorcist* (1973):** Author William Peter Blatty used his friend Shirley MacLaine as the inspiration for Chris MacNeil, the movie star whose daughter Regan is a victim of demonic possession, right down to giving the character a similar last name. When MacLaine signed a deal with producer Lew Grade, she tried to interest him in making the film version of *The Exorcist*. However, the producer made a lowball offer on the hot material, which was declined, and MacLaine ended up starring in another supernatural thriller, *The Possession of Joel Delaney* (1972). After other major actresses were considered by Blatty and director William Friedkin, the role eventually went to Ellen Burstyn, who earned an Academy Award nomination for Best Actress. In an odd

side-story, MacLaine has long maintained that the image on the novel's dust jacket cover was a distorted photograph of her daughter Sachi that was taken by Blatty, although the author has repeatedly denied this claim.

3. **Sterling Hayden as Quint in *Jaws* (1975):** The legendary star of *The Asphalt Jungle* and *Johnny Guitar* was selected by director Steven Spielberg to play the crusty shark hunter Quint in the adaptation of Peter Benchley's bestseller. (Lee Marvin was also briefly considered.) However, Hayden was in the midst of legal problems due to unpaid taxes, and his salary would have been subject to a levy by the Internal Revenue Service. Although several ideas were considered to circumvent the problem, none were deemed viable and Hayden ultimately passed. Veteran actor Robert Shaw (who called the script "shit") took the role and delivered what many consider the single finest acting moment in the film: Quint's monologue about the sinking of the USS *Indianapolis*.

4. and 5. **Gene Hackman and Michelle Pfeiffer as Dr. Hannibal Lecter and Clarice Starling in *The Silence of the Lambs* (1991):** Orion Pictures acquired the film rights to the bestselling Thomas Harris novel *The Silence of the Lambs* in 1988 because Gene Hackman expressed interest in directing and writing the movie version. He also planned to star as serial killer Dr. Hannibal "the Cannibal" Lecter (the role had previously been played by Brian Cox in Michael Mann's 1986 film *Manhunter*). By mid-1989, Hackman had dropped out of the project, and Jonathan Demme took over as director. Demme offered the role of FBI trainee Clarice Starling to Michelle Pfeiffer, with whom he had worked on the comedy *Married to the Mob*. Pfeiffer found the material too dark

and declined. When *The Silence of the Lambs* was finally made, Anthony Hopkins played Lecter and Jodie Foster played Starling. Both won Academy Awards for their performances.

6. Jodie Foster as Clarice Starling in *Hannibal* (2001): The massive success of *The Silence of the Lambs* virtually assured a sequel—however, it took Thomas Harris more than a decade to deliver one. When the novel *Hannibal* appeared in 1999, many readers were angered by the outré plot, which featured an ending that had Clarice Starling and Hannibal Lecter running away together as lovers. Among the outraged fans was Jodie Foster, who felt the novel's conclusion "betrayed" Clarice (director Jonathan Demme and screenwriter Ted Tally, both Oscar winners for *Lambs*, also passed; Ridley Scott was hired as director, and David Mamet and Steven Zaillian wrote the script). Foster later added: "Clarice meant so much to Jonathan and me, she really did, and I know it sounds kind of strange to say, but there was no way that either of us could really trample on her." Many actresses, including Hilary Swank and Cate Blanchett, were considered for the role, which ultimately went to Julianne Moore, who said: "Of course people are going to compare my interpretation with Jodie Foster's . . . but this film is going to be very different." It was. And, despite modifying the controversial ending, the movie proved as polarizing to fans as the novel.

—S.B.

RAY BRADBURY'S FIVE HORROR FILMS
THAT MOST INFLUENCED HIM AS A YOUTH

A native of Waukegan, Illinois, Ray Bradbury is the author of The Martian Chronicles, Fahrenheit 451, The October Country, Dandelion Wine, Something Wicked This Way Comes, The Illustrated Man, *and countless other classic works of science fiction, fantasy, and horror. He has also been the recipient of numerous awards, including a star on the Hollywood Walk of Fame in 2002, and the National Medal of the Arts in 2004.*

The following was dictated to Del Howison on September 16, 2007, at Ray Bradbury's home in Los Angeles, California.

1. *The Hunchback of Notre Dame* (1923): I was three years old when I saw this film. It made me want to be a hunchback.
2. *The Phantom of the Opera* (1925): I was five years old when this came out. It made me want to be Lon Chaney.
3. *The Lost World* (1925): It made me fall in love with dinosaurs. I've loved them all my life. I wrote all kinds of things about them. John Huston read something I wrote about them and it caused him to hire me to write the screenplay for *Moby Dick*.
4. *King Kong* (1933): I fell for Fay Wray. She's the best. Years later my friend Ray Harryhausen got to go up to the top of the Empire State Building with her. That's something, isn't it?
5. *The Mummy* (1932): The one with Boris Karloff. I wanted to be a mummy strolling out of a tomb.

MATCH THE HORROR FILM WITH ITS TAGLINE

_____ 1. *The Blob* (1958)

_____ 2. *Last House on the Left* (1972)

_____ 3. *The Texas Chainsaw Massacre* (1974)

_____ 4. *Dawn of the Dead* (1978)

_____ 5. *Halloween* (1978)

_____ 6. *Alien* (1979)

_____ 7. *The Amityville Horror* (1979)

_____ 8. *Friday the 13th* (1980)

_____ 9. *The Shining* (1980)

_____ 10. *An American Werewolf in London* (1981)

_____ 11. *Cannibal Ferox* (1981)

_____ 12. *The Howling* (1981)

_____ 13. *Scanners* (1981)

_____ 14. *Poltergeist* (1982)

_____ 15. *The Thing* (1982)

_____ 16. *A Nightmare on Elm Street* (1984)

_____ 17. *Gothic* (1986)

_____ 18. *Manhunter* (1986)

_____ 19. *The Exorcist III* (1990)

_____ 20. *Hardware* (1990)

_____ 21. *Se7en* (1995)

_____ 22. *Hannibal* (2001)

_____ 23. *House of 1000 Corpses* (2003)

_____ 24. *Shaun of the Dead* (2004)

_____ 25. *Hostel* (2006)

_____ 26. *Snakes on a Plane* (2006)

A. "In the 21st Century there will be a new endangered species . . . Man."

B. "Break the Silence."

C. "Man is the warmest place to hide."

D. "Do you dare walk these steps again?"

E. "Sit back. Relax. Enjoy the fright."

F. "Let he who is without sin try to survive."

G. "Indescribable . . . Indestructible . . . Nothing can stop it!"

H. "Welcome to your worst nightmare."

I. "A romantic comedy. With zombies."

J. "The night HE came home . . ."

K. "Who will survive and what will be left of them?"

L. "Imagine your worst fear a reality."

M. "The monster movie."

N. "A masterpiece of modern horror."

O. "For God's sake, get out!"

P. "Conjure up your deepest, darkest fear . . . now call that fear to life."

Q. "In space, no one can hear you scream."

R. "It's just you and me now, sport . . ."

S. "Banned in 31 countries."

T. "To avoid fainting, keep repeating 'It's only a movie . . . It's only a movie . . .'"

U. "A 24-hour nightmare of terror."

V. "When there's no more room in Hell, the dead will walk the Earth."

W. "They're here."

X. "If Nancy doesn't wake up screaming, she won't wake up at all."

Y. "The most shocking tale of carnage ever seen."

Z. "10 Seconds: The Pain Begins. 15 Seconds: You Can't Breathe. 20 Seconds: You Explode."

JOHNNY RAMONE'S TOP TEN FAVORITE HORROR MOVIES

Johnny Ramone (left) on the set of *Bride of Re-Animator* with actor David Gale. (Photograph © the John Family Trust. All Rights Reserved. Reprinted by permission. www.johnnyramone.com.)

Johnny Ramone was the guitarist for the legendary punk rock group the Ramones. In 2003 he was named the sixteenth Greatest Guitarist of all time by Rolling Stone *magazine. A lifelong horror fan, he compiled the following list himself prior to his death in 2004. Johnny's widow, Linda, provides additional insight within the quotes below.*

1. *Bride of Frankenstein* (1935): The James Whale–directed classic was Johnny Ramone's favorite horror movie of all time. Acquiring an original half-sheet from *Bride* was one of his happiest moments as a collector. Possessing one of only five known surviving copies of the incredibly rare "style B" half-sheet issued by Universal in 1935, Johnny even secured one of the best in the business to meticulously restore some minor imperfections in the vintage piece. Another of the five pieces in existence is owned by Johnny's friend and fellow collector, Kirk Hammet, of Metallica, who coincidentally bought Johnny an original pressbook from *Bride* one year for his birthday.

   "Johnny never thought he would own an original piece from this film. That *Bride* half-sheet was his most cherished piece in his huge memorabilia collection. It was also the most money he ever spent on a poster."

2. *The Invisible Man* (1933): Another Universal classic directed by James Whale makes the top two in the legendary punk guitarist's top ten list.

   "He thought Claude Raines was amazing in the part because he had a great voice with such a strong presence that you felt he was there even when you couldn't see him on screen."

   Johnny had an original 1935 insert from *The Invisible Man* in his memorabilia collection.

3. *The Texas Chainsaw Massacre* (1974): The Ramones debut album released in April of 1976 on Sire/Warner Brothers includes a song titled "Chainsaw," based on this cutting-edge classic directed by Tobe Hooper.

"Johnny loved it. He thought it was crazy! He went to visit Ed Neal (the hitchhiker) at his house and kept in touch with him. After they met, Johnny said he thought Ed was a really nice guy, so different from his character the hitchhiker."

4. *Night of the Living Dead* (1968): "Johnny felt this movie [directed by George Romero] was shot amazingly and looked genuinely scary. He really got a kick out of seeing the footage from *Night of the Living Dead* intercut with footage of Ramones fans in Buenos Aires swarming the band's van and trapping them inside." (See the "Night of the Living Pinheads" scene from *Ramones Raw*, directed by John Cafiero.)

5. *King Kong* (1933): "Johnny said that when he first saw it as a kid, *King Kong* seemed really scary to him. Whenever he liked something he'd watch it over and over again. He watched *King Kong* all the time on WOR's Million Dollar Movie. Years later he would write to Fay Wray to get autographed photos for his collection."

Johnny is immortalized in an eight-foot tall bronze memorial statue located in the "Garden of Legends" at the Hollywood Forever Cemetery in Los Angeles alongside the final resting place of Fay Wray, who passed away the same year, 2004.

6. *Re-Animator* (1985): "He *loved* this film. He watched it all the time. Anytime anyone would come over to our house, he would always push it on them and try to get them to watch it. He thought the lead [Jeffery Combs as Herbert West] gave a great performance and he met him at a poster show in L.A. He even visited the set of the sequel (1990's *Bride of Re-Animator*) while it was shooting here in Hollywood."

7. *The Evil Dead* (1981): "He really enjoyed the inventive camera work in this one. Johnny always said he felt the director [Sam Raimi]

had started a new technique in the way people were shooting horror films."

8. *The Wolf Man* (1941): "He had the one-sheet, and whenever he collected an original poster from a movie he loved, it was a big thing for him. He thought the makeup for the original Wolfman looked great and was hard to compete with even in modern movies. He loved the Universal monsters and the look of those classic films."

9. *Freaks* (1932): The line "Gooble Gobble" from the infamous wedding scene in Tod Browning's cult classic (released by MGM and later banned for years), inspired the soon-to-be equally infamous phrase "Gabba Gabba Hey" penned by the Ramones in the song "Pinhead" from their 1977 sophomore release *Leave Home*. The band's fascination with pinheads would also carry over into their live show. A masked pinhead mascot appearing on stage wielding a "Gabba Gabba Hey" sign quickly became a staple in their live performances. The Ramones would revisit the *Freaks* theme with photos of many real-life oddities featured in the packaging of the album *Animal Boy* (1986). A UK 12-inch single ("Something to Believe In") from the 1986 release included *Freaks* star Prince Randian aka "the Living Torso" on the sleeve.

"Johnny owned two different original 1932 half-sheets, the one-sheet, and a set of the original lobby cards from this film. He loved *Freaks* and so did the Ramones."

10. *Psycho* (1960): Rounding out the list at number ten is Alfred Hitchcock's classic starring Anthony Perkins.

"Johnny thought Janet Leigh looked great in it and that the shower scene was one of the scariest ever shot. He was a big fan of Bernard Herrmann, who did the score for the movie."

Thanks to Ron Moore and John Cafiero for their assistance.

PROFESSOR LEO BRAUDY'S ELEVEN FAVORITE MOMENTS OF HORROR VS. TERROR IN FILM

 Professor Leo Braudy teaches seventeenth- and eighteenth-century English literature, film history and criticism, and American culture at the University of Southern California. He has written the books The World in a Frame: What We See in Films, The Frenzy of Renown: Fame and its History, *and* From Chivalry to Terrorism: War and the Changing Nature of Masculinity. *He also coedits, with Marshall Cohen, the widely used anthology* Film Theory and Criticism, *now going into its seventh edition. His most recent book is* On the Waterfront *in the BFI Film Classics series, and he is working on a book about the idea of the monstrous.*

In the late eighteenth century, when folktales, novels, and paintings were busy spreading the fear of darkness in contrast with the Enlightenment proclamations of progress and a new world, horror was considered a lesser form than terror, not just the synonym it is today. To inspire horror was to cause a physical reaction, much as the word itself came from a Latin root meaning to make your hair stand on end.

Terror, as in Matthew G. Lewis's *Tales of Terror* (1801), was a different matter entirely. The physical might enter into terror, as it did in the period of the French Revolution called the Terror, when thousands were sent to the guillotine. But in essence terror was a spiritual reaction, a sense of awe and dread that sank into one's soul. Writers who produced a sense of horror in their readers were doing something lower-level, akin to a skeleton popping out of closet in a fun house. Horror made you fear for your own safety, while terror shook the foundations of your belief in an orderly universe and a benevolent God.

It's easier to choose my favorite moments of horror than terror in the movies, perhaps because movies depend so much on what my wife calls "the jumping out effect." She means mere surprise, the gruesome figure beyond the frame you didn't know was there, the unexpected dump into a pit filled with poisonous snakes, the seemingly comfortable easy chair that turns out to be a torture device. But the moments of juicy horror must have a bit of terror in them, something eerie and unexplainable.

Horror

1. Alfred Hitchcock was the master of anticipation. One of his great moments occurs when Arbogast, the detective in *Psycho* (1960), goes up the stairs to investigate the room of Norman Bates's mother, and Norman (disguised as his mother, although we don't know that yet) comes out with chef's knife raised to kill him and slashes away. Hitchcock shoots this from overhead in longshot until we are close up on Arbogast's bloody face. All of us (except Arbogast) knew it was going to happen, but it still chilled the blood when it did.

2. Another anticipation moment is the first sight of the Thing in Christian Nyby's *Thing from Another World* (1951). After its body has been chopped out of the arctic ice, it escapes when a fearful soldier drapes the ice cake with a working electric blanket, only to have Its arm ripped off by sled dogs. But that severed arm revives on its own, and so the motley crew of scientists and military people in the polar station know it's still around. Their Geiger counters show that it's in the greenhouse behind the door. They open the door and there it is. I never knew what it looked like in that scene until years later when I taught the film. I guess my ten-year-old eyes must have been closed the entire time when it came out of the greenhouse door and they slammed the door on its arm, chopping off its chitinous fingernails.

3. Another, even more gruesome moment, from *The Thing*, this time the John Carpenter remake (1982), which goes back more closely to John W. Campbell Jr.'s original short story. The inhabitants of the isolated polar station have this time gradually realized that there is a shape-shifter among them (no Tom Corbett outfit this time!) and suspicion falls on the outsider MacReady, the helicopter pilot, whom they try first to freeze outside and then to gang up on. In the fight, one of the men has what seems to be a heart attack. They put him on a gurney and the doctor applies the obligatory paddles. Suddenly his chest opens into a mouth with giant teeth and bites off the doctor's arms at the elbows, as the patient's head turns into the body of a crab that scuttles out of the room pursued by flamethrowers. (I've left out a few gory details.) A Rob Bottin triumph.

4. In the first scenes of George Romero's original *Dawn of the Dead* (1978), paramilitary police attack a ghetto apartment building where radicals have holed up, at the same time that a disease has begun to rage, which animates the recently dead. One of the men killed by the police rises up and staggers back into his apartment. His wife, overjoyed that he is still alive (or seems to be) rushes into his arms to embrace him. He hugs her enthusiastically and then bites a huge chunk out of her bare shoulder. A large part of the rest of this film takes place in one of those big shopping malls, which was a rarity at the time, and I saw it in something called the Golden Ring Mall outside of Baltimore. That's the film's eerie side, the potential horror that lurks in otherwise bland public spaces.

5. Two moments in Mario Bava's *Black Sunday* (1960) stand out. In the first, before the credits, the witch Princess Asa Vajda is being executed by the Inquisition. She is bound to a post and the executioner approaches carrying a metal mask furnished with

enormous spikes that will pierce the face of whoever wears it. From Asa's point of view we see the mask placed over her face. Then a well-muscled executioner lifts a huge hammer and, with an enormous thump, smashes the mask into her face and the stake behind her (all oddly reminiscent of the beginnings of J. Arthur Rank films). A century later, a skeptical professor manages to destroy the crucifix that kept her body in bondage, cutting his hand on the glass front of her tomb in the process. We watch her dead face with the bugs crawling in her empty eye sockets until the vivifying blood does its work, and her eyes float up into place from inside her skull.

Terror

I associate the purer forms of terror with the lack of special effects, now infrequent in this age of CGI. Terror traffics more in eeriness, which connects it to what the eighteenth century called the sublime. It makes you feel small and alone. It doesn't usually jump out; it advances slowly, inexorably, and lets your imagination fill in the blanks. Maybe horror is more the mode of film, with its overwhelming visual immediacy, while terror is more the mode of fiction, pioneered by writers like Poe, Le Fanu, and Lovecraft, for whom almost every monster was unspeakable and indescribable.

1. In *Les Diaboliques* (1955), directed by Henri-Georges Clouzot, the murdered tyrant husband, whose body keeps appearing and disappearing much to the fright of the mistress and wife who murdered him, finally appears to his wife fully dressed and floating in a bathtub. He then begins to rise from the bathtub, *slowly*, with no jumping out, like the slowness with which the naked ghost woman rises from the bathtub in room 237 to meet Jack Torrance in Kubrick's *The Shining*. It's the slowness that gives you time to wonder

"what is going on here?" The wife finally has a heart attack, and if you haven't seen the film, I won't spoil it by telling you the rest.

2. Virtually any late scene in the original *Invasion of the Body Snatchers* (Don Siegel, 1956) would qualify as terror because, except for the pods in the backyard greenhouses, it all seems so normal. Lovely suburbia, dear hearts and gentle people, the best friends and acquaintances of a perfect small town—except for the fact that they have all been turned into pod people by extraterrestrial visitors and want to convince the hero and heroine to join them. If I had to pick one scene, I suppose it would be the one in which the townspeople gather at the village intersection to welcome unsuspecting bus riders from nearby and bring them into their fold. The 1978 remake has its charms, but the whole sense of a seemingly normal world gone terribly wrong is gone. It was set in San Francisco, after all!

3. Stephen King hated Stanley Kubrick's version of *The Shining* (1980), and I have a lot of trouble with it myself, especially when Kubrick and/or his coscreenwriter Diane Johnson seem to go to such great lengths to show that "shining" makes no difference at all. But there are still a lot of great things in it. I love that helicopter shot behind the credits with the tiny Torrance Volkswagen making its way amid the sublime scenery of the mountains, while Berlioz plays on the soundtrack. But the great terror moment for me is when Jack gazes down at the model of the maze in the lobby of the Overlook and we gradually realize we are seeing the tiny figures of Wendy and Danny walking in it. It's the first moment that it's clear that the hotel has started to take Jack over and absorb him into its malevolent spirit.

4. Horror often comes when we are tied to the victim's point of view and don't know when the monster is going to jump out.

Maybe terror comes when we are associated with the monster's point of view, or at least the point of view of some monsters. An early scene in John Carpenter's *Halloween* (1978) delivers some of that. It begins with a leafy suburban street, perhaps descended from *Invasion of the Body Snatchers*, with a young boy and his babysitter strolling along talking about Halloween and horror movies. Then they come to the Myers house, vacant since the horrific events of fifteen years before. As they talk about the house, we get a shot from inside the house. Just a cinematic convenience? No, there is heavy breathing on the soundtrack, and the shadowy side of a face and shoulder come into the frame. Someone is there. The young woman walks down the street and the heavy breathing continues. Whose side is this movie on?

5. Maybe I should take another moment from *Halloween* for this entry. Films like this are often called "slasher" films because they deal in knives and blood, lots of it. But as many bad horror films show, a lot of killing doesn't necessarily make a memorable film. Spookiness, perhaps another word for terror, is required as well. And that is there in the final combat in *Halloween*. Laurie, the plucky babysitter—a figure that Carol Clover has dubbed "the last girl"—has succeeded in outwitting the monster Michael Myers and has seemingly killed him right through his mask with a cleverly bent coat hanger. She leans against a door jamb, worn out from the battle, while his body lies behind her. Then of course he gets up. Monsters are inexorable and implacable. That's why there are sequels.

6. I'll wind up with another last girl, Kristen, in *Nightmare on Elm Street 4* (directed by Renny Harlin), a series with more pleasures of both horror *and* terror for me than the *Halloween*s and the *Friday the 13th*s. Initially a shy, self-effacing girl, as Freddy swallows up her friends, Kristen actually becomes more power-

ful herself, a kind of doppelganger for the mephitic janitor who is her rival. Entering her dreams to fight him, Kristen finds herself in front of a movie theatre. She begins watching the film until a sucking wind pulls her into it, like something out of Buster Keaton's *Sherlock, Jr.* But this isn't comedy; this is horror (or perhaps terror). As she runs to meet her boyfriend, the sequence begins over and over: they are caught in a time loop and she has to break out. Like the rest of us in the audience, she is in a dream and the dream is the movies, with continuous performances.

ANTHONY TIMPONE'S TEN MOVIES I WISH I NEVER PUT ON THE COVER OF *FANGORIA*

Anthony Timpone is the longtime editor of Fangoria *magazine (affectionately known as "Fango") and its Web site, www.fangoria .com, as well as the author of the book* Men, Make-up and Monsters *(St. Martin's Press).*

As editor of *Fangoria*, the toughest question I face every month is what to put on the cover. Each time, I must balance commercial decisions (potential hit movie tie-ins) with creative ones (what's the best image?). I strive to find the most enticing cover ghoul to catch the prospective buyer's eye and convince them to take our magazine home.

When horror is popular at the US box office (the current boom has been going strong since 1996's *Scream*), the choice becomes easier, as there are plenty of films to pick from for each issue. When product is lean, you see a *Buffy the Vampire Slayer* cover and the gorehounds scream for blood—mine!

Looking back at nearly three decades' worth of magazines, I noticed *Fango* gave national newsstand exposure to more than a few clunkers. Many times, since we don't see the films before they come out, we have no idea if they will be good or not. So it's a matter of luck and instinct. Despite the Herculean efforts of executive art director Bill Mohalley, who has designed every *Fango* cover since 1983, our "front and center" can only be as strong as the images that are supplied to us by the studios. Some bad movies have made great covers (#74, *Critters 2*), while great movies have made bad covers (#262, *Death Proof*). Reviewing over 200 editions that I edited since 1986 (you can't blame me for the pre-Timpone #4's Mr. Spock or #6's C–3PO covers, thank you very much!), I've chosen this rogues' gallery of the 10 Movies I Wish I Never Put on the Cover of *Fangoria*.

1. *Maximum Overdrive*, #56: Author Stephen King made his directorial debut in 1986 on this self-described "moron movie," in which the machines of the world strike back at mankind. He also said he was "coked and drunk out of (his) mind" while he helmed this movie based on his short story "Trucks." Wish I had a similar excuse for putting this ridiculous movie (which features a killer soda can vending machine) on the cover, but I don't.

2. *Bad Dreams*, #72: The 1980s were littered with Freddy Krueger imitators, none quite as blatant as this 1988 *Nightmare on Elm Street* wannabe, in which a hideously burned cult leader returns from the dead to haunt survivors of a mass suicide. Real-life burn victim Richard Lynch starred as the scarred baddie, making *Bad Dreams* an exercise in Bad Taste.

3. *Night Life*, #82: This obscure 1989 direct-to-video zombie movie, about a young kid getting mixed up with zombies at his uncle's mortuary, is a good little sleeper. What I hate about this cover, which was photographed specifically for the magazine, is that the prop corpse looks so darn fake. That femme ghoul sports the chintziest eyelashes since Tammy Faye.

4. **Dolly Dearest, #102:** Another cover born of desperation! Few major studio horror films were produced during the late eighties/early nineties, so I frequently had to come up with special theme issues (e.g. Lovecraft Movies, Vampires, Werewolves, Big Bugs), direct-to-video releases, or cable premieres for *Fango* cover subjects. In this case, I chose an awful *Child's Play* knockoff to herald our Women of Horror issue.

5. **Batman Returns, #114:** Only once during my entire tenure as *Fango* editor was a cover ever imposed on me by my publisher, Norman Jacobs. The blockbuster *Batman* had set company sales records in 1989 for our sister magazine *Starlog*, so when the sequel rolled around in 1992, Norm insisted I put this non-horror release on *Fango*'s front to boost circulation. The hardcore readers rebelled, the movie underperformed at the box office, and we probably lost subscribers instead of gaining them.

6. **The Craft, #153:** This lightweight 1996 teen witch movie inspired one of the dullest *Fango* covers (utilizing the film's poster campaign) of all time. We also found that cover shots of sexy girls and distaff monsters rarely translate into sales for us. Readers prefer 'em male-specific, plus, the bloodier the better.

7. **Species II, #172:** One of the worst sequels from the nineties (a decade cluttered with bad sequels), this 1998 sex-and-tentacles flick killed the franchise until the Sci-Fi Channel got into the Saturday night schlock market.

8. **Virus, #175:** This terrible 1999 Jamie Lee Curtis movie, about alien pack rats battling a tugboat crew, deserved to be lost at sea. Like the flop film, the cover's a garish mess too.

9. *Psycho*, #179: Inarguably cinema history's most notorious mistake, Gus Van Sant's ill-advised shot-for-shot 1998 remake of Alfred Hitchcock's classic film led to this equally dreary and uninspired cover.

10. *The Haunting*, #184: The failure of Van Sant's *Psycho* didn't scare away producer Steven Spielberg from redoing the great 1963 Robert Wise ghost film a year later. The original film garnered praise for it subtlety and sense of dread; the CGI-inflated redux is lifeless and boring. What were they thinking? What was *I* thinking? A bad cover for a bad movie.

BARRY GIFFORD'S FIFTEEN FAVORITE LATE-NIGHT TINGLERS (IN NO PARTICULAR ORDER)

Essays by Barry Gifford on these films may be found in his books Out of the Past: Adventures in Film Noir *(2001) and* The Cavalry Charges *(2007). His novels include* Wild at Heart *(1990), which was filmed by David Lynch,* Night People *(1992), and* Memories from a Sinking Ship *(2007). He has written screenplays for numerous films, including* Lost Highway *(1997),* Perdita Durango *(1997), and* City of Ghosts *(2003).*

1. *Island of Lost Souls* (Erle C. Kenton, 1933; big nod to H. G. Wells)
2. *I Walked with a Zombie* (Jacques Tourneur, 1943; big nod to Val Lewton)
3. *Sunset Boulevard* (Billy Wilder, 1950)
4. *Stranger on the Third Floor* (Boris Ingster, 1940)
5. *Nosferatu* (F. W. Murnau, 1922)

Cesare the Somnambulist (Conrad Veidt), in *The Cabinet of Dr. Caligari* (1920)

6. *The Cabinet of Dr. Caligari* (Robert Wiene, 1920)
7. *Night of the Hunter* (Charles Laughton, 1955; big nod to Davis Grubb)
8. *Repulsion* (Roman Polanski, 1965)
9. *Cult of the Cobra* (Francis D. Lyon, 1955)
10. *Cape Fear* (J. Lee Thompson, 1962)
11. *Lost Highway* (David Lynch, 1997; big nod to myself)
12. *Invasion of the Body Snatchers* (Don Siegel, 1956; big nod to Jack Finney)
13. *Invaders from Mars* (William Cameron Menzies; 1953)
14. *Serie Noire* (Alain Corneau, 1981)
15. *The Red House* (Delmer Daves, 1947)

ALAN BEATTS'S FIVE COMMON TACTICAL ERRORS IN HORROR FILMS

Alan Beatts is the owner of Borderlands bookstore in San Francisco, which specializes in horror, fantasy, and science fiction. He's been running the shop for ten years, but started off in a very different business—working as (among other things) a bodyguard, private investigator, and firearms instructor. The best thing about his current job is that people hardly ever shoot at him. He loves horror movies, and he wishes there were more like John Carpenter's The Thing, *in which the characters are all smart, do the right things, and mostly die anyway.*

If you've ever found yourself thinking the characters in a horror movie are being stupid, you might be right. Below are five basic combat principles that are commonly violated in horror films. Although it's understandable when inexperienced characters make mistakes, it's surprising how often characters who should know better (like cops and soldiers) blow it.

1. Ensure that a firearm is loaded after it's been out of your control.

You should never assume that a firearm is loaded or unloaded. Anytime a firearm has been out of your direct control (e.g., left in a room or with another person) you should check to see if it's loaded (or not).

When Burt (Michael Gross) gives Melvin (Robert Jayne) an unloaded gun in *Tremors* (1990), it might have been better for Melvin to find out that it's empty sometime *before* he tries to shoot one of the graboids. At least he survived, which is a good trick when you're being chased by a twenty-foot-long burrowing worm with jaws like a shark.

2. Do not ignore your instincts.

One of the basic tenets of tactical awareness is that you should be guided by your instincts, unless there is a compelling reason not to do so. In short, if you have a "bad feeling" about something or some situation—stop, reassess, and if possible, choose another course of action.

An example of this is in *The Howling* (1981), when Karen White (Dee Wallace) goes out in the woods. At night. By flashlight. In a nightgown. To see what is howling outside. You needn't have very well-developed instincts to know that's a bad idea.

3. Maintain 360-degree awareness.

When operating in a risky environment, you must be aware of your surroundings. This especially includes areas beyond your normal line of sight (i.e., above and behind you). Before entering an area, you should look up and check the ceiling area for threats. When operating alone, check your back-trail at least every 30 seconds. If you're working with a trusted partner, you should split the directions of responsibility such that one person is primarily responsible for observing the forward area and the other is focused on the rear area.

Despite their formidable attitude and obvious training, the unit of Colonial Marines in *Aliens* (1986) pays the price for not looking up in the first battle with the title critters under the atmosphere plant. There are plenty of other examples of this mistake in film but the sheer degree of the ugly consequences of this one are a standout—sergeant and more than half the unit killed plus a fusion reactor ready to explode. That's a bad day by anyone's measure. It's not like they should have been surprised when the nasties started in on them. After all, they'd just watched something chew its way out of someone's chest.

4. Secure your exit route.

You should be aware of possible exits at all times. In a dangerous environment you should not enter any area without identifying at least one method of exit and ensuring that the exit will remain useable (e.g., making sure that doors cannot be locked behind you).

Horror films are full of bad places to get stuck—crypts, houses, ships, towns, toilets . . . you name it. Sometimes you can't avoid getting trapped, but this rule would've saved the day in *Jeepers Creepers* (2001). The sibling protagonists are smart enough to realize what a bad situation they are about to get into when they first look at the sinister chute leading underground. Smart enough, in fact, that Trish (Gina Philips) comments to Darry (Justin Long), "You know the part in horror movies when somebody does something really stupid, and everybody hates him for it? This is it." But they still aren't smart enough to think about how the hell Darry is going to get out of that hole in the ground if something goes wrong.

5. Confirm your kills.

A threat should never be considered neutralized without verification. An unverified kill should be treated as a threat until verified. This can take many forms, ranging from handcuffing unresponsive subjects that have been shot to keeping weapons on target and maintaining a safe distance after the threat has stopped moving . . . all the way to "safety" shots into the head of previously engaged and motionless targets.

Halloween (1978) is the classic example of this. Michael Myers (Nick Castle) is stabbed in the neck with a knitting needle, stabbed in the stomach with a butcher knife, and shot multiple times. Each time he gets up and goes at it again until he falls out a second story window (and he still vanishes at the end of the film). Based on subsequent events, perhaps even a bullet between the eyes wouldn't have put him down for good, but it might have helped. More important, a set of handcuffs (or even better, parking a car on top of him) might have made life much better for poor Laurie Strode.

EDGAR WRIGHT'S TOP TEN *"OUCH! I'M SORRY, BUT THAT HAS GOT TO HURT!"* MOMENTS IN HORROR FILMS (PLUS ONE VERY HONORABLE MENTION)

Edgar Wright is a key figure in contemporary British film. He directed Hot Fuzz *and* Shaun of the Dead, *both of which he cowrote with Simon Pegg. He also directed the UK Channel 4's* Spaced, *a sitcom that quickly gained cult status and changed the landscape of English television in the late 1990s.*

Chances are neither you, nor your family, friends, nor even friends of friends have been groped by a poltergeist, raped by a tree or had their head exploded in a million pieces by a naughty telepath.

But I'd wager you all know the sheer agony of a paper cut from an envelope. Ouch. That's nasty. You wouldn't wish it upon your worst enemy. (Ironically, that's exactly what Frank Whaley's vengeful assistant does to the studio boss from hell, Kevin Spacey, in *Swimming With Sharks*. More on that later.)

There's a distinct level of audible sympathy when somewhat everyday injuries crop up in films. You can hear an audible "ewww," gasp, or intake of breath when such tribulations are depicted.

What is even more interesting is how such moments can provoke the biggest audience reactions in the goriest, most outlandishly violent, fantastical genre films.

This is true peeking-through-your-fingers material. . . .

1. *The Thing* (1982): John Carpenter's classic remake has some of the most vividly gruesome creature effects of all time. It's wildly gory and deeply unsettling. But what moment unites the audience in a collective shudder? Why, the scene when Kurt Russell forces his entire team to undergo a blood test and takes a scalpel to each of their thumbs. It may be only a drop of red stuff compared to the remainder of the film, but it never fails to make even the most hardened moviegoers wriggle in their seats.

2. *The Evil Dead* (1982): As mentioned before, it's unlikely we can truly empathize with someone enduring a nasty case of molestation-by-trees. Equally, you won't quite be able to have the sense memory of what it feels like to be hacked to pieces whilst possessed by Candarian demons. But can you imagine how painful it would be to have a sharpened no. 2 pencil jammed into your ankle? Of course you can. We've all been there. Admittedly your demonic soon-to-be-ex-girlfriend didn't wield the pencil. But still, a loud and very hearty *ouch*.

3. *Dawn of the Dead* (1978): Foreheads have been sliced off, necks have had lumps taken out of them, and zombies have been chowing down on humans all over the shop (literally in this one too). One of our protagonists, Roger, has already had a meaty chunk taken out of his ankle by a hungry flesh eater. That's quite an *ouch* already. But later, salt is poured into that very gash, when another equally ravenous zombie grabs poor Roger's now-bandaged leg and needlessly fingers the open wound. That's just not cricket. It's pure *ouch*.

4. *The Exorcist* (1973): The second half of William Friedkin's legendary shocker contains some of the strongest, most disturbing material to ever feature in a studio picture. There's masturbation with a crucifix, for one. Let alone a little girl saying the c-word

in an English accent whilst possessed by El Diablo. Some pretty hot stuff. But the CAT scan scene where little Linda Blair is subjected to some nasty-looking injections has all needle-phobes hiding under their seats. Couple that with the thunderous noise of the procedure, plus some truly terrifyingly industrial-looking medical apparatus, and I'll wager 1970s audiences were looking at alternative medicines for a good while afterwards.

5. *Audition* (1999): A fair few people have never had acupuncture. They are understandably not comfortable with the idea of needles, no matter how fine, being inserted into the flesh. The climax of Takeshi Miike's *Audition* is not going be a good way of convincing them otherwise. The notorious denouement of this film features an extended scene of the deranged Eihi Shiina torturing a drugged and paralyzed Ryo Ishibashi by poking needles into his chest and face. When I saw the film, this provoked several walkouts, even before she cut off his foot with a piano wire. The dismemberment was extreme, but the needles? That was quintessential *ouch*.

6. *Deep Red* (1975): A clairvoyant hacked to death and impaled on broken glass? Yep, quite nasty. A man dragged along the street behind a garbage truck? That's pretty *ouch*. A recently stabbed woman drowned in a bath of scalding hot water? Now, we're getting warmer. Okay, how about a psychiatrist being menaced by a spooky robotic doll, then struck around the head by a mystery killer who then . . . then . . . proceeds to bash his teeth out on a hard wooden mantelpiece? The doll is scary as shit, but I can take that. The teeth being deliberately knocked out? That is just *ouch*. Unforgettable *ouch*.

7. *Misery* (1990): In Stephen King's novel, deranged superfan Annie Wilkes cuts off romantic novelist Paul Sheldon's foot, punish-

ing him for having the audacity to try escaping her suffocating clutches. Screenwriter William Goldman was attracted to the adaptation because of the shocking power of this scene. But who knew that a softened version of the scene would somehow have twice the *ouch*? In Rob Reiner's film, Kathy Bates cripples James Caan by placing a block of wood between his ankles and then thwacking them with a sledgehammer. This practice, usually employed when impeding the movement of farm animals (or disobedient workers), is known as "hobbling," as Annie helpfully explains. The unanimous cries of the audience immediately made the practice infamous. A bigger crunch has never reverberated around auditoriums.

8. *Zombi 2* (aka *Zombie* aka *Zombie Flesh-Eaters*) (1979): Zombie movies generally center on a few key, shocking images: walking corpses and people getting munched. That's enough of a raison d'être to spawn hundreds of great zombie movies. (Okay, maybe eleven good ones, thirty-two great bad ones, and countless bad, bad ones.) It's ironic, then, that Lucio Fulci's notorious Italian splatter-fest gains its infamy from one moment that doesn't have a whole lot to do with flesh-eating. I'm talking of the scene when poor Olga Karlatos gets out of the shower, hears an intruder, locks the bathroom door and then . . . *bang.* A moldy zombie hand bursts through the wooden door, grabs her painfully by the hair, and then slowly pulls her face towards the door, her eye inching ever-closer to a huge, fourteen-inch splinter. The eventual penetration of said eye by big splinter is unmatched in its nastiness. Poor lady. Frankly, if I had a choice between eyeball-puncture and being eaten alive, I'd choose the latter. Leave my eyes out of it; just eat me, already.

9. *The Fly* (1986): David Cronenberg is truly the king of body horror. A large part of his oeuvre is dedicated to surreal distortions of the

human form. Classic images, such as Max Renn pulling a flesh revolver out of an abdominal vagina (in *Videodrome*), are seared onto the brains of many horror fans. His fevered imagination of parasites in armpits, mutant afterbirths, and the aforementioned exploding heads are gloriously twisted. But sometimes Cronenberg can get the biggest *ouch* from the most everyday of terrors. In *The Fly*, the fast-disintegrating Seth Brundle stands in front of the bathroom mirror, horrified and fascinated by his decaying fingers. He first squeezes an obscene amount of pus from one of the digits. Cue audience, freaking out. This is then topped by Brundle casually peeling off one of his fingernails. Somehow this small moment combines the unease of every anxiety dream of rotting teeth with the sheer agony and ecstasy of picking a scab. It's truly unmatched for sheer squirm and audible wince.

10. *Grindhouse* (2007): In Eli Roth's hilarious faux-trailer for the non-existent *Thanksgiving*, there is a moment that proudly aspires to match Italian horror cinema's limitless depths of misogyny. There is no real reason why a scene in which a cheerleader bouncing on a trampoline does the splits in the air and lands naked onto the killer's knife would feature in a holiday-centric slasher flick. You thankfully don't even see the collision of the skyward-pointing instrument and the young lady's young lady-parts. But good God, if the entire audience I saw it with didn't raise the roof with a deafening "OOOOOOH!" A moment so wince–inducing, it causes both sexes to cross their legs. That's some powerful *ouch*.

Very Honorable Mention: *Jackass: The Movie* (2002): It's not a horror film per se, but the honor of surely one of the biggest collective shrieks of pain I've ever heard in a cinema goes to the big-screen version of *Jackass*. *Swimming With Sharks* sadly loses its title of "Best Paper Cut Scene" to Johnny Knoxville and his merry band of pranksters. The scene involves the Jackass team inflicting paper cuts on each other, climaxing with the lunatic Steve-O getting a paper cut on his tongue. I saw this in a packed house and I'm not sure I've ever heard such a loud reaction. Simple, yet brutally effective. Truly the death of a thousand *ouch*es.

ELI ROTH'S TOP TEN NASTIEST HORROR MOVIE GENITAL MUTILATIONS

Eli Roth burst onto the horror scene in 2002 with Cabin Fever. *He then wrote, produced, and directed* Hostel, *which was a smash hit worldwide.* Hostel *was voted the #1 scariest film of all time on Bravo's "Even Scarier Movie Moments" and earned rave reviews around the globe. Roth made the sequel in 2007, cementing his reputation as one of the most profitable yet uncompromising horror filmmakers working today. His works to date have been produced for a combined total budget of $16 million, and have earned over $160 million at the box office alone. He has been profiled in the* New York Times, GQ, Interview, *and* Rolling Stone, *and has been a guest on* Late Night with Conan O'Brien, Jimmy Kimmel Live, *and* The Howard Stern Show.

Between *Cabin Fever*, both *Hostel* films, and *Thanksgiving*, I've chopped up my fair share of body parts. However, there's nothing more satisfying than filming a gore scene where you chop up the naughty bits. Genital mutilation always, *always* gets the biggest reaction from the crowd, and the scenes become those moments that everyone talks about years and years later. When I was a kid, if I saw a film with a great head explosion, it was cool, but nowhere near as thrilling as a realistic on-camera castration. So here are the nastiest genital mutilations—the ones that made me cross my legs and squeal like a little girl.

1. *To Be Twenty*—The Final Scene

I watched Fernando Di Leo's little-seen classic and am simply amazed he had the balls to make this film. Di Leo was an incredibly smart director who loved making genre B-movies, and never cared to make Italian so-called art films. He made great crime movies, but the film that for me defines his career is *To Be Twenty*, a movie that for eighty-five minutes is a sexy comedy, until the last five minutes when it all goes horribly, horribly wrong. Di Leo set out to make a film that showed the change in attitude towards open sexuality in Italy in the early seventies, when the hippie movement was dying down, and the older generation wanted to punish the kids for their open sexuality. He cast two of the most popular actresses from "sexy" comedies—Gloria Guida and Lili Carati—and for eighty-five minutes, the girls run around Rome, having fun, having lots of sex, and teasing men and getting away with it because they're so beautiful. That is, until they tease the wrong group of men at a diner. The men chase the girls into the woods, rip their clothes off, and rape them. The scene is so real and horrific, you can only imagine what they went through when they filmed it. One of girls is held upside down by two men, spreading her legs like a wishbone, and the leader of the gang vaginally stabs her to death with a giant stick. Her friend is then beaten to death, and the men walk away, accidentally stepping on the girls' portable radio, turning on disco music. The girls are left naked and dead in the woods, and the credits roll over the frozen image, accompanied by the disco music. Even knowing what's coming, the film has genuinely the most shocking and disturbing ending I've ever seen. When the film came out in theaters, crowds went to see it expecting a fun sexy comedy, and they got it . . . until the end. By the end of the first day every single print of the film was recalled, and the entire film was recut. Only one print of the film survived, and was used to make a DVD, which has both versions of the film. People were outraged, and it isn't until only recently that critics have been reexamining the film, and appreciate it for what it is. Di Leo was grossly misunderstood, as was his film, which was made with great intelligence and care, and was intended to be disturbing. It's a hard film to watch, but a brilliant one if you can get past the shock of what happens and see what Di Leo was saying about culture and society in Italy at the time.

2. *The New York Ripper*–The Nipple-Slicing Scene

Despite his writing and directing masterpieces in so many different genres (watch *Lizard in a Woman's Skin*, *Don't Torture a Duckling*, and *The Beyond* for proof), critics and fans have never quite forgiven Lucio Fulci for his early eighties Times Square sleaze-fest, *The New York Ripper*. Fulci went on an amazing run starting in 1980 with *Zombie*, and made some of the most violent but beautiful and surreal horror films that fans are only now truly beginning to appreciate. However, he abandoned this craft for pure sadism, shock, and violence in *The New York Ripper*, a film even the most hardcore horror fans feel they need to take a shower immediately after watching. Fulci made this film without two of his longtime collaborators—cinematographer Sergio Salvati and composer Fabio Frizzi—and somehow the film just feels "dirtier." There are many brutal murders in this film, done by a pervert who hangs out in Times Square sex clubs and kills in a comical Donald Duck voice, but nothing is more cruel and disturbing than Daniela Doria's slow death by razorblade in her apartment. The film has already had a girl stabbed in the vagina with a broken bottle and a nymphomaniac tied up in a motel room before being stabbed to death, but this killing "the Little Duck" makes extra special. The killer calls the police inspector on the case, and slowly slices open the inspector's prostitute girlfriend, played by Daniela Doria, with a razor blade. But just when you think it's over—the killer, in graphic close up, carefully slices into her nipples, before finally, *slooooooowly* bringing the razor over her eyeball. It's a relentlessly brutal death, and you just get the sense that Fulci was pushing himself to see how far he would dare go to on camera. The beautiful Daniela Doria was one of Fulci's favorite victims—she was the first to die in *House by the Cemetery*, she literally puked her guts out in *City of the Living Dead*, and Fulci ties her up naked to a bed before killing her here, and later gives us a full shot of her carved-up corpse. It's unfortunate the term "misogyny" got applied to Fulci, because if you see his feminist masterpiece *Beatrice Cenci*, you know how absurd that label is, but if you saw only this film, you'd understand why people don't go seeking more of his work, which is truly a shame. Fulci was a genius, and this simple killing is far more disturbing than seeing the same woman endlessly throwing up her own intestines. *Viva* Fulci!

3. *Ricco the Mean Machine*—The Cock-and-Ball Gag

If you live in Italy in the 1970s, it's a real bad idea to sleep with the mafia boss's wife, no matter how hot she is. In this case, it's the lovely Malisa Longo, who's forced to watch the boss's henchman hold down her lover, Manuel Zarzo, as they chop off his manly bits and shove them down his throat, before tossing the poor eunuch into a vat of acid. This scene caused great outrage in 1973, when the film was released, and the scene was cut, so to speak, for many years. The level of violence in this scene is fairly disproportionate to the rest of the film, which plays like a fairly tame seventies Italian gangster revenge film. Suddenly, out of nowhere, you're treated to this giant close-up of a knife ripping through the genitals, and then you see them stuffed into his mouth. I'd put this castration on par with the penis-removal in *Cannibal Holocaust*, in which the penis is presumably also eaten, just not on camera. (Like how I worked another castration in there? Clever, eh?)

4. *Cannibal Holocaust*—The Stone Dildo

Director Ruggero Deodato spent many years as Italian neorealist master Roberto Rosselini's assistant director, and took what he learned and applied it to the cannibal genre. With a camera, a skeleton crew, and a jungle full of savages who had never before even seen a movie camera, Deodato made a film that today still holds up as probably the most disturbing film of all time. I cast Deodato as the cannibal in *Hostel: Part II* not only as a nod to *Cannibal Holocaust*, but also so I could ask him questions about how he filmed this stuff. Deodato made it seem like it was no big deal, that he just asked the jungle savages to do something and they did it, but the performances are just too good for people who live in trees and hunt with poison darts. In one scene, our main character, a professor from New York University, stumbles upon a villager whose wife was unfaithful. The villager ties the woman's legs to a tree and stuffs her vagina full of mud, and then proceeds to repeatedly stab her in the vagina with a giant phallic stone until she's dead. The villager puts her corpse in a canoe, and sends her down the river, presumably as a message to the village, but also probably so they can later enjoy her as a snack. The professor is suitably horrified by the savagery, and we as audience members are equally horrified that someone could film such a scene. However, composer Riz Ortolani's music is so groovy that you can't help but later sing it and reenact it at highly inappropriate moments with your brothers when you're at dinner with your parents. It happens.

5. *Ichi the Killer*—The Nipple Slice

There are so many over-the-top deaths in Miike's Splatter Manga Massacrepiece that the film very quickly becomes a cartoon. But even after you've seen naked men hung up by hooks in their flesh while boiling oil is poured over them, tongues cut out, and people sliced in half, the scene where a woman's breasts are put under a table through two holes and her nipples are sliced off still makes me queasy. It's just so simple and sick, and to stand out in a film like this is a feat indeed. The movie never takes a serious tone, and is meant to be a nonstop, over-the-top orgy of cartoonish violence, but this one kill feels somehow more painful than slicing off your own tongue.

6. *Last House on the Left*—The Blow Job With Extra Teeth

In a wonderful twist of events, the mother of murdered rape victim Mary Colinwood goes so far as to not just seduce the psycho serial killer/rapist (played by Fred Lincoln), she actually goes down on him, and finishes him off with a final chomp. The kill isn't nearly as graphic as Mary's mutilation, when you see the killers spool out her intestines like a garden hose, but you hate this bastard so much it's fun to see him get it. It's also worth noting that Fred Lincoln (under the name F. J. Lincoln) went on to direct a number of porn films, which makes this death that much more appropriate.

7. *Cannibal Ferox*—The Meat Hook Brassiere

Those troublemaking twentysomethings should know better than to go playing around in a cannibal village in the jungle— especially since this film was made as a response to the success of *Cannibal Holocaust*. When they're finally captured and punished, director Umberto Lenzi, in a bid to outdo director Ruggero Deodato, has the cannibals hang up actress Zora Kerova by her breasts with large metal hooks. You can see her flesh stretching—my nipples hurt just thinking about it. It's all done in plain daylight right on camera, and the effects are pretty sick. It should be noted that Zora Kerova—just a year later—gets a broken bottle stabbed into her crotch in Lucio Fulci's sleaze-fest *The New York Ripper*, presumably in a bid by Fulci to outdo Lenzi.

8. *Cannibal Holocaust*—The Abortion by Hand

I could fill up this entire list with genital mutilations from Deodato's neorealist grindhouse classic, but I'll try to keep it to the most painful ones. A villager is pregnant, and we witness the other girls hold her down, reach up inside her, and pull out a baby. These are not the village midwives, this is some kind of punishment, and since we know they're cannibals, we can only assume they're preparing dinner. It's as disgusting as it sounds. The camera doesn't flinch, but you will.

9. *Mother's Day*—The Axe in the Balls

This is one of the most satisfying kills in all the eighties slasher movies, because the girls who've been held captive and raped by the hillbillies get their revenge and hit one of the rapists where it hurts the most. I showed this film at my bar mitzvah after-party (because I wasn't friends with enough girls to have a dance) and we replayed this scene over and over, frame by frame, laughing and cheering at the meaty testicle-lump that spills out over the blade. A great kill.

10. *Night Train Murders*—The Switchblade Tampon

Two creepy Italian guys and a demented rich woman torment two girls traveling home for Christmas in Aldo Lado's tense, atmospheric ripoff of *Last House on the Left*. The more unstable of the two psychos pushes the envelope by holding a switchblade at the crotch of one of the girls, and as the train goes into a tunnel they bump on the tracks and he accidentally stabs the knife into her. The scene's played very, very realistically, and we realize the psychos didn't mean for it to go that far, but now that the damage is done, they have to finish the girls. The girls are so sweet and likable that you really want them to survive, so when that moment comes it's extremely difficult to watch. What makes it more nauseating is that you feel the killers are as sick about it as the audience is.

JAMES GUNN'S NINETEEN FAVORITE REASONS
GOD MADE HUMANS SO SQUISHY

James Gunn likes horror movies. He's made a few movies that seem like horror movies but aren't really all that horrific—including writing the 2004 remake of Dawn of the Dead, *which is kind of more of an action film than a horror film, and writing and directing 2006's* Slither, *which is really kind of a comedy more than a horror film. Currently, he is writing and directing* Pets, *which also isn't a horror movie, and writing and directing the Internet series* PG-Porn *(guess what—not horror). Most recently, he wrote this biography, which he really wouldn't recommend to anyone. You can be one of his 30,000 closest friends at www.myspace.com/slithermovie.*

These are a few of my favorite gory moments in movies. Some of these movies I don't even like—but each of these moments in particular is transcendent. A word of warning: many are over-the-top and funny, but a few are disturbing and not for the fainthearted (however, I suppose if you're fainthearted it's kind of stupid to be reading *The Book of Lists: Horror*).

1. Charles Hallahan's head detaches itself from his body, sprouts spider legs, and scurries around all over the damn place in John Carpenter's version of *The Thing* (one of three or four scenes from *The Thing* that could be on this list).

2. A lawyer gets sliced in half by a sliding glass door—then, for fun, the front of his body slides down the glass so we can see into the back half of his body—in *Thir13en Ghosts*.

3. Bruce Campbell cuts off his own possessed hand, and yet the little bastard keeps coming, in *Evil Dead 2*.

4. John Hurt gives birth to an adorable baby alien—through his stomach—in *Alien*.

5. A straight razor cuts open Simone Mareuli's eye in *Un Chien Andalou* (from 1929!!).

6. An almost completely decapitated zombie jolts his body forward so that his head flips back up like a Pez dispenser's to bite an unsuspecting victim in *Land of the Dead*.

7. James Kirk (not the Captain) is flattened Wile E. Coyote–style (only a lot bloodier) by a falling pane of glass in *Final Destination 2*.

8. Bill Moseley gets all Jim Henson-y on Kate Norby when he taunts her by using her husband's face as a puppet, and then forces her to wear it as a mask, in *The Devil's Rejects*. The nut!

9. Eihi Shiina gleefully saws off Ryo Ishibashi's foot with piano wire—for a good long while—in *Audition*.

10. A lovable zombie baby plays peekaboo with a woman's face in *Dead-Alive* (laugh away—it's only funny till it happens to you).

11. A falling church steeple crushes Adam Buxton's head into his body, yet he continues to stumble around for a few moments (presumably looking at his own intestines), in *Hot Fuzz*.

12. Cerina Vincent shaves the hair—and skin—off her legs in a super-squirm-inducing scene in *Cabin Fever*.

13. Paul McCrane, in *Robocop,* is doused by toxic waste, making his body all soft and pulpy, so that he explodes like a wet paper bag when he's hit by a car.

14. Michael Ironside uses his kick-ass telekinetic powers to make a dude's head explode in *Scanners* (and, oh, did I fantasize about having those powers when Dr. Callici would drone on endlessly about erosion in my high school earth sciences class).

15. Samantha Eggar eats the placenta from the bloody fetus growing out of her torso in *The Brood*.

16. Travis Bickle uses a gun to blow off a deserving scum-bucket's hand in *Taxi Driver*.

17. A North Korean ice skater attempts the difficult "Iron Lotus," only to accidentally decapitate his partner, in *Blades of Glory*. (Why do I feel like I'm going to be the only dude mentioning *Blades of Glory* in *The Book of Lists: Horror*?)

18. An unhappy housewife uses steel wool to scrub her lips until they're bloody, then uses scissors to cut them off in the short film *Cutting Moments*.* (This scene almost made me faint when I saw it at Montreal's Fantasia Film Festival in 1997.)

19. Albert Dupontel uses a fire extinguisher to bash another dude's face into pulp—in one glorious, awful shot (almost certainly the most violent shot in movie history)—in *Irréversible*.

*The editors note that *Cutting Moments*, written and directed by Douglas Buck, can be found on the DVD *Family Portraits: A Trilogy of America*.

TIM SULLIVAN'S THIRTEEN FAVORITE "SPLATSTICK" MOMENTS

Tim Sullivan began his career pumping fake blood for the horror flick The Deadly Spawn *(1983). In 1990, Tim moved to L.A., where he worked in development at New Line Cinema for five years. It was there that he first encountered* Detroit Rock City *(1999), which he eventually coproduced, finding himself yet again pumping fake blood—though this time for Gene Simmons of KISS. Having formed New Rebellion Entertainment, Tim made his directorial debut with the horror-comedy* 2001 Maniacs *(2005), followed by a complete flip in vibe,* Driftwood *(2006), a character-driven supernatural teen thriller described as "Stand by Me meets* Ghost Story." *Next up was a double dose of* 2001 Maniacs: *first, the graphic novel from Avatar Press, followed by* Beverly Hellbillys, *the film's much-anticipated sequel.*

Horror and comedy have brushed shoulders for quite some time, be it the subtle gallows humor darkly shading the films of James Whale, or the not-so-subtle hijinks of Abbott and Costello's raucous encounters with Frankenstein, Dracula, the Wolf Man, and so on. For my buck, however, it wasn't until "Godfather of Gore" Herschell Gordon Lewis came on the scene in 1964 that death became the actual punch line of a murderous joke, giving birth to what I've always referred to as *splatstick*.

It's just a joke, ye would-be offended viewers and critics alike! Vaudeville with violence! Burlesque with blood! A gruesome illusion, not unlike the mustachioed magician sawing his nubile assistant in half. Blood, boobs, and laffs, decidedly *not* drawn out in cringe-inducing sequences of realistic torture—but cartoonish blasts of splat where the victim "dies" before he or she even knows what hit 'em!

And then the boulder falls and crushes the unsuspecting lovely lady below! Drum roll please . . . Groan. Laugh. Ba da bump!

I've always preferred this type of mayhem in my horror, hence the homage to Herschell with *2001 Maniacs*. But between HGL's original and my remake, many others have left a bloody mess on the silver screen with their own brand of splatstick. In chronological order, here are my personal favorites. . . .

1. *Two Thousand Maniacs!* (1964)
Directed by Herschell Gordon Lewis

Okay, okay. An obvious choice, I know, but c'mon! How could this list *not* begin in Pleasant Valley?! Although *Blood Feast* was Herschell's first foray into this warped turf, it is here that he perfects and defines the splatstick genre with creatively gory setups and payoffs right out of a Warner Brothers Road Runner cartoon. Blood-soaked and feather-plucked, of course.

Highlight splatstick moment: The Barrel Roll, complete with railroad spikes to "tickle ya a little on the way down." And for those diehards who missed this scene in *2001 Maniacs*—don't'cha worry yourself none! We've got ya covered in the sequel, *Beverly Hellbillys*. Yee haw!

2. *I Drink Your Blood* (1970)
Directed by David Durston

Though it was no doubt hard to laugh through the turbulent and tragic tail end of the sixties, this delirious grindhouse classic, produced by the aptly named Jerry Gross, offers drug-induced splatstick as a shocking antidote to the real-life horrors of the likes of Charlie Manson. For doubters and haters, you might want to take the advice of the film's villain, the one and only Horace Bones: "Satan was an acid-head. Drink from his cup. Pledge yourselves, and together we'll all freak out!"

Highlight splatstick moment: Between rabies, meat pies, dead goats, stray electric carving knives, and hippie maniacs, it's kind of hard to choose just one, but ever since I saw this on a double bill with *I Eat Your Skin* at my local drive-in as an impressionable youth, the image of that skinny old man in his nasty long johns puking up his dirty dentures while being choked to death remains burned into my brain like a bad trip. Not that I would know . . .

3. *Theatre of Blood* (1973)
Directed by Douglas Hickox

William Shakespeare plus Vincent Price equals . . . splatstick? You bet your bum! There's definitely something rotten here in Denmark—the foul stench of Price's victims in this delicious British delight that masterfully combines wit, intelligence, and some of the most gruesome splatstick ever seen in a studio film, astonishingly, made by highbrow talent both behind and in front of the camera.

Highlight splatstick moment: For anyone who ever doubted that Billy Shakespeare was a sick bastard, check out the scene inspired by his play *Titus Andronicus*, where Price force-feeds glutton Robert Morley the creamed corpses of his dead, beloved poodles. Hmmm. To bleed or not to bleed. Is there really any question?

4. *Dawn of the Dead* (1978)
Directed by George A. Romero

Ten years after his own über-serious, groundbreaking *Night of the Living Dead*, the ever-socially aware George Romero injected a heavy dose of humor into his follow-up, a "goregasm" of blood-drenched levity much welcomed as the seventies came to a close, a decade scarred by both the aftermath of Vietnam and

Watergate, as well as celluloid exorcists, omens, and Amityville horrors inspired by "true-life stories." Both metaphorically and on screen, Romero literally threw a pie in the face of his zombies, taking movie gore to never-before-seen levels and to a height of popularity that would make a superstar out of FX artist Tom Savini, spawn the birth of horror's New Testament, *Fangoria* magazine, and single-handedly set the stage for the most prolific splatstick decade yet—the eighties.

Highlight splatstick moment: Hands down, the helicopter decapitation. Fucking classic. If you don't know the scene, you're probably not reading this book! One wide shot with no edits and no CGI. This is how they do it old school, folks. It worked then. It works now. And it'll work forever. Bless you, George.

5. *Motel Hell* (1980)
Directed by Kevin Connor

A twisted tale that could truly have come straight from the crypt, this was a breath of fresh air in the wake of unimaginative *Halloween* rip-offs. Kicking off the eighties' Golden Era of Splatstick, this quirky, colorful, perverse treat threw down the gauntlet and raised the bar for inspired mayhem. To this then 16-year-old, bored by a routine diet of kitchen knives, machetes, and hockey masks, this gourmet feast of Farmer Vincent Fritters was one helluva Happy Meal!

Highlight splatstick moment: Brother and Sister Vincent and Ida lovingly and meticulously harvest their "crop"—a garden of shell-shocked victims buried neck-deep in the dirt, their throats slit so they can't scream for help! And all in the new process of Ultra Stereo! Are we having fun yet?

6. *An American Werewolf in London* (1981)
Directed by John Landis

Hands down, the greatest horror comedy ever made, this film gives it to you both ways, with serious scares that jolt you out of your seat and comic moments that make you piss your pants. Either way, you're on the floor in this one-of-a-kind return to "Monster Movie" territory helmed by a filmmaker as equally a Master of Comedy as he is a Master of Horror. And if that ain't splatstick, what the hell is?

Highlight splatstick moment: In an unforgettable scene that manages to be gross, frightening, and funny, hospital patient and werewolf victim David Naughton is visited from beyond the grave by his wisecracking best friend Griffin Dunne: "You ever try being a corpse? It's *boring!*"

7. *Return of the Living Dead* (1985)
Directed by Dan O'Bannon

Looking back, it's easy for me to see that no single period has had more impact on the type of movies I wanted to make than from the release of this film in summer of 1985 to the release of *Evil Dead 2* in 1987 a mere two summers later. From *Dead* to *Dead*, these two years were virtual nirvana for me, an adrenalin rush provided by filmmakers outdoing and out-grossing each other, pushing the genre to new heights of inspired bad taste in order to shake audiences out of their numb immunity to repetitive on-screen horrors. Simple knife slit ain't doing it for ya? How about chasing and chopping up a naked corpse? No? Okay, what do ya say to a living severed head actually giving head to a spread-eagled hapless chick? Still don't grab you. Okay . . . how about an eyeball popping out of its socket and landing in the wide open mouth of a gaping, shocked onlooker? Nope? Okay, Mr. Kaufman—I think it's up to you. You got Toxie with ya? Bring 'em on! You get the picture . . .

Highlight splatstick moment: For me, O'Bannon's film is the most consistently splatstick flick from beginning to end. There are so many highlights, it's hard to pick one. I can say that the Best All-Time Splatstick Performance Award goes to James Karen. That tireless old-timer truly understood what film he was in. And the gusto and glee he brings to the role is exactly what the splatstick vibe is all about. But forced to pick one, the classic moment for me is the zombie attack on the fleeing cops; that awesome overhead shot of the cops rushing in—only to run away as the zombies enter the frame, followed by a lovely bloodbath of flesh eating, then . . . wait for it . . . culminating in *the* all-time classic splatstick line of dialogue: "Send . . . more . . . paramedics!"

8. *Re-Animator* (1985)
Directed by Stuart Gordon

As if *Return of the Living Dead* wasn't enough to make one bust a nut in 1985, this gem came along and introduced us to Stuart Gordon and Jeremy Combs, while reacquainting us with goo master H. P. Lovecraft. Surely the most sexual splatstick, the gleeful depravity of Gordon's vision is both unsettling and seductive—which is just as it should be!

Highlight splatstick moment: Yeah, yeah, yeah—the aforementioned "head" scene is surely the first thing that comes to mind to most who have experienced this flick, but for my money (and God knows I have spent quite a bit of it over the years re-buying "new and improved" versions of this one!), the scene that completely won me over and made me a lifelong fan is the post-decapitation scene, where a petulant and annoyed Combs unsuccessfully tries to prop David Gale's severed head upright in a specimen tray before nonchalantly impaling it on a metal spike. Head on his shoulders and head on his desk indeed!

9. *Texas Chainsaw Massacre 2* (1986)
Directed by Tobe Hooper

Just as Romero reinvented his *Living Dead* baby with *Dawn*, here Tobe Hooper takes the solemn documentary tone of his original *Massacre* and gives it an eighties makeover. Anyone who expected a serious horror film and complained afterwards should be ground into chili. Didn't the movie's ad campaign, brilliantly parodying *The Breakfast Club*, give ya a clue? This was splatstick thru and *Grue*, where flesh was meat and Dennis Hopper was over-the-top and the counterculture was dead and Reagan was President and anyone who thought Steven Spielberg *really* directed *Poltergeist* deserved a slap in the face!

Highlight splatstick moment: Hmmm . . . Leatherface masturbating with his chainsaw or Bill Moseley's seminal Chop Top picking at the metal plate in his head with a molten wire hanger. I'm gonna piss off Joan Crawford and go with the wire hanger.

10. *Toxic Avenger* (1986)
Directed by Lloyd Kaufman

If Herschell is the Godfather of Gore, then Lloyd is its perverted uncle. You know, the kind that showed you and your buddies stag movies when your parents weren't around? And even gave you lube? Oh—that never happened to you? That's a shame . . . What can one say about a man who has made a lifelong commitment to splatstick, not just by churning out film after film, but by forming a company (more like a religion), Troma, whose sole agenda is to spread the Gospel of Splatstick throughout the world like some sick Scientologist with Apostles such as James Gunn and Joe Lynch? One can say—*thank you*, and embrace the world of Lloyd Kaufman and kneel at the feet of Toxie, the Son He has sent to live among us. As Keith Richards is to rock 'n' roll, Lloyd Kaufman is to splatstick, and when all the others have come and gone, Lloyd will still be there making us vomit with laughter.

Highlight splatstick moment: The moment I personally will always try to top in terms of milking a moment dry: the car crash. Gruesome, shocking, and outlandish enough as it is, but to then take it even further up a notch by having the witnesses, just when you are expecting them to help, instead whip out a Polaroid camera and begin snapping photos of the flattened victims? Genius. Fucked up, but genius nonetheless.

11. *Evil Dead 2* (1987)
Directed by Sam Raimi

Ah . . . the two-year bliss comes to an end with this, a truly screwball splatstick that has given many, myself included, whiplash from the sheer velocity of gore-rific pandemonium on display. Yes, Virginia, Sam Raimi once made films besides *Spider-Man*, and this masterpiece is a monument to his studio-unencumbered edge. With Bruce Campbell playing Johnny Depp to Sam's Tim Burton, there are few films that are such perfect incarnations of themselves. Everything works, and it all works without bloated computer effects and intruding studio executives and a five-month shooting schedule. It's organic. It's real. It's "on the spot" and it's eternally fresh. What punk rock is to music, *Evil Dead 2* is to horror. Dead by Dawn? Never.

Highlight splatstick moment: Hands down (bad pun intended): the sequence where Ash wrestles with his own severed hand. Jim Carrey, go home!

12. *Dead-Alive* (1993)
Directed by Peter Jackson

Proving Americans don't have the edge on mental illness, this import from New Zealand shows, like *Evil Dead 2* does, that budding filmmakers with dubious imaginations can go on to make multimillion-dollar movies and be awarded Oscars. So next time some preacher/teacher/parent wags their finger at you for playing with latex guts and Karo syrup in your basement and filming it all with your cell phone camera, just tell them to go talk to Sam Raimi or Peter Jackson!

Highlight splatstick moment: Guess I'm just a sucker for a scene of mayhem gleefully documented by a loony onlooker (see *Toxic Avenger* highlight), but my favorite *Dead-Alive* scene is at the zoo, when the rat monkey tears apart a guest—then cut to, of all people, Uncle Forry *"Famous Monsters"* Ackerman, zealously taking a picture with his outdated Brownie camera. Talk about a Kodak moment.

13. *Slither* (2006)
Directed by James Gunn

Anyone notice the gap between this splatstick and the last? Yep, thirteen years, folks. Thirteen years. Never has there been such a dry spell. (Sorry, but although so many of Freddy's nightmares and Jason's Fridays feature inspired splatstick deaths, the tired rehashes just don't rate "Top" anything, as Freddy and Jason were never intended to be silly or parodic.) After such an explosion of creativity in the eighties, the well ultimately dried up, yielding to an unfortunate nineties philosophy that horror was dead, and that the only way to approach the genre was with self-aware satires starring pouty Fox and WB starlets who had a week off from filming *Melrose Place* (thanks, Kevin Williamson). Talk about a cock tease—with their corporate studio fear of offending and a ruining desire to "play it safe," these flicks gave any card-carrying splatstick fan a bad case of blue balls.

Enter the New Generation. The kids reared on *Fangoria* and that Camelot period of the mid-eighties. Enter Rob Zombie and

House of 1000 Corpses. Eli Roth and *Cabin Fever*, Edgar Wright and *Shaun of the Dead*, Don Mancini and *Seed of Chucky* (doing to *Child's Play* what George and Tobe did to *Dead* and *Chainsaw*), Joe Lynch and *Wrong Turn 2*, Adam Green and *Hatchet*, me and *2001 Maniacs*. And yes, enter Lloyd Kaufman protégé James Gunn and *Slither*, a cult classic the instant it premiered.

Highlight splatstick moment: With a fearless performance from Michael Rooker that does James Karen, Jeffrey Combs, and Bruce Campbell proud, *Slither* plays as much eighties horror as it does *South Park*, and that's an interesting point, considering *South Park*'s gurus, Trey Parker and Matt Stone, also earned their wings at Troma. What could be more Troma and *South Park* than my highlight moment, in which the bewildered hicks come across an infected, bloated, giant Stella, looking like a cross between Jabba the Hut and *Willy Wonka*'s Violet Beauregard ("I'm so hungry, would you mind handin' me a piece of that possum over there?"). Kudos to Gunn for foregoing CGI and using on-set, old-school effects, courtesy of Rob Bottin. This is pure tip-of-the-hat to forty years of splatstick, yet entirely its own brand-new model for the new millennium. Like his aforementioned brothers in blood, Gunn understands the cathartic joy to be had from laughing at absurdity, turning tragedy into comedy (for isn't comedy tragedy plus time?), scares into social commentary. What else can one do in a world of 9/11, George W. Bush, and the so-called War on Terror other than finger paint with blood and guts? LONG LIVE SPLATSTICK!

STEPHEN VOLK'S TEN MOVIE FATES WORSE THAN DEATH

 Stephen Volk is the creator-writer of the multiple-award-winning British TV drama series Afterlife *and the notorious (almost legendary) BBC-TV "Halloween hoax"* Ghostwatch. *As screenwriter, his credits include Ken Russell's* Gothic, *William Friedkin's* The Guardian, *and* Octane, *starring Madeleine Stowe. His first collection of stories was* Dark Corners *(Gray Friar Press), from which the short story "31/10" was nominated for a Horror Writers Association Bram Stoker Award and for a British Fantasy Award.*

1. **Donald Sutherland in** *Invasion of the Body Snatchers* **(Philip Kaufman, 1978)**
   Can anything be more terrible than Sutherland in the final shot? A fisheyed pod-person keening to the rest of his tribe, and pointing at the camera as he does so, as if to say: "You're next!"

2. **Tyrone Power in** *Nightmare Alley* **(Edmund Goulding, 1947)**
   Depression-era drifter Stanton Carlisle thinks he's heading for the showbiz big-time with his fake clairvoyant act in this taut, excellently photographed film noir. But con-artistry is what you do while fate has other plans. And (ignoring the add-on happy ending) he ends up the very figure he abhors—the "Geek"—in this, the carny movie of all carny movies.

3. **Nick Nolte in** *Cape Fear* **(Martin Scorsese, 1991)**
   Yes, Robert De Niro (as Max Cady) might be dispatched into the waves at the end of Martin Scorsese's Biblical flood, but is it really a victory? The last we see of Nick Nolte, he is squatting like an ape-man in the primal sludge, with his head hung and

his arms covered in blood. Cady has turned him into himself—a murderer.

4. Jack Nicholson in *One Flew Over the Cuckoo's Nest* (Milos Forman, 1975)

Thank God the Chief threw that water cooler through the window and escaped the madhouse, because without that scene, the brain-dead blankness in rebel Jack's lobotomized countenance at the end of this brilliant satire would have been too much to bear.

5. Julianne Moore in *Safe* (Todd Haynes, 1995)

A sneeze, an itch, a visit to the dry cleaner's. Slowly, Carol White becomes allergic to everything around her and is drawn inexorably into a hell of her own creation (or is it?). The final frame, of her shielded from the outside world from head to toe, completely protected but utterly de-humanized, is abidingly chilling.

6. Jonathan Pryce in *Brazil* (Terry Gilliam, 1985)

In his imagination, bureaucratic drone Sam Lowry is a knight soaring with eagle's wings in romantic bliss. In reality, in this Brave New World, his head has been fucked by his smiling torturer/friend Michael Palin. Bold filmmaking by the most terror-driven Monty Python member, soaring to his own heights of absurdist horror.

7. Everyone in *Requiem for a Dream* (Darren Aronofsky, 2000)

Be careful if you go on this trip of trips with Jared Leto, Jennifer Connelly, Marlon Wayans, and Ellen Burstyn. You know within the first few minutes it's going to end badly; you can't imagine *how* badly. A relentless spiral sucks them, and us, down where we don't want to go. And their doom is all the more devastating for being undeserved.

8. Ray Liotta in *Hannibal* (Ridley Scott, 2001)

Perhaps the ultimate "look away" moment in recent cinema, this scene shows Anthony Hopkins's increasingly camp cannibal living up to his nickname, and taking epicurean delight in serving up loathsome Paul Krendler a tasty menu of his own cerebral hemispheres—while, of *course*, he is *still alive*. Porridge, anyone?

9. Christian Bale in *The Machinist* (Brad Anderson, 2004)

In this wonderfully unstable concoction of a movie, you are never quite sure what is reality and what is in the mind of the protagonist, skeletal Trevor Reznik. (Personally, I like that.) But when the truth comes rushing in, it is so powerful you feel the agony of a man whose very soul was altered irrevocably by a simple act of fate.

10. Michael Gambon in *The Cook, the Thief, His Wife, and Her Lover* (Peter Greenaway, 1989)

You may not have much sympathy for despicable Cockney gangster Albert Spica after you've witnessed the awful way he treats his wife (Helen Mirren), his minions, and an angelic cherub of a child. But the finale of this Jacobean revenge tragedy, served up with operatic flair and painterly precision, entails his being forced at gunpoint to eat Alan Howard's divinely cooked penis. *Bon appétit*!

REAL OR REEL? THE FACTS BEHIND FIVE HORROR FILMS THAT CLAIM TO BE BASED ON A TRUE STORY

1. *The Amityville Horror* (1979): On November 30, 1974, twenty-three-year-old Ronald DeFeo, Jr. killed his parents and four siblings in a house located at 112 Ocean Avenue in Amityville, New York. Thirteen months later, in December 1975, George and Kathy Lutz and their children bought the house (which had remained vacant since the murders) and moved in. Twenty-eight days after that, the Lutz family fled the house, claiming terrifying encounters with supernatural forces. Those are the events as recounted in Jay Anson's bestselling book (subtitled "A True Story"), and in a blockbuster film that spawned a prequel (which fictionalized the DeFeo killings) and numerous sequels. While the murders are a matter of public record (DeFeo, in fact, is still incarcerated at Green Haven Correctional Facility in New York) and the Lutz family did hastily leave their home, the veracity of many details in the story has been questioned by researchers. The infamous house still stands in Amityville, although the structure has been extensively renovated, and the street address changed to discourage sightseers. A remake of *The Amityville Horror* appeared in 2005 that took even greater liberties with the facts than the original version.

2. *The Mothman Prophecies* (2002): An adaptation of John A. Keel's account of his investigation of strange events in Point Pleasant, West Virginia, where an eerie, winged figure dubbed "Mothman" allegedly appeared to numerous locals and seemed to be a harbinger of doom. The film, directed by Mark Pellington, updates the real-life events (which took place in the sixties) to the present day, and streamlines the sightings of the Mothman into

a conventional narrative structure. It also creates a more reliably cinematic (and entirely fictional) protagonist in *Washington Post* reporter John Klein (played by Richard Gere), although the original author is referenced in Klein's initials, as well as in another fictitious character, played by Alan Bates, named Leek (Keel spelled backwards). The movie also eliminates the book's digressions into UFO sightings and *X-Files*-like conspiracy theories, but it is chillingly powerful and accurate in its depiction of one of the key events in the real-life case: The tragic collapse of the Silver Bridge between Point Pleasant and Gallipolis, Ohio, which occurred on December 15, 1967, and killed forty-six people.

3. *The Texas Chainsaw Massacre* (2003): In fairness to the original *Texas Chainsaw Massacre* (1974), cowriter/director Tobe Hooper, in interviews, cited only an influence from true events: the horrific crimes of "Plainfield Ghoul" Ed Gein. However, the 2003 remake, directed by Marcus Nispel, proclaimed on its poster that it was "Inspired by a True Story." While certain details in both films correspond with the real crimes—in particular, cannibalism, and the use of human skin and body parts as adornments and fetishes—the Gein case occurred in Wisconsin in the fifties, not in Texas in the seventies. Further, there was no murderous "family" involved in real life as there was in the *TCM* films. And, most pointedly, there were no reports of the use of a chainsaw. The official-sounding opening crawl of the original *TCM*, and the pseudo-documentary footage in the remake (both narrated by actor John Larroquette), also helped convince many viewers that the films depict a "true" story. The Gein case also inspired author Robert Bloch in the creation of Norman Bates in his novel *Psycho*, as well as Thomas Harris's serial killer Buffalo Bill in *The Silence of the Lambs*.

4. *The Exorcism of Emily Rose* (2005): This surprise hit—promoted as "Based on a True Story"—was a loose treatment of the case of Anneliese Michel, a young German woman who reportedly suffered from demonic possession and died in 1976 after a Catholic Church–authorized exorcism. Her parents, along with the two priests who oversaw the exorcism, were prosecuted and found guilty of manslaughter in the girl's death, since medical testing stated that the girl's problem was epilepsy, not possession. Director Scott Derrickson's movie set the story in the United States, renamed the girl Emily Rose, and featured the trial of one priest (and a profoundly different legal outcome). In 2006, German director Hans-Christian Schmid made the film *Requiem*, which was promoted as a more truthful (but still fictionalized) account of the case. Anneliese Michel's grave in Klingenberg am Main, Bavaria, Germany, is reportedly a pilgrimage site for some devout Catholics to this day.

5. *Wolf Creek* (2005): This Australian shocker, concerning three backpackers in the Outback who are stalked and tormented by a serial killer, was marketed as "Based on True Events." The events in question, however, did not take place near the Wolfe (note the actual spelling) Creek meteorite crater in western Australia as presented in the film, but rather in the northern part of the continent near Barrow Creek, in 2001. Two English tourists, Peter Falconio and Joanne Lees, were accosted by a drifter named Bradley John Murdoch, who killed Falconio and abducted Lees. She escaped and Murdoch was apprehended by authorities after a massive manhunt. In 2006, Lees published a non-fiction account of her ordeal titled *No Turning Back*. The film's killer is also reportedly modeled on another Australian serial murderer, Ivan Milat, who kidnapped and murdered hitchhikers in New South Wales in the nineties.

—*S.B.*

MARK GOODALL'S TEN REAL MONDO MOVIE DEATHS

Mark Goodall is a lecturer in media communications at the University of Bradford UK. He is the author of Sweet and Savage: The World Through the Shockumentary Film Lens *(Headpress), and* Crash Cinema *(CSP), and a member of the advisory board for the* Journal of Horror Studies. *He is a founding member the Firminists, an experimental writing group (http://firminists.blogspot.com/) and lead singer of Rudolf Rocker (http://www.myspace.com/rudolf rocker).*

"Real" "mondo" death: surely a contradiction in terms? The "shockumentary" or mondo film is one of the most controversial genres in cinema history. Eschewing virtually all of the rules of conventional documentary cinema, the mondo film blazed its way through the grindhouse, the arthouse, the domestic VCR revolution, the torrent of reality and actuality TV, and the Internet with its montages of shocking and repulsive human/animal behavior. Most mondo films concentrate on bizarre rituals around the globe, both sacred and profane. Yet in order to amplify the terror of the real, the mondo director occasionally sneaks in some "actual" death footage to jolt the viewer. While death scenes in the mondo film are often faked, they appear convincingly real and, as this list demonstrates, are some of the most unforgettable moments in film history. Is the shockumentary film a horror film? If horror can lurk in the cold brutality of everyday life, then mondo cinema is the place to find it.

1. Animal Apocalypse

Despite previous manifestations of "offbeat" documentary cinema, the first mondo film proper was Jacopetti and Prosperi's *Mondo Cane* (1963) from which the adjective "mondo" derives. A sequence in the film shows the disastrous results of atomic testing around the Pacific island of Bikini. The horrific effects of this contamination are demonstrated by the pathetic image of a turtle so disorientated by the pollution that she is unable to find the sea and is condemned to die slowly in the scorching sun. Mild stuff by today's standards, but an upsetting hors d'oeuvre of what was to come.

2. Flaming Corpse

The first human death in mondo cinema occurs in the sequel to *Mondo Cane*: *Mondo Cane 2* (1964). The iconic and haunting ritual immolation suicide of Quang Duc, a Vietnamese monk, in protest against the persecution of Buddhists during the Vietnam War is rendered in glorious Technicolor accompanied by an ominous two-note organ riff.

3. Speared to Death

Some may argue that the mistreatment of animals—a frequent mondo motif—is less traumatic than human suffering. Try watching Jacopetti and Prosperi's *Africa Addio* (1966), then. The shocking destruction of Africa by corruption and colonial neglect is symbolized by the emasculation and slaughter of the natural world. Lions lose their will to roar while hunters either blast elephants and crocodiles with high powered rifles or rip them to death with hundreds of spears. One of the worst scenes occurs when a hippopotamus is gradually speared to death by tribal poachers; in the end it resembles an enormous blood-drenched pincushion.

4. Shot for the Camera?

It's not just animals that are destroyed in *Africa Addio*. The Italian film crew narrowly escaped execution, then joined a group of alarming mercenaries trying to retake a Congolese village from rebels. After the mercenaries succeed, one of the rebel leaders, alleged to have raped and murdered dozens of innocents, is summarily shot—right in front of the camera. After the officer has a second shot blasted into his head, he is dragged into the bush. The incident caused a storm in Italy, where journalists accused the filmmakers of "conspiring in genocide to get good pictures," and the footage was sequestered.

5. Cannibal Deaths

There are close links between the mondo film and the cannibal and zombie films that exploded out of Italy in the late 1970s. The curious Italian/Japanese film *Guinea Ama* (*L'isola del cannibali,* 1974) includes convincing footage of cannibalistic practices as the tribal dead are suspended in slings, smeared in oils, and nibbled at. Some of this footage was later reused in the dire horror flick *Zombie Creeping Flesh* (1983), further cementing the link between mondo and gore cinema.

6. Death in America

One of the most intriguing aspects of mondo cinema is that the weird behavior captured by its lens is not just exotic and "Third World." The violence and insanity of the American psyche, for example, is examined in *Killing of America* (1979), scripted by the late Leonard Schrader (brother of Paul Schrader, screenwriter of *Taxi Driver*). This somber shockumentary is packed with caught-on-camera shootings, sniper attacks, hold-ups, suicides, and police killings. Bleak, depressing, with a powerful political message . . . and as traumatic as "death as entertainment" should be.

7. Killed by Comrades

In addition to a host of fascinating death rituals from around the globe, Thierry Zéno's superb film *Des Morts* (*Of the Dead*) (1979) captures the passing from life to death—and then to immortality. Amos Vogel praised the film for "breaking the last taboo," and the most shocking if not the most bloody moment is a scene where a Philippine rebel accused of treachery is machine-gunned by his former comrades. "He was a good friend," says the chief executioner afterwards, which makes the protracted killing (the victim is seen gasping and twitching in the background) all the more obscene. The notion of letting death unfold in front of the camera lens has since been copied but to lesser effect. The directors of the film later excised this sequence—the only section they had "bought in"—feeling its shock aspect too contrived.

8. Absurd Deaths

Most horror fans who are aware of mondo cinema will know it through the notorious and successful *Faces of Death* franchise. *Faces of Death* (1979) was the first mondo film to achieve success through the burgeoning home video market, even more so when it joined the list of "video nasties" drawn up by the right-wing British government of Margaret Thatcher. *Faces of Death* is so depressingly spurious (its sequence of a "Far East" restaurant serving live monkey brains is infamous) that when real deaths, such as the police footage of the carnage caused by a terrible plane crash, are shown, the viewer is left simply numb.

9. Tragedy in the Sky

A real death in *Sweet and Savage* (1983), an otherwise mediocre mondo offering, demonstrates that the gore-aspect of a film does not in itself make horror. Legendary trapeze artist Karl Wallenda is filmed attempting a highly dangerous walk across two towers in Puerto Rico. The wire sways and bends in the fierce winds. Upon reaching the center of the rope, Wallenda stumbles and hangs—agonizingly—for a few seconds before plunging to his death. The way in which this death is spliced with French tightrope-walker Philippe Petit's successfully negotiating his line makes the tragedy even more painful to experience: A horror that lurks in your mind long after you have witnessed it.

10. Suicide is Painful

The mondo film eventually morphed into the underground home-made compilation tape of atrocities, the most successful of which was the *Amok Assault Video* (1989). A staple of these *détourné* shock tapes was the live suicide of R. Budd Dwyer, who had been convicted of corruption and at a press conference called afterwards blew his brains out—live on American TV. The long version of this incident, including his speech comparing the U.S. to a gulag, is one of the most graphic and upsetting sequences in media history. It is arguably worse on second viewing, knowing what is to come. *Amok* guru Stuart Swezey has noted that the horror of the mondo film was (unlike the slasher movie) "truly an experiment in terror." Sometimes reality is more horrific than fantasy.

NANCY HOLDER'S THIRTEEN MOVIES SHE WISHES SHE'D NEVER SEEN BECAUSE THEY'RE TOO SCARY (YET CONTINUES TO WATCH REPEATEDLY. WHAT THE HELL IS WRONG WITH HER?)

Nancy Holder is a USA Today *bestselling author and former Trustee of the Horror Writers Association. She has received four Bram Stoker Awards, and her work has appeared on recommended reading lists by the New York Public Library; the American Reading Association; and the American Library Association. She has written many tie-in novels and authorized episode guides for shows such as* Buffy the Vampire Slayer, Angel, Smallville, *and others. She also* writes spookiness for children and young adults, most notably as Chris P. Flesh and Carolyn Keene.

1. *The Haunting* (1963, directed by Robert Wise)
2. *Hush . . . Hush, Sweet Charlotte* (1964, directed by Robert Aldrich)
3. *The Ring* (2002, directed by Gore Verbinski)*
4. *I Walked With a Zombie* (1943, directed by Jacques Tourneur)
5. *The Body Snatcher* (1945, directed by Robert Wise)
6. *Rosemary's Baby* (1968, directed by Roman Polanski)
7. *The Others* (2001, directed by Alejandro Amenábar)
8. *The Innocents* (1962, directed by Jack Clayton)
10. *Alien* (1979, directed by Ridley Scott)
11. *Tale of Two Sisters* (2003, directed by Kim Ji-woon)
12. *Suspiria* (1977, directed by Dario Argento)
13. *Curse of the Demon* (1957, directed by Jacques Tourneur)

* (I know, there's no explaining it.)

CERINA VINCENT'S TOP TEN HORROR MOVIES TOO SCARY FOR LITTLE GIRLS

Actress Cerina Vincent is best known to horror fans for her role as Marcy in Eli Roth's Cabin Fever *(for which she was nominated for the Saturn Awards' "Best Face of the Future"). Her other credits include the* Power Rangers Lost Galaxy *series (as Maya, the Yellow Power Ranger),* Not Another Teen Movie, *David Lynch's short film* Darkened Room, *and guest-starring roles on the TV shows* Malcolm in the Middle, Ally McBeal, *and* CSI. *She is also the coauthor (with Jodi Lipper) of the 2007 diet book* How to Eat Like a Hot Chick *(Collins Books). Her Web site is www.cerinavincent.net.*

Though I'm madly in love with the horror genre now, I have to admit that I was not always a horror fan. Unfortunately, between the tender ages of five and nine, I was exposed to horror films that terrified me until I was twenty. Maybe I had an overactive imagination, or maybe I just wasn't as cool as some other kids, but these movies screwed with my young brain; I worried and obsessed about these films daily, and spent too many nights falling asleep with the light on or sleeping in my parents' bed. It wasn't *my* parents who showed me these films too early—it was my *friends'* parents. These adults were renting frightening films for their daughters' slumber parties and had no clue of the terrible effect that these films had on our innocent little lives. I now realize what a compliment that is to these brilliant horror filmmakers, but I feel I wasted too many years thinking I hated horror, when what I really hated was my friends' parents. So, to stop turning chicks away from horror, and to ensure more female horror fans, here is a list of films that little girls should not watch until they are old enough to appreciate them.

1. *Poltergeist*: Anytime the TV went fuzzy, I thought I was going to die.
2. *Poltergeist II: The Other Side*: I prayed that my teeth would straighten out so my own braces wouldn't attack me.
3. *Poltergeist III*: That little girl died. Enough said.
4. *The Shining*: This made me fear my own father, and I was scared to ride my tricycle.
5. *The Exorcist*: I just saw pieces of this and . . . wow . . . bad, bad, bad stuff for little girls. I still won't eat pea soup.
6. *Alien*: Well, I knew for a fact that I didn't want to be an astronaut.
7. *Rosemary's Baby*: I was one of those little girls who wanted a baby when I was still a baby. Until I realized that it was possible to have Satan's baby. I was also really scared for my mom when she was pregnant with my sister.

8. *Child's Play*: Like many little girls, I was obsessed with dolls, and had fifty of them displayed in my bedroom. After this film, I'd lie in my bed and wonder which one was going to come to life and torment me. . . .

9. *A Nightmare on Elm Street*: I didn't sleep peacefully for many, many years.

10. *Jaws*: This ended up being my favorite movie by the time I was 12, but you can't make a little girl watch this and then throw her in the ocean and expect her to go snorkeling. I also was convinced that Jaws could get me in the bathtub, was under the drain in my swimming pool, and lived in Lake Mead.

JOE LYNCH'S TEN MOVIES MY MOTHER SHOULD HAVE NEVER LET ME WATCH (BUT THANKFULLY DID!)

Joe Lynch was born in Long Island, raised on a steady diet of horror films, novels, comics, and dirty-water hot dogs. Upon graduating from Syracuse University, Lynch was named "Filmmaker of the Year" in The Village Voice's *Best of Long Island issue for his short films and his first real first film job was as a grip/actor/third unit director/writer on the Troma cult classic* Terror Firmer, *which led to an in-house writing position at "The House that Toxie Built." Lynch created the hit show* Uranium *for FuseTV, and directed many a music video for artists like 311, Sugarcult, DevilDriver, and Strapping Young Lad.* Wrong Turn 2 *(2007) was Joe's first feature film and a dream come true for a die-hard horror fanatic. He currently resides in L.A. with his lovely (and tolerant) wife, Briana, and their manic pooch "Buckaroo" Banzai.*

My mother, Marina, will not be so keen on me exposing this list, but no matter. See, my mom, herself a horror nut as a teenager, is the red-handed culprit who passed on the virus of horror to me (as well as my two younger brothers) at a very susceptible age. It was that early exposure to the ghoulish that made me fall in love with horror, be it good, bad, or ugly. Yet, it was watching these movies that first clamped my eyes open like a reformed droog to the power of manipulative cinema and visual storytelling, and to how profoundly the medium had its grip on an audience.

So, this is the epitome of a "subjective list"—it's not for you to agree or disagree with . . . frankly, it's a chance for me to possibly embarrass my mom, but also thank her for giving me the gift of appreciating great genre filmmaking, both by watching and appreciating it, and now by making it.

Thanks for scaring the shit out of me, Mom . . . I wouldn't have had it any other way.

1. *Dawn of the Dead* (seen in theaters?): aka . . . THE MOST WATCHED VIDEO IN THE LYNCH HOUSEHOLD. No lie. With *Star Wars* and *Ghostbusters* coming in at a close #2 & #3, it was Romero's second zombie epic that made the top of the list, the default film my mom would bring home if they didn't have copies of *Dead Heat*, *Deadly Friend*, or *Aliens* in stock. At the very least she knew we'd be just as happy to watch some pasty green undead stroll through the Monroeville mall and get their melons sliced off by some bikers and flyboys. What's funny is that my first recollection of seeing *Dawn* was supposedly in theaters on my mom's lap, innocently watching scenes like the one where the Afro'd Zombo takes a nice chunk out of his lover's arm, and I was thinking "wow, the stuff under the skin is white?" I recall asking my mother later when I was a little older if I did in fact see Romero's classic in the cinemas, which would mean it was arguably my first film! I remember she admitted it to me then; however, now that her tastes and parenting skills are under the microscope, I doubt she'll fess up, and when I recently asked, she

said she didn't recall . . . was it *Popeye*? I think she's bullshitting me . . . I think it *was Dawn*!

I can hypothesize that the reason she brought me was that no babysitter was available, or so I'm assuming, and my mom needed her zombie fix, and by God and gore, was I to stop her? Never! Besides, what toddler would be able to understand what was going on up there anyway, right? I don't remember if I was "that baby" in the theater, the one screaming and hollering and making people whisper, "Who takes a baby into *this* movie?" (a sentiment shared between my wife and me while watching *The Mist* a few weeks back). I do remember barely being able to see over the seats at all those wide, dead eyes as they shuffled across the mall grounds to the delightful strains of Goblin's Muzak score. Somehow seeing that film at such an early age gave it a special importance to me, and multiple (and I mean multiple) viewings on VHS have secured it a place in my top films of all time, not just for nostalgic purposes, but because it is truly a masterpiece in horror cinema and art cinema as well. It's horror with meaning, with resonance. My mom's exposing me to *good* horror early on made me carefully develop my taste buds for the genre, giving me an early taste of what's to offer while injecting me with a love to scare, shock, and affect people which has been coursing through my veins ever since.

So while the truth might never be revealed, and I dare you to ask her one day without getting shot (yes, she carries a gun . . . but that's another story). But it was this film that made me fall in love with the horror genre, and the one I thank my mother every day for showing me.

2. *The Exorcist* (seen on VHS): One of my earliest memories is watching this film from the staircase of my parents' second house, not being able to *move*. So it was more my fault for sneaking an off-limits peek of this truly unsettling horror masterpiece from daring film-

maker William Friedkin, one of my childhood cinematic heroes (what kid references *Sorcerer* in social studies class?), than it was my mother's. But I couldn't believe what I had seen that first time I white-knuckled the banisters of the staircase as Regan ravaged her thingy with a crucifix, an image that no six-year-old should be absorbing. I needed to see it again, and one night, my mom rented the video and we planned on watching it over a huge bowl of Velveeta mac-n-cheese. My mother had told me that night that she got the chance to see the film at Radio City Music Hall when it premiered in 1974, when the bodies were hitting the floor/aisles and the vomit was flying, and not just on screen. Even she was unnerved seeing it then, saying it was scary because it felt so *real*, from the acting to the scenes in the hospital, and with my communion coming up soon that year, it made me think that this film was a lot more dangerous that I realized. It was *because* Friedkin kept the scares and the drama on a very grounded, human level that the film works, and being a just few years younger than Regan when I saw it again that night made me think I too could be next on Pazuzu's list of young nubile kids to visit. Seeing the film as a kid made me want to grow up *real* fast and skip that whole "pissing on the carpet" phase.

3. *The Toxic Avenger* (seen on VHS): This movie's a little Molotov cocktail of sickness, and I caught the bug very early. It had such a cheerful demeanor, like a child molester at a mall with a smile and a red balloon, who will pull his Dockers down to poke you with his pork. I remember my mother actually expressing real *anger* after watching this movie with us on a snow day home from school, as our jaws were floating in our hot cocoas, watching the Tromatic depravity on display with such reckless abandon. I was fascinated by how this tongue-in-cheek movie about New Jersey's first and only mutant superhero could offend her so much! Well, aside from the gratuitous head-crushing, the rape,

dismemberment, nudity, mutant intercourse, and, of course, obese evil-doer gut-crushing worthy of a Chas. Balun magazine cover, the movie was also very sweet and even good-natured in its message of peace and love amid barrels of toxic waste. It was the comedy that almost made the film *more* offensive, that it was having such a good time showing all this depravity, and I guess that was where my mom drew the line, but it was enough for me to be a Tromatic fan for life. I later had the honor to work as a writer for Troma and have a hand in the creation of the fourth installment in the Toxie saga (*Citizen Toxie*), and it was working with gonzo genius Lloyd Kaufman that I learned that you can make films no matter what the cost, what the risk, what the taste. Troma is true independent cinema, blood, boobs, and all, and it was that punk attitude that I guess just didn't agree with the madre at the time . . . which only made it cooler to love.

4. **Stephen King's *Silver Bullet* (seen in theaters):** One of the few films I got to see in the theater with both my mother *and* my grandfather (her father), who was a Big Gulp of a man (at least to a tyke like me, he was a skyscraper at 6'4") and at the time was dealing with the complications of ALS. It was a school night, so seeing a movie on a night homework needed to be completed (and barely was anyway), was already a no-no, but since my mom and I were big King fans, we said "screw it!" and dragged her father out for a night at the movies at this new thing called the "multiplex" that just opened up on the Long Island Expressway. Couldn't get in there (some strict policy of not letting anyone in after the lights go down), so we ended up in a small one-screen theater closer to town, and that night, even bookended with two people I felt secure with, I was terrified of this goddamned werewolf and the cycle of terror he wrought on the small town. The casting genius of pairing up Corey Haim and Gary Busey aside, this film started off with a gratuitous head-ripping, and by the end

I remember clutching my grandfather's side as they fought off the holy Lycan for dear life, my mom smiling the whole time. The film is deceptive in its almost "teen movie" tone with the kid scenes, yet when it comes to the scenes of murder and wolfy mayhem, the film gets dark and even nihilistic, like the scene when the fat guy gets pulled under his own shack or when the kid is killed on the veranda. Tough stuff, but a great night at the movies nonetheless. . . .

5. Fangoria's *Scream Greats, Volume 1: Tom Savini, Master of Horror Effects* (seen on VHS): I don't remember how this ended up in our cheapo Zenith VTR (sorry, no recording for us on the first machine) but this hour-long documentary on the FX master and his rise to splatter stardom was one the few films from the library that we rented on a regular basis, second only to *Dawn of the Dead*, which was like the grand thesis of Savini's handiwork. It was this documentary that made me first appreciate the intricate details an FX artist like Savini or Rick Baker would strive to achieve, a realism behind the latex and Karo syrup, and it only made me appreciate practical effects more in my own career. It also showed me how to stage an effective razor-blade slash (used in George Romero's *Martin*), which much to my mother's insanity and chagrin, gave her six heart attacks when I pulled it off one day in the kitchen. It was hilarious. But Savini's infectious, kid-like demeanor in the documentary made moviemaking seem like so much fun, and his job was the best on set. That's where I wanted to be . . . next to the buckets of blood!

6. *Maximum Overdrive* (seen on bootleg VHS): My mom's cousin/BFF, Donna, had somehow obtained a bootleg copy of this film to cheer me up after the death of my grandfather, whom I was very close with. What a twisted kid, huh? So to keep me and my cousins busy while they prepared food for the wake, she

gave us *Robocop* and this Stephen King–directed organ-grinder that even today feels underappreciated. My mother told Donna that I really wanted it after traveling with her to New York City one day and seeing posters with a looming, bearded King on it, daring us "I'm gonna scare you to death." Being a "Constant Reader" even as a child, I was pumped to see *MO* and disappointed it never came to our town. So when I finally saw it on a scratchy and poorly pan-and-scanned bootleg, I was shocked to discover that the film, while having its own forgivable flaws and unique charms as a slice of unfiltered King (for better or worse), had sucker-punched me by gleefully breaking a cinema taboo. The movie showed a little boy getting killed. Even when I was a kid, I remember thinking that it was a concept that was never approached or imagined to be broken, and that there was some rulebook in the mystical land of Hollywood that everyone abided by that stipulated that killing a young child, especially in a horribly sick, twisted, and deplorable way, like, oh, I dunno, say. . . . rolling over them with a frickin' *steamroller*, was strictly forbidden. This almost felt like King was saying, "Yeah? Well, fuck you and the horse you rode in on!" and the next thing I know, I'm watching a loving close-up of a Little Leaguer's dome being crushed. But what I remember more is how that one moment scared the shit out of me and filled me in a little bit about Death; he don't care 'bout *no body*. Adults, kids, dogs, Emilio Estevez . . . no one is safe from the trucks. But between my grandfather's wake and King's cinematic wake-up call to my senses, I got a little more up-close and personal with Death that day, which only makes one appreciate life more.

7. *Videodrome* (seen on VHS): Okay . . . honestly, of all the movies on this list, this is the most complex, the most sexually intense and the ickiest of the bunch . . . so why in God's good green gonads would any well-adjusted mother let her son watch this ambitious

and perverted thriller? I had seen *The Fly* in theaters with my dad, which was a hoot, but my mother was the guilty party for renting *VD* (how fitting) from the library and subjecting me to James Woods pulling a VHS out of what I later discovered was a giant vagina in his stomach. Hey, my mom was usually fine with the gore; it was the "making whoopee" stuff and the chick from Blondie burning her tits that prompted a fast-forwarding. Even then, I remember thinking how the film was so forward-thinking, that it felt like a real peek into the future, and it opened my eyes to how horror films could both sicken and provoke a deeper thinking. Plus it had an entrail-exploding television, and is what prompted my asking what the word "intestine" meant after watching the final scene with the "Sausage Vision" on TV. See kids? Learning *can* be fun!

8. *Evil Dead* (seen on VHS): That damned white box was what sealed the deal. If you remember, the old EMI videos would some- times come in white VHS hardcover plastic shells, and for some reason, I convinced my mother to heed Stephen King's claim that the film was "the most ferociously original film of the year" and just rent it . . . how bad could it be, right? Most of the horror videos at the time were in black hard cases or those huge porno boxes with the glossy cardboard finish displaying H. G. Lewis movies instead of *Little Oral Annie.* In our video store (which at the time was a kiosk in the King Kullen) the *Evil Dead* box was white, which to me meant "pussy" or "Rainbow Brite." So my mom relented, thinking "Well, Stephen King *did* see it . . ." and next thing I knew, I was having nightmares of trees going up my ass and spending years trying to figure out "How did they do that?" while my mother kept buying me *Gorezone* magazine and taking me to the magic store to buy latex and spirit gum. Thanks, Raimi. Then again, it was the film that taught me the word "disembowelment," so all was not lost!

9. *Last of the Mohicans* (seen in theaters): What??? Lynch, you're going soft on us! I know, I know. The reason this film is on this list is because it was one of the few flicks that Mom took us to that *wasn't* a horror movie, yet for some reason we were all in agreement that we would sneak into it after the action onslaught that was *Under Siege*. (God bless that birthday cake, huh?) But Michael Mann's sweeping and exciting adaptation of James Fenimore Cooper's novel also had multiple scalpings, numerous bloody battles, a graphic ambush with stabbings galore, one of the greatest third acts in cinema history, *and* the best kiss/make-out scene this side of *Rear Window*. So why is it on the list? To balance things out, guys . . . not all of these films have to be horror. My mother shouldn't have illegally snuck us into this movie, but the dramatic power the film had over her and her three psychotic boys was astounding. Mann not only shoots the hell out of this movie, but the emotional impact of characters' dying was to me what horror movies were missing at the time I saw it. Wait, we're supposed to feel bad when this character is burned at the stake, or when another sacrifices himself for his true love? All this violence, and my heartstrings are being tugged? I was confused, but also excited that a film like this had affected us so much in the theater. It has now become a family staple and I believe is my mother's favorite film. (I don't think her peer group would accept *The Exorcist*.) Plus, throw *Last of the Mohicans* in on a "movie night" date, and after the famed necking scene between Daniel Day-Lewis and Madeleine Stowe, I guarantee you'll be sliding into second base in no time.

10. *Psycho* (seen on TV): I remember this classic Hitchcock slasher from the many TV airings it had on New York's WPIX, Channel 11, but even more so from the poster my mom bought me for my bedroom before I even saw it. I admired the beauty of the framed pop-art-esque one-sheet daily when I stepped out of

the room. It reminded me that Hitch was a Cinema King and that Janet Leigh's undergarments defined "perk." One night my mother made an extended effort to make sure my homework was done early, then made a big buttery bowl of popcorn, and we sat down to watch *Psycho* together, even though its razor-sharp tension was dulled by commercial breaks for peanut butter Twix and Tab. No matter; even with the commercials and all the lights on in the house, we were both chilly with fright, from the rainy, fateful drive to the Bates Motel, to the final moments of the dark smile over Norman's face. The silent tension that precedes the most famous shower scene in film history is what sticks with me—that, and how a film that could play on public television without too many edits could still feel brutal and unflinching.

F. X. FEENEY'S TEN ESSENTIAL "CHILDREN OF HORROR" FILMS

F. X. Feeney is best known for his writings on film for L.A. Weekly *and the* Z Channel. *Feeney's credits as a screenwriter include* Frankenstein Unbound *(1990), which he wrote for director Roger Corman, based on the novel by Brian Aldiss; and* The Big Brass Ring *(1999), based on a story by Orson Welles, for director George Hickenlooper. His books include* Roman Polanski *and* Michael Mann, *both published by Taschen.*

I was tempted to call this list "Children, Grandchildren, and Stepchildren of the Damned." One scary kid on film breeds legions of others, it seems, in hit after hit—though it's fascinating to note that monstrous children never appeared onscreen until after 1945. Strictly speaking, they arrive in the late 1950s: but that's in keeping with the rebuilding of the world which followed Spain's civil war, the Nazi genocide against the Jews, Hiroshima and Nagasaki, and the whole of World War II. Humanity had never been obliged to consider so many displaced, lost children at one time before. The notion of "mutation" (for which we can thank our friend the atom) was also new. How better to dramatize these terrors and potential horrors than by focusing on children, whose potentials are by definition limitless?

1. *El Espiritu en las Colmena (The Spirit in the Beehive)* (1973): Ana Torrent (born in 1966) was barely five years old when Spanish filmmaker Victor Erice (born in 1941) cast her in the lead of this mysterious film-poem. Torrent's vulnerable presence and wondering, oceanic gaze are the epicenter around which the world of the film orbits—the bleak plateaus of remotest Spain circa 1940, in the silent aftermath of that country's civil war.

   She encounters a monster: James Whale's classic horror film *Frankenstein,* noisily projected on a bare wall—the very first movie she ever sees. The experience disturbs and obsesses her. The creature haunts her dreams—especially the scene where, in his own childlike enthusiasm at being accepted, the monster accidently (indeed, "innocently") drowns a child (the great Marilyn Harris). Ana begins sneaking out of the house at night, in efforts to contact the "spirit" of the monster—a quest that (with terrifying and poetic results that can make your hair stand) becomes her initiation to adult understanding.

   Although this is not, strictly speaking, a horror film, by invoking the experience of Whale's masterpiece—that most primal of the breed—the story, through the lens of Torrent's precocious capacities for terror, pity, and awe—for projecting grief to grown-up size—integrates the very meaning of "the horror tale" into *our* world, where the monsters preying upon us are the forces of history itself. This is a great gift to both lovers of horror, and poetry.

2. *The Bad Seed* (1956): One of the most charismatically horrid children in dramatic literature is Rhoda, the demon-next-door in Maxwell Anderson's play, *The Bad Seed*. She is an eight-year-old, blind of conscience, who murders without remorse and lies about it without batting an eye. Patty McCormack played this role—at age eight—on Broadway, and though she was arguably getting a mite long in the tooth (at age eleven!) by the time Mervyn LeRoy translated the play onto the screen, she remains the Iconic Evil Child of cinema. To these eyes, the secret of McCormack's precocious power is that she's so smart and funny, but never seems "knowing," and never *ever* plays for laughs. When she sets to work manipulating the adults around her, she is purely terrifying. Yet her energy is such that (innate, killer-comedic timing applied to horror will do this), over time, a ticklish anticipation at how far she will go may have you chuckling—in horror.

3. *Village of the Damned* (1960): "They're *children*," says the humane man of science, played by George Sanders.

   "Don't be sentimental," replies the military commander. "They must be destroyed!"

   Sanders is, of course, father to one of this terrifying brood— "Or perhaps not," he drily adds. Imagine a whole gang of *Bad Seed* Patty McCormacks: A circle of children—conceived in a weird multiple instance of Immaculate Conception—are born in the English village of Midwich on the same day, after a four-month gestation, and proceed to mature ten years in a matter of two or three. Similar incidents are taking place in remote villages around the world, though in those cases the locals (including the Soviets) have killed the children in their cradles. Here in more humane England, scientific curiosity prevails—until it is clear that these little telepaths are not just "otherworldly" but literally extraterrestrial, and bent on world conquest.

   At a mere seventy-seven minutes, the film has a fairytale

power in its brevity. Any longer, and it might have become "psychological"—obliged us to identify too strongly with either Sanders or the alien kids, and wrecked the clean flame of the outcome—which can fill your memory with puzzling and disturbing shadows for years after.

4. **"Toby Dammit" from *Histoires Extraordinaire (Spirits of the Dead)* (1968):** Terence Stamp plays actor Toby Dammit in the throes of a wildly decadent meltdown. "I'm not an actor!" he insists, as he clutches the trophy at an awards ceremony and kneels, hoarding it close to his chest amid a standing ovation. His even greater prize is the sleek, devilishly speedy sports car his admirers give him—and here master director Federico Fellini perhaps tips his hat to the late James Dean, for isn't it true that the shadow of all obsessive mass-admiration is subtly but forcefully a wish for our beloveds *to die,* youthfully and beautifully, so we might love them forever? One hates to think so, but the historic record is rather comically on the Devil's side of the ledger, as Fellini conceives it. Freely adapted from Edgar Alan Poe's story "Never Bet the Devil Your Head," we follow Toby as he roars through the streets of the night city, tempted toward Destiny (be it an orgasm, be it death) by a devil who repeatedly appears to him in the form of an angelic child (Marina Yaru, perfect), whose sinister, half-dead, half-sexualized gaze hints at infinities of possibility.

5. **_Don't Look Now_ (1973):** Although a young actress named Sharon Williams inhabits the red coat during this film's terrifying beginning, and Adelina Poerio (details withheld!) wears it at the horrifying finale, the child in the red coat is less the result of a performance than of a masterfully evoked *idea*. Her little red coat is the only way we know her, because (just as for the grieving father played by Donald Sutherland, who is catastrophically

undone by his ache to have her back in his life) she embodies both a heart-rending memory and a hope, always just one step ahead of us, always out of reach.

6. *The Exorcist* (1973): What child in jeopardy could be more iconic than one in the grip of Satan?

Nearly everybody sees this film sooner or later, so it needs little celebration from yours truly, but several strokes of genius must be acknowledged. First, there is the Jesuit-educated novelist, William Peter Blatty, whose bestselling novel tapped into a deep need for religious faith in an American public tested by a decade of political assassinations and civic turmoil, and a comparable need in the world at large, tested constantly by wars and social collapse. If there's a Devil, there must be a God, right? This is exactly the primal, unspoken logic Blatty tapped into. Second, there is filmmaker William Friedkin, whose own storytelling genius was so engaged by Blatty's screenplay that he applied every sensitivity, every ounce of craft and ingenuity, into creating a film which provokes the imagination as richly, if not more so, than the novel. Together, they made us see the devil in actress Linda Blair. Despite that she must work at the center of a brilliant maelstrom of diabolic effects, from the sounds of pigs being slaughtered to the husky voice of Mercedes McCambridge, her possession would not be scary or moving if Blair were not so sweet, so spontaneous and authentic.

7. *The Shining* (1980): I have this image in my head of Stephen King reading Blatty's *The Exorcist* in 1971 and thinking, "I can top this." After all, why stop at a kid being possessed by Satan when you can explore the ecstatic equivalent, a boy who is psychic and can handle it, menaced by a father who is just as psychic, but can't? Top this with the fact that Stanley Kubrick was offered *The Exorcist* and turned it down, only to regret this decision

when he saw what a mega-hit Friedkin made of it. When King's bestselling novel later crossed his desk, Kubrick brought all of his passion and precision to bear on realizing it as a film.

The result is yet another iconic "child in jeopardy," whose signature moment comes when Danny Torrance (played by young Danny Lloyd, of the thousand-yard stare) pilots his winged tricycle through the empty corridors of the Overlook Hotel, only to come upon the ghosts of twins his own age (Lisa and Louise Burns). They used to live in this place, until *their* father axemurdered them. They invite him to "come and play with us," and that is their final warning. Never underestimate the capacity of kids to stick up for one another, whatever their states of being.

8. *City of Lost Children* (1995): A young boy dreams that Santa Claus has come. But then, dream grading into nightmare, another, then another, and still other identical Santas come down the chimney. The room fills with them before the boy awakens with a cartoon howl.

So begins this comical, poetic nightmare of a film by Marc Caro and Jean-Pierre Jeunet (the latter of whom has gone on to direct such excellent films as *Amélie* [2000] and *A Very Long Engagement* [2005]). In *City of Lost Children,* the gaunt, decrepit villain is a stealer of children's dreams. He kidnaps kids, wires them up to a strange helmet matching the one on *his* head, and eavesdrops on whatever unfolds while they sleep. He's no longer capable of having dreams himself, or even of shedding his own tears—a textbook definition of adulthood, in the context of this movie. His only opponents are a circus strongman who has the mind of a child, and an orphaned nymphet who has the street-smarts of a miniature adult—a platonic pair of storybook lovers in a dinghy, like the owl and the pussycat. They row across the toxic-looking sea, under its perpetual full moon, to rescue the little boy from the first scene—but they also mean to liberate the villain, and this is the beauty of this film's ethical core. Adults, it is implied, are the children of this world most in need of rescuing.

9. **The Sixth Sense (1999)**: We've seen kid psychics—*The Shining* (1980)—and movie children have long been magically anointed into lives of special destiny—from the legends of King Arthur to the libraries of Harry Potter—but if there's a more original rite-of-passage in fantasy or horror than *The Sixth Sense*, which so movingly elevates a mortal child to the role of ghostly ambassador between this world and the next, I'm not aware of it.

Many celebrate the ingenious twist with which this film delivers our hero's protector (Bruce Willis), and us, to a new understanding in the film's final moments. In the realm of fantasy, only *Planet of the Apes* (1968) has so effectively hidden such a jaw-dropping shocker in plain sight. But the greatness of *The Sixth Sense* derives instead from the depths at which it charts both the terrors of childhood, while dramatizing the astonishing practical strength with which children everywhere master their fears. Haley Joel Osment is essential to this—he has, precociously, the gravitas of James Stewart in *Vertigo* as he probes the maze of shocks with which his great gift confronts him. (*"I see dead people!"*) More wonderful than any wild final twist is the simplicity he summons in himself at the film's most horrifying moment—hiding under a tent of blankets, he finds he has company, the outraged soul of a young murdered girl (Mischa Barton). This moment hits every nerve in a viewer, because each of us has, when small, feared what might lurk under our beds, and when grownup, felt a stab of animal panic at that floorboard which creaks for no reason at four in the morning. Haley gets a grip, and simply asks the ghost: "Can I help you?"

Can't beat that for a role model. Ever since, roused, braindead and primally afraid, from safe sleep, above the age of 50, I've asked the squeaky floors in my place the same thing—and it never fails to relax both me, and the Unseen.

10. *The Silence of the Lambs* (1991) and *Manhunter* (1986): What are *these* two movies doing here? one might ask.

Although we often fear for Will Graham's son in *Manhunter*, and whole families are attacked (children included), the action centers around the doings of adults, and the same goes for *Silence of the Lambs*, where no child is in immediate evidence.

And yet—jeopardized childhood, and monstrous transformations, are at the very heart of the horror in both films. Think of how Hannibal Lecter probes Clarice, the young detective in *The Silence of the Lambs*, fishing for clues to the child she used to be, and in many ways still is. He's not merely being a murderous, cannibal psychiatrist hunting his next mental meal, though that's the surface tension. At his core, he is seeking evidence that somewhere in this hideous world, one rare child has managed to achieve adulthood, with what's best in her, unspoiled. He is riveted by Clarice's tale of attempting to rescue lambs from slaughter. He even makes a pencil sketch, in the manner of a religious icon; for that's the feeling she's aroused in him—a restored belief. Every clue we detect of Lecter's early life (like that jumble of strange maternal stuff in his storage unit) hints at a world of child abuse so deep we'd do better not to fathom it, only trust that it's there. This is why *Hannibal* and *Hannibal Rising* inevitably failed. No one—not even Hannibal's creator, Thomas Harris—can mine the darkness behind such evil without trivializing the causes into sentimentality. It is what is *unknown* about evil acts, and what is unknown about the world we each confront as children, that is most terrifying, and therefore most cathartic, about stories involving children and horror.

In *Manhunter,* when FBI-man Jack Crawford accuses detective Will Graham of going soft—"feeling sorry" for the "Red Dragon" serial killer they're pursuing—he replies: "As a child, my heart bleeds for him. Someone took a kid and manufactured a monster. But as an adult, he's irredeemable. He murders whole families in pursuit of trivial fantasies. As an adult, someone should blow the sick fuck out of his socks."

This clear-cut, remarkably sane statement sums up the moral core inseparable from any film in which children must act in relation to horror. Heroism is a response, not a fact of nature: We may not be responsible for the horrors perpetrated upon us, but we are always accountable for how we respond.

DOUGLAS BUCK'S TEN FAVORITE FAMILIAL HORROR MOVIES

With his disturbing short films, including the notorious Cutting Moments, *Douglas Buck has been a continuing presence at international genre festivals for over ten years. With the theatrical release in France and New York of his first indie feature,* Family Portraits: A Trilogy of America, *to outstanding critical reception (including raves in both the cinephile bible* Cahiers du Cinéma *and the mainstream* Premiere*), and the completion of his second feature* Sisters, *starring Academy Award nominees Chloë Sevigny and Stephen Rea, it appears Buck's time under the radar has passed. He's arrived.*

1. *The Corpse* (1970): English stockbroker daddy Michael Gough sadistically desires his teenage daughter and humiliates his pained wife and son to the point they decide to kill him. But is that

corpse really dead? Slow moving, maybe, but wonderfully perverse and terribly underrated.

2. **"Home" (1996), an episode of *The X-Files*, Season 4:** So disturbing the Fox Network vowed to never air it again (even though, of course, they did). Scully and Mulder wish they were dealing with the supernatural rather than with this limbless mother inbreeding with her three sons in an attempt to continue their "pure" family lineage. It also happens to share the name of one of my short films.

3. ***The Brood* (1979):** David Cronenberg's idea of a family drama. A mentally unstable mother gives birth to "id" dwarfs that kill her guilty parents and take back her daughter from the father who has custody . . . leaving him no choice but to strangle her to death. The birth sequence is a seminal Cronenberg moment—psychoanalytically and intellectually fascinating, while also totally disgusting.

4. ***Deathdream* (1974):** Junior has come back from Vietnam as a zombie, and Mom is so determined to deny it she's willing to kill Dad if necessary. Talk about the elephant in the room no one's willing to talk about. Plays like a John Cassavettes drama (including two stars from his 1968 *Faces*) with a monster.

5. ***Eraserhead* (1977):** Wild-haired Henry Spencer may not be married, but—with a newborn mutant child, a disturbing Thanksgiving dinner with his girlfriend's family that has to be seen, the constant presence of a mysterious massive maw resembling a birth canal, and a terrifying sexy female neighbor sinking into a literal black pool of desire—he lives in a landscape of male anxiety regarding family life. Surreal, amazing. My favorite David Lynch film.

6. *Parents* (1989): It's 1950s America and young Michael is starting to suspect his ever-merry suburban parents of a terrible secret—they may be cannibals. And, yes, they are. If you haven't seen it, I'm not giving away much about this blackest of comedies, as the success of it lies in its disturbing and subversive presentation rather than in its admittedly one-trick-pony idea.

7. *The Texas Chainsaw Massacre* (1974): The seminal crazy hillbilly family so many horror films continue to exploit, in all its original, epic, disturbing glory and pitch-black humor. Those dim-witted American backwoods families sure can be funny—when they're not robbing graves and hanging hot teenage girls from meat hooks. "Look what your brother did to the door!"

8. *Eyes Without a Face* (1960): How far will a doctor go to restore the beautiful face of a daughter destroyed in an accident he was responsible for? Enough to surgically remove the faces of kidnapped young women in an attempt to graft a new visage on to her head, that's how far. The fact the surgeries aren't working doesn't dissuade this loving father. Proving it's not just the Americans who are obsessed with beauty is this creepy, yet strangely tender, French classic.

9. *The Cement Garden* (1993): You can argue the film's inclusion on a horror list, but it certainly has its share of sexually perverse and baroque images. Soon after the death of her husband (in a scene linking a father's death with his son's random masturbation), a mother dies of an unknown illness, leading her three children to hide her body in the basement so they can get on with their adolescent games—including the youngest boy dressing as a girl while the barely teenage son and daughter flirtatiously cultivate an incestuous desire for each other. I felt less guilty *after* I learned Charlotte Gainsbourg was over twenty

when she made the movie. Somber, slow moving, yet deeply rewarding.

10. *Shock* (1977): Dora, recovering from a mental breakdown brought on by having viciously stabbed her abusive drug-addict husband to death and hidden the body, moves in with her young boy and new husband . . . but has her first husband returned, possessing both her *and* her son? Or is she is going insane from guilt? Or is the boy seeking revenge for his dead father? Lots of perverse family intrigue—and lots of gore—in this Italian shocker. Mario Bava's final film.

MICK FARREN'S TEN BEST OF HAMMER HORROR

During his long, checkered, occasionally hallucinatory and sometimes hell-raising career, Mick Farren has published over twenty novels, which range from the psychedelic fantasy of the DNA Cowboys *trilogy to the neo-goth vampirism of* The Renquist Quartet, *and the far future militarism of* Their Master's War. *An unreconstructed rock 'n' roller, he also continues to function as a recording artist and songwriter. He resides in Los Angeles where he writes a media column for* Los Angeles CityBeat. *Find Mick at http://doc40 .blogspot.com.*

Hammer Film Productions is arguably the best-known British studio. Founded in 1934, it staggered for more than twenty years making truly dreadful, low-budget second-features like *Death in High Heels*, *Crime Reporter*, and *Dick Barton Special Agent*. It wasn't until the mid–1950s, with innovative remakes of the Frankenstein and Dracula classics, that it hit a formula that would make it a legend in Gothic horror cinema. The strength of Hammer films lay in a repertory company of classically trained actors lead by Christoper Lee and Peter Cushing, and production techniques that turned cheap thrills into classy kitsch. One other factor played incredibly well for Hammer. They were the first English-language studio to make low-cost horror flicks in color, with the spilled blood a vivid red.

1. *Dracula* **(1958)**: An enormous success for Hammer, with huge trash-movie box-office returns in both the UK and the U.S. (where it was released as *The Horror of Dracula*), reviving the suavely immortal vampire count, saddling Christopher Lee with the part for the rest of his career (until he graduated to *Star Wars* and *Lord of The Rings*), and generating a slew of sequels. Directed by Terrence Fisher, and starring Christopher Lee and Peter Cushing.

2. *The Vampire Lovers* **(1970)**: Based on the J. Sheridan Le Fanu story *Carmilla*, this film initiated a whole new subgenre of lesbian vampire movies in which low-cut nightgowns and fangs in the neck proved an irresistible combination, and turned Polish starlet Ingrid Pitt—who, as a child, actually survived a Nazi concentration camp—into the Queen of Kink and Fang. Directed by Roy Ward Baker, and starring Ingrid Pitt and Peter Cushing.

3. *Countess Dracula* **(1971)**: Very loosely based on the historical murderess Elizabeth Bathory, *Countess Dracula* consolidated both the cult following for blood-sucking lesbians and Ingrid Pitt's supremacy as an icon at Hammer. Directed by Peter Sasdy, and starring Ingrid Pitt, Nigel Green, and Lesley-Anne Down.

4. *The Quatermass Xperiment* **(1955)**: Known as *The Creeping Unknown* in the U.S., this early Hammer drive-in hit was the movie version of a successful British TV sci-fi series, and one of the very

first films in which a nasty alien with bad intentions is brought back to Earth aboard an experimental space probe to wreak havoc on humanity. Directed by Val Guest, and starring Brian Donleavy and Thora Hird.

5. *Quatermass and the Pit* (1967): This third outing for the intrepid, alien-battling Professor Quatermass (U.S. title: *Five Million Years to Earth*) was again based on a Brit TV series. This time a prehistoric Martian spacecraft is discovered in an excavation under the London subway system, and, when revived, its ancient alien astronauts attempt to enslave humanity (which turns out to be the result of millennia-old Martian genetic experiments in the first place). Directed by Roy Ward Baker, starring Andrew Keir and Barbara Shelley.

6. *Rasputin, the Mad Monk* (1966): This film gave Christopher Lee time off from playing Dracula to cause occult chaos with a particularly sexy and alcoholic—but historically fanciful version—of the mystic madman running amok at the court of the last tsar, immediately prior to the Soviet revolution. Directed by Don Sharp, and starring Christopher Lee and Barbara Shelley.

7. *The Devil Rides Out* (1968): The occult adventure novels of Dennis Wheatley had a large following in the UK, but never gained a foothold in the U.S., despite their recurrent theme of Satanist conspiracy. Hammer attempted to turn one into a movie, but failed to attract a U.S. audience to the written works of Wheatley, despite supernatural and occasionally absurdist melodrama, and a U.S. title change to *The Devil's Bride*. Directed by Terence Fisher, and starring Christoper Lee and Gwen Ffrangcon Davies.

8. *The Camp on Blood Island* (1958): Hammer moved away from its usual fare of historical costume gore when it attempted to com-

bine the horror genre and the war movie. With World War II stereotypes prevailing, the inmates of a particularly bloody and brutal Japanese prison camp rebel against the torture and brutality of a sadistic commandant and guards. The formula was different, but the gore remained the same. Directed by Val Guest, starring André Morell and Barbara Shelley.

9. *She* (1965): Throughout the sixties, Hammer discovered that sex sold quite as well as shock and gore, and the combination of all three was irresistible. They cast around for suitable vehicles. One of the stranger ones was *She*—the H. Rider Haggard schoolboy adventure of the kind that inspired Steven Spielberg's *Indiana Jones* films—in which Ursula Andress (post–*Dr. No* hot) played Ayesha, "she who must be obeyed," the ruler of a lost city, who uses supernatural powers and human sacrifice to achieve immortality. Directed by Robert Day, starring Ursula Andress and Peter Cushing.

10. *One Million Years B.C.* (1966): This film ultimately became a trash-cult classic, with excellent Ray Harryhausen dinosaurs, battling cavemen, not a single word of English in dialogue—and, of course, Raquel Welch in an alarmingly twentieth-century fur bikini that was a hit all on its own as a dormitory poster for college boys the world over, which catapulted her to stardom. Directed by Don Chaffey, starring Raquel Welch and John Richardson.

LISA MORTON'S TOP TEN ASIAN HORROR MOVIES

Lisa Morton's fiction has appeared in many books and magazines, including the award-winning anthologies The Museum of

Horrors *and* Dark Delicacies. *She won the 2006 Bram Stoker Award for Short Fiction for her story "Tested." She has also written several films, including* Meet the Hollowheads, *and two nonfiction books,* The Cinema of Tsui Hark *and* The Halloween Encyclopedia.

1. *Song at Midnight (Ye Ban Ge Sheng)* **(1937):** This early mainland China talkie by the influential Ma-Xu Weibang riffs on *Phantom of the Opera* and still manages a few chills, despite its dated production values.

2. *Ugetsu (Ugetsu Monogatari)* **(1953):** Kenji Mizoguchi's Japanese masterpiece still contains some of the most quietly frightening images ever put on film.

3. *Kwaidan (Kaidan)* **(1964):** This classic from Japan's Masaki Kobayashi (based on stories collected by Lafcadio Hearn) may still be the best horror anthology movie ever made.

4. *A Chinese Ghost Story (Sien Nui Yau Wan)* **(1987):** Tsui Hark and Ching Siu-tung's breathtakingly beautiful and frantically paced classic is one of the quintessential Hong Kong films.

5. *The Untold Story (Baat Sin Faan Dim Ji Yan Yuk Cha Siu Baau)* **(1993):** Half of Herman Yau's lunatic Hong Kong serial-killer movie is admittedly not good—but the half that works, starring the brilliant Anthony Wong, earns it a place on this list.

6. *The Ring (Ringu)* **(1998):** This Japanese chiller not only firmly placed Hideo Nakata in the ranks of horror's great directors, it also launched a flood of sequels, remakes, and rip-offs . . . and none of them come even close to the original.

7. *Battle Royale (Batoru Rowaiaru)* **(2000):** Kinji Fukasaku's Japanese science fiction/thriller/social commentary/action mash-up is intense, fast, deeply disturbing, and not for the squeamish.

8. *A Tale of Two Sisters (Janghwa, Hongryeon)* **(2003):** Kim Ji-woon's South Korean masterwork is quite simply the best horror film of the last twenty years, with an astonishing performance from Yeum Jeung-ah as the psychotic stepmother.

9. *The Host (Gwoemul)* **(2006):** South Korea's Bong Joon-ho scored a smash hit with this funny, action-packed, and exquisitely made monster movie.

10. *Dog Bite Dog (Gau Ngao Gau)* **(2006):** This Hong Kong thriller from Cheang Pou-soi forces the traditional killer-on-the-run motif through a horror filter and creates one of the most nihilistic and uncomfortable films ever made.

JÖRG BUTTGEREIT'S TOP TEN
JAPANESE MONSTER MOVIES

Jörg Buttgereit is the director/cowriter of the legendary art house horror films Nekromantik, Nekromantik 2, Der Todesking, *and* Schramm. *He has also directed music videos, TV shows, and stage productions, and written the books* Monster Island *and* Nightmares in Plastic. *Find out more at www.myspace.com/joergbuttgereitofficial.*

1. *Frankenstein Conquers the World* **(1965):** The heart of Frankenstein mutates in the atomic fires of Hiroshima into a giant Japanstein creature.

2. *Godzilla vs. the Smog Monster* (1971): Godzilla saves the day by defeating the giant vomit-monster Hedorah! Director Yoshi-mitsu Banno was thrown out by the producer after he created this hilarious Greenpeace-monster-feast.

3. *King Kong Escapes* (1967): Poor old Kong has to fight his robot clone and falls in love with a cute American scientist. The beautiful Mie Hama, from the James Bond film *You Only Live Twice*, is also in this movie.

4. *Matango: Attack of the Mushroom People* (1963): On a deserted island, members of a shipwrecked party eat strange mush-rooms and turn into walking mushrooms. Strangest drug movie ever.

5. *Gamera vs. Guiron* (1969): Two boys get kidnapped by two sexy females from planet Tera. The girls (named Barbella and Flo-bella) want to eat the little boys' brains to get their knowledge. But the giant superturtle Gamera appears and has to fight with the knife-shaped monster Guiron to save the boys. Must be seen to be believed.

6. *Mothra* (1961): Two 6-inch fairies (the pop duo the Peanuts) get ex-ploited by a capitalist in Newkirk City. The beautiful giant moth Mothra flies to the rescue. Very sweet family entertainment.

7. *Goke, Bodysntacher From Hell* (1968): Aboard an Air Japan com-mercial jet, a terrorist is infected by spores from outer space and turns into a bloodthirsty vampire.

8. *Godzilla* (1954): The grim black and white classic that started the Kaiju eiga genre. Gotta have this in the list. Otherwise they don't take you seriously.

9. *Gamera 3—Revenge of Irys* (1999): The atomic turtle's most con-vincing adventure, featuring stunning FX. Even people who normally laugh at Japanese monsters like this film.

10. *Godzilla, Mothra, King Ghidorah—Giant Monsters All-Out Attack* (2001): Stupid title, but the most convincing Godzilla movie ever, made by Shusuke Kaneko, who also did *Gamera 3*.

RICHARD STANLEY'S TEN FAVORITE ITALIAN HORROR MOVIES (PLUS THREE BORDERLINE CASES)

Richard Stanley's films include the visionary science fiction thriller Hardware *(1990) and the mystical Africa-based horror film* Dust Devil *(1992). He was the original writer/director of* The Island of Dr. Moreau *(1996), starring Marlon Brando and Val Kilmer, before departing the production after a few days. He cowrote the screenplay for* The Abandoned *(2006), directed music videos for Public Image Ltd. and Fields of the Nephilim, penned articles for* Projections 3 *and* The Fortean Times, *and made documentaries on such diverse topics as Afghan freedom fighters, Haitian voodoo, and Nazi occultism. He is also a trained anthropologist and a voodoo houngon. More is available at www.myspace.com/richardstanley13.*

1. *Kill Baby . . . Kill!* (1966)
Director: Mario Bava
Stars: Giacomo Rossi-Stuart, Erika Blanc

Mario Bava can be considered to be the godfather of the Italian Gothic, having innovated many of the conventions later "borrowed" by American franchises like *Friday the 13th* and *Scream*. Despite its extraordinary title, this is one of the director's most restrained entries, relying on a skillfully maintained otherworldly atmosphere rather than the physical frissons of his earlier work. The plot concerns a cursed aristocratic family at the center of a series of supernaturally motivated murders. The ghost story, reminiscent of the work of Bava's mentor Riccardo Freda, serves as an excuse to crank up the dry ice, stirring the usual clichés into a vortex of Kafkaesque dreamscapes, exemplified by the sequence in which the protagonist literally pursues *himself* through a series of identical chambers, slowly but surely gaining ground, only to find he has gained nothing at all. Being a ghost story there is—of course—a ghost, and while I hate to give the game away, this does feature one of the scariest specters ever committed to celluloid. You've been warned!

2. *Four Flies on Grey Velvet* (1972)
Director: Dario Argento
Stars: Michael Brandon, Mimsy Farmer, Bud Spencer

The *giallo* is one of Bava's innovations, a species of "whodunit" on which a great many of his disciples were to distinguish themselves, among them future "maestro of the macabre" Dario Argento. Known as *gialli* in the old country because of the yellow covers of the original pulps, the tradition has more in common with Edgar Wallace and Alfred Hitchcock than Agatha Christie, radically re-inventing the mousetrap while paying lip-service to its archetypes—faceless gloved assassins, scantily clad victims, baffled cops, and inspired amateur sleuths who sift through the red herrings before unmasking a killer in the last reel, invariably as a result of a misperceived, seemingly insignificant clue trailed in the title or first act. An engaging generic quirk dictates that the plot nearly always turns on a titular animal that fails to appear in the film itself and whose non-existence or non-appearance holds the key to the mystery (*The Bird with the Crystal Plumage* [1970], *The Black Belly of the Tarantula* [1971], *The Scorpion with Two Tails* [1988], etc.).

While neither the first nor the most accomplished of its kind, *Four Flies* finds a place on this list thanks to its byzantine plotting, warped sexual politics, swaggering set pieces, and—of course—that title. Michael Brandon plays a permanently stoned drummer who spends the film believing he's a killer in a series of bizarre, paranoid events. He's teamed with a gay private eye, who's hired on the strength of his claim to having "never solved a case," and Bud Spencer is a mysterious dropout named God whose appearances are signaled by an appropriately messianic Ennio Morricone choral motif. Add to this a recurring dream involving an execution in a sun-drenched Middle Eastern marketplace, a laser process for retrieving images from the eyes of the dead, and the most elegantly eroticized auto accident ever committed to film, and you have one of my favorite flicks of all time, nationality and taxonomy aside.

3. *Don't Torture a Duckling* (1972)
Director: Lucio Fulci
Stars: Florinda Bolkan, Tomas Milian, Irene Papas

Fulci's finest hour and a half, and a further sampling of the transgressive possibilities of the *giallo*. The victims this time are pubescent schoolboys rather than the usual fashionably underdressed women; the string of murders tears apart the social fabric of a sleepy southern Italian village. The bewildered parents turn on the local witch, beating her to death before a tabloid journalist and the town slut succeed in unmasking the real culprit. To give away more would do the film's all-too-plausible "twist" a disservice. Suffice to say, this distinctly personal work is one of the earliest films to tackle pedophilia head-on and levels the finger of accusation squarely at the hypocritical town elders who shelter the killer, the local censor, and the Catholic Church itself. A brace of strong performances, striking location photography, and a powerfully understated score by Riz Ortolani all combine to make the central set piece of Florinda Bolkan's Christlike scourging and martyrdom one of the strongest sequences of its kind in Italian cinema. *Cinema Paradiso*'s stolen kisses will never seem so innocent again . . .

4. *Lisa and the Devil* (1972)

Director: Mario Bava

Stars: Telly Savalas, Elke Sommer, Alida Valli

Some movies, like wars, can only be understood when inebriated or under the influence of powerful mind-altering substances. This one caught me unawares one Halloween under the influence of a particularly good crop of magic mushrooms, and it simply knocked me for six. To say it tickled my funny bone would be putting it mildly; I couldn't get up off the floor. . . . Every time I tried, another off-kilter moment or non sequitur would knock me straight back on my ass again. This is quite simply one of the strangest films ever made. Dazed blonde Elke Sommer strays from a tour group viewing a fresco, which shows the devil carrying away the dead, to meander through a string of encounters with a ghostly aristocratic family and their demonic servant, Leandro, played with impish relish by Telly Savalas, complete with lollipop, kid gloves, and a fetching range of quasi-Masonic accessories. The entire film seems unstuck in time and place, with names, identities, and relationships fluctuating alarmingly. (A special mention to Alida Valli, whose deranged matriarch is played as blind in some scenes, while plainly sighted in others.) But as all are apparently dead to begin with, this seems quite in keeping with the nightmare logic conjured from the multicolored chaos by Bava's swooning lens. At times it appears the cast are simply making it up as they go along, and one can only imagine the director's imperfect grasp of English allowed some of the weirdest dialogue in cinema history, including mangled chunks of Jim Morrison lyrics and even the Rice Crispies jingle, to find its way into the script. Apparently, Bava's dad made mannequins for shop windows, and here, the director's tendency to portray human beings as living dolls reaches its lunatic apogee in one of the most overblown acts of sustained necrophilia ever inflicted on the viewing public. Bracing stuff—too bracing for the producers, who cut the film by nearly half its length and shot additional scenes involving a bewildered exorcist played by Robert Alda, who strives to make sense of the diabolic shambles. It was released in some territories as *House of Exorcism* and credited to fictional director Mickey Lion (had to get an animal in there somehow!). The original, while admittedly an acquired taste, remains unsurpassed in all its baffling glory.

5. *Deep Red* (1975)
Director: Dario Argento
Stars: David Hemmings, Daria Nicolodi, Gabriele Lavia

The *giallo* comes of age with a cinematic tour de force that turned the genre on its head. David Hemmings gives arguably the most nuanced performance of his career as a concert pianist who witnesses the brutal murder of a German clairvoyant by persons unknown. Convinced he holds the key to the killers' identity, Hemmings finds himself compelled to return to the scene of the crime as his curiosity tilts into an obsessive monomania fanned by the attentions of ambitious reporter Daria Niccolodi, who senses a scoop in the making. Like a demented hall of mirrors, the film's surfaces conceal countless games of gender, perception, and identity. Among its highlights is the exposure of the assassin's face in the opening reel (hidden in plain sight, so to speak); the hugely influential score by Argento's "in-house" band Goblin, which deploys rock 'n' roll percussion and keyboard rhythms with an intelligence and confidence hitherto unknown in cinema; and the unforgettable "house of the screaming child," whose labyrinthine corridors look like Gaudi after a hit of Black Pentagram LSD. A bleeding masterpiece.

6. *Suspiria* (1977)
Director: Dario Argento
Stars: Jessica Harper, Alida Valli, Joan Bennett, Udo Kier

Argento's breakthrough success burst like a thunderbolt over the heads of international audiences, who simply hadn't seen it coming and had no prior knowledge of the dark tradition from whence it was spawned. From its opening frames, the viewer is propelled into an utterly different world, where normal rules no longer apply. Conventional narrative logic and even the reassuring tropes of the *giallo* gleefully abandoned, the story, characters, and dialogue are subservient to a full-throttle assault on the senses; sound and constantly shifting multicolored lighting are amped to the max. Written with Argento's former spouse, actress Daria Niccolodi, *Suspiria* and its sequel concern witchcraft, sharing a weird, private cosmology only partly accessible to the casual viewer, and drawing on real-life figures such as Helena Blavatsky, G. I. Gurdjieff, Rudolf Steiner, and decadent romantic poet Thomas De Quincey to weave the grimmest of grim fairytales. The gossamer-thin script details Jessica Harper's attempts to flee the clutches of a witch cult secretly thriving in an eldritch dance school in the Black Forest. While the young American's plight is engaging enough, the school is the *real* star of the show: the academy's baroque velvet-lined corridors winding ever inwards, the spaces between their walls charged with a malignant intensity, an atmosphere where, in Argento's words, "the air is thick and hard to breathe. . . ." Initial suspicions that the wallpaper has overwhelmed not only the cast but the plot itself are weirdly borne out when, in true *giallo* tradition, the wallpaper is found to contain the vital clue to the lair of Mater Suspiriorum, hidden in plain sight all along! As *il maestro* succinctly puts it, "Magic is everywhere!"

7. *Zombie Flesh-Eaters* (1979)

Director: Lucio Fulci
Stars: Tisa Farrow, Ian McCulloch, Richard Johnson

Rushed into production to capitalize on the success of George Romero's *Dawn of the Dead*, this dime-store imitation is to some extent an improvement on the original. Attempting to re-connect the series to its Caribbean roots, Fulci's unofficial sequel opens with the arrival of a plague-ridden ghost ship in New York Harbor before the action shifts to the godforsaken atoll from whence it came. Trapped on the island, the dim leads throw in their lot with flaky Dr. Menard and his sidekick as they come under siege from a growing legion of the ugliest, skankiest dead-folk the world has ever seen. These shuffling, messed-up zombies are of the old-fashioned, slow-moving variety, which forces the director to keep the plot moving instead—and move it does! It may well be the greatest exploitation movie of all time, a title richly deserved on the basis of one sequence alone: To capitalize on the recent success of *Jaws*, an otherwise extraneous episode is grafted onto the plot, in which a hot chick goes swimming only to be menaced by a shark. As this is Fulci, not Spielberg, the young lady is topless and the shark is completely real, albeit presumably of a harmless variety. Then, in a twist designed to showcase the undoubted box-office superiority of the zombie, a man in convincing makeup emerges from the sea bed and attacks the shark. He's not wearing a respirator and probably can't see a damn without goggles, but he grabs that big, scary-looking fish and sinks his teeth in like a pro, while the naked nymphet flaps her limbs in distress and the weird disco score (courtesy of Fabio Frizzi) throbs on the soundtrack! Things like this usually happen only on posters! Then there's that bit of business with Olga Karlatos's eyeball. Words fail me . . .

8. *Cannibal Holocaust* (1980)
Director: Ruggero Deodato
Stars: Robert Kerman, Francesca Ciardi, Gabriel Yorke

No overview of the genre would be complete without mention of what many consider the most infamous horror movie ever made. Deodato began his career as an assistant to Roberto Rossellini, though few could have guessed to what ends his grounding in neo-realism would lead. This masterwork concerns four Americans who set out for a remote corner of the rainforest known as the "green inferno" to document the last tribes to practice cannibalism. Months later, a second expedition follows and succeeds in retrieving the film shot by the missing explorers, the cans left unopened by the superstitious natives who believe they contain "evil spirits." In a plot device "borrowed" to lesser effect by *The Blair Witch Project*, what follows purports to be the unedited rushes charting the explorers' demise. The "twist" in the tale comes with the revelation that the atrocities have been committed not by stone-age "savages" but by the filmmakers themselves in their rapacious quest for sensational footage. By the time the locals turn on the documentary crew in the last reel, their fate is richly deserved. While the self-reflexive structure serves as an apt metaphor for Western exploitation of the Third World, the apparent critique of the brutal methods employed by the fictional crew offers a copper-bottomed excuse for Deodato to duplicate their actions, committing to camera a series of scenes utterly beyond the pale of acceptable civilized human conduct in what amounts to—if not an actual "cinema crime"—then at the very least one of the most morally reprehensible motion pictures ever made and an enduring monument to mankind's capacity for evil. The convincing performances from a largely unfamiliar cast, the weirdly romantic score by Riz Ortolani, and sheer virtuosity of Deodato's camerawork only add to the outrage. After all, these are acts committed by sophisticated artists fully aware of their implications. Fortunately, the director has not made good on his repeated threats to helm a sequel, despite the slew of cheesy imitations that followed in its wake. As Robert Kerman's anthropologist puts it: "I wonder who the real cannibals are?"

9. *Inferno* (1980)
Director: Dario Argento
Stars: Leigh McCloskey, Irene Miracle, Daria Nicolodi, Alida Valli

Argento's follow-up to *Suspiria* provoked controversy, and doubtless its inclusion here will be as hotly disputed. Developing an idea from Thomas De Quincey's *Suspiria de Profundis*—the conceit of an infernal trinity akin to the three Norns or sorrows—Mater Lachrymarum, Our Lady of Tears; Mater Suspiriorum, Our Lady of Sighs; and Mater Tenebrarum, Our Lady of Darkness—the maestro turns in his most undisciplined and essentially dreamlike work, a lunatic farrago of murderous events that take place around a Gothic apartment building in New York which conceals the lair of the "Mother of Darkness." Within minutes, the plot collapses under the weight of the sumptuous, primary-colored imagery and the crazed Keith Emerson score, fragmenting into a series of virtuoso sequences that simply refuse to adhere into anything resembling a conventional narrative. Mumbling, dazed cast members are shuffled on and off or summarily dispatched in mid-flow as if the film can't even decide on a lead character, let alone a story, and when subtitles start to appear, such as "Later that same night in Rome," you know you're in trouble. Consequently, the film was savaged by critics and bombed at the box office, all but bringing the curtain down on Argento's American career. And yet . . . and yet . . .

In dispensing with the ramshackle plot (seemingly borrowed from Michael Winner's *The Sentinel* [1977] and H. P. Lovecraft's short story "The Dreams in the Witch House" [1937]), Argento liberates himself to create his finest set pieces, working at full throttle, completely off his trolley and at the top of his form. The opening scene, in which Irene Miracle plunges into the Stygian depths of a submerged basement to retrieve a key lost in the water, has an oneiric power unrivalled in cinema, reminiscent of Jean Cocteau at his very best and early masters of surrealism such as René Magritte. The collapse of the conventional aesthetic super-structure (reminiscent of the collapse of the house itself) forces us to deal with the essentially Jungian subtext, an approach that defeats critical approaches to the work along more traditional Freudian lines. The key lays in the text itself, in the stolen grimoire that floats in and out of this hazy fable, a fictive take on *The Mystery of the Cathedrals* by real-life alchemist Fulcanelli, whose narrative counterpart is literally discovered skulking beneath the floorboards in the preposterous (albeit strangely appropriate) finale. According to Fulcanelli, Gothic art and architecture are a secret symbolic language, and accordingly Argento's work acts as an encapsulation and a key to the genre as a whole, the dark art revealed as the art of light. While not a good movie by any conventional standard, *Inferno* is nonetheless a *great* movie and an authentic classic of Gothic cinema. Disregard it at your peril.

Rose Elliot (Irene Miracle) emerges from "the Stygian depths of a submerged basement" in Dario Argento's *Inferno* (1980). (*Inferno* © 1981 Twentieth Century Fox. All rights reserved.)

10. *The Beyond* (1981)

Director: Lucio Fulci

Stars: Catriona McColl, David Warbeck

Fulci's gumbo-flavored phantasmagoria takes off from familiar material (Winner's *The Sentinel*, Lovecraft's "The Case of Charles Dexter Ward," with a dash of *The Shining* and Clark Ashton Smith's *Book of Eibon* thrown in for good measure) to craft an incoherent fever-dream of a movie. A demonic surrealist painter in turn-of-the-century Louisiana opens the gates of Hell, only to be beaten to death for his efforts by disgruntled locals, who inter his crucified remains beneath a crumbling gingerbread-Gothic hotel. The action picks up in the present when the efforts of a young New Yorker to reopen the cursed hotel leads to a series of gruesome events that climaxes in the onset of a zombie-induced Armageddon and the descent of the leads into Hell itself. As with other examples of what Fulci and Argento term "total cinema" (a phrase "borrowed" from Truffaut), attempts to analyze or deconstruct events along traditional generic lines are hopeless. While throwing off countless literary allusions, the film itself (as evidenced by the DO NOT ENTRY sign prominently displayed on the mortuary door) remains stubbornly subliterate, with much of the attempted "dialogue" so gloriously cloth-eared that entire sequences pass without offering the slightest clue as to the character or motivation of the participants. All you can do is sit back and experience this mad dog of a movie until you either vow to put it behind you or submit to its weird rhythms. Of course, a six-pack of beers or liberal recourse to other intoxicants goes a long way towards disengaging the conscious mind so that this visionary epic can be enjoyed on its own freakish terms. Fulci's excremental opus is lurid and elusive by turns, a stumbling block to conventional notions of art, criticism, and rational thought. Quite simply: Wonderful beyond words!

"And you will face the Sea of Darkness and all therein that may be explored . . ."

—EIBON

Three Borderline Cases . . .

11. *Danger: Diabolik* (1967)
Director: Mario Bava
Stars: John Phillip Law, Marisa Mell, Michel Piccoli, Terry Thomas

While fantastical, this Bava masterpiece is by no means a horror film (which precludes its appearance in this roundup); still, it's far too much fun to go unmentioned. Based on a popular character from the Italian *fumetti* (comic books), this lil' firecracker details the deviant exploits of masked super-criminal Diabolik, who is hunted by both Mafiosi and corrupt *polizei* after repeatedly humiliating a futuristic right-wing government. Produced by Dino De Laurentiis as a follow up to *Barbarella*, the director turned in the project at a mere fraction of his given budget and simply handed back the balance, cheekily claiming that he "didn't need it," thus deliberately forfeiting a career in American cinema—an antiestablishment gesture reminiscent of the film's antihero himself! Admittedly, the action does slow down a tad in the second act, but the opening heist and resulting chase, involving helicopters and a string of gorgeous high-performance period sports cars in breathtaking Italian Riviera locations, not only rivals but outstrips anything to be seen in the early Bond movies. The Morricone score remains the essence of cool. And what schoolboy wouldn't dream of Diabolik's devoted blond assistant Marisa Mell, or the scene in which their love is consummated on a pile of stolen loot in the master criminal's high-tech underground lair? In fact I'm still dreaming of it now . . .

12. *Flavia the Heretic* (1974)
Director: Gianfranco Mingozzi
Stars: Florinda Bolkan, Claudio Cassinelli

Not a horror film so much as one of the "nunsploitation" movies that followed hot on the habit of Ken Russell's *The Devils*, this zoned-out feminist epic contains enough distinguishing characteristics to rise above its febrile peers. Set in fifteenth-century Italy, Mingozzi's Gothic potboiler concerns a typically "frustrated" nun incarcerated in a Byzantine monastery that's decorated by weirdly eroticized images of Saint Michael. Flavia (Florinda Bolkan, star of *Don't Torture a Duckling* and *Lizard in a Woman's Skin*) finds temptation in the unlikely form of hunky Jewish handyman Claudio Cassinelli (*The Scorpion with Two Tails*), leading to a series of visions and her eventual defection to the Muslim cause. Along the way, a tarantula cult shows up to inspire a pagan bacchanal, a black Madonna arrives by boat as a cover for a Muslim sneak attack, a naked nun emerges from the carcass of a dead cow, and people get impaled before the rebel nun is finally recaptured and skinned alive for her sins by resurgent Christians, thus restoring a patriarchal order of sorts to the beleaguered community. While fascinating, seductive, and thought-provoking by turns, Mingozzi's fractured polemic is not exactly a date movie, but then if boys will be boys, why can't girls be girls just once in a while?

13. "Toby Dammit" from *Histoires Extraordinaire (Spirits of the Dead)* (1968)
Director: Federico Fellini
Stars: Terence Stamp, Toto

The finest hour in Italian horror turns out to be exactly that, a short clocking in at just under sixty minutes and making up the final segment of an otherwise undistinguished anthology based on the works of Poe—*Spirits of the Dead*. Terence Stamp embodies the titular character as a failing, whiskey-sodden actor brought to Rome to star in the "first Catholic western," who succumbs to temptation when he accepts a coveted Ferrari in return for appearing at the Golden She-Wolf awards. It is as if the director's customary self-indulgence is held in check by the running time, and to my mind, Fellini delivers the best work of his career, with his usual supporting cast of grotesques being lent a cutting edge by the darker than usual material. The final passage, in which Stamp attempts to flee, only to become increasingly lost in the winding Neapolitan streets, is marvellously sustained. It becomes increasingly clear that on many levels the film is an homage to Mario Bava, a fact driven home by the reappearance of the irrationally terrifying ghost from *Kill Baby. . . Kill* (1967) at the *Grand Guignol* finale.

Which, like the unfortunate *Signor* Dammit, brings us neatly in a circle.

ALTERNATE INTERNATIONAL TITLES FOR EIGHT ITALIAN HORROR MOVIES

1. Original Title: *Cannibal Ferox* (1981)
   Alternate Titles: *Make Them Die Slowly*
                    Woman from Deep River
   Director: Umberto Lenzi

2. Original Title: *Zombi 2* (1979)
   Alternate Titles: *Zombie*
                    Zombie Flesh-Eaters
   Director: Lucio Fulci

3. **Original Title:** *The Beyond* (1981)
   Alternate Title: *Seven Doors of Death*
   Director: Lucio Fulci

4. **Original Title:** *Nightmare City* (1980)
   Alternate Title: *City of the Walking Dead*
   Director: Umberto Lenzi

5. **Original Title:** *City of the Living Dead* (1980)
   Alternate Title: *The Gates of Hell*
   Director: Lucio Fulci

6. **Original Title:** *Cannibal Apocalypse* (1980)
   Alternate Titles: *Cannibals in the Streets*
   Invasion of the Flesh Eaters
   Director: Antonio Margheriti

7. **Original Title:** *Tenebre* (1982)
   Alternate Title: *Unsane*
   Director: Dario Argento

8. **Original Title:** *Phenomena* (1985)
   Alternate Title: *Creepers*
   Director: Dario Argento

—Compiled by S.B.

MARK SAVAGE'S TEN FAVORITE
AUSTRALIAN HORROR FILMS

Mark Savage is an Australian director/writer whose most recent film, Defenceless, *finds its horrors along Australia's isolated southern coast. A lifelong horror fanatic (books and films), Savage maintains that his endless diet of international horror has made him a more balanced individual. He currently lives and works in Los Angeles, California.*

1. *Mad Max* (George Miller): This seminal exploitation classic plays like a futuristic *Death Wish*. Its fetishistic treatment of the automobile has echoes in David Cronenberg's film of J. G. Ballard's *Crash*.

2. *Razorback* (Russell Mulcahy): A visually stunning, highly stylized "*Jaws* on land" that captures the stunning Australian landscape and boasts some truly surreal sequences.

3. *The Last Wave* (Peter Weir): Weir's subtle brand of mystical horror is a fascinating, dreamlike experience. Heavy on suggestion, and not keen to provide easy answers for the viewer.

4. *Bad Boy Bubby* (Rolf de Heer): A grotesque and totally original fable with parallels to Hal Ashby's *Being There*. The sequences involving cat suffocation and incest are worth the price of admission.

5. *Shame* (Steve Jodrell): A criminally underrated, emotionally wrenching tale of a lawyer who goes to war with small-town elders harboring packs of teenage rapists. A modern western about a horrific situation.

6. *Picnic at Hanging Rock* (Peter Weir): A subtle, ambiguous, and enigmatic ghost story that earned Weir worldwide acclaim. A beautifully photographed, extremely erotic tale of schoolgirls who disappear into a canyon. It leaves the viewer in a state of high anxiety.

7. *Wake in Fright* (Ted Kotcheff): A schoolteacher's terrifying experience in Australia's hellish Outback. This is the most realistic

depiction of the country's darkest corners ever burned to film. The Canadian director captures the horror of absolute isolation and hopelessness, cleverly contrasted with beauty. A true classic.

8. *Vicious* (Karl Zwicky): An obscure, nasty, home-invasion low budgeter that recalls aspects of Sam Peckinpah's *Straw Dogs*. Extremely well acted and directed with ice-cold efficiency.

9. *The Cars that Ate Paris* (Peter Weir): An oddball drama about people living in isolation who prey on travelers. One of Weir's earliest films, it focuses on the dangers of small-town bigotry and, like *Mad Max*, explores Australia's fetishistic relationship with the automobile.

10. *Road Games* (Richard Franklin): The wide-open spaces are put to good use by director Franklin, who was a student of Hitchcock's and went on to direct *Psycho 2*. A creepy slasher in the *Halloween* vein that finds its horrors under the desert's harsh sun.

DAN MADIGAN'S TEN MOST INSANE, OUT-OF-THIS-WORLD MEXICAN HORROR MOVIES (IN NO PARTICULAR ORDER OF NUTTINESS)

Dan Madigan is the author of Mondo Lucha A Go-Go: The Bizarre and Honorable World of Wild Mexican Wrestling, *and screenwriter of the 2006 horror film* See No Evil *(starring wrestling superstar Kane). He's worked behind the scenes in professional wrestling, as well as in the movie industry and rock 'n' roll. In other words, he has done everything parents warn their children not to do.*

1. *The Brainiac* (aka *El Barón del Terror*): *Wow* . . . how else would you describe a film that has a reincarnated warlock who was burned at the stake three hundred years ago coming back to take revenge on the descendants of his accusers (echoes of Mario Bava's *Black Sunday*)? And not just a vengeful spirit, but a large-nosed, wiggly hook-handed, hairy forked-tongued demon that sucks the brains and souls from the back of its victim's necks. Just good ol' clean, wholesome fun. And director Chano Urueta had a role in Sam Peckinpah's *The Wild Bunch*! How's that for badass trivia?

2. *The Living Coffin*: Sometimes known as *El Grito De La Muerte* (*The Cry of Death*) in its native Mexico, this film has haunted haciendas, heroic cowboys and lazy sidekicks, hidden gold mines, ghosts . . . all the fixings of an old Monogram oater, something that fell out of the Sinister Cinema catalog. But it is a lot of fun. It's atmospheric and never tries to pull away from its B-movie status for what it is and what we want from it. Real-life matador Gastón Santos plays the hero in this moody set piece picture. You have to give them credit for trying to combine two popular genres, horror and western, which doesn't tend to work, but this is a gem from director Fernando Méndez, who could be called the Latino Terence Fisher.

3. *The Man and the Monster* (aka *El Hombre y el Monstruo*): Here's a great refried version of the Faustian metaphor with enough chilling atmosphere to cool down a jar of habañeros. It seems this guy Samuel wants to be the greatest piano player in the world, so much so that he is willing to sell his soul to Old Scratch himself. (I guess hard work and practice were too much to ask of him.) Anyway, things look rosy for good ol' Sammy-boy until that demonic loophole makes its way into the picture; it seems every time he plays his signature song, he turns into a monster, and of course a bloody rampage follows. With more than a passing nod

to *Dr. Jekyll and Mr. Hyde*, this neat little tale is doesn't get the recognition it deserves. Forget the fact that the makeup may not be up to par with what the great Jack Pierce used to produce; this is a fun film that should be enjoyed over a few cold *cervezas*.

4. **Wrestling Women vs. the Aztec Mummy**: Sometimes known by the more musical moniker *Rock 'n' Roll Wrestling Women vs. the Aztec Mummy*. Whatever you want to call it, this movie is *out there*, flying somewhere beyond the stratosphere. Any movie that gives you two female wrestlers in the buxom figures of Lorena Velázquez and Elizabeth Campbell in lieu of plot is okay in my book. In-ring action and wild fisticuffs with an ancient Aztec mummy and an Oriental villain named "Black Dragon" (whose evil epithet is out of a Doc Savage story) just adds to the surreal mulligan stew of this flick. Just sit back, switch your brain to OFF, and have a nice steamy bowl of wildness.

5. **Night of the Bloody Apes**: Come on . . . if the title alone doesn't get you, think about having that stick removed from your ass. . . . Director René Cardona not only remade his own 1962 deliciously demented film *Doctor of Doom*, he adds a nice amount of gratuitous gore and visceral nastiness (plus a hot Latina babe in a hot devil wrestling costume), actual footage of a graphic open heart surgery spliced in for good measure, and a crazed killer hybrid that is part leukemia-stricken boy and part crazed, murderous, woman-hating ape (read that last line again). This one is worth seeking out. You can keep your *English Patient*s and your *Brokeback Mountain*s. . . . I'll take this pinnacle of Mexican exploitation.

6. **Santo in The Treasure of Dracula (Santo en El tesoro de Drácula)**: Any way you put it, you have the greatest masked wrestler (*enmascarado*) in the world against the greatest undead bloodsucker of

all time, a classic match of Ali-Frazier proportions. Plus, some more hot chicks (a *lucha* movie staple), hidden treasure, a Wayback time machine so cool that it would make Mr. Peabody sell Sherman into white slavery to get a crack at it, and a heap of "wrasslin'" make this one a winner. This film has El Santo inventing a time-machine (I guess he has time to do all his scientific stuff between working out and wrestling matches) with the most obnoxious sidekick this side of Joe Besser—Perico (Alberto Rojas), who is a combination irksome Jerry Lewis and annoying Arnold Stang. There is a more "adult" version floating around (featuring more female flesh), which I am dying to see, but the idea of Dracula going a few rounds with El Santo is what makes this film a classic in any version.

7. *Frankenstein, the Vampire, and Company*: A Mexican version of *Abbott & Costello Meet Frankenstein*. Although stars Manuel "Loco" Valdez and Jose "Ojon" Jasso, of course, never come near the comic brilliance of Bud and Lou, this is a fun romp in south-of-the-border comedy and horror. The plot is virtually the same as the Abbott and Costello classic it apes, and there is a lot of fun in watching Frankenstein, the Vampire, and Wolfman envisioned through a Latino lens. This one is rarer than an honest man in a whorehouse; if you find even a half-decent copy, cherish it like the Shroud of Turin.

8. *El Vampiro* and *El Ataúd del Vampiro*: You might as well count these two films as one. *The Vampire* and its sequel *The Vampire's Coffin* are fun and moody journeys into the Dracula mythos. Although there is no Transylvanian count named Dracula, you get what the filmmakers were going for with German Robles reprising his role as Count Karol de Lavud in both films and star/producer Abel Salazar once again portraying the hero. You can tell that everyone behind the camera (including our old pal Fernando

Méndez assuming the directorial duties again) had a real fondness for the Golden Age of Horror films that Universal released in the thirties. Grave robbers, stolen corpses, wax museums with the usual rogues' gallery of waxen figures, large and empty hospitals dripping with atmosphere, vampires turning into large, obviously rubber, bats, and some unintentionally funny dialogue make these two worth adding to your international vampiric collection.

9. *El Violador Infernal* aka *The Hellish Rapist* (must have taken a team of Class-A writers to come up with that title): What a deranged movie, I mean *deranged*. I saw this beauty without subtitles and was still blown away by the insanity of it all. A career criminal on the electric chair is given another chance at a life of crime by the Queen of Hell. This miscreant is no prince to begin with, but with a new lease on life, he becomes the Hispanic "No More Mr. Nice Guy." The guy is an equal-opportunity rapist, buggering his dying gay boyfriend while carving "666" into the poor schmuck's behind, and violating women like it was going out of style. Sodomy and Satanism have never gone so well together, the peanut butter and jelly of antisocial behavior. Watch it with a loved one.

10. *La Vengaza de los Punks*: Bad hair, sub-substandard production values, an insane storyline, and enough eighties leather to outfit ten Krokus videos—how could you not want to see this one? Not so much a horror film as just plain horrific (as in, so horrifically bad that it is a must-see), this features a group of punks (hence the title) on a rape-murder-rape rampage (did I mention rape, the group's pastime?). This posse of juvenile delinquents (the youngest of whom is probably in his early thirties) is comprised of some outcasts from a *Surf Nazis Must Die* convention. The flick's rip-off of *Mad Max*'s visuals only shows how incredibly awesome

The Road Warrior really is. With a Mexican Lord Humongous (who changes from one dreadful costume to the next, practically scene by scene); his pudgy (no, excuse me, *fat*) leather-clad hell-wench; his gang of inept miscreants drenched in peroxide, studded leather wristbands, and magnificently god-awful makeup (if the Village People gang-raped Liberace, this group would be the offspring of that unholy union); anal impalements, death by scorpion-bites, bodies burned with a flamethrower, eyes gouged out—this is one for the books . . . if your books are geared towards bad taste bordering on trash.

MATTEO MOLINARI'S TEN FAVORITE
HORROR MOVIE BLOOPERS

Matteo Molinari was born in Genoa, Italy. Among his talents is Movie Watching, an activity at which he excels. After watching movies over and over again, Matteo has developed the uncanny ability of noticing things. Wrong things, mainly. That's why he's become one of the leading experts, if there is such a thing, on Movie Bloopers. After four books (two in Italy and two in the United States), Matteo is still searching for bloopers, even as he contemplates finding a real job just to pay some bills.

1. *Abbott & Costello Meet Frankenstein*: After a tug-o-war between the Wolfman and Count Dracula has left him spinning on a gurney in the lab, Chick (Bud Abbott) yells so loudly as to awaken the Frankenstein monster. Menacingly, the monster slowly turns his head . . . and the bolt on the right rips away from his neck! (01:16)

2. *Aliens* (also Director's Cut): When Ripley (Sigourney Weaver) opens the space door in order to expel the queen, little Newt (Carrie Henn) is sucked like everything else toward the shaft and she slides across the floor. The remaining half of Bishop (Lance Henriksen) reaches to grab the girl, and in doing so, reveals the hole on the floor where the still-in-one-piece actor is hiding. (02:11 / DC 02:28)

3. *Halloween*: Little Michael Myers spies on his sister and her boyfriend. They go in her room to make out, and the following Panaglide shot happens in real time. So, since the lights go off and then the boyfriend gets dressed and leaves, they make out for 65 seconds. Talk about a quickie! (00:03, 00:04)

4. *Jaws*: Brody (Roy Scheider) types the report on Chrissie's death: it states, "Date/Time Original III./Inc. 7–1–74, 11:50 PM" and "Date/Time Deceased Discovered 7–2–74, 10:20 PM." Later on, by the council chamber, a sign offers a reward to capture the shark that killed Alex M. Kintner on Sunday, June 29. But Alex was killed after Chrissie. Hmm . . . And, while we're at it, June 29, 1974, was a Saturday—not a Sunday. (00:09, 00:18)

5. *Jeepers Creepers*: During the closing credits, "Officer with Hole in Chest" is spelled "Office." (01:26)

6. *Jurassic Park*: Dr. Grant (Sam Neill) enters his trailer by opening a door with hinges on the left—but from the inside, they are on the right. (00:10)

   Dr. Grant stands in front of a velociraptor egg, which is delicately held by a computer-controlled arm—which proceeds to vanish before the next shot. (00:28)

7. *Manhunter*: On the telephone, Doctor Lecktor (Brian Cox) is able to get Graham's (William Petersen) address as "3680 DeSoto Highway." Later on, at the hospital, Graham is told they broke Lecktor's coded message to the tooth fairy killer: it reads, "Graham home, 3860 DeSoto Highway." Did he send the Tooth Fairy to another house just for fun? (00:31, 01:04)

8. *Maximum Overdrive*: The military vehicle with a machine gun arrives at the *Dixie Boy*, and as it drives by, it shows that the steering wheel has a small button as a horn. But when the vehicle starts honking the Morse code, in the middle of the steering wheel there is a horn the size of a pothole. (01:10, 01:13)

9. *The Terminator*: The Terminator (Arnold Schwarzenegger) looks for Sarah Connor's (Linda Hamilton) address in a phone book. There are three Sarah Connors, and their street numbers are 1823, 2816, 309. The first Sarah the Terminator visits lives at 14239. (00:15)

10. *Tremors*: Earl's (Fred Ward) horse gets grabbed from underground by one of the monsters, and fights to stand up again, but the tentacles hold it down—well, the tentacles *and* a cable that runs from its saddle and can be seen on screen left, that is. (00:32)

Earl's last name is Bassett, as mentioned by Valentine (Kevin Bacon) when he wakes him up (00:01), and as it appears written on the plate Earl himself removes (00:11) when they first attempt to leave Perfection, yet in the closing credits he's listed as "Earl Bass." (01:31)

BOB MURAWSKI'S TWELVE GREATEST
GRINDHOUSE HORROR ONE-SHEETS

Bob Murawski is a film editor who has worked with Sam Raimi for two decades, cutting Army of Darkness, The Gift, *and the three* Spider-Man *pictures. He has also edited films for directors John Woo, Scott Spiegel, and Kathryn Bigelow, and music videos for the Ramones and Motörhead. In 1996 he partnered with Sage Stallone to form Grindhouse Releasing, a Hollywood-based distribution company dedicated to the restoration and preservation of motion pictures historically held in very low regard (.e.g., low-budget horror and exploitation films). Grindhouse is committed not only to video distribution, but also theatrical release of the movies it acquires. Past releases include Lucio Fulci's* The Beyond, *and Ruggero Deodato's notorious* Cannibal Holocaust, *which have played to sold-out crowds throughout the U.S. For more information visit www.GrindhouseReleasing.com.*

1. *Blood Feast* (1963): The one that started it all. Crudely rendered artwork of a meat cleaver–wielding Einstein-haired killer standing over the mutilated torso of his bikini-clad victim in this two-color poster printed in stark black and blood-red. Herschell Gordon Lewis and David F. Friedman's immortal tag line— "Nothing so appalling in the annals of horror!"—fully delivered on its bold claim. "You'll Recoil and Shudder as You Witness the Slaughter and Mutilation of Nubile Young Girls." Indeed!

2. *Beast of Blood* (1970): A beautifully executed full-color painting of a rotting ghoul tearing off his own head, with viscera and gore galore! Hemisphere Films brought the classic Reynolds Brown–style monster art into the sleazy seventies with this striking one-sheet.

3. *Torture Dungeon* (1970): Lew Mishkin's lurid posters for Andy Milligan's threadbare Staten Island horror epics have their own

demented charm, and this is one of the sleaziest. A brightly hued combination of crudely colorized and overpainted scenes from the movie creates a nightmarish feeling of seediness, which perfectly conveys the movie's dingy aesthetic.

4. *I Drink Your Blood* (1971): Jerry Gross's spectacular one-sheet for David Durston's sordid tale of LSD-infested, rabies-infected hippies on a blood-crazed killing spree is appropriately printed in Day-Glo green and yellow fluorescent ink and actually glows under a black light! It was double-billed with Del Tenney's black-and-white zombie movie *I Eat Your Skin* to earn its well-deserved tag line: "Two great blood-horrors to rip out your guts!"

The one-sheet for the legendary exploitation double-bill of *I Drink Your Blood* and *I Eat Your Skin*.

5. *Orgy of the Living Dead* (1972): I was obsessed with this artwork from the time I saw the ad in the *Detroit News* drive-in listings, especially since the theaters playing this show were over 100 miles away and I was 8 years old. Touted as "A Triple Avalanche of Grisly Horror," the ad featured a vicious living corpse-head with sharp fangs, one eye, and one rotted socket. A large chunk of the skull was missing in the forehead to reveal the brain beneath. A disembodied, rotted hand reached forward, beckoningly. Behind this horror-head was a savage, busty vampire-woman, fangs and claw-like fingernails bared, chained like an animal. As if this weren't enough, a black–and-white photo of a screaming man in a straight jacket was also included, with the story of poor John Austin Frasier, who was driven insane by this explosion of terror. And the most shocking element of the entire program? Its PG rating! I later saw the one-sheet in full color and was even more impressed by this lurid gem, which was created by genre icon Alan Ormsby, writer of *Deathdream* and *Children Shouldn't Play with Dead Things*.

6. *Invasion of the Blood Farmers* (1972): A legendary exploitation title, a great tag-line—"they planted the LIVING and harvested the DEAD!"—and an incredible black-and-white photo-collage of pitchfork-stabbing, grave-digging action, all depicted in front of a blood-red moon. Another PG-rated treat from a kinder, gentler MPAA.

7. *Caged Virgins* (1973): Harry Novak's U.S. release of Jean Rollin's 1971 vampire art-film featured a poster with a hellish, full-color painting of scantily clad females (with a few in the background who were actually topless!) chained in a bloody pit of horror. No less than seven victims, "IN AN ENDLESS NIGHTMARE OF TERROR," are depicted, in ultra-lurid artwork that recalls the sixties men's magazine torture-chamber illustrations of such artists as John Duillo and Norm Eastman.

8. *The Texas Chainsaw Massacre* (1974): The classic! A simple, gruesome image of Leatherface, his chainsaw, and his helpless victim, dominated by the chillingly evocative tagline, "WHO WILL SURVIVE AND WHAT WILL BE LEFT OF THEM?"

9. *Zombie* (1980): Jerry Gross scored a major comeback with this minimalist masterpiece for Lucio Fulci's living dead classic. I'm not usually a fan of the "big head photo" style of movie poster, but the maggot-encrusted Gianetto De Rossi creation, with the blunt, cut-to-the-chase tagline, "WE ARE GOING TO EAT YOU!" made *Zombie* the must-see movie of 1980.

The one-sheet for Lucio Fulci's *Zombie*.

10. *Maniac* (1980): The best of all the slasher movies also had the best poster, a vivid painting depicting a waist-down shot of the killer holding a huge knife in one hand and a bloody scalp in the other. He is standing in a puddle of blood. In jagged white psycho-script, it reads "I WARNED YOU NOT TO GO OUT TONIGHT," and the title appears in big, bold, ugly letters. A hard-hitting piece of exploitation dynamite.

11. *Make Them Die Slowly* (1981): Exploitation master Terry Levine supercharged his U.S. release of Umberto Lenzi's Italian gore-fest *Cannibal Ferox* with a new 42nd Street–style, right-to-the-point title, and a one-sheet that takes the incredible Italian art and roughs it up for the grindhouse crowd, adding some grainy, violent stills from the movie and proudly labeling it, "The Most Violent Film Ever!" As if this weren't enough, Levine sealed the deal with the proclamation: "BANNED IN 31 COUNTRIES." Sublime.

12. *Pieces* (1983): A movie with two great tag-lines—"You don't have to go to Texas for a Chainsaw Massacre" and "It's EXACTLY what you think it is." A bright red poster depicting the surreal image of a chainsaw lovingly displayed on a satin platform, with a grotesque but sexy sewn-together blonde victim beneath. This one-sheet promised a lot and the movie delivered even more. I drove seventy miles to see *Pieces* and was not disappointed.

TIM LUCAS'S TEN HORROR FILMS
THAT AREN'T HORROR FILMS

Tim Lucas is an internationally recognized critic specializing in fantastic cinema. His work has appeared in Sight & Sound, Fangoria,

Film Comment, Cahiers du Cinéma, Cinefantastique, *and his own award-winning monthly,* Video Watchdog *(www.videowatchdog .com). He is the author of* The Video Watchdog Book *(1992), the monumental biography* Mario Bava—All the Colors of the Dark *(2007) and* Studies in the Horror Film: Videodrome *(2008). He is also the author of two acclaimed horror novels,* Throat Sprockets *(1994) and* The Book of Renfield: A Gospel of Dracula *(2005). He lives with his wife, Donna, in Cincinnati, Ohio.*

Throughout my life as a horror film devotee, I've taken silent note of a number of occasions when I have ventured outside the genre only to find myself unmistakably still in horror's presence. It's possible for a western, a drama, a love story, even a comedy to channel something of the atmosphere or undertow of the horror genre, be it through excessive violence, morbidity, a pronounced awareness or concern with matters of death, romance that takes a dark or unhealthy turn, or the surrealistic depiction of aberrant psychology and mental illness. It would also seem that elements of horror are virtually unavoidable in the realms of experimental cinema and European art cinema. What is most wonderful about these occasions, when they happen, is that they usually present us with ideas, approaches to the genre, that have not as yet been properly explored within it. The following (in chronological sequence) is a list of my favorite examples of non-horror pictures that nevertheless gave me some of the biggest cinematic scares of my life . . . or got deeply under my skin.

1. *J'Accuse!* **(1938):** Abel Gance's sound remake of his own 1919 antiwar classic stands out in my memory as the film that most made me believe in figments of terror that weren't there. This miracle is primarily achieved through the force of the lead performance by Victor Francen (*The Beast with Five Fingers*) as Jean Diaz, a World War I veteran so traumatized by his wartime memories that he withdraws from people and immerses himself

in the abstraction of work geared toward pacific solutions. However, as his work is subverted by a government determined to engage in another war, Diaz breaks down and pleads with the world not to live by the sword—out of respect for all those sons who gave their lives, their limbs, their faces for peace—and, as the world refuses to listen, the dead return to amass in defiance, summoned back by the vividness of Diaz's outrage. Francen's harrowing performance makes one believe that such a thing could actually happen. In a manner recalling Tod Browning's *Freaks* (1932), real disfigured war veterans were used in the climactic procession, which allows the most sincere horror to emerge from the most earnest and urgent of dramas.

2. *Pinocchio* (1940): The name of Walt Disney evokes all manner of family fun, but let us not forget that *Snow White and the Seven Dwarfs* (1938)—the very foundation of his empire—has some scary moments involving a huntsman ordered to cut the heart out of our virginal heroine, her flight into a forest made monstrous by the frenzied projection of her fears, and the wicked queen's transformation into a witchy crone dedicated to her rival's destruction. But this, Disney's next feature, based on the book by Carlo Collodi and widely touted as his masterpiece, is a harrowing parable about innocent life at the mercy of a corrupt, manipulative, exploitative world. I've seen screaming children carried out of screenings of this film. Lampwick's transformation into a donkey in the Pleasure Island sequence predates all but *one* werewolf transformation in the cinema (*Werewolf of London*, 1935) and, almost seventy years further on, it somehow remains more terrifying, more agonizing, than any other attempted to date.

3. *Sunset Boulevard* (1950): Billy Wilder's *noir*ish dramas had incorporated elements of horror before—notably *The Lost Weekend* (1945), with its unforgettable drunkard's hallucination of a bat

picking its way through a broken wall—but here, the prevailing moods are narcissism, paranoia, and necrophilia. The narrator (William Holden) tells us up front that he is dead, and his story sucks us into the living death that is silent screen star Norma Desmond's (Gloria Swanson) waxworks monument to her own past glory. Her final descent down the stairwell ("I'm ready for my close-up, Mr. DeMille!") is, importantly, the cinema's first fade-to-white and one of the rare instances of a scare that never loses its incendiary power, no matter how many times you see it.

4. *The Miracle of Our Lady of Fatima* (1952): In compiling a list like this, we mustn't overlook religious drama. This film is a predictably inflated Hollywood retelling of a true and rather more humble event that took place in 1917, when three children in the Portuguese village of Fatima claimed to have borne witness to a recurring vision of the Virgin Mary. Perhaps because the project was entrusted to director John Brahm—responsible for the horror classics *The Undying Monster* (1942), *The Lodger* (1944), and *Hangover Square* (1945)—the vision carries a charge as ghostly as it is "holy," and the titular miracle the Virgin enacts before an assembled crowd (causing the sun to momentarily plummet toward the Earth) terrified audiences in its day.

5. *The Night of the Hunter* (1955): Charles Laughton's only directorial venture has everything one might expect from a classic horror film, such as starkly expressionistic photography (by Stanley Cortez) and Robert Mitchum's ogreish performance as the Reverend Harry Powell, a money-grubbing con-man of the cloth who dramatizes the war between good and evil with letters tattooed on his own knuckles; he's as intimidating a Big Bad Wolf as you'll find in any fairy tale. Too stylized to fit comfortably into any genre, it nevertheless contains many frightening scenes, sometimes goosing its scares with flashes of comedy, and there

is one unforgettably, perversely lovely moment when a man in a rowboat finds the corpse of a woman at the bottom of a lake, her hair floating upwards, seated behind the wheel of her submerged Model T Ford.

6. *Susan Slade* **(1961):** Romantic melodrama of the 1950s and early sixties was actually a common source for some of the most shrill and sensational yet unexpected moments of horror. Who could forget the out-of-left-field cannibalistic climax of *Suddenly, Last Summer* (1959)? Or the moment in *Imitation of Life* (1959) when clean-cut Troy Donahue suddenly shows his own true colors as a sadistic racist by demanding of girlfriend Susan Kohner, "Is it true you're a nigger?" and slapping her to the ground in a back alley? There are dozens of like examples, but this Delmer Daves melodrama stands out in my memory—though I haven't seen it in decades—as especially horrific. Why? Well, there's a scene in which Connie Stevens, playing an unenthusiastic new mother, ignores the cries of her toddler until she can't stand it anymore and storms into the nursery . . . only to discover that the cigarette she accidentally dropped into her baby's crib had engulfed the wailing child in flames! (I wouldn't see anything quite so upsetting in a drama again until Bernardo Bertolucci's *1900*, made in 1976.) Visiting harm, especially such extreme harm, upon infants remains a place where horror films still generally refuse to go, and this hair-raiser shows why—which may have something to do with why it has become almost impossible to find in recent years.

7. *Last Year at Marienbad* **(1961):** From its introductory burst of funereal music, there is something vaguely but inescapably deathly about Alain Resnais's classic based on an original screenplay by novelist Alain Robbe-Grillet. The story is warm-blooded enough—a woman (Delphine Seyrig), vacationing with her husband, is approached by a debonair stranger (Giorgio Albertazzi)

intent upon seducing her with stories of their past affair at Marienbad, which may or may not have happened—but the cast are almost indistinguishable from a waxworks. Might the characters be inhabitants of a palatial afterlife in the wake of a tryst that culminated in homicide? Perhaps. Another explanation is that these characters are robots continuing to inhabit these geometric gardens long after their human creators have died, and that their tapes are finally beginning to corrode and break down. Whether it's horror, science fiction, or merely strange, it's as creepy as it's alluring. Notable for including the scariest fade-to-white since *Sunset Boulevard*.

8. *Persona* (1966): Because Ingmar Bergman was generally regarded as one of the most important filmmakers of his time, perhaps the greatest ever, the horror elements in his work were generally overlooked by the doting mainstream. *The Magician* (1958) contains some frightening, surreal moments; *The Virgin Spring* (1960) inspired Wes Craven's *Last House on the Left* (1972); *Through a Glass Darkly* (1961) is as harrowing a depiction of psychological disintegration as Roman Polanski's *Repulsion* (1965); and *The Hour of the Wolf* (1968) is most assuredly a horror film, an acknowledged influence on Oliver Stone's *Seizure* (1974) and David Cronenberg's *The Brood* (1979). This film is about loss of identity and the psycho-vampiric relationship that develops between a recuperating actress (Liv Ullmann) and her nurse (Bibi Andersson), who must fill the void left by her patient's refusal to speak. Throughout the film, Bergman shocks the viewer by playing with the mechanics of cinema—faking torn frames, projector burns, even inserting subliminal images of sex and violence. There is also a frightening flash of a satanic face, seven years before Captain Howdy popped up in William Friedkin's *The Exorcist* (1973).

9. *Gimme Shelter* (1970): David and Albert Maysles's film of the Rolling Stones' 1969 US tour culminates in chilling documentation of the free December concert held at the Altamont Speedway, the ugly antithesis of the paradisiacal Woodstock Music and Arts Fair four months earlier. Bad drugs and worse vibes infecting the audience, the Hell's Angels in charge of security (which they maintained by beating people with pool sticks), Marty Balin of Jefferson Airplane being pulled offstage mid-performance and knocked unconscious, and, when the Stones finally take the stage to play songs like "Sympathy for the Devil" and "Under My Thumb," they quickly realize their repertoire can only offer kerosene to douse the flames of discontent. A man aiming a handgun at the stage is stabbed to death on camera, and there were reportedly other deaths too, but the scariest moment (for me, anyway) is when a girl in the front row suddenly notices Mick Jagger looking in her direction and drops her look of concern to flip her hair and look flirtatious.

10. *The Green Room* (1978): This little-known film by acclaimed director François Truffaut is based on "The Altar of the Dead," a short story by Henry James (also responsible for "The Turn of the Screw," the inspiration for the 1961 horror classic *The Innocents*). It is a morbid love story, if you will, involving a young woman (Nathalie Baye) and an older widower (Truffaut) who writes the obituary column for a magazine. The more she probes into the life of this reticent man, she discovers that his private life is wholly dedicated to the maintenance of a private, candle-lit shrine originally built for his late wife, which he has expanded to accommodate all of those people beloved or admired by him who have died. In order for their relationship to exist, the woman must accept her lover's dead as her own and promise to look after them when his own photograph is added to the shrine. It's a morbid concept, but also a deeply human

one—and, for lovers of French cinema, one also deeply allied to the shrine to dead pets in René Clément's *Forbidden Games* (1952). Truffaut may have been forced to accept the lead part due to lack of funding, but I prefer to think that this project—made in the wake of the deaths of Truffaut's personal mentors Henri Langlois and Roberto Rossellini—was too intensely personal for him to entrust the role to anyone else. Acquired for U.S. release by Roger Corman's New World Pictures, this haunting parlor piece was slapped with a remarkably misleading ad campaign: "In the Green Room, everyone can hear you scream . . . but no one will help." No one came, either. Within a year of completing this commercial disaster, Truffaut began suffering from the migraines heralding the brain tumor that was to claim his life in 1984 at the age of fifty-two.

ANDRE DUZA'S TOP TEN HORRIFIC MOMENTS IN NON-HORROR FILMS

Andre Duza is a leading member of the bizarro movement in contemporary horror fiction, writing under the sub-style Brutality Chronic. His books include Dead Bitch Army, Jesus Freaks, *and* Necro Sex Machine. *His novelette "Don't F(Beep)k with the Coloureds!" is featured in* The Bizarro Starter Kit, *and he has contributed short stories to Permuted Press's zombie anthologies* Undead *and* Undead: Flesh Feast. *In addition to writing, Andre is an avid bodybuilder and a certified instructor of Spirit Fist Kung Fu.*

1. *Scarface*: Chainsaw scene
2. *American History X*: Curbing scene
3. *Looking for Mr. Goodbar*: Diane Keaton's death

4. *Requiem for a Dream*: "Ass to ass"
5. *Casino*: Joe Pesci's death
6. *To Live and Die in L.A.*: William Petersen's death
7. *Lady in a Cage*: James Caan's death
8. *Saló, or the 120 Days of Sodom*: Entire film
9. *Se7en*: "What's in the box?!"
10. *Pulp Fiction*: Ving Rhames doggy style

MITCH BRIAN'S TEN FAVORITE DISGUISED HORROR FILMS

Mitch Brian was born in Dodge City, Kansas, and raised on a steady diet of horror films, comic books, carnival freak shows, and family stories of frontier violence. He proudly cocreated and wrote episodes for Batman: The Animated Series, *and not-so-proudly wrote screenplays which became the grade-z horror flicks* Night Screams *and* Transformations. *His unproduced horror scripts include an adaptation of David Morrell's* The Totem, *rewrite work on* The Last Voyage of the Demeter, *and biopics dramatizing the true-life horrors of John Brown and George Armstrong Custer. He is a visiting Assistant Professor at the University of Missouri, Kansas City, where he teaches courses on the horror film and screenwriting. Please visit him at MitchBrianFilms.com.*

1. *Leave Her to Heaven* (1945)
Directed by John M. Stahl
Screenplay by Jo Swerling, based on the novel by Ben Ames Williams

Sold as a mainstream romance based on a bestselling potboiler, *Leave Her to Heaven* is filmed in a gloriously bright Technicolor palette that suggests psychological safety as hero Cornel Wilde happily falls in love with Gene Tierney. But under the gloss lurks a dark tale of an emasculating female bent on destruction. The perversity roars into high gear as Tierney's character is revealed to be a psychotic whose jealousy spells death for anyone too close to Wilde. Bedecked in virginal white, she drowns the hero's crippled brother, emerges snakelike from the lake in green skin-tight swimwear, and hits a masochistic high as she throws herself down the stairs to kill the baby inside her.

2. *The Virgin Spring* (1960)
Directed by Ingmar Bergman
Screenplay by Ulla Issakson

Bergman directs this medieval drama of predation, destruction of innocence, and revenge with rich, brooding intensity. In a deep-focus, black-and-white world where no good deed goes unpunished, we watch helplessly as a stern father's doting favoritism leads to a daughter's rape at the hands of outlaws. Wicked reversals abound. The virginal daughter's kindness is rewarded with savagery, the profound wisdom of the black-sheep daughter is callously ignored, and a loving father becomes a murderer, losing his soul in the process; though by this time we are sharing his sin and urging him on. Horror director Wes Craven would remake this film in 1972 as *Last House on the Left* . . . with far less sublime results.

3. *Performance* (1970)
Directed by Nicolas Roeg and Donald Cammell
Screenplay by Donald Cammell

This psychedelic, wantonly transgressive crime story soon morphs into a tale of psychic transference as ultraviolent gangster James Fox hides out at reclusive rock star Mick Jagger's pleasure dome. The once-powerful criminal's gradual loss of control is both funny and terrifying. And as one personality is subsumed into the other, polymorphous eroticism supercharges the growing sense of dread, making for dark, delicious pleasures (aided by the presence of Anita Pallenberg). Paint it black, indeed.

4. *Straw Dogs* (1971)
Directed by Sam Peckinpah
Screenplay by David Zelag Goodman and Sam Peckinpah, based on the novel *The Siege of Trencher's Farm,* by Gordon M. Williams

Few films have so successfully transposed elements of the Gothic horror story into modern drama. Instead of an innocent young woman, it's a petulant Dustin Hoffman who finds himself in a remote location on the moors where mental illness, familial abuse, angry villagers, and the unrestrained id are transmuted by Peckinpah's outlaw cynicism. Despite its dismissal by critics as sexist and exploitive (it both is and isn't), the film also explores marital sadism, psychological isolation, male inadequacy, and the human propensity toward senseless violence. As with all great horror films, we can both fear and revel in the cruelty and violence.

5. *Day of the Locust* (1975)
Directed by John Schlesinger
Screenplay by Waldo Salt—based on the novel by Nathaniel West

Novelist Nathaniel West's portrait of the denizens of Hollywood who have "come to Los Angeles to die" provides a rich landscape for a parade of grotesques, including sexually unidentifiable children, bitterly libidinous midgets, repressed homosexuals, emasculated suitors, and a queen bitch with a *vagina dentata*. Underscored by John Barry's underwater basso score and gauzy cinematography by Conrad Hall, this film is truly horrific in its apocalyptic portrayal of Hollywood at the height of the studio system, which it somehow manages to link (successfully?!) with rising fascism. Most distressing of all is how wonderful we feel when a child is trampled to death and how quickly that glee fades.

6. *Midnight Express* (1978)
Directed by Alan Parker
Screenplay by Oliver Stone, based on the book by William Hayes and William Hoffer

From the opening soundscape of gunshots, human wails, sinister electronic music, and a pulsing heartbeat, this "based-on-a-true-story" prison drama's horrific intentions quickly become apparent. Parker's documentary cityscapes (indebted to William Friedkin, himself indebted to Michelangelo Antonioni) give way to claustrophobic long-lens shots, violent slashes of night-time lighting, and sublimely baroque, smoke-filled interiors. Like 1975's *Salò*, this film manages to generate a palpable sexual undercurrent despite its horrifying situations . . . perhaps because "reality" has nothing to do with the hothouse ambiance of *this* Turkish prison, seething with homoeroticism and fetishized violence. By the time Brad Davis descends through Dante-like rings of hell to join zombified prisoners in a shuffling circle, we half-expect Bela Lugosi to be presiding over the proceedings.

7. *Cruising* (1980)
Directed by William Friedkin
Screenplay by Friedkin, based on the novel by Gerald Walker

Disguised as a police procedural, *Cruising*, through Friedkin's clinically distanced eye, creates a cold, growing sense of dread, as Al Pacino's supposed straight-arrow cop submits himself to the late-seventies gay leather bar scene to search for a serial murderer. Critics decried the film for being inaccurate; though I have no doubt that everything represented in the movie happened somewhere somehow, it sure didn't happen this way. The film see-saws from frames packed with Bosch-like decadence, all overheated and oversexed, to suddenly icy, disturbingly formalized compositions and enigmatic plot-turns. The result is dizzying and unnerving.

8. *Come and See (Idi i Smotri)* (1985)
Directed by E. Klimov
Screenplay by A. Adamovich and E. Klimov

We all know "war is hell," but the infernal crucible of war has never been so hypnotic as in this Russian odyssey of a twelve-year-old boy who is swept along through the Nazi invasion of Belarus. As in another great war odyssey, *Apocalypse Now*, humor and horror co-exist, shifting back and forth in the blink of an eye, but Klimov's vision has no room for heroics and is far more harrowing. There is never any hope that our young hero will control or dominate the proceedings and it is this helplessness that gives the film its exhausting, electrifying pull. Aleksei Kravchenko's face is an out-of-time mask of fear and pain, occasionally colored by wonder and fleeting joy. It is as rich and troubled as the war-torn landscape, a landscape both apocalyptic and eternal. Even when it's finished, it goes on. As Bertolt Brecht observed upon Hitler's end: "Do not rejoice in his defeat, you men, for though the world stood up and stopped the bastard, the bitch that bore him is in heat again."

9. *After Hours* (1985)
Directed by Martin Scorsese
Screenplay by Joe Minion

This nightmarish comedy of errors, directed with frantic glee, presents a human gauntlet of damaged city-dwellers who impede poor schlub Griffin Dunne's efforts to get back uptown to the safety of his apartment. Predatory camera moves and paranoid compositions ratchet up the tension so that even the tinkling music of an ice cream truck becomes sinister, as our hero's only hope of escape from an angry mob is to submit to premature entombment. The horrific has never been so funny . . . or the funny so horrific.

10. *Damage* (1992)
Directed by Louis Malle
Screenplay by David Hare, based on the novel by Josephine Hart

A bone-dry tale of a prominent man's sexual obsession with his son's fiancée becomes a morally slippery-wet meditation on trust, blame, and self-control. Juliette Binoche is a nearly silent, black-clad vampire, passively alluring, as Jeremy Irons falls under her spell. Or is it his own sense of inadequacy and self-loathing? Is he predator or prey? Nothing is explained, which intensifies the creeping dread as we watch and wait for the coming car-crash. As in so many vampire films, eroticism and violence result in the walking dead, and the desiccated remains revealed in this film's conclusion are both surprising and haunting.

ERIC SHAPIRO'S FIVE FAVORITE SCARY GENERATION X/Y–ERA MOVIES THAT AREN'T HORROR MOVIES

Eric Shapiro is an author from Tarzana, California. It's Only Temporary, *his short, apocalyptic novel, was on the Preliminary Nominee ballot for the 2006 Bram Stoker Award in Long Fiction. Shapiro also wrote the novellas* Days of Allison *(2006) and* Strawberry Man *(2007). His short fiction can be found in the anthologies* The Elastic Book of Numbers *(British Fantasy Award Winner for Best Anthology, 2006),* Daikaiju! *(Ditmar Award Winner for Collected Work, 2006), and* Corpse Blossoms *(Bram Stoker Award Nominee for Anthology, 2006), among other speculative fiction anthologies. In 2007, he directed the film* Rule of Three, *which depicts an assortment of sexual compulsives and predators.*

1. *Saló, or the 120 Days of Sodom* (1975): Promise me you won't watch this movie. Just advance to Number 2 on the list. This isn't even a movie; it's a beige-lit nuclear power plant of heinous emotion. You want to feel sick for three days? You want to drop some pounds through fasting? Then watch the movie. I'd give details, but I'm a being of class. Okay, okay, just one: *The wedding cake is made of feces.* I'd share more, but I'd rather die.

2. *United 93* (2006): You know that enemy of yours, the one who's afraid of both flying and terrorism? When it comes time to take revenge on that bastard, pry his eyes open Anthony Burgess–style and press PLAY on this motherfucker. Like *Salò*, in addition to showing humanity at its most extreme, *United 93* has some seriously upsetting lighting. Everything you see is washed-out and flat, just like the terrorists' consciences.

3. *Requiem for a Dream* (2000): The most topical movie ever made (minus the smirking self-back-patting that tends to accompany topicality). As somebody who's been sent around the bend and across the river by mis-prescribed medication, watching Ellen Bursytn's meltdown gets me crackling with panic. Add to this the fact that, my being a Jewish New Jerseyian, Bursytn resembles every single mother and grandmother that I met growing up, and my only recourse is to weep inconsolably.

4. *Bully* (2001): I don't know what's scarier: This realistic/low-budget/true-story depiction of a sociopathic Florida teenager being murdered by his peers, or director Larry Clark's shameless insistence on photographing his young cast minus clothing. Either way you slice it, the atmosphere in *Bully* is in-your-head harrowing, and the story is even more harrowing than that.

5. *Full Metal Jacket* (1987): As far as I'm concerned, one of the deepest reasons that this movie is so unsettling—beyond director Stanley Kubrick's maniac-perfect compositions and the shining-shower-knobs lighting—is its infinitely inscrutable and experimental two-act structure: We get a half hour of Marine boot camp, followed by ninety minutes of field action, and in the process, we're constantly adrift. This examination of warfare psychosis never allows you to settle into it, a technique that makes its leering faces and penetrating gunshots all the more disquieting.

RICHARD HARLAND SMITH'S TEN HORROR MOVIES
THAT SUGGEST LIFE IS UNLIVABLE

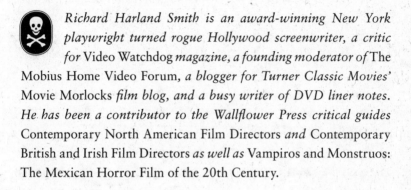

Richard Harland Smith is an award-winning New York playwright turned rogue Hollywood screenwriter, a critic for Video Watchdog *magazine, a founding moderator of* The Mobius Home Video Forum, *a blogger for Turner Classic Movies'* Movie Morlocks *film blog, and a busy writer of DVD liner notes. He has been a contributor to the Wallflower Press critical guides* Contemporary North American Film Directors *and* Contemporary British and Irish Film Directors *as well as* Vampiros and Monstruos: The Mexican Horror Film of the 20th Century.

1. *Night of the Living Dead* **(1968)**: The best of the bunch bears the worst possible news: when the chips are down and we need one another the most . . . we fail. Live with that.

2. *The Innocents* **(1961)**: Forget the "past is prologue" nonsense— the past is *epilogue* in this neck of the dark woods, and there's naught to do but turn around and go back the way we came. Except we're already there.

3. *The Cabinet of Dr. Caligari* **(1920)**: This German expressionist classic is so visually striking that we forget how unrelentingly grim a picture it paints of life in the modern age.

4. *Carnival of Souls* **(1962)**: The moral of this story is, no one gets out alive. And even if you do . . . you don't.

5. *Haunts* **(1977)**: Though we sense that the filmmakers didn't quite have a bead on the Big Picture, this obscure scissors-killer-on-the-loose psychothriller betters the instruction of *Repulsion*

with an overwhelming aura of repression, dreariness, and ennui that makes *you* wish you were dead.

6. *Let's Scare Jessica to Death* (1971): That we can't decide whether Jessica is cracked in the head or the victim of genuine supernatural events seems to be the point of this gently disturbing gem, in which there is no happy ending either way you slice the mole.

7. *Matango: Attack of the Mushroom People* (1963): This has got to be the most candied poison apple ever lobbed at horror film fans. Nobody dies, but everybody loses.

8. *Session 9* (2001): A masculine answer to the overstuffed "problem heroine" subgenre brings a refreshing blue-collar approach to the subject of psychic contamination.

9. *28 Weeks Later* (2007): This film takes *Night of the Living Dead*'s message even further . . . that those trying their best and even sacrificing their lives for the common good of humanity can't reverse the impossibility of living in a world gone mad.

10. *The Incredible Melting Man* (1977): Though it borrows heavily from *The Quatermass Xperiment*, this poor cousin distinguishes itself by the dead weight of its pessimism. And at the end, God gets out his hose.

TOMMY O'HAVER'S TOP TEN
WOMEN-IN-PERIL HORROR FILMS

Director Tommy O'Haver's movies include the comedy Billy's Hollywood Screen Kiss *and the romantic fantasy* Ella Enchanted. *His most recent film is* An American Crime, *starring Catherine Keener and Ellen Page—a dramatization of a horrific true-life murder case (which was also the inspiration for Jack Ketchum's novel* The Girl Next Door) *from the mid-sixties.*

1. *Shadow of a Doubt* (1943): Although Alfred Hitchcock has long been accused of hating women, he's actually given us some of the most dynamic heroines of the silver screen. In fact, he is arguably the grand master of the women-in-peril film—from *Rebecca* to *Suspicion* to *Psycho*, it's almost always his women we root for. This movie, Hitchcock's personal favorite and written by Thornton Wilder, is a particularly twisted treat, as teenager Charlotte Newton (Teresa Wright) discovers her beloved Uncle Charlie (Joseph Cotton) is a serial widow-killer—and in doing so, finds herself the next would-be victim on his list.

2. *Gaslight* (1944): Is Ingrid Bergman's timid young Paula Alquist going mad? That's certainly what her new husband, the mysterious and dashing Gregory Anton (Charles Boyer), wants her to think. As objects around the creepy old house disappear inexplicably, and gaslights flicker on and off without reason, poor Paula's pushed to the brink. But when the gig is up, she finds her strength and the tables are turned. Bergman got an Oscar for this one, and she deserved it, playing the quintessential heroine of the genre.

3. *Julie* (1956): This Doris Day–Louis Jourdan thriller was, surprisingly, also nominated for some Oscars—Best Screenplay and Best Song. In the tradition of *Gaslight*—and Doris's other, more famous woman-in-peril film *Midnight Lace*—our leading lady, a stewardess, marries bad, as she learns her new man actually killed her first husband! The climax—Julie manages to single-handedly land a passenger jet after her ex offs the pilot—is not to be missed.

4. *Eyes Without a Face* (1960): Georges Franju's obsessively gorgeous creep-fest scandalized the French establishment, reportedly making people faint when it was first released. At heart, it's the simple, sad story of Christiane (Edith Scob), a young woman left disfigured by a car crash, and her doomed relationship with her mad scientist father (Pierre Brasseur). Overwhelmed with guilt, he murders girls and attempts to graft their faces onto his own daughter's. This classic exposed the psychological horrors of plastic surgery long before we had *Nip/Tuck*.

5. *Strait-Jacket* (1963): Joan Crawford starred in what is perhaps the mother of all women-in-peril films, *Whatever Happened to Baby Jane?* But it's this William Castle film that really cemented her as a staple of the genre in her later years. Joan gives a terrific performance as Lucy Harbin, fresh out of the asylum after being locked up twenty years for a double murder. When she moves in with her daughter (Diane Baker), we begin to wonder whether she was ready to be released in the first place.

6. *Die! Die! My Darling!* (1965): In this brilliant *Baby Jane* rip-off, Tallulah Bankhead plays Mrs. Trefoile, the religious-fanatic mother-in-law of recently widowed Patricia Carroll (a very spunky Stephanie Powers). But when Patricia stops by to pay her regards to Mrs. Trefoile, and happens to mention she's planning to remarry, the overbearing woman locks the hapless "harlot" in the attic, determined to teach her a lesson. Seeing these two go at it is more fun than a *Showgirls* strip-off.

7. *The Big Cube* (1969): *Gaslight* meets *Beyond the Valley of the Dolls* in this outrageous acid-induced shocker. When well-to-do heiress Lisa (Karin Mossberg) meets ne'er-do-well gigolo Johnny (George Chakiris) it's bad news for her stepmom, aging actress Adriana (Lana Turner, of course). The couple begins "cubing"

her—replacing her Valium with LSD—to make her go insane so they can make off with the family fortune. The plot gets more absurd and convoluted—suffice it to say, this film satisfies, with its drug-trip visuals, ridiculous acid-claptrap dialogue, and a hilarious hippie wedding.

8. *Dressed To Kill* (1980): Brian De Palma's ode to *Psycho* is full of fun twists, as we find ourselves led from the milieu of a repressed Manhattan housewife (Angie Dickinson) into a not-so-distant underworld full of prostitutes, transsexuals, and anonymous sex. It's over the top and, as in most all De Palma films, almost every female character is in peril in one way or another.

9. *The Hand That Rocks the Cradle* (1992): This year brought two great returns to the genre, *Single White Female* being the other example. Curtis Hanson's *Cradle* narrowly beats *SWF* to make this list, if only because Rebecca De Mornay's evil nanny corners Ernie Hudson's simple-minded but suspicious handyman—and she threatens him with one of the most wicked and politically-incorrect lines in cinema history: "Don't fuck with me, retard."

10. *Safe* (1995): Paranoia is an essential element to all of these stories, and in Todd Haynes's strange and brilliant film, Julianne Moore's Carol White finds herself allergic to virtually everything—that's right, *everything's* trying to kill her. Her fear ultimately leads her to Wrenwood, a new-age retreat where she may find some peace—but for the audience, it's extremely unsettling.

EDWARD LEE'S TEN BEST HORROR MOVIES
WITH GRATUITOUS NUDITY

Edward Lee has had over thirty books published in the horror and suspense field, including City Infernal, Flesh Gothic, *and* House Infernal. *He is a Bram Stoker Award nominee, and his short stories have appeared in over a dozen anthologies, including* The Best American Mystery Stories of 2000, *the Hot Blood series, and the award-winning 999. His movie,* Header, *was filmed in late 2003 and will soon be released. Meanwhile, several others have been optioned for film. His Web site is at www.edwardleeonline.com*

1. *Erotic Nights of the Living Dead* (1980): Not even Joe (*Beyond the Darkness*) D'Amato's directorial expertise can save this dollar-store-budgeted effort (they couldn't afford lights, so they shot the night scenes during the day!) but what *does* save it are uncommonly original-looking zombies and a bunch of brazenly naked women, including Laura (*Emmanuelle and the Cannibals*) Gemser and Dirce (*Porno Holocaust*) Funari. The only thing more horrific than the zombies are the plainly visible genital warts on actor Mark Shannon, and it must also be mentioned that one actress in this flick sports *so much* pubic hair, you'll think she's got Don King in a leg-lock.

2. *A Virgin Among the Living Dead* (1971): The title blows the story as effectively as renaming *The Sixth Sense* something like *Bruce Willis is Really Dead*; however, this movie is, in my option, Spanish eroto-horror maestro Jess Franco's very best work, combining atmosphere, uncanny direction, lesbianism, vampirism, real dead bats on a bedspread, a talking hanged man, and howlingly attractive naked women into a brew of pulp horror perfection. It stars Franco supernu-

meraries Britt Nichols and Ann Libert, plus horror's answer to Marlon Brando, Howard Vernon. And we can only hope that protagonist Christina von Blanc was not a minor when this was filmed.

3. *Horror Rises from the Tomb* (1972): Naked women rise as well in this creepy doozy—perhaps, Paul (Jacinto Molina) Naschy's most notorious Gothic gem. A satanic baron, none-too-happy about being beheaded in the 1400s, personifies the phrase "payback's a bitch." Never mind the fake Styrofoam head in the decapitation scene, nor the barbeque-sauce-covered chicken thigh that stands in for a human heart. Good clean gory creepy naked entertainment doesn't get better than this.

4. *Graveyard Tramps* (1973): No graveyard but plenty of tramps in this campy sci-fi horror thriller formerly titled *Invasion of the Bee Girls* and oddly endorsed by Siskel and Ebert. Directed by Denis (yeah, I've heard of him) Sanders in California, this movie is actually brilliant in the way it takes its ludicrousness so seriously, and more brilliant still in its casting some of the *best-looking women you've ever seen in a movie*. Endowed female researchers who wear white lab coats and apparently nothing else "hump" government scientists to death, summoning incredulous, hip-talking federal agent Neal Agar, who does some humping of his own. This flick boasts one of the most scintillating lines of monologue in the history of cinema, when the proverbial overweight police captain says, "You're uptight, we're uptight, I'm uptight, we're all uptight." Kind of beats the heck out of "To be or not to be," huh? The gist: An evil plot to change earth's women into "bee girls" by cocooning their nude bodies in goo infused with bee enzymes. I'm *not* making this up. One actress here proves that breast implantation surgery had yet to be perfected in 1973.

5. *The Living Dead Girl* (1982): Impressionistic French director Jean Rollin's magnum opus of low-budget occult gold. Hell, I'll go you one better and say it is to horror what *Ben-Hur* is to classic film. . . . All right, maybe that's a bit of an exaggeration, but what's *not* an exaggeration is the movie's incontestable success in terms of viewer engagement, transitive atmosphere, and sheer cinematic beauty. You'll forget all about the opening scene's mock earthquake (jiggle the camera and have some off-screen stage hands lob rocks down the stairs—*that's* the earthquake) once the stunning Françoise Blanchard climbs out of her subterranean coffin and gets the blood-party started. She utters nary a word, and she doesn't need to because her body could make a 120-mph Amtrak slam on its brakes and back up for a second gander. If anything, her nude scenes are so captivating that you might find yourself distracted from the actual storyline. Miss Blanchard needs to be in some Naked Scream Queen Hall of Fame. Horror movies are rarely more effective and genuine than this.

6. *Satan's Slave* (1975): This movie asks the question: "Did women in colonial times have bikini lines?" while the branding scene provides the answer: "Evidently, yes." This very obscure Brit flick brings snappy hottie Candace Glendenning to a wonderfully creepy English manor house that turns out to be Party Central for old-school devil worshipers. The only element more abundant than things that go bump in the night are the naked women in nearly every scene. Horror virtuoso Michael Gough delivers a laudable performance, while every female cast member delivers a laudable pair of . . . forget it, and just take my word that this movie sits high on the list of must-sees for fans of sleazy seventies occult horror.

7. *Nude for Satan* (1974): One of the worst horror movies ever made but clearly one of the best titles. Italian pixie Rita Calderoni can

hardly "bare" the horrors of a ramshackle castle that seems to be a revolving door between the past and the present. Terrible storyline, *great* shower scene. Appreciators of feminine beauty will easily forgive the project's jaw-dropping flaws, due to Miss Calderoni's curvatures and professional mettle. Several women in this howler have doormat-sized pubic plots, and you can actually see the black chewing gum used to denote the missing teeth of the "Igor" character. Unabashed nudity and a spider made out of a football with pipe cleaners for legs (no lie!) earn this movie a top slot in the So Bad, It's Good category.

8. *The Devil's Nightmare* (1974): A creepy castle, a 600-year-old curse, and several women hotter than a rock in a campfire are the recipe for trouble in this Italian/Belgian Eurocult favorite. Pulp schlock or provocative thematic allegory? Probably the former, but, see, each character here represents one of the Seven Deadly Sins. When a tour bus misses the ferry, a field hand who happens to really be Lucifer directs our symbolic cast to the castle of one Baron von Rhoneberg, and little do they know a succubus is afoot, along with a lot of bad organ music. This movie is a ton of fun, pure and simple, and the bathtub scene steals the show. Veteran horror bombshell Erika Blanc treats viewers to not one but *two* trips to Nipple City.

9. *Blood Spattered Bride* (1974): This Spanish sleeper waxes Freudian in its rape-fantasy innuendo that tries at times to be a sleazier version of Polanski's *Repulsion* but throws in lesbian/vampiric undertones for kicks. High marks here for a preeminent Gothic atmosphere so important to successful movies from this era; this serves as the glue for a plot that's confusing and simultaneously captivating. There are only two nude scenes in this flick, but one of them—featuring bent-out-of-shape protagonist Maribel Martin—may well be the Mother of All Nude Scenes. This wom-

an's, uh, mammary carriage could make a monsignor kick out a stained-glass window, which is a more polite and less sexist way of saying that she's got the best tits to ever be bared in a horror movie. The other scene is an award-winner as well, as it begs the question: What do you do when you're walking on the beach and you see a snorkel and a pair of breasts sticking out of the sand? Answer: You dig!

10. *Toybox* (1971): What's more fun than a barrel full of monkeys? A Gothic mansion full of low-brow Hollywood strippers who *think* they're horror actresses. This Harry Novak clunker actually stands tall in the annals of sleaze horror, and afficionados of such fare will stare in awe at the bevy of female cast members who all possess rebel-yell-inducing physiques. The story kind of reminds me of that old *Outer Limits* episode about the handful of insipid dolts kept captive in a gloomy manse by an alien brain in the attic. There's no brain in this attic, however—there's "Uncle." See, Uncle's a perv with a penchant for voyeurism, and every week he pays his attractive relatives and their friends to participate in a role-playing orgy. Problem is, this week Uncle is dead but he's still directing the show. Nudity and the macabre have never proved more symbiotic. A zombie in a hot tub, a portentous giantess, dead naked chicks on meat hooks coming back to life, and a "handsy" bed—folks, this movie's got everything . . . everything, that is, except respectability.

ADAM GREEN'S TOP TEN HORROR MOVIE ACTRESSES WHO SHOULD HAVE GOTTEN NAKED . . . BUT DIDN'T

Writer/Director Adam Green made the films Hatchet *and* Spiral. *Awards he has won include second place in his sixth-grade poetry-*

reciting contest, an honorable mention in his third-grade diorama contest, and being just twenty-seven days shy of perfect attendance in the seventh grade.

Before I get castrated by the feminist right, let me lead this list off with a statement that this is all in good fun and in keeping with the themes of this book—it is just meant for a laugh. I have nothing but the utmost respect for each of these actresses and I do not think of women as objects—in fact, I even have one of my own that I keep around the house for stuff like laundry and sex.

For the guy who's gonna track me down and write to me, saying, "But dude! You forgot _____" . . . you need to get a grip, stop playing *Halo*, and kiss a girl. I don't really walk around keeping lists of actresses who I think should have gotten naked in a horror movie. This was a spur-of-the-moment notion, and what I came up with on the spot. So for those of you who *do* go through life keeping real lists of this sort of shit . . . um, wow.

And for the rest of you . . . thanks for having a sense of humor.

1. Jessica Biel in *The Texas Chainsaw Massacre* remake

Okay, I know I am not alone when I say that Jessica Biel and her body deserved two separate credits in this film. In fact, I would almost dare say that she was miscast, only because during the moments when I was supposed to be scared of the chainsaw wielding maniac . . . I was falling in love. Not to mention that this remake furthered the rumor that the character of Leatherface is gay, because no straight man would ever hurt a woman this beautiful. He should have been chasing after her with ice cream . . . not a chainsaw.

2. Kathy Bates in *Misery*

Just hear me out. Is it possible that perhaps Rob Reiner could have added a scene where Annie Wilkes shows up and stands over Paul's bed naked taunting him with her "dirty bird" talk and we see everything? Not because I needed to see Annie Wilkes' chesticles, but because perhaps it would have helped Kathy Bates get the "I should do full frontal nudity" thing out of her system before waiting it out another twelve years and doing it in *About Schmidt*. I love Kathy Bates and I think that she is arguably one of the most talented and beautiful women working in Hollywood . . . but if we were going to see her naked, I would rather it had been Kathy Bates circa 1990 over Kathy Bates circa 2002.

3. Heather Donahue in *The Blair Witch Project*

Did I really need to see Heather naked? No. But she makes this list because for a movie that went to such great lengths to seem realistic . . . there were some major logic issues. Someone explain to me how they had two stoners and an artsy film-school girl sleeping in the same tent night after night surrounded by video equipment . . . and not even some basic oral action got shot? Especially once they realized they were lost and that they might in fact die. Josh or Mike should have at least been able to talk Heather into some "just the tip," right? And once Josh was gone and Mike had her all to himself, a simple "look, we may not live through this" speech would have had her clothes off in an instant. I don't know about you, but any time I've ever had a near-death experience I didn't start thinking about *Gilligan's Island* or my mom's mashed potatoes. I thought about sex.

4. Lindsay Lohan in *I Know Who Killed Me*

I am very much a fan of Lindsay Lohan and I have often found myself in her corner and defending her when people have been bashing her. (So look out, because some actual thought went into this addition to my list.) After the recent wave of unflattering paparazzi shots that have surfaced online . . . it's not like there's much of Lindsay left that we haven't seen, save for perhaps the space in between her toes. Those asshole photographers have essentially Kodak-raped this poor girl at her every move just hoping to get some skin. So here, she's doing a movie where she plays a stripper . . . and could have taken the moment to really do nudity tastefully, perfectly lit, well made-up, and in a very sensual way in order to counteract those nasty paparazzi shots . . . but instead, she stayed covered up for the whole film. Not only did this prove to be frustrating for the audience . . . but it also condemned me to another year's subscription of *Playboy* just to check that goddamned "Potpourri" section for nipple slips.

5. Jessica Alba in anything she has *ever* been in

Christ, just do it already. I'd even watch the remake of *The Eye* if I thought there was a remote chance. But for now I'll just hold my breath for *Idle Hands 2* and keep chewing at my wrists because of *Good Luck Chuck*.

6. Mila Kunis in *American Psycho 2*

I mean, in the first *American Psycho*, we got more flesh-shots of Christian Bale showering than we did actual violence. Why did that trend have to change for part 2? I would have rather watched Mila wash her hair for ninety minutes. Think about it: here we have the remarkably beautiful and seductive Kunis in a serial-killer role inspired by one of the most graphic and disturbing books ever written . . . and all we get is Jackie's discarded lines from *That 70's Show* and a slightly more violent Priceline .com commercial with William Shatner? Even some Kunis side-boob could have elevated this film to a whole new level.

7. Jennifer Love Hewitt in *I Know What You Did Last Summer*

In the nineties, every pretty TV star got their own horror movie, where they got to wear tight white tank tops, not get naked, and yell useless threats at the sky. But Hewitt was one of those exquisite beauties that really stood out from the bunch, and her body looked like something out of Greek mythology. She's still gorgeous a decade later and, much like Jamie Lee Curtis, she will probably only get better with age. But *I Know What You Did Last Summer* could have been her prime moment of glory at the peak time in her life to finally give the boys what they wanted. In fact, I dare say that had she gotten naked in this film, it would have made the film epic enough to not need any sequels. They could have just kept repackaging this one and putting it out every six months when Anchor Bay rereleases *Evil Dead* . . . and I would have kept buying it.

8. Dakota Fanning in *Hide and Seek*

Relax, relax—I'm kidding! But let's just imagine for a second that. . . . Okay, fine, let's not. In fact, let's forget this joke entirely until it gets brought up in court as damaging evidence against me some day down the road.

9. Elisha Cuthbert in the *House of Wax* remake

Actually, now that I think about it, thank God she *didn't* get naked in this movie. First of all, I may not have been able to handle it and my head might have exploded in the theater all *Scanners*-style. And second of all, I think if Elisha could make it through *The Girl Next Door* (one of my favorite movies of all time) and play a porn star without showing her goods, then she certainly didn't need to show her stuff in this film. However . . . how happy would the world have been if she *had* done nudity? Perhaps the war in Iraq could have been avoided. Perhaps Osama would have turned himself in by now. This young woman may have the power to create world peace with her beauty . . . but I guess we'll never know. At least we'll always have the white tank top scenes from her performance as Kim Bauer in *24* to keep us satisfied. Oh, and that amazingly realistic and suspenseful sequence between Kim and the stock mountain lion footage.

10. Tamara Feldman in *Hatchet*

This was my fault and I apologize. Tamara is like a little sister to me and she is up there on my list of the most beautiful women I've ever known. I can't even begin to tell you about the hate mail I started getting when horror fans saw her scantily clad run on ABC's *Dirty Sexy Money*. "How did you have this goddess in a hardcore slasher movie and keep her all bundled up in layers the whole time—yet she's running around on this TV soap opera in her underwear?" OK—so I fucked up! I'm sorry! But let's not forget that I brought you perverted Whedon-loving dorks your beloved Harmony's bare chest in the very same movie. Did I get any love for that? No! Did I get any thank-yous for bringing you the gorgeous Joleigh Fioreavanti and an opening credit sequence that was nothing but gratuitous boobs? No! Instead, I got pelted with "why didn't Tamara show some skin?" mail from you greedy dicks. Sorry! All I can say is that if I have anything to do with the sequel . . . I'll see what I can do.

JOSH OLSON'S TEN BEST HORROR MOVIE SEX SCENES

Josh Olson wrote and directed the low-budget horror film Infested *in 2001. In 2006, he was nominated for both the American and the British Academy Awards for the screenplay to David Cronenberg's* A History of Violence, *the first studio film to feature what the French like to call* soixante-neuf. *He was the only second-grader in his class to see* The House that Dripped Blood.

1. Barbara Crampton and David Gale in *Re-Animator* (1985)

It's bad enough when the headless body of the evil, undead Dr. Carl Hill starts fondling the breasts of poor, naked Megan

Halsey as his disembodied head sits in a metal pan leering and drooling and giggling. But when his body picks up the head and starts running it over her body, you may see it coming, but you won't believe it. The most literal example of "giving head" ever put on film. Scary, funny, and creepy, this is the horror-movie sex-scene all others must be measured against.

2. Elisabeth Brooks and Christopher Stone in *The Howling* (1981)

No words are spoken as they undress and go at it by a campfire in the woods, tenderly at first, then savagely . . . then there are fangs, and drool, and hair, and growling, and finally, in one of the greatest acts of zoophilia in the history of cinema, they make the beasts with two backs—literally.

3. Amanda Donohoe and Chris Pitt in *Lair of the White Worm* (1988)

"Don't worry, I won't bite you," Lady Sylvia Marsh promises the dull-witted young boy scout she's picked up by the side of the road and is now bathing. She lies. The poor kid ends up literally paralyzed, a victim of his own schoolboy lusts, about to be fed to Donohoe's giant lizard-god, when the doorbell rings, and it's Hugh Grant, popping over for a spot of tea. Deranged sexual imagery abounds in this wonderfully zonked-out movie. Minor Ken Russell is still major league magic.

4. Julian Sands and Myriam Cyr in *Gothic* (1986)

And as long as we're on the topic of Ken Russell, who can forget Percy Shelley's encounter with Claire Clairmont in the billiards room? He approaches her, they embrace, and she opens her diaphanous gown to reveal her nipples, which open up to reveal—eyeballs! Oddly enough, three years later, Sands would star in another movie—*Warlock*—in which a woman's nipples open up to reveal eyes. Talk about subgenres. . . .

5. Taaffe O'Connell and an enormous slug in *Galaxy of Terror* (1981)

Pop screenwriting quiz: What do you get when you combine a planet that brings your greatest fear to life and a huge-breasted blonde nymphomaniac with a fear of bugs? Sid Haig's arm gets cut off, a maggot starts crawling around in the arm, then grows to enormous size, creeps onto said blonde, and, well. . . . If you're worried, she dies with a big smile on her face. Rumor has it that second unit director James Cameron actually directed this scene. We all started somewhere. . . .

6. Stuart Devenie and Brenda Kendall in *Braindead*, aka *Dead-Alive* (1992)

Easily the best zombie movie ever made—an over-the-top, blood-soaked, gore-stained obscenity that, somehow, you can show to your Aunt Matilda, because in its heart of hearts, it's not a zombie movie—it's a Warner Brothers cartoon. And contained in its madness is a zombie priest getting it on with a zombie nurse, a liaison which introduces the world to something we may have been better off never meeting—*a zombie baby*!

7. Sheryl Lee, Frank Silva, and Ray Wise in *Twin Peaks: Fire Walk With Me* (1992)

When Laura Palmer's demented lover Bob crawls into her bed and the two of them get down to it, it's genuinely disturbing, but David Lynch saves the worst for last—at exactly the right moment, Laura opens her eyes, and Bob's true identity is revealed, as he transforms into Leland Palmer—*her father*. For some reason, my own father took my then teenage sister to see this movie. I have to imagine that for at least a few seconds, those were the two most uncomfortable seats in the world.

8. Roger Periard and Marilyn Chambers in *Rabid* (1977)

Marilyn Chambers (in her first legit flick) gets checked into one of David Cronenberg's endless supply of creepy medical institutes, the Keloid Clinic, after a horrible motorcycle crash. For reasons that still aren't entirely clear (or necessary), her operation results in a spike that grows out of her armpit and does horrible things to whomever it impales. When one of her fellow patients wanders into her room and finds her writhing naked on the bed: "This is really weird," says the poor sap, just before he gets spiked.

9. **Nastassja Kinski and John Heard in *Cat People* (1982)**
Nastassja Kinski's got it bad for John Heard. Only problem is, Malcolm McDowell has informed her that the only person she can ever make love to without turning into a man-eating panther is him—her brother. Yuck. But she can't help herself, so she and Heard finally hit the sheets, and it is hot. Kinski has never looked sexier, and the scene just crackles. But then . . . it's over. Heard sleeps. Kinski stares at the ceiling. At the last minute, she turns into a panther, which gets in under the wire to earn it a place on this list, and sets us up for the climax of the film, another great sex scene that, sadly, takes place off-screen.

10. **Lana Wood and the invisible Satan in *Satan's Mistress* (1982)**
I saw this thing twice in the same year at Philadelphia's late, lamented Goldman Theater, both times with my comrade in schlock, Chris King. The first time, it was *Satan's Mistress*. A few months later, we went back to see *Succubus*, and I remember that sinking feeling we both had as the opening credits started running over a desolate beach on a gray day. The credits roll—Lana Wood again—and then we get to the title, and there's a skip in the film, the image of the beach vanishes, and a card—probably made out of cardboard—appears, "Succubus" written on it in Magic Marker (I may exaggerate), and we've been had. Used to happen all the time. All of which is a long way of saying that when I realized what was up, it dawned on me that at least I'd get to see the scene where the gorgeous, voluptuous and, most

importantly, *naked* Lana Wood has sex with an invisible dude again. It was worth it.

Honorable Mentions

SOLO CATEGORY

Linda Blair in *The Exorcist* (1973)

A good horror sex scene doesn't always involve two parties. Sometimes, the pleasures are more onanistic. Linda Blair. A crucifix. Movie history is made.

IS IT SEX IF ONE OF THEM'S DEAD? CATEGORY

Udo Kier and a corpse in *Andy Warhol's Frankenstein* (1973)

Dr. Frankenstein, doing obscene things to the body of his monster through a hole in his side, shouts out, "To appreciate life, you must first fuck death in the gall bladder." Truer words have never been spoken.

Special thanks to Michael Theobald.

SCOTT BRADLEY'S TEN ULTIMATE HORROR FILM CRUSHES

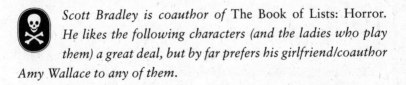

Scott Bradley is coauthor of The Book of Lists: Horror. *He likes the following characters (and the ladies who play them) a great deal, but by far prefers his girlfriend/coauthor Amy Wallace to any of them.*

1. **Lulu (played by Louise Brooks) in *Pandora's Box* (1929):** Not a horror film, you say? Perhaps not. But this German silent masterpiece—directed by the great G. W. Pabst—is plenty horrific. Former

Ziegfeld girl Louise Brooks defined a generation of flappers (and their hairstyle!) with her portrayal of Lulu, who manages to destroy everyone in her orbit with her untamed sexuality, and then gets snuffed by Jack the Ripper (also making her an early victim of the slasher movie policy of punishing promiscuity). Damaged goods never looked so good.

2. **Dorothy Vallens (played by Isabella Rossellini) in *Blue Velvet* (1986):** Ingrid Bergman's daughter plays the ultimate damsel in distress in writer/director David Lynch's mind-blowing autopsy on small-town America. That Dorothy also corrupts (educates?) our straight-arrow hero Jeffrey Beaumont (Kyle MacLachlan) only adds to her appeal: "Are you a bad boy? Do you like to do bad things?" Good girl Sandy (Laura Dern), while undeniably cute, never had a chance.

My runner-up in the vast universe of David Lynch hotties would be Audrey Horne (Sherilyn Fenn) in *Twin Peaks*. Cherry stem, anyone?

3. **Nicki Brand (played by Deborah Harry) in *Videodrome* (1982):** A super-pervy choice among pervy choices, I'll admit, but this pop shrink/pain freak in David Cronenberg's visionary techno-horror tale is about as sexy as it gets. When I fantasize about a life of sexual nihilism, it's always all about Nicki Brand. "Wanna try a few things."

4. **Irena Gallier (played by Nastassja Kinski) in *Cat People* (1982):** What's a gorgeous innocent to do if she turns into a murderous panther when she has sex—submit to an incestuous coupling with her similarly cursed and thoroughly crazed brother (Malcolm McDowell)? Or try a "normal" relationship with the zookeeper (John Heard) who admits that he "prefers animals to people"? Director Paul Schrader created an ultimate horror dream-girl in

this remake of the Val Lewton–produced classic, reinventing the original story as a perverse fantasia on Dante's *La Vita Nuova* with the beautiful Irena as a shape-shifting Beatrice.

5. **Baby Firefly (played by Sheri Moon Zombie) in *House of 1000 Corpses* (2002) and *The Devil's Rejects* (2005):** If writer/director Rob Zombie didn't want us to have nasty thoughts about his lady, he wouldn't have trained his camera on Sheri in the way he did in these two films—or maybe he just wanted us to see what a lucky guy he is. Take a gander at Baby's entrance into Red Hot Pussy Liquor and her flirtation with/humiliation of Goober in *Corpses*; that *is* the definition of a post-modern femme fatale. Build my gallows high, Baby (with apologies to Jane Greer in *Out of the Past*).

6. **Monika (played by Monika M.) in *Nekromantik 2* (1991):** Monika is gorgeous, charming, and smart. She's also a necrophile. But pretty much any guy would agree that if his dead body *had* to be molested, he'd hope it's by someone like Monika. This movie is amazing, right down to its jaw-dropping (and perversely moving) denouement. Would director Jörg Buttgereit, his collaborator Franz Rodenkirchen, producer Manfred Jelinski, and the lovely

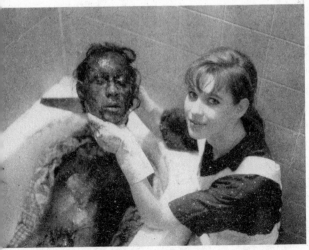

Monika M. privilege us with *Nekromantik 3* so we can find out what happens next?

Monika (Monika M.) on a hot date in *Nekromantik 2*. (Photograph by Jörg Buttgereit, used by permission.)

7. **Annie Brackett (played by Nancy Loomis) in *Halloween* (1978):** Sure, we all cheer for Jamie Lee Curtis as Laurie Strode in this classic from director John Carpenter. And get all horny about P. J. Soles as Lynda ("Totally!"). But I'll always go for Annie—the pothead daughter of Haddonfield's sheriff, Leigh Brackett (who's named after the legendary screenwriter of *The Big Sleep* and *The Empire Strikes Back*)—for both her understated sex appeal and her smart-ass remarks. Cutie Danielle Harris did a sexy riff on this character in Rob Zombie's 2007 remake, but I'll always go for the original Annie.

8. **Fran (played by Gaylen Ross) in *Dawn of the Dead* (1979):** Fran shouts down her boss in the TV studio when he wants to broadcast a list of inoperative rescue stations. She puts up with the ultra-obnoxious Flyboy (which alone should qualify her for sainthood). She learns to pilot a helicopter. She gets pregnant. And she shoots zombies. Fran is the gal that we all would want backing us up in the event of a zombie apocalypse. And she takes no shit from the boys. Ever.

9. **Billie Anders (played by Sally Conway) in "*Prologue*" from *Family Portraits: A Trilogy of America* (2004):** In writer/director Douglas Buck's conclusion to his devastating and brilliant trio of short films, Billie is the victim of a monstrous sex crime that left her wheelchair-bound and with a pair of hooks for hands. She returns to her hometown, and (in a single day!) talks to her former boyfriend, confronts and shames the man (William Stone Mahoney) who attacked her, and delivers a moment of transcendence to a homeless little girl. And Billie also looks like a red-headed Sarah Polley. What's not to love?

10. **Marla Singer (played by Helena Bonham Carter) in *Fight Club* (1999):** I am Jack's massive crush on this crazed hottie, who seems like

exactly the right person to be holding hands with as Western civilization comes to an end. "You've met me at a very strange time in my life," indeed. Where is my mind?

ANN MAGNUSON'S TWENTY-TWO SEXIEST MOVIE MONSTERS (HUMAN AND OTHERWISE)

Ann Magnuson is an actress, singer, writer, and performance artist. Her film credits include The Hunger, Making Mr. Right, Clear and Present Danger, *and* Panic Room. *She has appeared on the TV shows* Frasier, CSI: Miami, The Drew Carey Show, *the HBO miniseries* From the Earth to the Moon, *and was a regular on the sitcom* Anything but Love. *Her Off-Broadway credits include* The Vagina Monologues, Four Dogs and a Bone, *and her own one-woman shows,* You Could Be Home Now *and* Rave Mom. *She was the lead singer and lyricist for the psycho-psychedelic band Bongwater, with whom she released five albums. Her solo album* The Luv Show, *was released on Geffen Records in 1995, and her new CD,* Pretty Songs & Ugly Stories, *is distributed by Asphodel Records. Magnuson has written for magazines as varied as* Artforum, BUST, *and* Condé Nast Traveler, *and pens a monthly column for* Paper. *Visit www .annmagnuson.com for more information.*

1. La Bête in Jean Cocteau's *La Belle et La Bête*
   Cocteau's phantasmagoric film of the romantic fairy tale features impossibly handsome French actor Jean Marais as a Prince Charming trapped in the body of a courtly if exceedingly hairy Renaissance beast. La Belle's love eventually transforms La Bête into the blond Adonis of Cocteau's dreams, but I'm with Greta Garbo, who is said to have cried out at the film's end, "Give me back my beast!"

2. Frank Langella in *Diary of a Mad Housewife*

Although Langella was quite dreamy as Dracula in the 1979 vampire flick based on the hit Broadway play, his turn as George Prager, the narcissistic New Yorker who seductively toys with tormented housewife Carrie Snodgrass, was the sexier monster. Dracula couldn't hold a candelabra to this psychic vampire, who drained more than blood from his victims.

3. Christopher Lee in *The Wicker Man (1973)*

Lee portrayed many sexy vampires in many Hammer films, but he was at his most devilishly debonair in the role of neo-pagan cult leader Lord Summerisle, with his middle-aged John De-Lorean good looks. No man has made a turtleneck sexier.

4. Oliver Reed in *Curse of the Werewolf*

Oliver Reed, in or out of werewolf drag, is one sexy beast!

5. Peter O'Toole in *The Ruling Class*

Sure, he was cuddly as Christ, but when O'Toole's lunatic aristocrat turns bad and appears in undertaker-chic riding breeches, he seduces one and all. Those steel-blue eyes, that commanding voice, the punishing way he slaps a riding crop against his black leather boots while singing "Dem bones, dem bones, dem dry bones . . ."—all conspire to make this Jack one ribald ripper!

6. Thomas Kretschmann in *Downfall*

No one did evil like the Nazis. No one did leather like the SS. And no Nazi combined the two quite like Eva Braun's philandering brother-in-law Hermann Fegelein. Known as Himmler's "Golden Boy," Fegelein was a seductive fiend who believed any woman who did not succumb to his charms was his "enemy." *Downfall* is one of the only movies to commit the decadent Fegelein to celluloid, and the über-handsome Kretschmann

(who portrayed the lead Nazi in Roman Polanski's *The Pianist*)
does an excellent job conveying Fegelein's diabolically dissolute
ways.

7. Gary Oldman in *Bram Stoker's Dracula (1992)*

Oldman is a sexy monster in almost all his roles: Sid Vicious in
Sid and Nancy, the corrupt psychopathic cop in *The Professional*,
even Mason Verger in *Hannibal*. But when he shows up on the
streets of Victorian England in Francis Ford Coppola's 1992 film
Bram Stoker's Dracula, elegantly dressed in an absinthe-green
top hat and immaculately tailored waistcoat, I wanted to crawl
into that dandy Dracula's coffin for all of eternity!

8. David Hemmings in *Camelot*

A boyish *Blow-Up*–era Hemmings puts the Pan in Peter Pan
when he appears in a captivating cameo as Mordred, the mis-
chievous spawn of King Arthur and witch Morgan le Fey (or
was his mother Arthur's half-sister Morgause? Either way, young
Mordred is of dubious origin, and mythological to boot!). Sporting a Satan-esque ginger goatee and looking like a spry satyr in a
tight, modishly medieval leather ensemble, Hemmings gleefully
taunts Richard Harris and, in the process, seduces those of us
who like our imps mordant.

9. *The Creature from the Black Lagoon*

Green is my favorite color. Plus . . . those abs!

10. Anton Walbrook in *The Red Shoes*

No doubt about it, Powell and Pressburger's dance film *The Red
Shoes* is a horror classic. Distinguished Austrian actor Walbrook
plays a seductive yet cruelly controlling ballet master who drives
his dancers harder than Simon Legree. Think Balanchine gone
very, *very* bad. Just as tyrannical as my Belgian-born ballet

teacher but far sexier, Walbrook might have driven me to jump to my death on the railroad tracks had he been teaching ballet, baton, and tap in my hometown.

11. Patrick O'Neal in *Chamber of Horrors*

Little known and underutilized actor O'Neal made a startling impression on me in 1966, when us neighborhood kids were invited to a movie party to celebrate Marshall Jones's birthday. We were supposed to go see the latest James Bond film, but my parents forbade my brother and I from seeing those racy movies. Instead, Mrs. Jones took all us kids to *Chamber of Horrors*. Was seeing madman O'Neal chop his own hand off while handcuffed to a railcar, then use the stump as repository for an array of weapons, such as a hook, scalpel, and meat cleaver, more child-friendly than Bond? Was tingling in anticipation of the gruesome gore to follow the Fear Flasher and Horror Horn more wholesome than watching 007 bed buxom babes? You bet!

12. Jack Palance as Attila the Hun in *Sign of the Pagan*

Combine Palance's Ukranian bone structure (he was born Volodymyr Palanyuk) with swords, sandals, and an evil Fu Manchu mustache, and you got one yummy barbarian.

13. Jeff Goldblum in *The Fly (1986)*

Strangely enough, Goldblum is more appealing when he has been transformed into "Brundlefly"—a mutated heap of human/fly goo. How director David Cronenberg managed to make such a monstrosity so sympathetic is a mark of his genius. All I wanted to do was cradle that bloody morass of dripping marrow and tweaked fly-DNA in my arms, look into those sorrowful Brundlefly eyes, and kiss the pain away.

14. **Yul Brynner in *The Ten Commandments***

Pharaohs are hot. Brynner is hotter. Brynner as Pharaoh is as hot as it gets. Also: Brynner in *Westworld*: Evil, Wild West robot-gunslinger Brynner is almost as hot as evil, bare-chested, chariot-driving, Hebrew-oppressing Pharoah Brynner.

15. **Frederic March in *Dr. Jekyll & Mr. Hyde (1932)***

I first fell for this split personality in 1965, when gazing at photos from the film reproduced in my brand new issue of *Famous Monsters of Filmland*. March's transformation from the genteel Dr. Jekyll to that bad boy to end all bad boys was nothing short of mesmerizing. Plus, I just love a man in an opera cape!

16. ***The Phantom of the Opera***

Speaking of men in opera capes: Every Phantom in every version of *Phantom of the Opera,* with Lon Chaney Sr.'s 1925 silent classic at the top of the list and the Andrew Lloyd Webber musical at the bottom.

17. **All of Ray Harryhausen's stop-action animated creatures**

Special mention goes to the hunky Cyclops in *The Seventh Voyage of Sinbad* and the crazed Skeleton Warriors in *Jason and the Argonauts.* There is something mysteriously titillating about stop-action animation, especially when applied to mythological fantasy creatures!

18. **The centaurs in the pastoral sequence in Walt Disney's *Fantasia***

Granted, these centaurs are more mildly mythic than monstrous, but I can't help myself—centaurs are hot, hot, HOT!

19. ***Ghidorah, the Three Headed Monster (1964)***

Godzilla was my first love, but when we saw the previews for the new movie that introduced the latest in Japanese mutants to the world, my brother and I went nuts for the high-flying, three-headed, death-ray-shooting, gold-plated *daikaiju*. Ghidorah (or as we pronounced it in West Virginia, GHEE-dra) emits a high-pitched, otherworldly, three-toned shriek that translated into an irresistible mating call to one particular young West Virginny girl besotted with monsters.

20. Claude Raines in *The Invisible Man*

I love a guy with a sick sense of humor, and the Invisible Man knew how to deliciously torment his oppressors.

21. The gigantic green goons in William Cameron Menzies's *Invaders from Mars (1953)*

Super-tall invaders from outer space are damned sexy, no matter what planet they hail from. Mutant giants can so easily over-power their victims and carry them off to those unimagined lands that lay beyond the sandpits behind their boring suburban homes. These particular big lugs from Mars are especially ap-pealing due to the fact that their costumes resemble vintage one-piece pajamas with the feet in them . . . complete with zippers and sagging bottoms. They may not have had great seamstresses on Mars, but their foot soldiers really knew how to sweep a girl off her feet!

22. David Bowie in *The Hunger*

If you thought he was a sexy monster on screen, you should've seen him off!

C. COURTNEY JOYNER'S TOP TEN HORROR MOVIE SURGICAL BLUNDERS

C. Courtney Joyner is a screenwriter whose credits in-clude The Offspring *with Vincent Price,* Prison *with Viggo Mortensen,* Class of 1999, Dr. Mordrid, The Devil's Prey, Puppet Master III, Nautilus, *and more than twenty-five other movies and television shows. He has also written comic books as well as articles on genre films for* Fangoria, Famous Monsters, *and* Wildest Westerns. *He is the author of the upcoming book* The Westerners *and his latest movie is the action film* Cop War.

1. Facial replacement in *Eyes Without a Face*

Georges Franju's 1960 masterpiece treads over now-familiar story ground: The daughter of a brilliant surgeon is disfigured in a car accident, and he becomes obsessed with finding her a new face, which he cuts from young women he's captured. They all die in screaming pain, but it is worth it to him if the destroyed beauty of his daughter can be restored. Of course, the operations fail over and over, which only fuels the surgeon's madness and horror.

Franju's film is not just a stunningly atmospheric horror story; it's a fascinating look at the fragile mind of a genius that's warped beyond redemption by an obsession that plays itself out in the operating theater. Beneath the carnage are the bonds of family that no amount of blood-letting will ever dissolve.

Eyes Without a Face is true Grand Guignol committed to film, and we must be brave enough to watch it. Brilliantly (and graphically) shot by frequent Edgar Ulmer collaborator Eugen Shuftan, the film is the ultimate statement on the horror of medi-cine and the sometimes unstable minds of the men who practice it—we pray—only in the movies.

2. Gynecological procedures in *Dead Ringers*

One of David Cronenberg's most polished masterworks, the tale of the twin gynecologists goes from stylish noir seduction to the darkest realms of sexual torture. Cronenberg has explored the closeness of pleasure and pain before, but never with the romantic directorial eye he uses here. Unlike the smashed (and sexual) fenders of *Crash*, the polished metal that's pressed to skin in *Dead Ringers* is born from the mind of a doctor whose sexual indifference turns ultimately to rage, and the instruments he uses on his female patients become as twisted as he is. For Cronenberg, the blade of the scalpel is more than a tool for the surgeon; it becomes an organic extension of his body and the pain it causes is a sexual reward. The corruption of the body ("The New Flesh") is a theme the director has investigated before (in *The Brood* and *Videodrome*, among many others), but never with the subtle touch shown here. *Dead Ringers* is a violent story of medical perversion told in a whisper by one of cinema's true visionaries.

3. Hand replacement in *Mad Love*

It's a tried and true rule that romantic obsession and surgery don't mesh too well, and yet we see the tragic results over and over again. One of the finest examples is Peter Lorre's mad surgeon Dr. Gogol replacing pianist Colin Clive's destroyed hands with those of a knife-throwing killer, so that he can satisfy his love of music while Lorre tries to satisfy his love for Clive's wife, Frances Drake. The hands, of course, become their own entity with the instinct to kill, and Clive cannot control them—and eventually his target is Gogol. Once again, we witness a bizarre surgery that is successful, only to have dire circumstances. The great cameraman Karl Freund directs with more energy and glamorous élan than he displayed in his classic *The Mummy*. The gloss of MGM serves Freund's dark tale well, with every shot beautifully framed by the brilliant James Wong Howe.

The most remarkable sequence is when Lorre appears in a hideous disguise as a man who has had his own head and hands replaced. It is one of the great images of horror cinema, and Lorre's portrait of a medical genius pushed to the breaking point by unrequited love is one of the great performances.

4. Twin Separation in *Sisters*

The moment Dr. Breton (William Finley) savagely cleaves conjoined twins Danielle and Dominique apart, he kills one and splits the other's mind and personality completely in half. It's not the result he was hoping for, but it is a smashing moment in Brian De Palma's first major thriller. This quirky, violent, funny, and beautifully directed low-budget horror is a model of tension and craft. Although the fleshly connection between the girls is gone, they are joined forever in Danielle's mind, which is scarred (like her body) by the horrific surgery. Too influenced by Hitchcock? De Palma has never denied it, that's for sure, and this exercise is the director's indie masterwork. With a pounding score by Bernard Herrmann and a wonderful, troubling performance by Margot Kidder in the lead, *Sisters* remains a marvel of ingenious filmmaking from a director who has, sadly, had more than one misstep.

5. 1940s Brain Transplantation in *Black Friday*

Brain-switching has been a problem for mad doctors for decades, and no doctor dabbled in this procedure more than Boris Karloff. In this fast-paced Universal backlot gangster-horror combo, Karloff actually succeeds, but with (of course) tragic results. *Black Friday* is terrific fun. Doc Boris drops the brain of a gangster into a dying professor's body, only to have Jekyll-and-Hyde results, as the gangster's brain takes charge and the mild-mannered Prof goes on a killing spree.

Karloff's doctors seemed to start their experiments with the best of intentions, only to have everything go haywire by Act II. In *Black Friday*, Karloff is driven by ambition to show the world the wonders of his new surgical technique. But greed rears its head, and the good doc ends up shooting his patient in the guts and getting sentenced to the electric chair. Certainly, no other dedicated mad doctor went to the death house more times than Boris, and this time he deserves it.

Concocted by Curt Siodmak (several years before writing *Donovan's Brain*), this one is more gangster than horror, and more thriller than fantasy, and still manages to combine all the elements into one slick programmer package. Ably assisted by Stanley Ridges as the professor/gangster, Anne Nagel as a moll, and Bela Lugosi as a dapper hood, this little B is one of Dr. Karloff's mini-triumphs.

Karloff spent decades in the lab, as both creator and creation, making film history. His medico status was assured with the Columbia Pictures "Mad Doctor" series, which includes the terrific *The Man They Could Not Hang* and the wondrous *The Devil Commands*. As the years marched on, iconic Boris found himself cast as every doctor from Henry Jekyll to Baron Frankenstein, finally wrapping things up in scientist roles in the four U.S.–Mexican productions directed by Jack Hill. For all of these movie-medical ups and downs, *Black Friday* remains a little gem of the pre-war years.

6. **Victorian Brain Transplantation in *Frankenstein Must Be Destroyed***
There's no argument that Dr. Frankenstein's experiments are the greatest achievement in the history of horror-science in literature and film. When brought to the screen in its most famous incarnation, Universal emphasized Ken Strickfaden's wonderful machinery over scalpels and sutures, although the biggest "personality" problem with the monster was the result of his botched brain transplant. In the sequels, Universal often focused on the undead

monster's indestructible nature as a human machine rather than a human being—a classic miscalculation for all of the Frankenstein fathers, sons, and disciples.

When Hammer approached the story in 1957, they applied the realities of Victorian science to the scenario, adding a new sense of theatrical reality: The great Peter Cushing performed bloody surgery to put his monster together. And we saw it. After *Curse of Frankenstein*, Cushing's experiments brought him from the mere creation of life (*Revenge of Frankenstein* and *Evil of Frankenstein*) to the transference of the soul (*Frankenstein Created Woman*), and then back to brain transplantation in *Frankenstein Must Be Destroyed*. In *Destroyed,* the doctor's surgeries weren't part of the monster-creating process, but rather were done to save the life of a colleague in order get his scientific secrets. This is a story with roots in Stevenson and Conan Doyle rather than the Hammer archives.

A true, gaslit, Victorian melodrama without a trace of fantasy, *Frankenstein Must Be Destroyed* is Terence Fisher and Peter Cushing's elegant summation of their work at Hammer. Beautifully shot and cut, the film boils away all traces of lightning bolts or resurrection of the dead. Instead, this is a tale of medical horror that is grounded in time, place, and character. Cushing played scores of medical men in his career, but he has never been more commanding in his signature role than here. As the doctor's tragic patient, Freddie Jones is no lumbering monster, but rather "a victim of everything Frankenstein and I ever advocated." This is the true yin and yang of the Frankenstein saga as creator and creation face off against one another, and both actors are superb.

Although Cushing and Fisher opted for one last dance with the fragile *Frankenstein and the Monster from Hell*, their *Frankenstein Must Be Destroyed* is the energetic, full-throttle, bloody masterwork of the Hammer Frankenstein series.

7. Head Transplantation (and Removal) in *The Thing with Two Heads* (1971)

Dr. Cadavan Griffiths is credited as "medical advisor" on this American International Pictures backdoor classic. Griffiths obviously knew his stuff, since the procedure of putting bigot Ray Milland's head on Rosey Grier's body is a success. The problem is that Rosey refuses to have his own head removed so Ray can have his massive body all to himself. Sadly, the attitude of the patient can mean a lot in the recovery process, and Rosey just ain't going to cooperate with the plans of Ray's doctors. This culminates in a wonderful two-headed motorcycle chase with the cops, and all kinds of silly hell breaking loose around L.A. With the drive-in-gutsy direction of producer Wes (*Race with the Devil*) Bishop, a two-headed gorilla courtesy of Rick Baker, and wonderfully funny work by its two leads, *The Thing with Two Heads* is a great AIP time capsule from the seventies, and a demonstration of the stumbling progress of head transplant surgery.

8. Glandular Transplants Performed by John Carradine in *Captive Wild Woman* and *The Unearthly*

Any time John Carradine began working with glands, there seemed to be a problem. In the fast-paced *Captive Wild Woman* he created a she-gorilla who reverted back to animal form when her sexuality was aroused. In *The Unearthly*, John's botched glandular work resulted in a basement full of scarred and twisted half-wits.

In the intervening years between the films, Carradine seemed to have learned very little working beside docs like Bela Lugosi or forging ahead with his own research in *Revenge of the Zombies* and *The Invisible Man's Revenge*.

Universal's mad doctors of the 1940s tended to be double-breasted smooth-talkers with a streak of egomaniacal insanity that pushed their experimentation into "realms man should leave alone." Carradine, Lionel Atwill, and George Zucco were the studio's mad doctor co-op whose unconventional procedures resulted in one medical disaster after another, and Dr. Carradine lead the way with his ape-girl creation.

While *Captive Wild Woman* is slick fun from the forties horror factory, *The Unearthly* is a low-rent rehash that Carradine decided to play to the absolute hilt. This time, the doc's sanity is as elusive as the reasons for his glandular transplants. In one botched operation after another, Carradine creates a "Hercules with the mind of a chicken" (Tor Johnson), destroys Sally Todd's face, and puts a patient into a state of "living death." Thank God tough-cop Myron Healey is on hand to stop Carradine before he takes a knife to neurotic (and always hot) Allison Hayes. A grungy little hoot and one more horrifying chapter in John Carradine's checkered cinematic medical career, *The Unearthly* provides ample proof that pulsating glands are nothing to monkey around with.

9. Brain Exploration in *The Black Sleep*

Reginald LeBorg's sometimes stodgy but always atmospheric medical-horror featured (in the words of producer Aubrey Schenk) "every goon in Hollywood." By casting Lon Chaney, John Carradine, and Tor Johnson as prime examples of Dr. Basil Rathbone's surgical skills, it's obvious that Basil needed to refine his technique. Unlike more expensive swashbuckler-horrors like *The Black Castle*, this little period piece is a full-tilt horror story, with Rathbone as yet another doc whose surgical obsession is fueled by sexual desire. In this case, the former Wolf Frankenstein wants to find a way to revive his comatose wife, and his research leads to one failed brain surgery after another. Although hurt by some production penny-pinching, there are still some solid moments, such as when (dull) hero Herbert

Rudley discovers a dungeon of disfigured patients, or when John Carradine sets Rathbone's nurse on fire. Rathbone's controlled hamminess is the film's centerpiece, while Chaney projects rage and Carradine lets his acting dogs loose. With a script by noir specialist John Higgins, *The Black Sleep* is an effective little B nightmare about surgery leading to deformity and madness—or is it the other way around?

10. Head Re-Assignment in *The Brain that Wouldn't Die*

For sheer gonzo fun, few medical sagas can compete with Joseph Green's ditty about a hot-shot doc (Herb Evers, aka Jason Evers) whose beautiful fiancée gets decapitated in a car accident. What else can he do except keep her head alive in a dish while searching for another body to attach it to? Seems "drive-in logical," but the doc's ego keeps getting in the way: A stern warning from Dad about "taking too many chances in the operating room" goes ignored (naturally), and none of the babes he sees really turn him on until he finds the magnificent (and magnificently scarred) Adele Lamont. Also, our hero (?) seems to have a tiny problem with surgical after-effects, whence the twisted flesh-heap he practices on and keeps locked in a closet. Meanwhile, his head-only fiancée is getting royally pissed waiting for her new body! It all ends with the flesh-heap escaping, a lab fire, an arm yanked from the socket, a cheek bitten off, and the now-crazy fiancée/head laughing like hell as gallons of coffee-essence blood is smeared everywhere. This is one of those wonderfully grungy, adults-only-styled New York flicks from the sixties, and a real cautionary lesson for anyone contemplating head transplantation.

MIKITA BROTTMAN'S TEN FAVORITE HORROR MOVIE PSYCHOANALYSTS

Mikita Brottman is the author of numerous books on the horror film, including Meat is Murder *and* Hollywood Hex *(both from Creation Books) and* Offensive Films *(Vanderbilt University Press). She is a professor in the Department of Language and Culture at the Maryland Institute College of Art in Baltimore, and a psychoanalyst in private practice.*

Good Shrinks

1. **Dr. Constance Petersen (Ingrid Bergman) in Alfred Hitchcock's *Spellbound* (1945)**
Petersen is a shy, bookish psychoanalyst who performs brain surgery on pajama-clad paranoiacs. Gregory Peck also stars as the gorgeous, genteel new head of the mental asylum. Too bad he turns out to be an amnesiac patient in disguise.

2. **Dr. Sam Loomis (Donald Pleasence) in *Halloween* (John Carpenter, 1978)**
Loomis is solely responsible for the care of escaped lunatic Michael Myers, whom he follows to the quiet, leafy suburb of Haddonfield on Halloween night. Loomis, who shares his name with Marion's boyfriend in Hitchcock's *Psycho*, is the only one astute enough to sense the danger posed by his errant patient, and with a little help from "final girl" Jamie Lee Curtis, puts an end to the killer's rampage. Until the sequel, that is.

3. **Dr. Mark Kik (Leo Genn) in *The Snake Pit* (Anatole Litvak,1948)**
Poor Virginia Cunningham (Olivia de Havilland) finds herself in a terrifying state mental hospital after losing her memory.

Luckily, she's put under the care of the handsome, caring Dr. Kik, who saves her from shock therapy and treats her kindly even when she bites one of his colleagues.

4. **Dr. Stewart McIver (Richard Widmark) in *The Cobweb* (Vincente Minelli, 1955)**
McIver is the head of a swanky mental hospital that's looking a little worse for wear. He's so concerned to involve his patients in the running of the asylum, he even lets them design the drapes—with terrifying consequences.

5. **Dr. Bondurant (Charles Lanyer) in *The Stepfather* (Joseph Ruben, 1987)**
Dr. Bondurant is the kind of psychoanalyst that only exists in the movies—quiet, genuinely affectionate, and, most importantly, *believes* his young patient when she tells him she thinks her perfect new stepfather is actually a serial killer. Too bad he gets slaughtered soon afterwards.

Bad Shrinks

6. **Dr. Louis Judd (Tom Conway) in *Cat People* (Jacques Tourneur, 1942)**
Dr. Judd is suave, urbane, and sophisticated. It's a shame he's such a bad psychoanalyst, trying to seduce his strangely troubled patient (Simone Simon). But then, you can't blame him for not believing her when she claims to turn into a panther at night.

7. **George Sims (Boris Karloff), master of the eponymous London asylum in *Bedlam* (Mark Robson, 1946)**
Karloff oozes fake sincerity, scarcely glossing over the sadism lurking right beneath the surface. Still, you can't help sympathizing with him when his patients revolt and wreak horrible vengeance.

8. **Dr. Robert Elliott (Michael Caine) in** *Dressed to Kill* **(Brian De Palma, 1980)**

Elliot is much more than just an ordinary shrink—he's a psychopathic cross-dresser who's compelled to slash up any female who arouses his sexual desire, reminding him that he's still very much a man. Physician, heal thyself!

9. **Dr. Hannibal Lecter (Anthony Hopkins) in** *The Silence of the Lambs* **(Jonathan Demme, 1991)**

Dr. Lecter may not be typical, but he reminds us that all psychiatrists are essentially cannibals who feed their morbid curiosity with intimate details of other people's private lives.

10. **Dr. A. N. Lewis (Michael Powell) in** *Peeping Tom* **(Michael Powell, 1960)**

Lewis, played by the film's director in an uncredited cameo role, performs terrifying experiments in fear on his vulnerable infant son (played by the director's real-life infant son), who grows up into—what else?—a homicidal maniac obsessed with fear.

NEIL MARSHALL'S TEN BEST MOVIE BOVINE FATALITIES

Neil Marshall is the writer and director of the horror films Dog Soldiers *(2002) and* The Descent *(2005), as well as the postapocalyptic action adventure* Doomsday *(2008). He is a self-confessed movie junkie.*

Inspired by gruesome cow deaths in two of my own films, *Dog Soldiers* (cow attacked by werewolf, falls off cliff into fire) and *Doomsday* (cow run over by tank) I thought I'd pay tribute to the other unfortunate cows who've bought the farm on screen, and although some of these choices aren't horror movies, what they do to the cows can be pretty horrific!

1. *Apocalypse Now*: Coppola filmed an authentic tribal ritual outside the temple to suggest what's happening to Kurtz inside. Real cow, real blades, real death!
2. *Jurassic Park*: Unwitting cow fed to raptors for midday snack . . . "Clever girl!"
3. *Starship Troopers*: Unwitting cow shoved in a cage with an alien bug only to be sliced and diced!
4. *Three Kings*: Unwitting cow steps on land mine and is blown sky high and spread over a wide area!
5. *Tremors*: Entire herd is attacked by underground worms known as Graboids!
6. *Oh Brother Where Art Thou?*: Cow gets in the way of fleeing felons and is brutally hit by a speeding car!
7. *Twister*: Cow is picked up by tornado and is liberally tossed about, presumably coming to an unhappy landing!
8. *Mars Attacks!*: Herd of cows set on fire by evil aliens and proceeds to stampede through farmyard!
9. *The Howling*: Cows have their throats ripped out by werewolves . . . Slim Pickens indeed!
10. *Lake Placid*: Cow is led to the shore and fed to the giant alligator by a crazy old woman!

STACI LAYNE WILSON'S TOP TEN "KILLED BY KITTY" MOMENTS IN HORROR FILMS

Author Staci Layne Wilson was raised by wild cougars in the Everglades, where she got her taste for cinema spotlighting killer cats by peering through the foliage at the nearby drive-in movie theater. She later moved further east and lived with a tribe of tigers, where she wrote her book, Animal Movies Guide, *using nothing but palm fronds and ink derived from black orchids.*

1. *Inferno* (1980): Italian Grand Guignol maestro Dario Argento directed this macabre, very gory story of a witch known as the "second mother" who lives in a cursed building in New York. Look for an homage to *The Birds*, which substitutes chucked cats for the famous feathered fiends. There is also a beautiful Persian cat who's a familiar for the "third mother" witch, and a coven of murderous felines who are drowned by a crippled antiques dealer . . . but don't worry: Karma comes back to bite him!

2. *The Tomb of Ligeia* (1965): Starring Vincent Price, directed by Roger Corman, scripted by Robert Towne, and based on an Edgar Allan Poe tale, how can you go wrong with *The Tomb of Ligeia*? Apparently, you can't: This atmospheric ghost story, complete with an eerie and evil black feline at the ready to torment a soul or two, is a must-see for fans of the genre.

3. *Eye of the Cat* (1969): Borrowing heavily from Hitchcock, *Eye of the Cat* unfolds a tale of terror about a laid-back hippie type and his girlfriend, who have larceny in their hearts. The couple plans to rob the mansion of the man's eccentric, wealthy, wheelchair-bound aunt, but as it turns out, Auntie keeps dozens of cats in her home—and it just so happens that the man suffers from feline-o-phobia. What a catastrophe! Be careful which cut you see: The original features a veritable swarm of cats, while the pared-down TV version shows just one lonely (albeit formidable) kitty!

4. *The Uncanny* (1977): Writer Wilbur Gray believes that the feline species is made up of supernatural creatures, and as a warning to the world, decides to prove it by authoring three horror stories that illustrate the truth about cats. This trilogy of terror stars Peter Cushing, Donald Pleasance, Samantha Eggar, and Ray Milland.

5. *Two Evil Eyes* (1990): *Two Evil Eyes* is a pair of back-to-back filmettes; one directed by George Romero, and one by Dario Argento. Argento's is the tale of a black cat that drives a photographer insane. There's also a meat cleaver and a razor-sharp pendulum involved. Based on the short story by Edgar Allan Poe.

6. *Tales from the Darkside: The Movie* (1990): A child tells three stories of horror to keep from being eaten by a witch in this anthology flick, based on the hit television series. One of the stories, "The Cat from Hell," is about—you guessed it—a feline born and bred in fire and brimstone. Animal rights activists will appreciate the storyline of the merciless moggy getting even with a pharmaceuticals billionaire for all the cats he killed to test his products.

7. *Strays* (1991): "They have nine lives. We only have one." That's the tagline for this not-so-scary horror movie about some very bad cats living in the basement of the newly acquired home of the Jarrett family (Timothy Busfield, Kathleen Quinlan, and twins Jessica and Heather—the latter of whom went on, coincidentally, to star in a naughty-type movie called *Cybersex Kittens*). We never do learn why these cats are so mad and murderous, but they're good at what they do. The industrious pusses manage to cut off the phone service, open vents, and murder the family's hapless hound.

8. *Night of a Thousand Cats* (1972): Psycho playboy Hugo lures unsuspecting babes to his old Gothic abbey-cum-mansion, makes sweet love to them, and then kills them. He feeds his army of ravenous cats with their tender vittles, but keeps their heads in a crystal cage as part of a grisly collection. This low-low-budget flick could not afford all one thousand cats, so don't bother counting.

9. *Crimes of the Black Cat* (1972): A mysterious killer is murdering fashion models by using a black cat whose claws are dipped in curare. The Grand Guignol set pieces will have horror fans growling [purring?] with delight.

10. *The Crawling Hand* (1963): When a medical student hacks off the hand of a dead space explorer to keep as a sickening souvenir, he doesn't know that an alien life-force has possessed the appendage, making it murderous. But the hand is no match for the hungry neighborhood cats!

This list originally appeared in Animal Movies Guide *by Staci Layne Wilson; reprinted by permission of the author.*

CAITLÍN R. KIERNAN'S THIRTEEN OF THE TOP TEN LOVECRAFTIAN FILMS NOT ACTUALLY BASED (OR ONLY LOOSELY BASED) ON THE WORKS OF H. P. LOVECRAFT

Born in Skerries, Dublin, Ireland, Caitlín R. Kiernan is the author of such novels as Silk, Threshold, *and* Murder of Angels, *the short story collections* Tales of Pain and Wonder *and* From Weird and Distant Shores, *and the novelization of the 2007 film version of* Beowulf. *She is also a trained paleontologist (with publications in the* Journal of Vertebrate Paleontology *and the* Bulletin of Zoological Nomenclature*), a comics writer (for Neil Gaiman's* Sandman*), and an accomplished vocalist and lyricist.*

1. *Alien* (Ridley Scott, 1979): Few films have managed to so perfectly convey the sheer *alienness* of extraterrestrial life or of alien worlds as the original *Alien*. The exploration of H. R. Giger's derelict biomechanoid starship by Dallas, Lambert, and Kane

remains one of the most sublimely Lovecraftian moments in movie history.

2. *The Thing* **(John Carpenter, 1982):** Though actually based on John W. Campbell's "Who Goes There," Carpenter's remake of Howard Hawks's *The Thing from Another World* (1951) gets high Lovecraftian marks for its portrayal of the beginning of the end of the world in the shadow of the "Mountains of Madness."

3. *The Creature from the Black Lagoon* **(Jack Arnold, 1954):** So, maybe the bug-eyed Devonian survivor in the Amazon is best described as a "Shallow One," but there's no denying the film's debt to "The Shadow Over Innsmouth."

4. *Lemora: A Child's Tale of the Supernatural* **(Richard Blackburn, 1975):** This little-known gem of Southern Gothic vampirism takes some of its best bits from HPL, most notably, Hy Pyke's performance as the demented bus driver who delivers Lila Lee to the haunted town of "Astaroth."

5. *Dark Waters* **(Mariano Baino, 1994):** Again, a film that borrows much from "The Shadow Over Innsmouth," the supremely atmospheric *Dark Waters* is sometimes cited as the first Western film shot in the post-Soviet Ukraine.

6. *Ghostbusters* **(Ivan Reitman, 1984):** "Gozer the Traveler will come in one of the pre-chosen forms. During the rectification of the Vuldronaii, the Traveler came as a very large and moving Torb. Then, of course, in the third reconciliation of the last of the Meketrex supplicants they chose a new form for him, that of a Sloar. Many Shubs and Zuuls knew what it was to be roasted in the depths of the Sloar that day, I can tell you." 'Nuff said.

7. *Event Horizon* (Paul W. S. Anderson, 1997): Though clearly inferior to many of the films from which it borrows (such as *Solaris, 2001: A Space Odyssey*, and *The Haunting*), *Event Horizon* offers up a pretty effective look at mankind come face-to-face with Azathoth, "who gnaws hungrily in inconceivable, unlighted chambers beyond time and space."

8. *King Kong* (Merian C. Cooper and Ernest B. Schoedsack, 1933): Surprisingly few seem to have picked up on the notable parallels between the first half of *King Kong* and the plot of "*The Call of Cthulhu*." Considering that the latter first appeared in 1928, one must wonder if Merian C. Cooper had read the particular issue of *Weird Tales* in which it was first published.

9. *Solaris* (Steven Soderbergh, 2002): Along with *Alien*, the remake of *Solaris* is one of the most sublime examples of man's (disastrous) contact with a truly alien "Other" yet filmed.

10. *Smilla's Sense of Snow* (Bille August, 1997): based upon Peter Høeg's bestselling novel (1992), this film moves the action from New England to Greenland and Denmark, but retains much of the basic premise of "The Colour Out of Space."

11. *Hellbound: Hellraiser II* (Tony Randel, 1988): A marked improvement over the first film in the long-exhausted *Hellraiser* franchise, *Hellbound* takes us to some very Lovecraftian regions that Lovecraft implied, but never quite had the nerve to visit himself.

12. *Hellboy* (Guillermo del Toro, 2004): This adaptation of Mike Mignola's comic culminates in one of the most visually delightful encounters with the Great Old Ones ever filmed.

13. *The Blob* (Irvin S. Yeaworth Jr., 1958): When all is said and done, this archetypal fifties horror flick owes much to the pernicious meteorite from "The Colour Out of Space" and the shoggoths of *At the Mountains of Madness*.

ROBERT KURTZMAN'S TEN FAVORITE CREATURE FEATURES

Robert Kurtzman is a director/producer and award-winning FX creator. He directed such horror films as Wishmaster, Buried Alive, *and* The Rage. *He wrote the original storyline for Quentin Tarantino's script* From Dusk Till Dawn, *and coproduced the film as well. He was also executive producer of the Albert Brooks/Leelee Sobieski film* My First Mister *for Paramount Classics. In 1988 he opened KNB EFX Group with partners Howard Berger and Greg Nicotero. His credits appear on hundreds of movies, including John Carpenter's* Vampires *and* In the Mouth of Madness, *Sam Raimi's* Army of Darkness *and* Evil Dead 2, *and Wes Craven's* New Nightmare.

1. John Carpenter's *The Thing* (1982): This film still stands up after twenty-five years and in my opinion is the greatest rubber-monster film ever made. With outstanding creature effects by a then very young Rob Bottin, it was one of the films that made me want to become an FX artist. The effects were created practically before the advent of CGI. It came out the same summer as *ET* and *Poltergeist*. I was seventeen and so blown away by the film and the effects that I went to see it every day for a solid week.

2. James Cameron's *Aliens* (1986): I saw this film while working on *Evil Dead 2* and it brought tears to my eyes. I love the original

film and was skeptical a sequel would be as good. But the mixing of sci-fi, action, and horror created a whole new direction. The film is a nonstop, adrenaline-fueled slice of movie heaven, and isn't just one of the best creature effects films, but one of my favorite films of all time. The Queen Alien, designed by James Cameron and executed brilliantly by Stan Winston's FX team, is one of the best creature creations ever put on film. The power loader fight between Ripley and the queen mixes one-quarter-scale miniature cable-controlled puppets with a life-size animatronic version to perfection.

3. **Ridley Scott's *Alien* (1979):** My mom dropped me and a friend off at the movies on a Saturday afternoon while she went shopping. We told her we were seeing a different film, and snuck in. We'd seen the trailer with the egg cracking and the green light coming out and truthfully, we weren't sure what we were getting into. We just loved the title and you could count us in for anything sci-fi with monsters and special FX; after all, it was only two years after *Star Wars* came out. We got our popcorn and Cokes and took our seats. We were only ones in the theater. The lights dimmed and the movie began. For the first half-hour or so we felt pretty secure, intrigued but on familiar ground . . . until the chest-burster scene. After that, all bets were off. We had no clue where it was going to go. We were horrified, but our eyes were glued to the screen. We were never the same again. That image would be burned into my mind's eye forever. And I'm thankful for that.

4. **Steven Spielberg's *Jaws* (1975):** This is one of those films that, no matter when it's on, I *have* to watch it. I was only 11 years old when it came out, erupting into a summer of shark fever. It was the first of the big summer blockbusters and it changed the summer movie experience forever. To me, it's a perfect film, even

though the mechanical shark doesn't really hold up by today's animatronic standards. It's Spielberg's masterful handling of suspense and minimalist approach to how he shows the shark which keeps *Jaws* from showing its age.

5. **Jack Arnold's *Creature From the Black Lagoon* (1954):** The technical perfection of the Creature suit was way ahead of its time. Beautifully sculpted, designed, and constructed by Milicent Patrick under supervision of Bud Westmore, it is still to this day one of movie history's greatest creature suits, both in design and execution. From the time of its release to today, it has inspired generations of effects artists.

6. **Merian C. Cooper and Ernest B. Schoedsack's *King Kong* (1933):** Willis O'Brien's stop-motion Kong was completely convincing at the time and even for me as a child, in the sixties, I was completely mesmerized. It was on TV every Thanksgiving and every year I couldn't wait to sit with a bowl of chips and a Coke and enjoy the magic. It was one of the earliest films I'd seen that stirred my imagination and my interest in visual effects.

7. **Gordon Douglas's *Them* (1954):** I first saw this film on a late Friday night as a kid. I was watching a late night horror host show, and at the time, my dad was working second shift and he got in a little after midnight every night. The night my dad came home and found me watching *Them*, he told me a great story about when he first saw the film as a kid. He'd saved up his money to go see it at the local theater in my hometown called the Crest Theater. It was a 1950s single-screen theater in the center of town. He and his friends were terrified after seeing it, and he had to walk all the way home from the theater that night, which was about a mile. It was a windy night with tree branches creaking all around him. He ran all the way home, terrified that "Them"

were right behind him, ready to snatch him up in their pinchers! He told me it was the scariest film he'd ever seen as a kid. For me, those giant ants were a marvel to behold as a kid. I'll never forget the cold stare of the little girl when she sits up in the car after hearing the sounds from the ants out in the desert.

8. **Franklin J. Schaffner's** *Planet of the Apes* **(1968):** John Chambers won an honorary Oscar for his makeup FX work in creating a future planet Earth ruled by talking apes. The performances brought the makeups to life and elevated what could have been a really cheesy concept to a sci-fi classic. It was also one of the first films that introduced me to the idea of a paradox. The film was followed by numerous sequels and was one of the first films to take advantage of mass merchandising. I remember having the *Planet of the Apes* action figures and lunch boxes as a kid. A few years ago I purchased the re-issue of the figures in yet another attempt to recapture my youth, or at least, on occasion, glimpse at it.

9. **Peter Jackson's** *Lord of the Rings* **trilogy (2001–2003):** Peter Jackson and his FX team, led by Richard Taylor, had to be very creative and frugal early in their careers while working on no-budget horror films in New Zealand. They put every dime onto the screen, no matter what they had to work with. It's that ability to make movie magic with limited resources that made Peter and Richard the perfect team to tackle *Lord of the Rings*. Don't get me wrong; the series is far from cheap at $300 million for three films, but Peter and Richard and their partners and collaborators put $600 million on the screen. They packed so much heart, incredible images of Middle Earth, and fantastic creatures into those films that it brought back the child in all of us. It reminded me of the first time I'd seen *King Kong* or *Jason and the Argonauts* as a kid and how blown away and inspired I'd felt. The trilogy is one of the best cinematic experiences I've ever witnessed

and features some of the most incredible creature FX, both CGI and practical, ever achieved.

10. **Ridley Scott's** *Legend* **(1985):** Darkness and Meg Mucklebones: two incredible creatures and two amazing performances (Tim Curry as Darkness and Robert Picardo as Meg Mucklebones). Rob Bottin, hot off his groundbreaking work on Joe Dante's *The Howling* and John Carpenter's *The Thing*, creates more classic movie creatures.

BOB BURNS'S EIGHT WORST MONSTER MOVIE COSTUMES

Bob Burns began his career as an apprentice to legendary makeup man Paul Blaisdell in the mid-fifties, working on the monsters in Invasion of the Saucermen, The She Creature, *and* It Conquered the World. *Burns serves as the technical consultant for the Discovery Channel's* Movie Magic *series, and co-hosts the "Bob's Basement" segments on the Sci-Fi Channel's news magazine* Sci-Fi Buzz. *He lives in Burbank, where he curates the Bob Burns Museum, which contains one of the largest collections of movie props and antique toys in the United States.*

1. *Creeping Terror*: It looks like a rolled-up rug that goes around eating people by sucking them into it. I think it *was* an old, used rug.
2. *Phantom Planet*: The monster looks like Goofy or Pluto with a rubber body that has craters on it. His tongue is even sticking out.

Phantom Planet
(Photograph provided
by Bob Burns)

3. *Beast from the Haunted Cave*: A chicken-wire frame covered with a bunch of angel hair. The rest of the body is anybody's guess.
4. *Giant Leeches*: They look like black rain coats with doughnut-size tentacles glued on.
5. *Frankenstein's Daughter*: One of the worst makeups in history.

Frankenstein's Daughter
(Photograph provided
by Bob Burns)

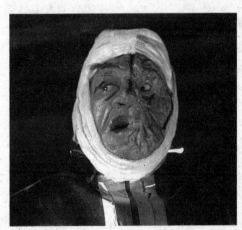

Killers from Space (Photograph provided by Bob Burns)

6. ***Killers from Space***: These guys wore tights and hoods, and had ping pong balls for eyes.

7. ***Night of the Blood Beast***: This monster had a big head that looked like a parrot's, and the body looks like a piece of crap with horse hair glued on it.

8. ***Eye Creatures***: This is a horrible remake of *Invasion of the Saucermen*, and the costumes are really bad. They look like jumpsuits with eyeballs glued all over them, and big heads with gaping mouths. It also looks like they could only afford one complete costume, as the rest are only the top torso with jeans for the rest of the suit. This film is so bad that it makes the original *Saucermen* that Paul Blaisdale and I worked on look like an A-film.

PROFESSOR PAUL M. JENSEN'S TEN FAVORITE TWO-CHARACTER SCENES FEATURING BORIS KARLOFF (PLUS ONE BONUS)

Professor Paul M. Jensen teaches courses in film history and appreciation at SUNY–Oneonta. He is the author of four books: The Cinema of Fritz Lang *(1969),* Boris Karloff and His Films *(1974),* The Men Who Made the Monsters *(1996), and* Hitchcock Becomes "Hitchcock" *(2000). He has also contributed articles on film-related subjects to numerous periodicals, including* Film Comment, Films in Review, Scarlet Street, Headpress, *and* Video Watchdog. *He appears in documentaries on the DVD releases of seven Universal Studios horror classics—*Frankenstein, Bride of Frankenstein, The Mummy, The Invisible Man, The Phantom of the Opera, It Came from Outer Space, *and* Creature from the Black Lagoon—*and also provides an audio commentary for* The Mummy. *Paul also memorably played "the Blind Man" in the classic grindhouse horror film* Last House on Dead End Street *(1973), written and directed by the late Roger Watkins.*

1. With Clark Marshall, in *The Criminal Code* (1931)

Karloff is consistently impressive as Galloway, a hardened criminal who nonetheless projects a kind of unsentimental decency in this prison story. The scene in which he "executes" Runch, a squealer, is played in long shot, with Karloff's back to the camera, emphasizing the dynamic stillness and abrupt, compact movements of his lean frame. In this *pas de deux*, he flicks a knife into view, then blocks his cringing quarry's attempts to escape, first with a slight shift to the right, then four graceful steps to the left, and finally a slow advance that herds Runch into a back room—while the sound of yelling prisoners outside provides counterpoint to the silent stalking within.

2. With Edward G. Robinson, in *Five Star Final* (1931)

Karloff has several notable scenes as Isopod, an unctuous newspaper reporter who is also a sexual predator. It is especially gratifying to see him share the screen with Edward G. Robinson, playing his editor. Isopod has tricked some embarrassing information out of an inoffensive couple, and now, heavy-lidded inebriation heightens his smug self-satisfaction and phony moral indignation as he declares, "I was shocked, Mr. Randall, shocked!" The vibrant Robinson takes it all in, as Karloff dominates the scene and, for the moment, his boss.

3. With Robert Young, in *The Guilty Generation* (1931)

An early scene between a successful gangster (Karloff) and the son who has disowned him (Robert Young) captures more nuances than its creators may have expected. The smooth-faced youth is righteous, preachy, and sure of himself. His father, seriously flawed as a person and a parent, shifts between relaxed openness and a mixture of hurt and anger, with anger dominant. The muscles in Karloff's face tense as the son describes how horrible it was to have him as a father, making this "bad" man more complex and comprehensible than his "good" but shallow offspring.

4. With Zita Johann, in *The Mummy* (1932)

When Ardath Bey (Karloff) and Helen Grosvenor (Zita Johann) first meet, they feel a riveting connection without either person knowing why. Locked in a mutual, hypnotic stare, they speak mundane, polite dialogue ("I called to see Sir Joseph."; "He's in the study.") that is belied by the haunted quality of their voices and the strength of their gaze. Time seems to stand still as they hover in the dimly lit room, interacting in the present, yet existing apart from the concrete world around them. For once, Karloff is granted a scene with a woman who, like him, looks and sounds exotic but in a muted, natural way.

5. With Lawrence Grant, in *The Mask of Fu Manchu* (1932)

The first encounter between this Chinese villain-hero (Karloff) and an Englishman introduces some surprising racial implications. Sir Lionel Barton (Lawrence Grant), as if unaware that he is a prisoner, automatically talks as if he has power and authority. "I want to know the meaning of this!" he demands. "You'll answer my question!" When Barton asks, "You're Fu Manchu, aren't you?" his captor responds, "I am a doctor of philosophy from Edinburgh. I am a doctor of law from Christ College. I am a doctor of medicine from Harvard. My friends—out of courtesy— call me 'Doctor.'" This elicits only sarcasm and condescension from Barton, and when the Doctor speaks of having some ancient artifacts returned, Barton snaps back, "Our English people like to look at them on holidays!" In short, Fu Manchu, for all his mercilessness, has dignity, wit, and polite sophistication— qualities alien to the Englishman's knee-jerk assumption of natural superiority. As a result, whether intended or not, the film makes clear why Dr. Fu Manchu could resent what he later calls the "accursed white race."

6. With Bela Lugosi, in *The Raven* (1935)

Although this movie as a whole belongs to Bela Lugosi, in their first scene together Karloff (as Bateman, a murderer) and Lugosi (as Dr. Vollin, a surgeon) are perfectly balanced, so that the reluctantly violent Bateman's helpless physicality contrasts dramatically with the enthusiastic sadism of the intellectually superior Vollin. In the process, Karloff speaks what has become one of my favorite catch-phrases, Bateman's sad rationalization of his brutality: "Sometimes you can't help—things like that."

7. With O. P. Heggie, in *Bride of Frankenstein* (1935)

In his second scene with the elderly blind man (O. P. Heggie), the Frankenstein Monster (Karloff) experiences a wide range of emotions—including that rarity, happiness—and passes through several compressed stages of education. We have the privilege of watching this dangerously bewildered victim gain knowledge and insight. The scene is an audacious one that courts absurdity, but director James Whale and his actors maintain a steady tone of honest feeling and human comedy instead of slipping into sentimentality and broad parody.

8. With Karloff, in *The Black Room* (1935)

Karloff plays twin brothers with very different personalities, so seeing them interact is both a technical accomplishment and, more important, an acting achievement. True, at this point the arrogant Gregor is pretending to be friendly to the naïve Anton, so the scene does not strike the hoped-for confrontational sparks. Nonetheless, it provides a gratifying contrast between the disheveled, sprawling crudeness of Gregor and the gentle, rather prim stability of his brother, and between the guttural speech of the former and the latter's softer tones.

9. With Henry Daniell, in *The Body Snatcher* (1945)

Two of the most resonant voices in film history—belonging to a pair of powerfully intense actors—speak this script's literate dialogue when Cabman Gray (Karloff) and Dr. MacFarlane (Daniell) converse in a pub. Many complex qualities emerge during the second such scene, including the men's mutual hatred and equally mutual need for each other. As they discuss the difference between knowledge and understanding, the grave robber and sometime murderer reveals a sensitive, even gentle, side, while the healer emits icy ruthlessness. It's safe to say that neither actor was ever better, as each builds on what the other provides.

10. With Peter Bogdanovich, in *Targets* (1968)

In a scene of fictional autobiography, Karloff portrays an aging horror star and Peter Bogdanovich, this film's writer/director, plays his on-screen writer/director. In one scene, we spend several minutes with what appears to be a relaxed, natural, and very human Karloff, as well as a relaxed, natural, and very human Bogdanovich. The scene also brings Karloff's career full circle when the two men watch *The Criminal Code* on television and react to the very scene cited above. Bogdanovich disappointedly declares, "All the good movies have been made," and Karloff states that he couldn't "play a straight part decently anymore," but these comments are belied by the very film we are watching.

Bonus: *Playhouse 90*'s production of *Heart of Darkness* (1958)

In the mid-1950s, when his movie roles were at best undemanding, Karloff found rewarding material in the theatre and on television. The theatre performances are forever unavailable, but some of the television work is accessible, with live productions preserved in kinescope form. This *Playhouse 90* adaptation strays far from the Joseph Conrad source, and Roddy McDowall is not my idea of Marlow, but his climactic encounter with the enigmatic Kurtz is highly satisfactory. Perfectly cast as Kurtz, Karloff is still a forcefully physical figure, and it is worth much to hear that intelligent, passionate, understated voice speak a variation on Conrad's lines: "Exterminate all the brutes! Exterminate me! Horror, the horror!"

DAVID WALLECHINSKY'S SIX
OVERLOOKED HORROR FILMS

David Wallechinsky created the Book of Lists series in 1977 with his father Irving Wallace and sister Amy Wallace. He is also the co-creator of the People's Almanac books, and author of The 20th Century: History with the Boring Parts Left Out, Whatever Happened to the Class of '65? *(with Michael Medved),* Tyrants: The World's 20 Worst Dictators, *and numerous other titles. Wallechinsky is also a columnist for* Parade *and blogs on the Huffington Post.*

1. *A Page of Madness (Kurutta ippeji)*—Japan, 1926

   A Japanese silent classic, *A Page of Madness* takes place in an insane asylum. A man whose wife is incarcerated there takes a job as a janitor with the intention of helping her escape. The director, Teinosuke Kinugasa, made at least 100 films, the most famous of which was the Oscar-winning *Gate of Hell* (1953). *A Page of Madness*, a prime candidate for a modern remake, was thought to be lost for forty years until Kinugasa found a print in his garden shed.

2. *Titicut Follies*—USA, 1967

   Like *A Page of Madness*, *Titicut Follies* takes place in an insane asylum. But Frederick Wiseman's groundbreaking *cinéma vérité* feature documents life inside a real mental hospital, the State Prison for the Criminally Insane in Bridgewater, Massachusetts. Wiseman exposed such appalling conditions inside the prison, including abuse of naked prisoners, that the film was banned from public showings for twenty-three years.

3. *Demon Woman (Onibaba)*—Japan, 1964

   During a time of war, an old woman and her daughter-in-law lure soldiers into a covered pit, kill them, and trade their armor and weapons for food. One of their victims, a general, wears a demon mask, which the old woman uses to scare her daughter-in-law into not running away.

4. *Pulgasari*—North Korea, 1985

You don't see a lot of monster movies from North Korea, and this one has one of the most unusual backstories in the history of cinema. The current dictator of North Korea, Kim Jong-il, kidnapped South Korean director Shin Sang-ok and forced him to make movies in North Korea. *Pulgasari* was Shin's last work before he escaped while on a trip to Vienna. Pulgasari the monster begins his life as a doll made of rice and clay, but grows whenever he eats metal. Soon he is protecting oppressed villagers from the evil warlord. But then he grows so big that he becomes a burden to the citizenry he is supposed to be protecting. As for Shin, after being debriefed at length by the CIA, he made his way to Hollywood, changed his name to Simon Sheen, created the *3 Ninjas* series and even managed to get *Pulgasari* remade as an American children's film called *Galgameth*.

5. *Dead of Night*—UK, 1945

Probably the first horror anthology film, *Dead of Night* consists of five separate tales successfully tied together as one story. My favorite episode is "Golfing Story," which many horror fans hate because it is a comic yarn in which character actors Basil Radford and Naunton Wayne reprise their sporting-obsessed roles from Alfred Hitchcock's *The Lady Vanishes*. However, "Golfing Story" relieves the tension before the creepiest segment, "The Ventriloquist's Dummy," in which Michael Redgrave plays a ventriloquist who appears to be controlled by his dummy.

6. *Witchcraft Through the Ages (Häxan)*—Denmark/Sweden, 1922

In this precursor of both surrealism and docudrama, writer/director Benjamin Christensen, who also plays The Devil, presents a weird and shocking history of witchcraft, with emphasis on the Middle Ages, mass hysteria, and the dangers of superstition. An abridged version, with narration by author William S. Burroughs, was released in 1968.

FRANZ RODENKIRCHEN'S TEN PERSONAL ENCOUNTERS WITH THE HORROR GENRE (PLUS A CODA)

Franz Rodenkirchen is married to writer/translator Sanna Isto, with whom he has two daughters. He heads the consulting department at the German script development company Script House. As script advisor, he regularly works for the Binger Filmlab, Amsterdam; the European workshop Script & Pitch; CineLink, the co-production market of the Sarajevo Film Festival, and many others. Franz co-wrote four legendary horror films—Nekromantik, Nekromantik 2, Der Todesking, *and* Schramm—*with director Jörg Buttgereit, and helped in bringing them to the screen. By now, he has worked on well over 100 international film projects, predominantly with writer/directors.*

I realize this is more of a story than a list, but stories are my life . . .

1. *1967*: My earliest memory of seeing a movie was at the age of four, when I watched *The 7th Voyage of Sinbad*, by Nathan Juran, on TV. I distinctly remember the scene with the Cyclops roasting humans on a spit. As it turned out later after we met, Jörg Buttgereit's earliest film memory is the same, so, given we are the same age, he must've seen the same broadcast.

2. *1977*: At school, as a preteen, I was thrilled but also scared to hear of all the horror films my friends talked about—especially

the moment when Vera Miles touches the shoulder of Mrs. Bates and stares into the face of death. That struck me as the most horrible sight imaginable. Needless to say, when finally I saw *Psycho* for the first time, as an adult, I was quite disappointed with that particular effect.

3. *1980*: Lucio Fulci's *Zombie Flesh-Eaters* played, and though my anxiety was strong as ever (oh, those days of puberty . . .), I agreed to go see it with my fourteen-year-old girlfriend. For the length of the movie I tried to both see and not see what was going on. Afterwards, my girlfriend walked home alone through dark fields, while I spent the night with the lights on and seeing zombies in every corner . . .

4. *1981*: Age seventeen, and looking fifteen, I tried unsuccessfully to pass for eighteen to see *Dawn of the Dead*. All my friends got in and another legend was born. But this time I promised myself I'd get a handle on that anxiety problem. As for the looks—time would help.

5. *1984*: Now twenty and living in Berlin, I made good on that promise. One night I attended a triple feature at the legendary Sputnik Cinema in Berlin (where we'd have most of our premiere screenings later): *Night of the Living Dead*, *The Texas Chainsaw Massacre*, and *Carrie*. After seeing *TCM*, I was sure I'd seen the best horror film ever made. And from that day, I launched into a full exploration of the genre.

6. *1984*: Some weeks later, while grating carrots, I managed to cut off the tip of my right index finger and, after receiving a tetanus shot at the hospital, I finally went to see *Dawn of the Dead*. Unlike *Psycho*, this film lived up to its reputation. I loved it, and still do.

7. *July 1988*: At the horror all-nighter "Shock Around the Clock," at the wonderful Scala Cinema in London, the first international screening of *Nekromantik* propelled our cheap little movie out into the world—where it still enjoys a healthy life.

8. *1990*: After a full day of casting for *Nekromantik 2*, we had not found an acceptable leading lady. Frustrated, I went to a triple-bill midnight screening, including Lucio Fulci's *House by the Cemetery*. There I saw a woman I wished had shown up at our casting. I followed her out, approached her in a dark alley, and, in a complete cliché moment, asked if she had ever thought about starring in a film. That's how I met Monika M., who became the star of *Nekromantik 2*.

9. *1993*: We were banned from screening our films at the "Love and Anarchy" Film Festival in Helsinki (due to reputation only), so the organizers of the festival put everybody on a ferry to Tallinn to screen *Nekromantik 1* and *2* (in a triple bill with Abel Ferrara's *Driller Killer*). I dedicated the screening to the festival's top guest John Woo, who was nice enough to accept and sit through the whole thing.

10. *1994*: Returning to the Helsinki Film Festival for the screening of our last film, *Schramm*, I attended a screening of Tsui Hark's *Green Snake* and was afterwards accosted by a woman who remembered me from the year before. That's how I met my wife.

Coda: 2007: On one of the rare occasions when I'm home alone these days, I watched *Wolf Creek*—it had quite a reputation, and I felt a new hunger to delve back into my favorite genre, after years of sagging interest. I stopped the film after the first time they knock out the bad guy, with no intention of ever seeing the rest. I could find nothing in me that wanted to continue watching.

VINCE CHURCHILL'S TOP TEN LIST OF FILMS IN WHICH, WOW, THE BLACK GUY LIVED!

Vince Churchill is the author of two horror/science fiction novels: The Dead Shall Inherit the Earth *and* The Blackest Heart. *He contributes a regular column, "The Splatter Pattern," to* The Hacker's Source *magazine. Next up is a horror novella called* Condemned, *scheduled to be published by Daystar Studios in the fall of 2007. His next novel, a dark end-of-the-world love story called* Good Night My Sweet, *is slated for completion in early 2008.*

Back in the day, if there was a black character in a horror film, odds were they were there strictly for the sake of the body count. A black guy was the horror equivalent of the red-uniformed guys on *Star Trek*. So here's my list of the best horror flicks where the black guy (or gal) overcomes all until the end credits. And there were so many films to choose from, don't you know.

1. *Bats*: He's no Madonna, but the single-named Leon, best known for the Jamaican bobsled classic *Cool Runnings*, backs up leads Lou Diamond Phillips and Dina Meyer and manages to not bite the big one.

2. *Halloween H20*: Rapper-turned-actor Will Smith, uh, no, I mean LL Cool J plays a security guard at a private school with a bulls-eye on his back so big he might as well have been driving by a KKK meeting with Paris Hilton on his lap. But he does live to bust a rhyme another day.

3. *Deep Blue Sea*: Well, Samuel L. Jackson might have become shark chow, but that rapper-turned-actor Tupac, uh, I mean LL Cool J, plays a God-fearing cook with a parrot who finds a way to

survive intelligent killer sharks and also the ocean. We all know brothers can't swim, so this ought to count for two. Mr. Cool J is one lucky Negro.

4. *Thir13een Ghosts:* Rah Digga plays Maggie, a useless housekeeper/nanny whose abrasive personality makes Florence from *The Jeffersons* seem like Alice from *The Brady Bunch*. Most viewers of the film probably wished her character dead, but miraculously she lives to the end.

5. *Dawn of the Dead:* Ken Foree decides suicide is not the answer, then kicks zombie ass (accompanied by cheap action music) up to the roof to hitch a ride with the pregnant helicopter-flying chick. It ain't his baby, so no sweat.

6. *Day of the Dead:* Terry Alexander portrays our island-accented chopper pilot John and manages to fly off into the sunset with the girl in a way reminiscent of the previous *Dawn of the Dead*. Hey, Zombie Mon, get your dark meat elsewhere.

7. *28 Days Later:* By far the most attractive of our survivors, Naomie Harris's Selena has a cute English accent and is handy with a machete too. Hubba, hubba.

8. *Anaconda:* Rapper-turned-actor Ice T, uh, I mean Ice Cube, takes a trek into the jungle and defies stereotype by not letting the big snake be his downfall. Plus, he gets to work with a sweaty J. Lo. Better than a free basket of hot wings.

9. *The Thing:* Keith David literally chills out with Kurt Russell and waits to see what happens when the home fires burn low at the end of John Carpenter's classic remake. But honestly, what good can come from a brother working in the Arctic?

10. *The House on Haunted Hill*: In the remake of the old William Castle/ Vincent Price shocker, Taye Diggs enters the house a simple baseball player, but by the time the credits roll, he's not only survived, but is stranded on a ledge with the sexy Ali Larter and has an envelope filled with million-dollar cashier's checks made out to *cash*. He not only lives, he lives large!

JOHN SKIPP'S FIVE FAVORITE BENIGN "FACE OF GOD" MOMENTS IN HORROR FILMS (PLUS TEN HONORABLE MENTIONS)

John Skipp is one of America's most cheerfully perplexing renaissance mutants: New York Times *bestselling author-turned-filmmaker, satirist, cultural crusader, musical pornographer, purveyor of cuddly metaphysics, interpretive dancer, and all-around bon vivant. With* The Long Last Call, Conscience, *and the Bram Stoker Award–winning anthology* Mondo Zombie, *he has returned to the front ranks of modern horror fiction. Other books include* The Light at the End *and* The Bridge *(both with Craig Spector),* Stupography, *and* The Emerald Burrito of Oz *(with Marc Levinthal). He lives in L.A. and thinks you should visit him at www .johnskipp.com, just for fun.*

1. *Santa Sangre* (1989): Nobody in the history of transcendence-based cinema has used horrific imagery more abundantly or profoundly than Alejandro Jodorowsky.

Death, morbidity, cruelty, madness, and the spiritual perils that the flesh must endure on their way to godhead are continually invoked throughout *El Topo* and *The Holy Mountain*: not to mitigate the sacred, but to propel it forward through a landscape of corruption and dread—fighting all the way—until it actually earns the transcendence it craves.

But these are not horror films, in any conventional sense.

So it wasn't until *Santa Sangre* that he flipped the coin, and used nearly conventional horror tropes (e.g., "He's a serial killer, and this is how it happened") as a kick-start toward ultimate, truly staggering enlightenment.

Those moments are far too abundant to count, coming in both sideways and right in your face. (The boy and the bleeding elephant, anyone?)

But I'd have to pick the sequence in which our incredibly broken murderer/antihero buries his latest victim, and a white horse emerges from the grave. Must be seen to be fucking believed. And total genius, no matter how (or how many ways) you slice it.

2. **The Shining** (1980): Legend has it that Stanley Kubrick called to wake up Stephen King in the middle of the night and ask, "Excuse me, but I need to know . . . do you believe in God?" And when King replied that actually, yes, he did, Kubrick went, "Oh," and hung up the phone.

So how fascinating is it that the self-professed atheist/existentialist/agnostic-at-best—whose *2001: A Space Odyssey* turns out to be one of the greatest face-of-God movies ever made—would choose to represent transcendent love and grace almost exclusively through the smile of Scatman Crothers?

But there it is: beneficent and loving and beautiful beyond compare, in extreme close up, as he talks to young Danny. And even though this face of God might have to die (it didn't happen in the novel) in order for others to be saved, there is no denying the power of that smile.

(Note: Spielberg tried to use the same Scatman modalities in "Kick the Can," his installment in *Twilight Zone: The Movie.*

But one film's radiance is another film's treacle; the smile is still undeniable, but it plays more flim than flam.)

3. *Twin Peaks: Fire Walk with Me* **(1992):** If you were to ask me what the greatest horror film ever made was, I would probably say *Twin Peaks*. The only thing is that it's about thirty-some hours long; most of it ran episodically, on TV, in hour-long increments; and almost nobody called it horror.

But, of course, that's just crazy, because I've never seen anything *down-to-the-soul scarier*. Between the inimitable "Bob," Leland Palmer, Leo, Windom Earle, and the Black Lodge itself, there's hardly a devastating note left unhit in the entire horror lexicon.

And so it comes down to the closing moments *of Twin Peaks: Fire Walk With Me*—David Lynch's posthumous theatrical prequel/final entry in the series—to nail the face of God forever and completely.

In the Black Lodge. With Agent Cooper and Laura Palmer, smiling at each other. While an angel hovers overhead.

Letting us know that—on a certain level of Heaven—everything is already all right.

And that Hell, however dark and deep, is not the end.

4. *Hardware* **(1990):** There's no better place to hit the high notes of transcendence than in an actual death scene: when a character literally parts the veil between this world and the next one, then walks us through the changes.

And this has never been done more expertly than writer/director Richard Stanley does it with the death of Mo (Dylan McDermott) in *Hardware*: a psychedelic segue so intimate and willful that you'd be proud to die that way, too.

Far too few other filmmakers—Douglas Trumball with Louise Fletcher in *Brainstorm*, Ralph Bakshi with the pool-shooting crow in *Fritz the Cat*—have bothered to convey such intimacy with this penultimate moment.

But since Mr. Stanley brought both brilliance and a badass killer robot to the proceedings, he definitely takes the cake. Horror filmmakers, please take note.

5. *Jacob's Ladder* (1990): This is, to my mind, the inarguable high point of transcendent horror cinema.

Who would have thought that Adrian Lyne—the director of *Flashdance*, *9½ Weeks*, and *Fatal Attraction*—would parlay the Hollywood leverage he bought with those successes into such an unadulterated masterpiece?

And who would *ever* have thought that the face of God would be conveyed, so thoroughly and convincingly, by Danny Aiello and Macaulay Culkin?

But there it is.

When they smile—or dispense their wisdom—they do everything that the horror genre could ever hope to do, in terms of radiant gnosis.

Dispensing truth that the soul cannot ignore.

Transcending genre.

And achieving true greatness, in the process.

Honorable Mentions

28 Days Later (2002): The scene with the horses, flat out. Brendan Gleeson blowing the kiss is the icing on God's cake.

The Exorcist (1973): As much Christian iconography as there is throughout the film, it's the scene at the end—when the post-possession Linda Blair hugs the priest—that says it all for me.

Rosemary's Baby **(1968)**: It's all about the look on Mia Farrow's face when she comforts her little monster. Talk about transcendence. . . .

May **(2002)**: The very last shot of the film—the comforting gesture from the patchwork-corpse pal of the amazing Angela Bettis—is a gorgeous God-surprise, and seals the deal on this little indie gem.

Blade Runner **(1982)**: Roy Batty's dying speech. No more needs to be said.

Creature from the Black Lagoon **(1954)**: Similar monster-loves-woman moments can be clocked, from the original *King Kong* on. But there's such poetic grace in the swimming sequence—the creature mirroring Julia Adams from below—that it takes things beyond the obvious lust to a grander sense of God's weird design.

The Bride of Frankenstein **(1935)**: One word: "Friend . . ."

Dawn of the Dead **(1979)**: The beautiful, pure Romero moment, down in the mall, between Gaylen Ross and the zombie in the Arco-Pitcairn softball uniform. Just looking at each other, through the barrier of glass. Always makes me wanna cry.

Day of the Dead **(1985)**: My vote would be for Terry Alexander's smile, every bit as beautiful as Scatman's. But Scott Bradley would never forgive me if I didn't also include the final climb up the missile silo, a literalized ascension of pure redemptive truth.

Cannibal Ferox **(1981)**: Who would have thought this callous shit-burger of a movie would feature the face of God? But when the two doomed white women sing "Red River Valley," even the cannibals are moved.

(And though Ruggero Deodato's *Cannibal Holocaust* [1980]— the movie this one shamelessly rips off—is the far superior film, it's interesting to note that God never shows up for Deodato. Maybe God was off with Terrence Malick at the time, spending twenty years prepping *The Thin Red Line*?)

VICTOR SALVA'S TEN THINGS WE HAVE LEARNED FROM HORROR MOVIES

A California native, Victor Salva is the writer/director of Jeepers Creepers, Jeepers Creepers 2, Clownhouse, *and* Powder. *He also directed the 2006 film* Peaceful Warrior, *starring Nick Nolte.*

1. If your car breaks down in the rain outside a spooky old house, sleep in the car.
2. Short cuts, back roads, and any lakes or resorts you're warned of by crusty, indigenous strangers should be avoided.
3. Skinny dipping or any other kind of nudism or sexual activity is punishable by death.
4. Never, ever, throw down and step away from the gun, knife, or any other weapon you have just used to kill the monster. You will need it again, trust me.
5. When bodies start to pile up or people go missing, the smartest thing to do is to split up the remaining group into easier targets and hope nothing bad happens to them.
6. Most monsters are warded off by fire, a bright light, or a smaller budget, which makes it ill-advised to glimpse the creature in any great detail.

7. Always assume the calls are coming from inside the house—wherever you are.
8. Radiation causes gigantism in everything but human intelligence.
9. Aliens are creatures whose main interest is the human heart. Other organs are considered side dishes.
10. No creature will ever really be destroyed until its box office potential is pronounced dead as well.

THE ORIGINAL TITLES OF FIFTEEN HORROR FILMS

1. Original Title: *The Cuckoo Clocks of Hell*
   Final Title: *Last House on Dead End Street* (1977)
   Director: Roger Watkins

2. Original Title: *Orgy of the Blood Parasites*
   Final Title: *Shivers* (1975)
   Director: David Cronenberg

3. Original Title: *Network of Blood*
   Final Title: *Videodrome* (1982)
   Director: David Cronenberg

4. Original Title: *The Babysitter Murders*
   Final Title: *Halloween* (1978)
   Director: John Carpenter

5. Original Title: *Headcheese*
   Final Title: *The Texas Chainsaw Massacre* (1974)
   Director: Tobe Hooper

6. Original Title: *Charlie's Family*
   Final Title: *The Manson Family* (2003)
   Director: Jim Van Bebber

7. **Original Title:** *Burned to Light*
   Final Title: *Shadow of the Vampire* (2000)
   Director: E. Elias Merhige

8. **Original Title:** *Phobia*
   Final Title: *I Drink Your Blood* (1971)
   Director: David Durston

9. **Original Titles:** *Zombie*
   Voodoo Bloodbath
   Final Title: *I Eat Your Skin* (made 1964, released 1971)
   Director: Del Tenney

10. **Original Title:** *Star Beast*
    Final Title: *Alien* (1979)
    Director: Ridley Scott

11. **Original Titles:** *The Anderson Alamo*
    The Siege
    Final Title: *Assault on Precinct 13* (1976)
    Director: John Carpenter

12. **Original Title:** *Code Name: Trixie*
    Final Title: *The Crazies* (1973)
    Director: George A. Romero

13. **Original Title:** *Scary Movie*
    Final Title: *Scream* (1996)
    Director: Wes Craven

14. **Original Title:** *Sex Crime of the Century*
    Krug and Company
    Final Title: *Last House on the Left* (1972)
    Director: Wes Craven

15. **Original Title:** *Grave Robbers from Outer Space*
    Final Title: *Plan 9 from Outer Space* (1959)
    Director: Edward D. Wood, Jr.

—*Compiled by S.B.*

NACHO CERDÁ'S TEN MOST PROFOUND
CINEMATIC HORROR EXPERIENCES

Nacho Cerdá was born in 1969. He became interested in filmmaking at an early age, shooting Super 8 and video home movies. After graduating from journalism school in Barcelona, he studied film at USC. There, he shot his first 16mm short, titled The Awakening. *In 1994, he and his partners founded Waken Productions, a production company for which Cerdá directed his second short film, the controversial* Aftermath. *He has also produced two other shorts,* Doctor Curry *and* Dias sin Luz. *These were followed by his world-acclaimed short* Genesis *which earned a Goya (Spanish Academy Awards) Nomination for Best Short Film in 1998. The* Abandoned *(2006) was his feature film debut and was voted "Audience Favorite" at the first After Dark Horror Fest.*

1. *Jaws* **(Directed by Steven Spielberg; 1975):** The film that marked me for life, period—not only as an aspiring filmmaker, but as a fan of horror films. I was only six when my uncle snuck me into an afternoon show. An amazing sense of anticipation started to build as I was just looking at the lobby cards, where a great white shark's mouth was on full display. I felt like we were stepping into forbidden territory, a place where the most unimaginable horrors were to unfold . . . and they did. Halfway through the picture, I was totally glued to the screen watching Richard Dreyfuss dive through a wreck in the middle of the night. As he rummaged through the sunken remains, a severed head popped out, sending a chill through my spine. I jumped in my seat, so scared that I instinctively grabbed another spectator's hand, making him jump even more. I freaked that guy out so much that he was about to slap me before realizing that I was only a child. "Keep your nephew on a leash!" he snarled to my uncle. After

that memorable experience, unconnected scenes and images kept coming back to me, to the point of reconstructing in my mind a version of the movie created from visual memories. Of course, back then we did not have home video to watch films over and over again, so I was stuck with that memory for years to come— seven, to be precise. When I turned 13, I picked up a bootleg at my local video store, and I couldn't wait to relive the excitement. It was then that I realized film was able to keep the emotions intact, and also, the possibility of reprising them over and over. Besides all this, I could share the horror with my friends. I believe that's when I was born to be a filmmaker and create those fantasies for other people.

2. *The Living Dead at the Manchester Morgue* (Directed by Jorge Grau, 1974): When Chicho Ibañez Serrador (director of *Who Can Kill a Child?*) hosted a Spanish TV show consisting of a fine selection of horror films, none of us knew what we were in for. It had been only a few years since my Spielberg experience, and although I got scared to death, my fears circled around creatures, monsters, or vampires. After watching these resurrected human beings eating flesh and stalking the living, I realized how much that fear was indeed not only coming from the outside but from the inside. I became familiar with my own mortality at the sweet age of ten. Death has been an obsession for me ever since. I basically could not understand why a living form with an intellect (us) could hold such an enormous amount of viscera inside. I believe much of this conflict confronting soul and body erupted in my own school, which was of a hardcore Catholic sort. After the film was over that Monday night, I could not sleep at all, tucked under my bed sheets, looking into the darkness of my bedroom in search for an answer to those questions that we all keep asking to this day.

3. *El Espanto Surge De La Tumba* (Directed by Carlos Aured, 1973): This one might sound a bit funny, but I swear to God that it happened this way. Before home video was introduced in the Spanish market, my family used to rent Super 8 movies to basically make me shut up. I was the very insistent type, always asking my parents to take me to a movie or get specific titles for my home enjoyment. Little did they know what sort of flick they had just picked up for their 7-year-old child! My uncle had taught me how to operate the projector, so I could be in total isolation in the darkness of the screening room. I remember inviting Pablo, a friend from school, who later became my long time companion in watching horror flicks. He and I started projecting *El Espanto*, starring Paul Naschy, and by reel 2, we literally had to stop the movie because we were shitting our pants. It was so ridiculous . . . neither of us would dare to thread the next reel . . . what sort of nightmares were still to unfold through that lens? I looked at the projector like it was some sort of machine from hell. I believe that also developed my fascination for the damn thing.

4. *The Evil Dead* (Directed by Sam Raimi, 1982): It's one of those classics that I have yet to watch on the big screen. Again, it was back in the eighties, when home video was bursting in Spain; because of my young age, this option became a way to watch R-rated films. It was like being a child again and sneaking in to see *Jaws*. I remember pressing play with a sense of dread running through my spine, and sure enough, twenty minutes in, I had to stop the thing again! Just like with the Naschy flick a few years back. This time the horrors were bigger and meaner. It was the ultimate mix of reanimated corpses, now possessed and shooting out all sorts of internal fluids. My Catholic school had already pushed the envelope teaching us the concept of Hell. And this damn movie gave me the whole enchilada. I used both this film and *Jaws* as a way to torture my classmates, inviting them over

to my place and playing both movies to witness their reactions. When the U.S. DVD came out, the menus proclaimed "Begin Horror" for the play function, and that's exactly how I felt the very first time I pushed that button.

5. *The Thing* (Directed by John Carpenter, 1982): Yes, we all know . . . the same year as *ET*. But this one was way more pissed off and nasty. Maybe it was this film that first combined both my obsessions for human metamorphosis and identity. My old pal Pablo, who had previously watched it, came along with me. "You're in for a ride," he said. I remember an early scene where Kurt Russell finds the Norwegian corpse with all those weird tentacles coming out of his arms. He told me: "You ain't seen nothing yet." That set me up for good. The film's isolation, loneliness, and the fear of death were all elements that I believe somehow influenced so much of my future work. After *Jaws*, it's probably the film that I've seen more than any other and still to this day remains a classic for me.

6. *The Legend of Hell House* (Directed by John Hough, 1973): My first haunted house movie ever! Once more, it involved my sneaking into a summertime afternoon screening. There are a couple of scenes that kept creeping up on me years after. First, it was a ghostly silhouette showering, but underneath the cabinet, blood was leaking out. Once the main character opens the door, we see there wasn't a person, but a slaughtered cat in the basin. The second were those little trips the characters take down to that hellish chapel with cobwebs and nightmarish paintings. It was scary as shit. Of course, that's when I realized that all our Catholic iconography was as twisted and dark as the Middle Ages. When I returned to a church on my own, nothing was the same anymore. The outstanding production design, sound, and electronic music were especially haunting, and they also helped to

set up my future standards as a genre filmmaker. I rushed to my local video store when it came out and quite honestly, the atmosphere was so well accomplished that it still holds up.

7. *The Good, the Bad, and the Ugly* (Directed by Sergio Leone, 1964): I also spent half my childhood watching American westerns in the repertory cinema across the street from home. John Wayne was usually the king of the show, and for some reason, in those films there was always a fine distinction between the good and bad guys, mostly Indians, bank robbers, or ruthless criminals. It was later that I found out about these other kinds of westerns that didn't look quite the same. The landscape, the cast, the way they were shot . . . somehow when I was a child they started making an impression on me with how radical and different they were compared to the American ones. Good and evil were no longer separate entities, and I really liked that. It was very interesting for me how they mixed and confused those sacred terms. Now we had three ruthless people going after a sum of money buried in some distant cemetery. It was particularly striking the way Leone turned violence into beauty, blending both with a haunting score that would remain in my soul to this day. I never thought that you could find beauty in Hell, but I believe Leone found it. I particularly remember a very touching scene where Clint Eastwood grants a last wish to a dying soldier. He gives him a cigarette and sees it consume in his lips until the soldier dies. For a moment, amongst all that violence and crazy battle that preceded this scene, time seemed to stop for a second to watch that man die. It was only one life out of hundreds being killed in a battle. Absolutely beautiful.

8. *Se7en* (Directed by David Fincher, 1995): When *Alien*[3] was released, I happened to be in Los Angeles. Being a huge fan of the series, I immediately bought my ticket to an evening show at a West-

wood cinema to check out how in the world they would top what Ridley Scott and James Cameron had so expertly crafted before. To tell you the truth, I was not disappointed at all. Although the film was a bit uneven, it definitely possessed a unique and moody style that had me totally glued to the screen. Everyone I knew trashed that movie back then, but the name David Fincher started to pull certain strings in some of us. Not much later came this absolute masterpiece called *Se7en*. Being a filmmaker myself, it's often difficult to get involved just like a regular member of the audience. You just know too much about the craft, too much about the technical aspects, making it hard to approach a film from a fresh perspective. But sometimes, and I mean *really* rarely, you find a film that throws all that out the window. Fincher's masterwork did it. For the first time in a long time, the roles were inverted, and the film took control of me. The third act in film took on a whole new meaning, with the scene of John Doe leading the main characters to the desert.

9. *United 93* (Directed by Paul Greengrass, 2006): An absolute masterpiece and one of those once-in-a-lifetime cinematic experiences that shouldn't be missed. It constitutes for me what the essence of cinema should be: an emotional journey. When people talk about films, they usually overestimate the story elements—I've heard people saying, "Oh, you already know what's going to happen, the bad guy is such and such, the girl will die . . ." and I think: "So what, stupid? Do I care about that? No!" Movies are not so much about where you're going as about the emotional journey of *how you get there*. We each know our own life is going to end, don't we? Yes, of course, we will definitely die. But does it take way the excitement or surprises to come? No. Why shouldn't it be the same in a movie? *United 93* is not trying to make a political statement or surprise the audience by any means, it's just trying to involve you emotionally in that crazi-

ness that happened back then. Muslims, Jews, Catholics, Americans, Europeans, Asians . . . that didn't really matter. They were all a bunch of human beings trying to survive, and that's what made it special to me. As I said, as a filmmaker, it's hard for me to detach from the technical aspects of a movie, but, once again, I was totally blown away. In fact, I had to pinch myself halfway through to realize I was in a movie theatre. A magic experience.

10. *Lonesome Gun* aka *My Name is Nobody* (Directed by Tonino Valerii, 1973): Actually, this was my first doppelganger movie, and one of those westerns that I could not quite understand as a child. Its haunting geography and, again, Morricone's score to portray the poetry of solitude and despair in the old West, left a mark on me. After a few viewings, I began to realize how much of an existential ride this really was. It was about an old gunslinger who accepts his own death and the coming of a new generation. Basically, it talked about the passing of time and how we grow old. Despite the fact that this Sergio Leone–produced film was supposed to play as a comedy, it made me cry several times. Leone's hand crept in at certain times, inflicting a sense of nostalgia and sadness. There is one memorable scene when Henry Fonda confronts a wild bunch of 150 horsemen, putting on his old pair of glasses to focus. It was a man alone against his destiny. A long shot booms up over him to frame the vast desert while the bunch throttle ahead. If you ever watch this one, you'll understand why I could not hold my tears.

SARAH LANGAN'S TOP TEN STUPIDEST
HORROR MOVIE DECISIONS QUIZ

Sarah Langan is the author of the New York Times *Editor's Choice first novel,* The Keeper *(2006) and its sequel* The Missing *(2007), which won a Bram Stroker Award and received a starred review from* Publishers Weekly. *Langan's stories are forthcoming from* Cemetery Dance, Shivers, *and* Darkness on the Edge: Stories Inspired by Springsteen Songs. *She has an MFA in fiction from Columbia University, and is pursuing her master of science in environmental toxicology. She lives in Brooklyn, where she is trying to teach her rabbit how to fetch while writing her third novel,* Audrey's Door.

Name the Film in in Which the Following Things Happen

10. Befriending a Nazi monkey.

9. Hanging out in the Antarctic with Wilford Brimley.

8. Having sex, smoking pot, and generally enjoying adolescence.

7. Falling asleep while these pods are growing all over your house, and everybody keeps making pig sounds, especially if you're married to a dork, when you could be making the nookie with Donald Sutherland.

6. Giving the taxidermist next door a peep show, you tramp.

5. Going to the prom with Bobby, when you *know* he's only going to pour pig's blood on your new dress.

4. Letting your shipmate out of quarantine, even though he's got a bony intergalactic space-vagina stuck to his face. . . . Because in space, no one can hear you scream!

3. Eating that chocolate mousse that tastes like chalk, and makes you dream you're having sex with Satan, and now carrying his love child. Especially if you're married to an out-of-work actor.

2. Playing with a Ouija board, especially when it's named Captain Howdy.

1. Not figuring out he's calling from inside the house, Carol Kane.

Answers

10. *Raiders of the Lost Ark* (1981)

    Half point for *Monkey Shines* (1988)

9. *The Thing* (1982)

8. *Halloween* (1978), *Friday the 13th,* (1980), *A Nightmare on Elm Street* (1984), and all their progeny, from *Scream* (1996) to *Hostel* (2006)

7. *Invasion of the Body Snatchers* (1978)

6. *Psycho* (1960)

5. *Carrie* (1976)

4. *Alien* (1979)

3. *Rosemary's Baby* (1968)

2. *The Exorcist* (1973)

    Half point deducted for any mention of Dee Snider's craptacular *Strangeland* (1998)

1. *When a Stranger Calls* (1979)

FOUR HORROR WRITERS ON THE FILM
ADAPTATIONS OF THEIR WORK

1. **Stephen King on Stanley Kubrick's film adaptaion of** *The Shining* **(1980):** "There's a lot to like about it. But it's a great big beautiful Cadillac with no motor inside. You can sit in it, and you can enjoy the smell of the leather upholstery—the only thing you can't do is drive it anywhere. So I would do everything different. The real problem is that Kubrick set out to make a horror picture with no apparent understanding of the genre. Everything about it screams that from beginning to end, from plot decision to that final scene—which had been used before on *The Twilight Zone*" (quoted in *Stanley Kubrick: A Biography*, by Vincent LoBrutto).

2. **Colin Wilson on** *Lifeforce* **(1985), the film adaptation of** *The Space Vampires*, **directed by Tobe Hooper:** "John Fowles once told me that the film of *The Magus* was the worst movie ever made. After seeing *Lifeforce* I sent him a postcard telling him that I had gone one better" (from *Dreaming to Some Purpose*, by Colin Wilson).

3. **F. Paul Wilson on Michael Mann's film adaptation of** *The Keep* **(1983):** "Michael Mann, who seems to have a great visual sense, had no sense at all of this type of story and how to tell it. He doesn't seem to have much sense of how a story is constructed. He just wanted to do what he wanted to do, and he did not want any mention of a vampire in the movie. Even though a vampire is just a red herring in the book, he wanted no mention of it at all. So if you do that, you take away the very reason that the book is set in the Transylanian Alps (which is to high-

light this red herring). As a result, things start to crumble" (from an interview with the author on http://www.the-keep.ath.cx/default_en.htm).

4. **William Peter Blatty on William Friedkin's film adaptation of *The Exorcist* (1973):** "With the film, the people were just getting the rollercoaster ride. Let's face it—the message was adroitly snipped out of the film. It wasn't there. On the most basic level, the film argues for some kind of transcendence: if there are demons, why not angels? Why not God? And one religion, the Catholic Church—if not others as well—seems to have power to command the evil spirit, which seems a validation of religious belief. But the real point of the book is nowhere to be found in the film" (from an interview with the author in *Faces of Fear,* by Douglas E. Winter).

—*Compiled by S.B.*

CHAPTER 2

"For the Love of God, Montresor!"

THE LITERATURE OF DREAD

TWENTY GREAT OPENINGS IN HORROR FICTION

1. "Last night, I dreamt I went to Manderlay again."

    —*Rebecca,* by Daphne du Maurier.

2. "This is what happened."

    —"The Mist," by Stephen King.

3. "This morning I put ground glass in my wife's eyes. She didn't mind. She didn't make a sound. She never does."

    —"The Dead Line," by Dennis Etchison.

4. "What was the worst thing you've ever done? I won't tell you that, but I'll tell you the worst thing that ever happened to me . . . the most dreadful thing."

    —*Ghost Story,* by Peter Straub.

5. "Jack Torrance thought: *Officious little prick*."

    —*The Shining,* by Stephen King.

6. "You think you know about pain?"

   —*The Girl Next Door*, by Jack Ketchum.

7. "It was the last morning the four of them would ever be together: the man and his wife, his daughter and his son."

   —*Testament*, by David Morrell.

8. " 'I see,' said the vampire thoughtfully, and slowly he walked across the room towards the window."

   —*Interview with the Vampire*, by Anne Rice.

9. "Sometimes a man grows tired of carrying everything the world heaps upon his head."

   —*Exquisite Corpse*, by Poppy Z. Brite.

10. "ABANDON ALL HOPE YE WHO ENTER HERE is scrawled in blood-red lettering on the side of the Chemical Bank near the corner of Eleventh and First and is in print large enough to be seen from the backseat of the cab as it lurches forward in the traffic leaving Wall Street and just as Timothy Price notices the words a bus pulls up, the advertisement for *Les Miserables* on its side blocking his view, but Price, who is with Pierce & Pierce and twenty-six doesn't seem to care because he tells the driver he will give him five dollars to turn up the radio, 'Be My Baby' on WYNN, and the driver, black, not American, does so."

    —*American Psycho*, by Bret Easton Ellis.

11. "Fetish? You name it. All I know is that I've always had to have it with me . . ."

    —*The Scarf*, by Robert Bloch.

12. "Egnaro is a secret known to everyone but yourself."

    —"Egnaro," by M. John Harrison.

13. "When a day that you happen to know is Wednesday starts off by sounding like Sunday, there is something seriously wrong somewhere."

    —*The Day of the Triffids*, by John Wyndham.

14. "The most merciful thing in the world, I think, is the inability of the human mind to correlate all its contents."

    —"The Call of Cthulhu," by H. P. Lovecraft.

15. "No live organism can continue for long to exist sanely under conditions of absolute reality; even larks and katydids are supposed, by some, to dream. Hill House, not sane, stood by itself against its hills, holding darkness within; it had stood so for eighty years and might stand for eighty more. Within, walls continued upright, bricks met neatly, floors were firm, and doors were sensibly shut; silence lay steadily against the wood and stone of Hill House, and whatever walked there, walked alone."

    —*The Haunting of Hill House*, by Shirley Jackson.

16. "There was something large and wet and dead in the middle of the road."

    —*Animals*, by John Skipp and Craig Spector.

17. "See the child. He is pale and thin, he wears a thin and ragged linen shirt. He stokes the scullery fire. Outside lie dark turned fields with rags of snow and darker woods beyond that harbor yet a few last wolves."

    —*Blood Meridian, or the Evening Redness in the West*, by Cormac McCarthy.

18. "Kenny Dorchester was a fat man."

    —"The Monkey Treatment," by George R. R. Martin.

19. "My first experience? My first experience was far more of a test than anything that has ever happened to me since in that same line."

    —"The Swords," by Robert Aickman.

20. " 'Whatever are you doing?' demanded the first Mrs. Henry Ridout, being surprised to find her husband easing her over the side of the boat."

    —"The Love of a Good Woman," by William Trevor.

                               —Compiled by A.W. and S.B.

THE FIFTY-SIX BESTSELLING HORROR BOOKS SINCE 1900

In order to compile this list, we examined each year's national hard-cover bestsellers as determined by Publishers Weekly *and pulled not only horror books, but also books that changed horror and horror writing in some way.*

   Below are the years in which each book appeared on the best-seller list, and its ranking on the list for the year.

1902 #7— *Hound of the Baskervilles*, by Sir Arthur Conan Doyle: Sherlock Holmes's only real foray into horror and probably the most enduring of his tales.

1923 #1— *Black Oxen*, by Gertrude Atherton: A tale of youth rejuvenated.

1934 #10—*Seven Gothic Tales*, by Isak Dineson: The consummate storyteller.

1938 #4— *Rebecca*, by Daphne du Maurier: The ultimate Gothic novel.

1939 #3— *Rebecca*, by Daphne du Maurier: She's still here!

1946 #10—*The Snake Pit*, by Mary Jane Ward: The first big "real-life" horror story. A precursor, in many ways, to Stephen King's tales of horror in modern life.

1952 #5— *Steamboat Gothic*, by Frances Parkinson Keyes: Not horror by any stretch of the imagination, but true Gothic. A lifestyle vanishing.

1957 #8— *On the Beach*, by Nevil Shute: A frightening futuristic vision of the horror that the atomic age might bring.

1967 #7— *Rosemary's Baby*, by Ira Levin: Contemporary horror rears its ugly head again. Vietnam is in full swing and the devil made me do it.

1969 #10—*The House on the Strand*, by Daphne du Maurier: Thirty years later and she can still write a spooky tale for the masses.

1971 #2— *The Exorcist*, by William Peter Blatty: Everything is different from here on out.

#9— *The Other*, by Thomas Tryon: Completed a year that messed with our minds and turned our focus away from the headlines.

1974 #3— *Jaws*, by Peter Benchley: Proved that horror didn't have to be supernatural. Just when you thought it was safe to read another book.

1979 #6— *The Dead Zone*, by Stephen King: The beginning of the most incredible reign of horror ever!

1980 #5— *Firestarter*, by Stephen King: Mind-play in horror. King loved doing that.

1981 #3— *Cujo*, by Stephen King: Man's best friend as enemy.

1982 #7— *Different Seasons*, by Stephen King: The first horror collection to make it into the year's top ten since Isak Dineson's, in 1934.

1983 #3— *Pet Sematary*, by Stephen King: Children, animals, and dead things. What more could you want?

#5— *Christine*, by Stephen King: Two in one year. Another record.

1984 #1— *The Talisman*, by Stephen King and Peter Straub: With the help of Peter Straub, King gets his first yearly #1.

1985 #5— *Skeleton Crew*, by Stephen King: His second collection to climb the charts.

1986 #1— *It*, by Stephen King: #1 on his own. The eighties belong to King.

1987 #1— *The Tommyknockers*, by Stephen King: UFOs?

#4— *Misery*, by Stephen King: Disguised autobiography?

#10—*Eyes of the Dragon*, by Stephen King: Three in one year, and twelve in nine years. Another record.

1988 #7– *Queen of the Damned*, by Anne Rice: Bet you thought it would be her other book, eh? This came twenty years after the previous female author made it.

1989 #2– *The Dark Half*, by Stephen King: He's back and he isn't finished yet!

1990 #2– *Four Past Midnight*, by Stephen King: Yet another collection!

#7– *The Stand*, by Stephen King: Expanded and resold.

#9– *The Witching Hour*, by Anne Rice: A shift from writing about vampires.

1991 #3– *Needful Things*, by Stephen King: Another book the size of a brick.

1992 #1– *Dolores Claiborne*, by Stephen King: Another #1!

#3– *Gerald's Game*, by Stephen King: They say sex sells, even if it's dead.

#7– *The Tale of the Body Thief*, by Anne Rice: Back to the vampires.

1993 #5– *Nightmares and Dreamscapes*, by Stephen King: And yet *another* short story collection! Where does this guy get his ideas?

#7– *Lasher*, by Anne Rice: If it ain't broke, don't fix it.

1994 #5– *Insomnia*, by Stephen King: No wonder he can't sleep. He's up all night writing!

1995 #7– *Rose Madder*, by Stephen King: The third lady rears her head.

1996 #3– *Desperation*, by Stephen King: A novel point of view.

#5– *The Regulators*, by Richard Bachman: Why does this seem so much like Desperation?

1998 #3– *Bag of Bones*, by Stephen King: The nineties go to him as well.

1999 #2– *Hannibal*, by Thomas Harris: The controversial return of Hannibal the Cannibal beats out King.

#3– *Assassins*, by Jerry B. Jenkins and Tim LaHaye: Religious horror scares the masses.

#6– *Hearts in Atlantis*, by Stephen King: Hannibal plays the lead in the film version!

#7– *Apollyon*, by Jerry B. Jenkins and Tim LaHaye: If you're not with us, you're against us!

2000 #2– *The Mark*, by Jerry B. Jenkins and Tim LaHaye: The Beast rules the world.

#4— *The Indwelling,* by Jerry B. Jenkins and Tim LaHaye: The Beast takes possession.

2001 #1— *Desecration,* by Jerry B. Jenkins and Tim LaHaye: Morality is scary!

#4— *Dreamcatcher,* by Stephen King: Aliens or gods or us?

#6— *Black House,* by Stephen King and Peter Straub: Missed #1 this time.

2002 #4— *The Lovely Bones,* by Alice Sebold: The dead solve their own murder from the grave.

#9— *Everything's Eventual,* by Stephen King: Like another bestseller.

2003 #5— *Armageddon,* by Jerry B. Jenkins and Tim LaHaye: The end is near.

#9— *The Lovely Bones,* by Alice Sebold: That pesky dead person just won't go away.

2004 #4— *Glorious Appearance,* by Jerry B. Jenkins and Tim LaHaye: It's about time he got here!

2005 #8— *The Historian,* by Elizabeth Kostova: In search of Dracula.

—D.H. *(source: Publishers Weekly)*

STEPHEN KING'S TEN FAVORITE
HORROR NOVELS OR SHORT STORIES

Stephen King is the most popular writer of horror fiction in the history of literature. His numerous bestsellers include Carrie, The Shining, Cujo, The Dead Zone, *the* Dark Tower *series,* Misery, Pet Sematary, *and* The Green Mile; *he also wrote the novellas on which the films* Stand by Me, The Shawshank Redemption, *and* The Mist *are based. He penned the screenplay for* Creepshow, *and wrote and directed* Maximum Overdrive. *His nonfiction includes a history of the horror genre called* Danse Macabre, *and the autobiographical* On Writing: A Memoir of the Craft. *King was the guest editor of* The Best American Short Stories 2007, *and won the O. Henry Prize* for his short story *"The Man in the Black Suit."* Among his recent works are The Colorado Kid, Cell, Lisey's Story, *and* Duma Key.

1. *Ghost Story,* by Peter Straub
2. *Dracula,* by Bram Stoker
3. *The Haunting of Hill House,* by Shirley Jackson
4. *Dr. Jekyll and Mr. Hyde,* by Robert Louis Stevenson
5. *Burnt Offerings,* by Robert Marasco
6. "Casting the Runes," by M. R. James
7. "Two Bottles of Relish," by Lord Dunsany
8. "The Great God Pan," by Arthur Machen
9. "The Colour Out of Space," by H. P. Lovecraft
10. "The Upper Berth," by F. Marion Crawford

—*Originally appeared in* The Book of Lists 3 *by Amy Wallace, Irving Wallace, and David Wallechinsky (1983)*

DON D'AURIA'S TEN BOOKS THAT CHANGED THE HORROR GENRE

Don D'Auria is Executive Editor at Leisure Books, where for more than a decade he has directed the horror line that Rue Morgue *called "the champions of paperback horror." During that time he's been lucky enough to work with some of the leading authors in the field. Born and raised in suburban New Jersey, he was the quintessential horror kid, growing up on a steady diet of TV's Chiller Theater on Friday nights, Creature Features on Saturday nights, and horror novels and* Famous Monsters *magazine the rest of the time. He is the recipient of an International Horror Guild Award for his contributions to the horror genre.*

1. *The Monk,* by Matthew Lewis (1796): Arguably the first horror best-seller. This mix of monks, nuns, demons, and Satan was a phenomenon in its day, so famous (or infamous) that its author was known as "Monk" Lewis for the rest of his life.

2. *Dracula,* by Bram Stoker (1897): Sure, there were vampires before *Dracula*, but this is the book that established them firmly in the public's consciousness and created a cultural icon in the process. Count Dracula is as recognizable today as Mickey Mouse or Snoopy and is the inspiration for countless subsequent novels and stories, as well as movies, TV shows, plays, breakfast cereals, cartoons, even a *Sesame Street* puppet. Without Dracula and his vampire kin, the horror genre would be a very different animal today.

3. *Tales of the Grotesque and Arabesque,* by Edgar Allan Poe (1840): The father of American horror. Poe's horrors didn't come from monsters, ghosts, or demons; they came from inside the mind. (He's also often credited with being the father of the detective story.) This book was the first collection of his work. It was hardly a success upon its release, but its influence grew and spread, largely after Poe's death. Today his work is part of the canon of American literature and is taught in schools across the country—influencing and inspiring countless young future horror writers.

4. *The Outsider and Others,* by H. P. Lovecraft (1939): Though Lovecraft wasn't very popular during his lifetime, his influence has grown exponentially since his death—thanks largely to this book and other Lovecraft collections published by Arkham House. When Lovecraft died, August Derleth didn't want to see his friend's writing go out of print, so he created Arkham House to publish Lovecraft's work, previously only printed in the pulp magazines. Gradually Lovecraft developed a (posthumous) following

and eventually became recognized as one of America's greatest horror authors. His brand of "cosmic" horror and the Cthulhu mythos created a whole subgenre, Lovecraftian horror. But it might never have happened without the Arkham collections. This is the prime example of what a small publisher can do.

5. *The Exorcist,* by William Peter Blatty (1971): Blatty took the oldest bad guy in literary history, the Devil, plucked him out of his usual Gothic and religious settings, and let him loose in a contemporary Georgetown brownstone so he could terrorize a society that didn't much believe in him anymore. Suddenly the Devil seemed to be everywhere. Almost overnight the floodgates opened to a slew of demonic possession books and movies, and "religious horror" was born. Inspired by a true story!

6. *Carrie,* by Stephen King (1974): The first book by the most influential horror author of the twentieth century. A phenomenon not just in horror but publishing in general, at one time King described his fiction as the equivalent of a Big Mac and fries, but that sells his work short. His fiction is literature with the common touch, aimed squarely at the Everyman, and it hits its mark. His arrival on the scene—coupled with his enormous sales—was a major factor in the huge horror publishing boom of the 1980s. Basically, there's horror fiction before King and horror fiction after King.

7. *Interview with the Vampire,* by Anne Rice (1976): Rice created a whole new type of vampire: romantic, erotic, often homoerotic, sympathetic, conflicted, but still frightening. Her lush, neo-Gothic style was a dramatic counterpoint to King's recognizably contemporary horrors. Her vampires seduced fans by the millions, and brought a lot of new female readers into the horror market.

8. *The Books of Blood,* by Clive Barker (1984): The most visible and bestselling book in the revolutionary movement that came to be known as "Splatterpunk." As the name implies, young authors like Barker and the team of John Skipp and Craig Spector took things to extremes in terms of gore, grittiness, and sex, and gave the genre a jolt of electricity. It was horror pushed over the top. This stuff was definitely not playing it safe. From this point on, all bets were off when it came to how far you could go in horror fiction.

9. *Welcome to Dead House,* by R. L. Stine (1992): The first in Stine's *Goosebumps* series. Not only did the immense success of the books convince publishers that kids read horror (a lot), it also introduced millions of young readers to the genre and created a whole new generation of horror fans.

10. *Guilty Pleasures,* by Laurell K. Hamilton (1993): The first novel in the long-running Anita Blake, Vampire Hunter series. Depending on your point of view, they injected a large dose of romance into horror, or horror into romance. Hamilton's books broke down walls, blurred distinctions, and dramatically changed not one but two genres.

BENTLEY LITTLE'S TEN HORROR ONE-HIT WONDERS THAT EVERYONE SHOULD READ

Hailed by Stephen King as "the horror poet laureate," Bentley Little was born in 1960. He is the Bram Stoker Award–winning author of The Burning, Dispatch, The Policy, The Town, The Store, The Vanishing, *and many other novels, as well as an acclaimed short story collection titled* The Collection. *His short story "The Wash-*

ingtonians" was the basis for an episode of Showtime's Masters of Horror *series. The son of a Russian artist and an American educator, Bentley Little and his Chinese wife were married by the justice of the peace in Tombstone, Arizona.*

1. *The Auctioneer,* **by Joan Samson:** Joan Samson made a huge splash with this stunning debut and then promptly dropped from sight. The story of an auctioneer who moves into a small town and gradually takes it over by first selling the unwanted items of its populace and then demanding increasingly steep tithes from the local citizens, *The Auctioneer* is social satire masquerading as horror, and it works on many levels. I read it in high school and never forgot it. A brilliant book.

2. *Burnt Offerings,* **by Robert Marasco:** The novel that was made into one of the seminal horror films of the 1970s. Richer and more subtle than the movie, the book, by Tony Award–winning playwright Marasco, tells the story of the Rolfe family, who rent a summer house at a shockingly low price with the stipulation that they must care for the owner's invalid mother, who never comes out of her upstairs room. *Burnt Offerings* may not have the critical cachet of Shirley Jackson's *The Haunting of Hill House* or Richard Matheson's *Hell House*, but it belongs in the company of those classics, and in its neo-traditionalist updating of haunted house tropes, it set the stage for much of what was to follow.

3. *The Cook,* **by Harry Kressing:** The rumor in the early 1960s was that this was John Fowles writing under a pseudonym. There are echoes of *The Magus* here in both style and theme, and Fowles blurbed the book, which was thought at the time to be a clever bit of self-referential post-modernism. It turned out that Kressing *wasn't* Fowles, but that didn't detract from the power of this hugely influential yet now largely forgotten masterpiece,

in which a mysterious cook uses food to gain control over the wealthy family for which he works. A great book.

4. *Falling Angel,* by William Hjortsberg: The basis for the atmospheric film *Angel Heart*, Hjortsberg's novel is an innovative synthesis of the horror and hardboiled detective genres. The mysterious Louis Cyphre hires detective Harry Angel to find a missing pop singer, and the gumshoe is drawn into a terrifying world of black magic and evil. The book's once-startling originality may not seem quite as fresh as it once did, since over the years numerous other authors have followed the same template, but *Falling Angel* remains impressive and extremely compelling.

5. *The House Next Door,* by Anne Rivers Siddons: This novel became a hit primarily because of Stephen King's enthusiastic endorsement in his horror overview *Danse Macabre*. Siddons quickly parlayed that triumph into a successful string of Southern soap operas and has never returned to the horror genre. That's a shame. *The House Next Door* is a very original and contemporary haunted house story, completely free of ghosts. Unique.

6. *Magic,* by William Goldman: A one-hit wonder only in that it's the hugely successful William Goldman's lone horror novel, *Magic* tells the story of Corky, a ventriloquist whose mind and personality are being taken over by his dummy, Fats. The movie made from the novel was good (and the commercial for the film was genuinely scary), but it's the page-turning book, with its powerful ending, that has stuck with me all these years.

7. *Maynard's House,* by Herman Raucher: I'm cheating here. Raucher's huge hit was *The Summer of '42*, and many readers think he dropped from sight after cashing in with that ubiquitous weepie. But he also penned this eerie and surrealistic tale of a Vietnam

veteran who is willed a cabin in the Maine woods by his army buddy Maynard. Thought-provoking and at times confusing, *Maynard's House* works as both a supernatural horror story and a study of an emotionally wrecked vet dealing with post-traumatic stress syndrome.

8. *Platforms,* by John R. Maxim: Maxim has gone on to have success in other genres, but to my knowledge, this paperback bestseller from 1982 is his sole horror outing. And it's terrific. In a New England suburb, train commuters are behaving strangely and becoming violent, while the dead are starting to appear to the living. That's the starting point for a complex and epic horror novel that also postulates an intricately detailed afterlife. Personally, I was hugely influenced by the book, and my first (mercifully unpublished) novel owes a huge debt to *Platforms.*

9. *Ratman's Notebooks,* by Stephen Gilbert: Before Carrie there was Willard, another socially maladjusted misfit wreaking horrific revenge on his tormentors. Willard befriends the rats in his cellar that his mother wants him to kill and then trains them to do his bidding. A surprisingly touching and sensitive story, despite the ick-factor, it paved the way for a slew of similarly themed books and movies.

10. *Replay,* by Ken Grimwood: Not exactly horror, but close enough for rock'n'roll. This is one of my favorite books of all time, and I've bought numerous copies over the years and given them away to friends, family, and even casual acquaintances. The basic premise has been used subsequently in films such as *Groundhog Day* and *The Butterfly Effect,* but nowhere has it been utilized more brilliantly than in Grimwood's melancholy tale of a man blessed with the opportunity—or cursed with the burden—of reliving his life over and over again. Profound, moving, and unforgettable.

KIRBY MCCAULEY'S TEN BEST HORROR ANTHOLOGIES

Kirby McCauley is a veteran literary agent. He has edited a number of anthologies, including Dark Forces *and* Frights *(both of which won the World Fantasy Award). He also coedited* Nightmare Town, *a collection of stories by Dashiell Hammett.*

1. *The Omnibus of Crime,* edited by Dorothy L. Sayers
2. *Sleep No More,* edited by August Derleth
3. *They Walk Again,* edited by Colin De La Mare
4. *New Terrors,* edited by Ramsey Campbell
5. *Great Tales of Terror and the Supernatural,* edited by Herbert A. Wise and Phyllis Fraser
6. *The Fontana Book of Great Ghost Stories,* edited by Robert Aickman
7. *Terror by Gaslight,* edited by Hugh Lamb
8. *Terror in the Modern Vein,* edited by Donald Wollheim
9. *And the Darkness Falls,* edited by Boris Karloff with Edmund Speare
10. *The Dark Descent,* edited by David G. Hartwell

REVEALED! THE PSEUDONYMS OF SEVENTEEN HORROR WRITERS

1. Stephen King—Richard Bachman; John Swithen
2. Dean Koontz—K. R. Dwyer; Leigh Nichols; David Axton; Owen West; Brian Coffey; Aaron Wolfe
3. Dennis Etchison—Jack Martin
4. David J. Schow—Oliver Lowenbruck; Chan McConnell
5. Douglas Clegg—Andrew Harper
6. Whitley Strieber—Jonathan Barry (this pseudonym "collaborated" with Strieber on the novel *Catmagic*)
7. Ramsey Campbell—Carl Dreadstone; Jay Ramsay

8. John Skipp—Maxwell Hart
9. Shaun Hutson—Robert Neville; Nick Blake; Frank Taylor; Tom Lambert; Samuel P. Bishop; Wolf Kruger; Stefan Rostov
10. Douglas Borton—Michael Prescott; Brian Harper
11. Anne Rice—Anne Rampling; A. N. Roquelaure
12. Robert Bloch—Collier Young
13. Bentley Little—Phillip Emmons
14. Richard Matheson—Logan Swanson
15. Kim Newman—Jack Yeovil
16. Harlan Ellison—Cordwainer Bird
17. Rick Hautala—A. J. Matthews

—Compiled by S.B and R.P.

MICHAEL SLADE'S HORRIFIC INSPIRATIONS
FOR HIS THIRTEEN NOVELS

Michael Slade is the pen name of a lawyer and a historian. Of the 100-plus murder cases the lawyer has been active in, fully one-third involved issues of insanity: psychosis and psychopathology. When a satisfied client offered to kill anyone he wished "as a tip," Slade switched to writing horror-thrillers. More information on Michael Slade and his work is available at www.specialx.net.

1. *Headhunter:* In 1978, I took a 3,350-mile road trip around Britain. On arriving in York, I could have bowled down the streets at night and not hit anyone. The Yorkshire Ripper was loose. That inspired me to release a headhunting psycho in my home town, and on the day I began writing, the Clifford Olson case broke. The Mounties were investigating eleven serial killings, so I fictionalized their manhunt.

2. **Ghoul:** Alice Cooper praised *Headhunter* and invited me back-stage. That spawned Slade's rock 'n' roll thriller. It plays off allegations that rock drove real-life psychos to kill: AC/DC's *Highway to Hell* and the Night Stalker; the Beatles' "Helter Skelter" and the Manson family; and so on. It's my homage to Lovecraft.

3. **Cutthroat:** Time for a Monster Mash: Bigfoot and the Wendigo will do. To suspend disbelief, let's start with the Zodiac Killer, bring back the Mad Mountie for Custer's Last Stand, and serve up the culinary tastes of China. We're hunting the Missing Link in human evolution.

4. **Ripper:** In 1962, my mom took me to London. Once I mastered the Underground, I went searching for Jack the Ripper's killing sites. In 1967, Scotland Yard let me into the Black Museum. The plot for *Ripper* grew out of that: a carnival of carnage on Deadman's Island, with killing machines. It's my take on Agatha Christie's classic *And Then There Were None*.

5. **Zombie (North American title: *Evil Eye*):** My all-time favorite battle is the defense of Rorke's Drift: 100 British Redcoats against 4,000 African Zulus who must either rip out their guts or go without sex for years. That provides the juju for a modern psycho who is disemboweling Mounties, and took me on safari to Zimbabwe and the Okavango Delta of Botswana to act out the naked prey chase.

6. **Primal Scream (British title: *Shrink*):** There was to be no sequel to *Headhunter*. Readers disagreed. Finally, to silence the persistent question, "What about Sparky?" (the killer's name came from a real mad dog that attacked me when I was five), I wrote this tale of a psychotic archer hunting "bum boys" in the snowy Northern woods. It's based on a real Canadian skull-crusher who sod-

omized American tourists because the U.S. Army rejected him as "too violent" to fight in Vietnam.

7. *Burnt Bones:* Sherlock Holmes has Moriarty. The 87th Precinct, the Deaf Man. Let's give the Mounties an arch-nemesis: Mephisto. My early trips to Stonehenge were when you could still walk among the megaliths. The search in *Burnt Bones* goes back to Coliseum gladiators, Hadrian's Wall, headhunting Picts, and those sneaky Campbells who butchered my ancestors at Glencoe.

8. *Hangman:* As a lawyer, I argued the last hanging case in the Supreme Court: a cop-killing "for fun." The State of Washington retains the gallows. That gave me the setup for a cross-border jury killer who plays the game Hangman in reverse with the police. A wrong guess makes the next victim lose an extra limb.

9. *Death's Door:* In 1977, I climbed illegally to the top of the Great Pyramid of Cheops in Egypt—what a view!—and almost got pushed off by a gang of Cairo street punks. That gave me the mummy plot for the return of Mephisto—a plastic surgeon gone mad. Some say this book's darker than *Ghoul.*

10. *Bed of Nails:* Slade's cannibal feast. I was a Guest of Honor at the World Horror Convention in Seattle in 2001. The outside world worries we're a bunch of bloodthirsty freaks. Playing to that dread—and setting a novel at the WHC—was too delicious to resist. To experience the climax, I flew to the Cook Islands in the South Pacific, and talked my way into Atiu's secret skeleton cave.

11. *Swastika:* My mom died in 2003. In cleaning out her house, I found my dad's Bomber Command archive. He flew forty-seven combat missions against the Nazis, with 2-in-100 odds of sur-

viving, and trained the crews that struck SS *Sturmbannfuhrer* Wernher von Braun's V2 rocket factory at Peenemunde. Twenty thousand prisoners of war died in the concentration camp that built his missiles so I could watch von Braun—as a whitewashed Tomorrowland hero—on Disney's TV show as a boy. The secret behind the Roswell Incident.

12. *Kamikaze:* My mom worked as a nurse in the Pacific during the war. In college, I delved into the atomic bombing of Hiroshima. There's a strong motive for revenge. In *Kamikaze*, a Japanese soldier lost three generations to the blast, and was sterilized by radiation. Now head of the Yakuza, he suicide-crashes the Pacific War Veterans' Convention so the sushi chef can fillet a surviving crewman of the *Enola Gay*.

13. *Crucified:* The death of my dad when I was nine shook my faith in God. The real-life Beasts of Satan trial has the Vatican training exorcists by the hundreds. *Crucified* is a Christian's worst nightmare come true. Golgotha, the Crusades, the Inquisition, the Witch Hunt, Satanism, the Reichskonkordat, and a trial lawyer's eye for the Achilles heel.

GEORGE CLAYTON JOHNSON'S TEN HORROR, SCIENCE FICTION, AND FANTASY WRITERS WHO INSPIRE HIM

George Clayton Johnson is the coauthor (with William F. Nolan) of the novel Logan's Run, *which was the basis for the film of the same name. He also wrote episodes of many classic genre television shows, including* Alfred Hitchcock Presents, The Twilight Zone, *and* Star Trek, *as well as conceiving the storyline for the movie* Ocean's 11.

These ten great writers have inspired me with their writings and their character. They have influenced my thinking and decorated my life. I knew them all. I loved them all.

1. A. E. van Vogt
2. Ray Bradbury
3. Theodore Sturgeon
4. Rod Serling
5. Charles Beaumont
6. Richard Matheson
7. William F. Nolan
8. Jerry Sohl
9. Robert Bloch
10. Dennis Etchison

THIRTEEN SURPRISING HORROR WRITERS

We all know Winston Churchill as the Prime Minister of England. Agatha Christie's name is synonymous with murder mysteries, and John Lennon's with rock and roll. But did you know that they all also—at one time or another—tried their hand at writing horror fiction?

1. Winston Churchill—"Man Overboard"
   Few recall that Churchill was a journalist and short-story writer before he became a politician and statesman. This harrowing tale of a sailor fallen overboard and praying for death is the only

horror story he wrote. It was published in the late 1880s in *The Harnsworth Magazine*, a popular British journal.

2. Patricia Highsmith—"The Snail-Watcher"

There's an argument to be made that most of Highsmith's work, including the novels *Strangers on a Train* and *The Talented Mr. Ripley*, would qualify as a certain kind of existential horror. However, one short story, "The Snail-Watcher," stands squarely in the genre. Along with Highsmith's usual psychological insights, in "The Snail-Watcher," creepy, gory things happen as she tells the tale of a henpecked husband who takes up snail-breeding. The new hobby takes over his life, and . . . we won't spoil the end, except to say that a snail crawls up his nostril. After reading it, you'll want to take a shower. "The Snail-Watcher" has become extremely popular and is often anthologized. In real life, Highsmith did breed snails and often traveled with her "pets."

3. John Lennon—"No Flies on Frank"

At the height of his popularity, the internationally famed Beatle published a collection of stories and poems titled *In His Own Write*, which features this short and frequently anthologized bit of macabre surrealism about the fate of a rotting corpse. A husband kills his wife, and then notes with surprise that she is soon covered with flies while he is not. He bundles up the body and delivers it to his mother-in-law.

4. Evelyn Waugh—"The Man Who Liked Dickens"

Waugh is famous for such classic novels as *Brideshead Revisited* and *Scoop*. Among his short stories, "The Man Who Liked Dickens" is particularly disturbing: the tale of a man who falls ill in the jungle and is nursed back to health by an illiterate recluse with a passion for the works of Charles Dickens. The recluse forces his "guest" to read to him—and you'll never forget the haunting trick-ending. This short story provided the seed for Waugh's 1934 novel *A Handful of Dust*.

5. Truman Capote—"Miriam"

While Capote is certainly famous for the true-life horrors recounted in the famed *In Cold Blood*, he is only known to have made a single excursion into short horror fiction. This is the creepy tale of a seemingly innocent child who appears on the doorstep of a kindly middle-aged woman who is willing to help the waif. The little girl haunts and taunts her hostess, who is too well-bred to force out the demon child, who subtly reduces her to servitude. Blood-curdling, without a trace of gore.

6. Raymond Chandler—"The Bronze Door"

According to the late Peter Haining in his book *The Lucifer Society*, the legendary creator of private eye Philip Marlowe "loved fantastic fiction and his biographers have disclosed that he wrote quite a number of 'strange' stories . . . primarily for his own satisfaction. He allowed only a handful of these to be published, among them 'The Bronze Door', which was the very first and appeared in 1939." Reading this tale makes us regret that the rest of Chandler's horror fiction remains unobtainable. "The Bronze Door" epitomizes a revenge fantasy most of us would . . . kill for.

7. F. Scott Fitzgerald—"The Curious Case of Benjamin Button"

First published in 1926, this is the popular story of a man who grows in reverse back to babyhood. Throughout Fitzgerald's body of work there are touches of the fantastic and macabre, but this piece stands alone as truly supernatural.

8. Robert Graves—"Earth to Earth"

Graves is widely known as a British poet, novelist, and scholar. He wrote only one humorous disturber, "Earth to Earth." This four-page piece of nastiness, written in 1955, is the tale of an organically minded couple, Mr. and Mrs. Hedge, who fall under the spell of master composter Dr. Eugen Steinpilz and his secret method.

9. Edith Wharton—*The Ghost-Feeler*

The great Edith Wharton is so well known for her marvelous novels (including *The Age of Innocence and The House of Mirth*) that only her dedicated readers know she was, as evidenced in this collection, a master of the supernatural tale. Her brilliant ghost stories include "Afterwards," "The Triumph of the Night," and many more. She referred to herself as "a ghost-feeler," one who senses the unknown. So delicate was Wharton's imagination that she was unable to sleep in a room containing spectral stories, and destroyed any she came across at home. This did not, however, stem her wonderful output of the supernatural.

10. Paul Gallico—"The Terrible Story"

A bestselling author in his day, Gallico is today most remembered for his novel *The Poseidon Adventure* (the basis for two film versions). "The Terrible Story" is the only work of horror in his considerable oeuvre. It is an early work about the power of computers. Professor Haber spends a final night with his creation, the Mark IV, a giant computer. Having renounced all human love, Haber refers to the Mark IV as "*liebchen.*" After a night of communion with the activated computer, Haber receives his comeuppance for his rejection of humanity and his power-madness.

11. John Steinbeck—"An Affair at 7 Rue de M—"

Steinbeck, author of classics such as *The Grapes of Wrath*, wrote one horror story, although his body of work is usually concerned with cruelty and suffering. "An Affair at 7 Rue de M—" is a humorous tale with a touch of the macabre. It is about an evil piece of bubble gum, and its fight to the death.

12. Tennessee Williams—"Desire and the Black Masseur"

A playwright best known for *A Streetcar Named Desire* and *Cat on a Hot Tin Roof*, Williams also published a few spooky stories. "Desire and the Black Masseur" so frightened horror anthologist Peter Haining that he called it the most terrifying story he'd ever read. It is a purely psychological tale about a depressed middle-aged white man who finds masochistic release in a sauna bath at the hands of a muscular black masseur. Barely a word is exchanged between the men, and as the client begins to come regularly, the pain deepens with each visit.

13. Doris Lessing—*The Fifth Child*

The author, who won the 2007 Nobel Prize for literature, published this subtle but insidious shocker in 1988. It tells the tale of a middle-class English family whose existence is turned upside down by the arrival of a decidedly abnormal fifth child named Ben. Lessing penned a sequel to the novel in 2000 called *Ben in the World*.

—A.W. and S.B.

JACK KETCHUM'S TEN BEST HORROR NOVELS THAT DON'T CALL THEMSELVES HORROR NOVELS

Jack Ketchum is the author of such classic novels as The Girl Next Door, Off Season *and its sequel* Offspring, *and* Red. *His work has earned four Bram Stoker Awards from the Horror Writers of America. Prior to his writing career, he was a soda jerk, actor, teacher, and Henry Miller's literary agent. Film versions of his novels* The Girl Next Door *and* The Lost *have been released to wide acclaim,* and a film of Red *is in the works. More information can be found at* www.jackketchum.net.

1. *Heart of Darkness,* by Joseph Conrad

   Novel, novella, what's in a name? Congo, Kurtz and . . . *The horror! The horror!*

2. *Doctor Rat,* by William Kotzwinkle

   Animal researchers, pit bull enthusiasts, beware—this rat has teeth.

3. *The Collector,* by John Fowles

   My own book *The Girl Next Door* owes a debt to this one. So, probably, do butterflies.

4. *Maldoror,* by the Comte de Lautréamont

   The Godfather of Surrealism contemplates the tenderness of a baby's flesh in the first couple of pages, with evil intent. Take it from there.

5. *One Hundred Years of Solitude,* by Gabriel García Márquez

   Welcome to Macondo and the Buendía family—haunted and haunting. Magical realism at its amazing best.

6. *Moby-Dick,* by Herman Melville

   Ahab to universe: *"Have ye seen anything of a white whale?"* Arguably the most enduring flop of all time. Asks the question, who's more terrifying, Moby or the Captain? I know who I like.

7. *The Siege of Trencher's Farm,* by Gordon M. Williams

   Peckinpah hated the novel but adapted it into *Straw Dogs* anyway. The book's scarier, and a lot of it made its nasty way into *Off Season.*

8. *The Painted Bird,* by Jerzy Kosinski

One boy's harrowing survival story in war-torn Poland. Liked it so much I stole Mr. K's first name for my early nom de guerre, Jerzy Livingston.

9. *Grendel,* by John Gardner

Miscreant intellectual monster contemplates the meaninglessness of life while eating villagers. 'Nuff said.

10. *Child of God,* by Cormac McCarthy

The ultimate outsider. With dead girls.

RAMSEY CAMPBELL'S THIRTEEN NOVELS
ON THE EDGE OF HORROR

The Oxford Companion to English Literature *describes Ramsey Campbell as "Britain's most respected living horror writer." He has received more awards than any other writer in the field, including the Grand Master Award of the World Horror Convention, the Lifetime Achievement Award of the Horror Writers Association, and the Living Legend Award of the International Horror Guild. Among his novels are* The Face That Must Die, Incarnate, The Overnight, Secret Story, *and* The Grin of the Dark. *His collections include* Waking Nightmares, Alone with the Horrors, Ghosts and Grisly Things, *and* Told by the Dead, *and his nonfiction is collected as* Ramsey Campbell, Probably. *His novels* The Nameless *and* Pact of the Fathers *have been filmed in Spain. His regular columns appear in* All Hallows, Dead Reckonings, *and* Video Watchdog. *He is the president of the British Fantasy Society and of the Society of Fantastic Films. Campbell lives in Merseyside with his wife, Jenny. His pleasures include classical music, good food and wine, and whatever's in that pipe. His Web site is at www.ramseycampbell.com.*

1. *Dan Leno and the Limehouse Golem,* by Peter Ackroyd (1994)
   Ackroyd has written several novels that deserve a mention here—the darkly occult *Hawksmoor*, the rurally weird *First Light*, the alchemical *House of Doctor Dee*—but *Dan Leno and the Limehouse Golem* is still a revelation: a fast-paced Victorian serial-killer novel, witty and ingenious and suspenseful.

2. *The Deadly Percheron,* by John Franklin Bardin (1946)
   What was Bardin's secret? According to the introduction by Julian Symonds to a Penguin omnibus of the first three novels, Bardin's mother was a schizophrenic, which may suggest a reason for the author's focus on abnormal psychology. *The Deadly Percheron* is the tale to which the Robbie Coltrane character keeps referring in Neil Jordan's film *Mona Lisa*. It begins like a story from *Unknown Worlds*, with the narrator attempting to psychoanalyze a patient who receives mysterious instructions from a dwarf. Soon the narrator is attacked and robbed of his identity. Philip Marlowe would have swapped clothes with his neighbor in hospital and made his escape, but Bardin's protagonist recognizes how paranoid his story sounds and becomes a victim of it. The book progresses further into nightmare and never quite emerges, even to the point that it extends into Bardin's second novel, *The Last of Philip Banter*. Read that too, and the third, *Devil Take the Blue-Tail Fly*. Alas, his later novel *Purloining Tiny* is perverse, but reads like someone imitating Bardin.

3. *The Unnameable,* by Samuel Beckett (1953)
   Beckett at his most austere and intense. Deirdre Bair's biography reveals that he wrote the novel as a way of surviving the imminent death of his mother. If it's a vision of any kind of afterlife,

it's a truly terrifying one, and is best read in a single sitting. Characters and memories (if that's what they are) rise out of the disembodied monologue and vanish like ghosts, bearing fragments of the narrative and the narrator. It may not be an experience for all readers, but if you can take it, it's unforgettable.

4. *Committal Chamber,* by Russell Braddon (1966)

"Three men and their women are brought to face the truth about themselves in the committal chamber of a crematorium." So says the blurb of the British hardcover, accurately enough, but it avoids mentioning that the book is a variation on one of the earliest classic short horror stories. Its understatement only adds to the intensity, and it rises to a fine pitch of terror.

5. *The Death Guard,* by Philip George Chadwick (1939)

This nightmare vision of a new kind of warfare has seen only two editions. The Hutchinson hardcover is even rarer than the first and only paperback, published in 1992 with an introduction by Brian Aldiss. The novel grew out of the horrors of the First World War, and proposes the creation of a humanoid race bred simply to kill. The humanoids finish off a war and then proceed to overrun humanity in scenes that amply justify Karl Edward Wagner's inclusion of the book in his list of the best science fiction horror novels. A thread of racism runs through it, but it's still richly deserving of revival.

6. *The Plague Court Murders,* by Carter Dickson (1934)

This was John Dickson Carr's first novel under this transparent pseudonym. Most of Carr's work is detective fiction influenced by Chesterton, especially in a fondness for apparently impossible crimes. He had a strong sense of the macabre, not least in his titles—*The Hollow Man, Skeleton in the Clock, He Who Whispers, It Walks by Night* (his very first novel, close to Poe in its Gothic atmosphere and gruesomeness). Another influence is the ghostly fiction of M. R. James—the short story "Blind Man's Hood" is a spectral tale in that tradition—and this is apparent in *The Plague Court Murders*, which even quotes James's "A School Story" near the end. While the murders are solved, the book conveys an almost palpable sense of evil and dread. The haunted house of the title feels oppressively authentic, and a chapter devoted to its history never explains away the supernatural horror. Under both his names, Carr is worth reading, but don't read *The Hollow Man* first; it includes a chapter that lists many of the solutions to his tricks.

7. *Magic,* by William Goldman (1976)

Don't see the film, read the novel. It is indeed magic in a variety of ways. Goldman often plays brilliant tricks on the reader—in *Control*, for instance, and in the book (though not the movie) of *Marathon Man*—but this is the most ingeniously sustained. In fact, this reader didn't immediately catch it when it was revealed. As an account of a mind at and beyond the end of its tether, the book far outstrips the film (for which the author has to take some blame, since he wrote the screenplay).

8. *Hangover Square,* by Patrick Hamilton (1941)

John Brahm's film *Hangover Square* stars Laird Cregar as a deranged Victorian pianist and composer who is sent into murderous fits by high-pitched sounds. It's a compelling melodramatic thriller, rendered all the more intense by Bernard Herrmann's score, and an absolute travesty of the novel by Patrick Hamilton, author of *Gaslight* and *Rope*. In the book the protagonist William Harvey Bone suffers blackouts in 1939 London and imagines acts of violence that perhaps he will commit. He's a precursor of *American Psycho*'s Patrick Bateman, disintegrating in an England as bleak as anything in Graham Greene, without even that writer's hints of religious redemption. By all means see the film, but don't let it put you off the novel.

9. *The Day the Call Came,* by Thomas Hinde (1964)

A black comedy of paranoia narrated by the man who's waiting for the call. Here and in "The Investigator" (in his collection of two novellas *Games of Chance*) Hinde conveys how the deranged can pass as sane, not only to themselves.

10. *A Kiss before Dying,* by Ira Levin (1954)

Levin is best known in the field for *Rosemary's Baby*, a tour de force of a horror novel, told very largely through dialogue. *A Kiss before Dying* is more compulsive still—a study of a sociopath driven by ambition to kill and kill again. The serial killer is today's fashionable monster, with authors outdoing one another in attempts to elaborate the monstrousness (and too often the unlikeliness). Not the least of Levin's achievements is to show a murderer as murderers tend to be—inadequate and self-obsessed, with an exaggerated sense of their own worth and a compulsion to prove it—and still make the tale absolutely compelling. It was decently filmed by Gerd Oswald, but the remake begins with a miscalculation as basic as starting *Psycho* with the first appearance of Mrs. Bates. Seek out the book, which is a classic of edgy suspense.

11. *The Hole in the Wall,* by Arthur Morrison (1902)

My friend, the poet Richard Hill, brought this to my notice, and I can't improve on his description of it as a nightmare version of *Treasure Island*. Morrison specialized in social realism (*Tales of Mean Streets*, *A Child of the Jago*), and his view of crime and its sources was much less romantic than Stevenson's. The child's viewpoint from which we see events adds to the sense of dread, and the quicklime scene tips the book into real horror.

12. *The Art of Murder,* by José Carlos Somoza (2001, published in English 2004)

At the time of writing most of my readers may be far less familiar with Somoza than he deserves. Three of his novels are available in English. *The Athenian Murders* is a detective story Nabokov might have been proud to devise, while *Zig Zag* invents an impressively malevolent new kind of ghost born of an experiment in string theory. *The Art of Murder* is perhaps the most disturbing of the three, however. Promoted as crime fiction, it's primarily speculative fiction about a near future (now the recent past) in which human beings are sold as art objects. The psychological insight into their state—in particular the central character's—is at least the equal of Ballard.

13. *Savage Night,* by Jim Thompson (1953)

Noir fiction sometimes ventures into horror—Cornell Woolrich's *Black Alibi*, for instance, filmed for Val Lewton by Jacques Tourneur as *The Leopard Man*—but none of its proponents takes the tendency farther than Jim Thompson. The ending of *The Getaway* appears to have been too grotesque even for Peckinpah, because what waits over the border in the last chapter of the novel is the territory of Poe. Sometimes Thompson's work barely contains its excesses—the incestuous sadism that surfaces in *King Blood* is particularly troubling—but *Savage Night* is probably the book best suited to the present list. By the final pages it has become either a ghost story or a living nightmare, however living is defined in the context. "In the end," Geoffrey O'Brien writes, "only the voice remains." He could be writing about Beckett—indeed, to the very Beckett book I've listed—but he has *Savage Night* in mind.

MICHAEL MARSHALL SMITH'S TEN BEST HORROR BOOKS THAT YOU WON'T FIND ON THE HORROR SHELVES

Michael Marshall Smith is a novelist and screenwriter. He is a three-time winner of the British Fantasy Award for best short story, and his collection More Tomorrow and Other Stories *won the International Horror Guild Award. After three science fiction novels as Michael Marshall Smith, he wrote the internationally bestselling* Straw Men *crime thriller trilogy (and his most recent novel,* The Intruders*) as Michael Marshall.* The Servants, *a supernatural novel under yet another name—M. M. Smith—will be published next year.*

1. *Dead Babies,* by Martin Amis

   Amis has always had a dark side, and the third of his early novels really shows it. I mean, even the title isn't a walk in the park. The story of a drug-fuelled weekend in the 1970s which spirals badly out of hand, it shows some of the horror genre's shock-meisters for the wimps they are.

2. *The Killer Inside Me,* by Jim Thompson

   Jim Thompson is someone every horror fan should read—for tone, if nothing else. This is really a crime novel, kind of—the story of a local sheriff's shady dealings in a small town. But it's also one of the best and most restrained evocations of a deranged and amoral intelligence you will ever find: and note the intriguing little ontological shift at the end . . .

3. *The Informers,* by Bret Easton Ellis

   Ellis is another literary guy whose toe always seems to be in the dark end of the pool. *American Psycho* would be the obvious inclusion in this list, almost too obvious—so instead, try this collection of loosely linked short stories: and watch how they slowly degrade (like damaged film stock) into implied and sometimes even very literal horror. . . .

4. *Flicker,* by Theodore Roszak
Speaking of film stock, this superb conspiracy novel about the hidden meaning of film would sit perfectly happily in the horror section too, if it wasn't too busy being the novel everyone *should* have bought and read (along with Umberto Eco's *Foucault's Pendulum*) instead of that piece of **** *The Da Vinci Code*!

5. *The Wasp Factory,* by Iain Banks
The themes, imagery, and reveals in Banks's justly celebrated (literary) debut would not be out of place in any full-on horror novel—showing a morbid distrust of the mind, and, in particular, of the body, that would have David Cronenberg nodding in approval. . . .

6. *Something Nasty in the Woodshed,* by Kyril Bonfiglioni
Kyril Bonfiglioni's Mortdecai trilogy is one of the most criminally under-known series in any genre. So okay, it's not horror, at the start; more the wildly amusing story of everyday portly, dissolute, and immoral art-dealing folk. In the first novel, the Honorable Charlie Mortdecai comes across like some modern and lunatic brother of Sherlock Holmes, but by this third volume—a bizarre investigation into the "old religion" on Jersey—it's become very, very dark indeed. . . .

7. *Lunar Park,* by Bret Easton Ellis
Yep, Ellis again. But this really is a horror novel, pure and simple. Okay, it's hip and knowing and postmodern too: but that doesn't stop it's being a horror novel, okay? So how come this (admittedly very good) book winds up on the tables in the front

and center of the store, when horror people end up exiled to the shelves in back? Hmm?

8. *In the Electric Mist with the Confederate Dead,* by James Lee Burke

It's got ghosts in it. It's a great crime novel, of course—one of Burke's magisterial David Robicheaux series, set in and around New Orleans—but it also shows a deft touch with the super-natural, bringing the otherworldly close enough to center stage that if *we* did it, it'd be horror.

9. *A Christmas Carol,* by Charles Dickens

More ghosts—along with alternate realities, the pain of missed opportunities, and an ultimate redemption. Sure, it's got a happy ending, but there's no reason why horror shouldn't—it's the ten-sion of not knowing which way our lives will go that scares us the most. . . .

10. *The Bible,* by various authors

No disrespect meant or implied, but seriously . . . The loons who campaign for the banning of fantasy or horror novels ought to try reading this baby from cover to cover. There's some very heavy stuff in there, and the unearthly spirit concerned can sometimes seem kind of . . . *touchy.* And that Revelations section at the end—can't you just see it filmed in jittervision, with a pounding Marilyn Manson soundtrack?

DEL HOWISON'S TEN FAVORITE BOOKS THAT SOUND LIKE THEY'RE HORROR BUT AREN'T (IN NO PARTICULAR ORDER)

Del Howison is coauthor of The Book of Lists: Horror, *and proprietor of Dark Delicacies in Burbank, California.*

1. *The Supernatural History of Worms,* by Marion C. Fox, published by Friends' Book Center (1930)

2. *Barbs, Prongs, Points, Prickers, & Stickers,* by Robert T. Clifton, published by University of Oklahoma Press (1970)

3. *Rats for Those Who Care,* by Susan Fox, published by TFH Publications (1995)

4. *The Transitive Vampire,* by Karen Elizabeth Gordon, published by Times Books (1984)

5. *Public Performances of the Dead,* by George Jacob Holyoake, published by London Book Store (1865)

6. *The Onion Maggot,* by Arthur L. Lovett, published by Agricultural Experimental Station (1923)

7. *Reusing Old Graves,* by Douglas Davies and Alastair Shaw, published by Shaw & Sons (1995)

8. *The Man with Iron Eyebrows,* by Edouard Charles, published by Royal Magazine (1902)

9. *Flushing and Morbid Blushing,* by Harry Campbell, published by H. K. Lewis (1890)

10. *My Invisible Friend Explains the Bible,* by J. G. Bogusz, published by Branden Press (1971)

ROBERT BLOCH'S TEN FAVORITE
HORROR-FANTASY NOVELS

Born in 1917, Robert Bloch was one of the grandmasters of twentieth century horror fiction. He is perhaps best known for his 1959 novel Psycho, *which was the basis for the legendary Alfred Hitchcock film. Bloch also wrote many screenplays, teleplays (including for the original* Star Trek *series), hundreds of short stories, and more than twenty-five novels before his death in 1994.*

This classification excludes, by definition, science fiction, humor, or horror with fantasy element—tricky distinctions!

1. *Dracula,* by Bram Stoker
2. *Frankenstein,* by Mary Shelley
3. *Conjure Wife,* by Fritz Leiber
4. *Dr. Jekyll and Mr. Hyde,* by Robert Louis Stevenson
5. *Burn, Witch, Burn,* by A. Merritt
6. *The Werewolf of Paris,* by Guy Endore
7. *Là-bas,* by J. K. Huysmans
8. *To Walk the Night,* by William Sloane
9. *The Phantom of the Opera,* by Gaston Leroux
10. *A Mirror for Witches,* by Esther Forbes

—Originally appeared in The Book of Lists 2, *by Irving Wallace, David Wallechinsky, Amy Wallace, and Sylvia Wallace (1980)*

POPPY Z. BRITE'S TOP TEN "DINE 'N' DIE" STORIES IN HORROR FICTION

Poppy Z. Brite is the author of eight novels, both horror and non-genre. Some of her works include Lost Souls, Exquisite Corpse, Liquor, Prime, *and* Soul Kitchen. *She has also published four short story collections and assorted nonfiction. A native New Orleanian, Brite was one of the first 70,000 people to repopulate New Orleans after the post-Katrina failure of the federal levees. She currently lives there with her husband, Chris, an award-winning chef. Keep up with her daily doings and psychotic responses to the U.S. government's treatment of south Louisiana as a Third-World country at http://docbrite.livejournal.com.*

When I posted in my online journal that I was stuck for an idea for this book, reader Gaynor Newman suggested that I combine two of my great literary interests—horror and cuisine—to make a list of horror stories in which characters are killed by food items. I loved the idea, and here are the results. (I regret that I was unable to find copies of several stories suggested by other readers, so this list is in no way complete; it just represents a few of my favorites . . . and one nonfavorite that was nevertheless important to me, as you'll see).

1. *Flowers in the Attic*, by V. C. Andrews. Not a good novel, but a strangely compelling (and hugely popular) one, this was the first thing I read—at age thirteen—that made me realize, "I can already write better than this"—an important moment in any young writer's life. Four siblings are locked in an attic by their cruel grandmother and weak mother, later to be slowly poisoned by arsenic-laced powdered doughnuts.

2. *The Long Lost,* **by Ramsey Campbell.** A couple traveling in Wales happens upon Gwendolyn, a strange elderly woman who claims to be a distant relative of the husband. Upon her return to England with them, Gwen prepares cakes—"an old recipe"—for a barbecue, with various adverse effects for the guests. Chapter 29 of this novel has what may well be the single most chilling scene I've ever read. Beware of the Tor hardcover, an otherwise nice edition whose jacket copy gives away nearly the entire story.

 3. **"Lamb to the Slaughter," by Roald Dahl.** Perhaps the most famous example of this odd little subgenre, Dahl's unforgettable tale features a woman who brains her husband with a frozen leg of lamb, then pops the murder weapon in the oven and feeds it to the investigating policemen.

4. *We Have Always Lived in the Castle,* **by Shirley Jackson.** Two sisters live with their elderly uncle in a remote old house, shunned by the villagers because one sister poisoned the rest of the family at dinner years ago.

 5. **"Sunbird," by Neil Gaiman.** A cadre of hilariously drawn food-snobs in search of the ultimate dining experience find a rare bird, consume it, and are in turn consumed by it.

6. **"Gray Matter," by Stephen King.** We all know beer is food. In this short story, it's also a medium for a nasty spore that turns a hard-drinking man into a quivering, sentient mass of gray jelly.

7. *Thinner,* **by Stephen King (writing as Richard Bachman).** I had planned to limit this list to one entry per author, but surely the King of Horror deserves two spots, particularly since this novel was orig-

inally published by his late alter ego. A Gypsy curse can only be removed by feeding someone a Gypsy pie—but be careful who gets a slice.

8. **"Tight Little Stitches in a Dead Man's Back," by Joe R. Lansdale.** Post–nuclear-apocalyptic survivors dine on radioactive whale meat. "Crawling on their bellies like gutted dogs" is one of the milder effects.

9. *The Amulet,* **by Michael McDowell.** The late McDowell is surely one of the genre's most underrated writers. This tale of a small Alabama town menaced by an evil piece of jewelry isn't his best work, but it's still enjoyably nasty, and concludes by having its long-suffering protagonist take revenge on her cruel mother-in-law by feeding her bandage-swathed, possibly comatose husband a fatal mixture of applesauce and lye.

10. *From Hell,* **by Alan Moore.** Possibly the finest graphic novel ever published, a Masonic/architectural take on Jack the Ripper set in Eddie Campbell's wonderfully drawn Victorian London. At least one of the prostitutes is dead from Dr. Gull's laudanum-tainted grapes before the ritual mutilation is performed on her.

THOMAS LIGOTTI'S TEN CLASSICS OF HORROR POETRY

Thomas Ligotti is the author of five collections of horror stories. Conspicuous features of his works include an idiosyncratic prose style and inventive narrative structures as well as subjects and themes of a uniformly grim nature.

1. **"A Dream within a Dream," by Edgar Allan Poe.** In this poem, Poe says all there is to say about the horror and unreality of human existence.

2. *The Flowers of Evil,* **by Charles Baudelaire.** Tribute must be paid to the collection that inspired all others of a lavishly degenerate and fantastical kind that followed. Without Baudelaire's flowers, those of George Sterling, Ambrose Bierce, Clark Ashton Smith, David Park Barnitz, and Richard Tierney (among other luminaries past and present of American small-press horror poetry) would not exist.

3. **"City of Dreadful Night," by James Thomson ("B.V.").** In the greatest horror poem ever written, Thomson guides the reader on a tour of nightmarish illuminations. As Dante's *Inferno* is an excursus on how awful it is to be in hell, "The City of Dreadful Night" expatiates on how awful it is to be at all. The bad news: Life is a farrago of madness and suffering. The good news: God does not exist.

4. *Lead (Plumb),* **by George Bacovia.** Poems from a Romanian backwater town where the season is either autumn or winter, the time of day is twilight, the atmosphere is thick with anxiety or melancholy, the streets and parks are deserted, claustrophobic rooms look out on cemeteries and slaughterhouses, and there is always a funeral to attend. Some titles: "Autumn Twilight," "Winter Twilight," "Violet Twilight," "Black," "Grey," and "Ancient Twilight."

5. *The Fungi from Yuggoth,* **by H. P. Lovecraft.** A summation of Lovecraftian themes and sentiments in thirty-six sonnets. The horrors are all here as well as the dreams. Gods cavort in a Godless cosmos. New England serves as both a landscape of infinite doom and as charmed ground where one may "stand alone before eternity."

6. *Something Breathing,* **by Stanley McNail.** The standard for horror poetry as a genre. Spooky and macabre tales in verse. Things gibber and shamble. McNail specialized in miniature ballads of evil little girls.

7. *Nightmare Need,* **by Joseph Payne Brennan.** As a writer, Brennan's best work is represented by his poetry rather than by his fiction (with a few classic exceptions like "Canavan's Back Yard" and "Levitation"). *Nightmare Need* is his most distinguished collection and extensively demonstrates his signature subjects: desolate scenery, crummy ruins, lamentations for departed pets, loneliness and alienation, agonizing nostalgia, and death, death, death.

8. **"Mr. Blue," by Tom Paxton.** An unrivaled poetic fantasy of sociopolitical paranoia. Paxton's words might have been spoken by Big Brother to Winston Smith in George Orwell's *1984.* It begins: "Good morning, Mr. Blue / We've got our eyes on you."

9. **"In the Court of the Crimson King," by King Crimson (lyrics by Peter Sinfield).** One of the great examples of the Symbolists' rule that poetry does not have to make sense to make an impression. In this case, the impression is that of sardonic grandeur.

10. *Paper Mask,* **by Thomas Wiloch.** This is but one, almost arbitrarily chosen, collection among the numerous volumes of prose poems by Wiloch. He is the best at what he does, and what he does is seduce his readers into a world of quiet apocalypses, bitter ecstasies, and tiny derangements. While the prose poem form is compact by its nature, Wiloch's imagination is vast with sinister conceits.

JAMES D. JENKINS'S TEN WEIRDEST
GOTHIC NOVELS

James D. Jenkins is founder/publisher/editor of Valancourt Books (www.valancourtbooks.com), a small press specializing in new editions of rare Gothic, supernatural, and decadent novels. Since 2005, Valancourt has published over fifty works originally published between 1790 and 1950, and has dozens more titles in the works. In addition to new editions of well-established classics, Valancourt has reprinted novels so rare that they survived in only one known copy worldwide prior to republication.

1. *The Witch of Ravensworth* (1808), by George Brewer
   The hideous Witch of Ravensworth is the clear precursor to more famous literary monsters such as Dracula and Frankenstein's monster. But even more entertaining than her propensity for sacrificing infants and drinking their blood is Brewer's bizarre, darkly comic style, with its rapid-fire staccato sentences and delectably gruesome descriptions, not to mention the exclamation "It was the Hag!!!" every time she appears on scene.

2. *Horrid Mysteries* (1796), by Carl Grosse, translated by Peter Will
   Jane Austen immortalized this book by including it among the "horrid novels" read by her heroines in *Northanger Abbey*, and Thomas Love Peacock joked that Shelley slept with a copy under his pillow. Don't worry if you find the plot (which involves multiple murders and a secret society) incomprehensible. The author or translator apparently lost track of the plot too, as evidenced by the beautiful Elmira's dying no fewer than three times in the course of the novel.

3. *The Necromancer; or, The Tale of the Black Forest* (1794), by Peter Teuthold

Another of the "Northanger Novels," and only slightly more intelligible than *Horrid Mysteries*. This one is a series of interconnected tales set in Germany's Black Forest, centering on the mysterious figure of Volkert the Necromancer.

4. *The Animated Skeleton* (1798), by Anonymous

Set in France during the Dark Ages, where the good Count Richard has disappeared, and lawlessness, including wanton rape and murder, reigns. Surreal in its narration, this strange story culminates with a moving, talking skeleton that reveals Richard's fate and leads to the exposure of the guilty.

5. *The Demon of Sicily* (1807), by Edward Montague

THE
DEMON OF
SICILY

Edward Montague

Foreword by
New York Times Bestselling Author
Jo Beverley

VALANCOURT BOOKS

Satan comes to the Convent of St. Catherina, determined to win the souls of Sister Agatha and Father Bernardo. This process is drawn out over a couple hundred pages, and to keep things lively in the meantime, Montague tosses in kidnappings, imprisonments, impalings, decapitations, drownings, rendings asunder by demons, and burnings at the stake.

The Demon of Sicily by Edward Montague (Design by Ryan Cagle, used by permission of Valancourt Books)

6. *The Mysterious Hand; or, Subterranean Horrours!* (1811), by Augustus Jacob Crandolph

Not to be missed is the great scene in the first volume, where the evil Count d'Egfryd inveigles the beautiful and innocent Julia Bolton into a hot-air balloon, and takes her up several miles in the air in an elaborate and ill-fated scheme to rape her.

7. *Manfroné; or, The One-Handed Monk* (1809), by Mary Anne Radcliffe

Although the author's pen name recalls the more famous Ann Radcliffe and the title evokes Lewis's *The Monk, Manfroné* is hardly the derivative plagiarism one might expect. It's worth the cover price for the opening scene alone, in which a sinister monk enters Rosalina's room at night in an attempt to rape her and suffers the gruesome severing of his hand in the process.

8. *Santa-Maria; or, The Mysterious Pregnancy* (1797), by Joseph Fox Jr.

Besides its wonderful title, this novel is intriguing because, as Montague Summers puts it, it is "a tornado of circumstances and events curiously reminiscent of Sade."

9. *Deeds of Darkness; or, The Unnatural Uncle* (1805), by G. T. Morley

This probably has one of my favorite titles among all Gothic novels (what exactly is that unnatural uncle *doing* in the darkness?), although one contemporary journal was quick to state that "the sentiments in this tale are proper, and the moral is good." But don't let that deter you from reading it—the most shocking of the early Gothic novels tended to justify themselves with claims of "morality."

10. *Rosalviva; or, The Demon Dwarf* (1824), by Grenville Fletcher

The title pretty much says it all.

MARK VALENTINE'S TOP TEN WORKS
OF DECADENT HORROR FICTION

Mark Valentine is the editor of Wormwood, *the literary journal of the decadent and fantastic, and creator of the* Connoisseur, *an aesthetical occult detective whose curious adventures are recounted in* In Violet Veils *(1999) and* Masques and Citadels *(2003).*

1. *The Picture of Dorian Gray,* by Oscar Wilde: The cornerstone book of the brief flame of English decadence in the 1890s, and a languorous and dangerous account of how to sin in style.

2. *The Hill of Dreams,* by Arthur Machen: Described as "the most decadent book in the English language," a sensuous and searing account of the fate of the artist and dreamer in a dreary and Philistine world.

3. *Studies of Death,* by Eric, Count Stenbock: Sombre and ironic stories by an Estonian nobleman described by W. B. Yeats as "Scholar, connoisseur, drunkard, poet, pervert, most charming of men."

4. *Shapes in the Fire,* by M. P. Shiel: Highly ornate, original, and refulgent prose in a set of tales that outdo Poe in their grotesquerie, by the Montserrat-born king, philosopher, and fantasist.

5. *The Golem,* by Gustav Meyrink: The finest example of middle-European decadence in the dying days of the Austria-Hungarian Empire, an occult tale drawing on the rich traditions of Jewish folklore.

6. *The Book of Jade,* by Park Barnitz: Poems by a Midwest pastor's son who died young after creating the most nihilistic and doom-ridden volume ever.

7. *Flower Phantoms,* **by Ronald Fraser:** A golden-haired young woman with the look of a sly page at the Russian court achieves a high hothouse communion with a strange orchid.

8. *Doctors Wear Scarlet,* **by Simon Raven:** A rich, riotous, and erudite thriller by the best exemplar of twentieth-century decadence, creator of memorable cads and haughty scholars learned in the ways of evil.

9. *An Itinerant House,* **by Emma Frances Dawson:** Moody and atmospheric ghost stories from the enigmatic young woman whose work is the epitome of the flourish of San Francisco Decadence.

10. *The Stone Dragon,* **by R. Murray Gilchrist:** Strange tales by a recluse who lived in a candlelit manor house in the English Peak District and made this one book of high decadent weirdness among regional and folk fiction.

KARL EDWARD WAGNER'S THREE LISTS OF THE THIRTEEN BEST HORROR NOVELS

Karl Edward Wagner trained as a psychiatrist before becoming a writer of horror and fantasy. Wagner created the fantasy hero Kane, recounting his exploits in three novels and many short stories. He also wrote novels featuring the Robert E. Howard characters Conan the Barbarian and Bran Mak Morn. Among his other works are the novel Killer *(with David Drake), and the collections* In a Lonely Place *and* Why Not You and I? *With David Drake and Jim Groce, Wagner also founded Carcosa Press to preserve the work of great pulp authors. He was the editor of* The Year's Best Horror Stories *anthologies from 1980 until his death in 1994.*

I. The Thirteen Best Supernatural Horror Novels

1. *Hell! Said the Duchess,* by Michael Arlen
2. *The Burning Court,* by John Dickson Carr
3. *Alraune,* by Hanns Heinz Ewers
4. *Dark Sanctuary,* by H. B. Gregory
5. *Falling Angel,* by William Hjortsberg
6. *Maker of Shadows,* by Jack Mann
7. *The Yellow Mistletoe,* by Walter S. Masterman
8. *Melmoth the Wanderer,* by Charles Maturin
9. *Burn, Witch, Burn,* by A. Merritt
10. *Fingers of Fear,* by J. U. Nicolson
11. *Doctors Wear Scarlet,* by Simon Raven
12. *Echo of a Curse,* by R. R. Ryan
13. *Medusa,* by E. H. Visiak

II. The Thirteen Best Science Fiction Horror Novels

1. *The Death Guard,* by Philip George Chadwick
2. *Final Blackout,* by L. Ron Hubbard
3. *Vampires Overhead,* by Alan Hyder
4. *The Quatermass Experiment,* by Nigel Kneale
5. *Quatermass and the Pit,* by Nigel Kneale
6. *The Cadaver of Gideon Wyck,* by Alexander Laing
7. *The Flying Beast,* by Walter S. Masterman
8. *The Black Corridor,* by Michael Moorcock
9. *Land Under England,* by Joseph O'Neill
10. *The Cross of Carl,* by Walter Owen
11. *Freak Museum,* by R. R. Ryan
12. *Frankenstein,* by Mary Shelley
13. *The Day of the Triffids,* by John Wyndham

III. The Thirteen Best Non-Supernatural Horror Novels

1. *The Deadly Percheron,* by John Franklin Bardin
2. *Psycho,* by Robert Bloch
3. *Here Comes a Candle,* by Fredric Brown
4. *The Screaming Mimi,* by Fredric Brown
5. *The Fire-Spirits,* by Paul Busson
6. *The Crooked Hinge,* by John Dickson Carr
7. *The Sorcerer's Apprentice,* by Hanns Heinz Ewers
8. *Vampire,* by Hanns Heinz Ewers
9. *Fully Dressed and in His Right Mind,* by Michael Fessier
10. *The Shadow on the House,* by Mark Hansom
11. *Torture Garden,* by Octave Mirbeau
12. *The Master of the Day of Judgment,* by Leo Perutz
13. *The Subjugated Beast,* by R. R. Ryan

— Originally appeared in the June and August 1983 issues of Rod Serling's Twilight Zone Magazine; *reprinted by permission of the Karl Edward Wagner Literary Group.*

MARK JUSTICE'S SEVEN FAVORITE HORROR STORIES FROM THE BLOODY PULPS

Mark Justice is the author of Deadneck Hootenanny *and* Bone Songs, *as well as coauthor (with David T. Wilbanks) of* Dead Earth: The Green Dawn. *He produces and hosts horror's top podcast, the aptly named Pod of Horror. He lives in Kentucky with his wife in a house filled with cats, DVDs, books, and stacks of beautiful, moldering pulps.*

1. **"The Call of Cthulhu," by H. P. Lovecraft.** *Weird Tales,* **February 1928.**
In compiling a list of pulp horror stories, I've found the biggest problem was deciding which Lovecraft stories to include. After all, he's the granddaddy of pulp fear fiction. His impact on the genre cannot be overstated. And he's #1 on our Hellish Hit Parade. "The Call of Cthulhu" is noteworthy for the only HPL-written appearance of the tentacled elder god and for the disturbing sunken city of R'lyeh. Cosmic horror began here.

2. **"The Shadow Kingdom," by Robert E. Howard.** *Weird Tales,* **August 1929.**
King Kull. Reptile men who can pretend to be human. Sorcery. A palace filled with hidden passages. Chill-inducing fantasy by one of the masters.

3. **"The Case of Charles Dexter Ward," by H. P. Lovecraft.** *Weird Tales,* **May and July 1941.**
One of Lovecraft's longer pieces, this novella was written in 1927 but not published until 1941. Lovecraft set this story of madness and necromancy in his hometown of Providence, Rhode Island. In addition to the author's dense, melancholy prose, "The Case of Charles Dexter Ward" includes the first mention of the Great Old One, Yog-Sothoth.

4. **"Let's Play Poison," By Ray Bradbury.** *Weird Tales,* **November 1946.**
Another of Bradbury's early children-are-evil stories (see "The Small Assassin") finds a teacher who grows certain that kids are demons from Hell. While Bradbury could successfully make children the heroes in his writing, he also understood too well how alien some adults might find them.

5. **"For Fear of Little Men," by Manly Wade Wellman.** *Strange Stories,* June 1939.

Wellman, the king of regional tales of terror, spins a moody, evocative yarn about Native American myths. "For Fear of Little Men" gets bonus points for its Minnesota setting—a rarity in horror, then and now—and for the sheer coolness of tiny little Indians attacking the hero with tiny little arrows.

6. **"Johnny on the Spot," by Frank Belknap Long.** *Unknown,* December 1939.

In a change of style for Long, this is a hard-boiled tale of the Eternal Hitman. Brief, with an impact like a sharp stick to the eye.

7. **"Death and The Spider," by Novell Page writing as Grant Stockbridge,** *The Spider Magazine,* January 1942.

Though not strictly a horror title, Page's Spider novels were always crazy, surreal, and almost hallucinogenic, with the title character engaged every month in a bloodbath that often killed thousands. In the 100th issue, the Spider battled Death himself, and the high-strung crimefighter finally died. But by the end of the novel, he got better.

J. F. GONZALEZ'S TOP THIRTEEN OBSCURE SHOCKERS FROM THE PULPS AND BEYOND

J. F. Gonzalez was born May 8, 1964, and ten years later, almost to the day, he read his very first pulp horror story. It was "Sweets to the Sweet," by Robert Bloch, and he's been hooked on horror ever since. He writes in addition to reading and collecting pulps. He is the coauthor of such novels as Clickers *(with Mark Williams) and* Clickers II: The Next Wave *(with Brian Keene), both homages* to those classic fifties hybrid sci-fi/horror films. His other novels include Shapeshifter, Bully, The Beloved, Survivor, and Hero (co-written with Wrath James White), among others. His short fiction is collected in Old Ghosts and Other Revenants and When the Darkness Falls.

1. "Claimed," by Francis Stevens, from *The Argosy*, March 6–20, 1920.
2. "Beyond the Door," by J. Paul Suter, from *Weird Tales*, April 1923.
3. "The Copper Bowl," by George Fielding Elliot, from *Weird Tales*, December 1928.
4. "They Bite," by Anthony Boucher, from *Unknown Worlds*, August 1943.
5. "The Man Who Cried 'Wolf,'" by Robert Bloch, from *Weird Tales*, May 1945.
6. "Island of the Hands," by Margaret St. Clair, from *Weird Tales*, September 1952.
7. "Call Not There Names," by Everill Worrell, from *Weird Tales*, March 1954.
8. "The Other Side," by Arthur Porges, from *Fantastic*, Feb 1964.
9. "After Nightfall," by David Riley, from *Coven 13*, 1969.
10. "Screaming to Get Out," by Janet Fox, from *Weirdbook* #12, 1977.
11. "Window," by Bob Leman, from *Fantasy & Science Fiction*, May 1980.
12. "Bagman," by William Trotter, from *Night Cry Magazine*, Fall 1985.
13. "14 Garden Grove," by Pierre Comtois, from *The Horror Show*, Winter 1986.

SARAH PINBOROUGH'S "ROUGH GUIDE" TO HORROR TRAVEL LIST

Sarah Pinborough is a British author of four horror novels and several short stories. Her next novel, Tower Hill, *is due out in 2008 from Leisure Books, and she also has a novella,* The Language of Dying, *due from PS Publishing at the end of 2008. Sarah is a member of the writers' collective MUSE with fellow writers Sarah Langan, Alexandra Sokoloff, and Deborah LeBlanc. She is currently working on her next novel, a screenplay, and stroking her cats. She is* not *planning a vacation in the near future.*

Vacationing can be a precarious business. Plan wisely and take care where you choose to stop a while and take in the view. What seems pleasant on the surface may have a nasty surprise lurking. Whether you're a thrill-seeker wanting a vacation with an edge (although I warn you that edge may be rather sharp), or a more squeamish traveler who wants to know where to avoid to stay relaxed and breathing on your two weeks off . . . you need to read on . . .

1. *Got a luxury budget? Then why not try a night or two in the Overlook Hotel? Located in an isolated Colorado resort, the hotel promises old-style glamor and guaranteed privacy. You'll find you like it so much you might not want to leave . . . or maybe the Overlook just won't let you.*

   The Overlook Hotel is, of course, the setting for Stephen King's *The Shining*. The hotel has a grisly past and almost a life of its own, enjoying the company of the long-dead and manipulating the living, until they join the ranks of those that have already been consumed by its malevolence. This is a hotel that's definitely worth a visit, but perhaps only through the pages of that book.

Incidentally, the Overlook Hotel was based on the Stanley Estes Hotel, which is only a few miles away from where the horror and crime writer Tom Piccirilli now lives. Let's hope the hotel doesn't work any of its black magic on him!

2. *Feeling the pinch and don't have the cash for a flash hotel? Driving late into the night and your eyes are starting to burn? Well, look here . . . there's a flashing neon sign coming up . . . a motel . . . just what you need. A cheap room and a hot shower . . .*

If you see a sign for the Bates Motel, just keep on driving, or your stay may be longer than you expect. Famous as the setting from Robert Bloch's *Psycho*, and the home for Norman Bates and "Mother," the iconic shower scene in the movie destroys any enjoyment to be had in a long, hot shower for at least a month after viewing. However, it is great for keeping the water bills down, and even years after seeing it, I'm always wary of having the curtain pulled totally shut. But really, what do we expect from an author who stated, "Despite my ghoulish reputation, I really have the heart of a small boy. I keep it in a jar on my desk," eh?

3. *Wanting a longer vacation than the normal two weeks that fly by before you've blinked? Perhaps you and a group of friends want a home away from home for a month or so? Somewhere to relax? Maybe a summer rental is just for you . . .*

Shirley Jackson's Hill House, from *The Haunting of Hill House*, may well appeal to you and your friends, but as you walk through its ordinary rooms, someone—or something—may take your hand and lead you places you're not sure you want to go. If you do find yourself a resident there, you might do well to consider parking your car far away from its boundaries to avoid any temptation to do yourself harm. Hill House may not want you to leave. It seeks out lost and lonely souls to keep it company, and that constant companionship will not be good for you. For as Ms. Jackson states in the novel's first paragraph: "Hill House, not sane, stood by itself against its hills, holding darkness within; it had stood so for eighty years and might stand for eighty more." Don't say you weren't warned . . .

4. *Been feeling a little under the weather of late? Needing a vacation full of brisk air and cliff-top walks? Are your lungs crying out for the salty tang of fresh sea air? Beware . . . some seaside towns aren't so good for your health. . . .*

A. Two towns spring to mind in this category. The first is Innsmouth, Massachusetts (from "The Shadow Over Innsmouth," by H. P. Lovecraft). Should you wander too far into this town and find yourself tempted to stay, be warned that interbreeding is the norm in this quaint town, and we're not talking about mixing genes with the neighboring village. The Deep Ones want to interbreed, and if you're not willing to go that far, you may well find that the locals sacrifice you for endless gold and fish. And getting there can be difficult. As one traveller was told: "You *could* take the old bus, I suppose . . . but it ain't much thought of hereabouts. It goes through Innsmouth—you may have heard about that—and so the people don't like it."

B. Second comes Whitby, in Yorkshire, one of the easier places to find on this list because it actually exists on a map. If you look across the harbor toward East Cliff, you will be able to see the view that inspired Bram Stoker while writing *Dracula* during his stay in the Royal Hotel. I can think of nowhere spookier than an old-fashioned English seaside town, and it was in this sleepy town that Count Dracula first landed on British soil and disappeared in dog-form into the graveyard. Cold, English sea mists and vampires . . . what more could you want in a town? It's top of my list for a romantic weekend away, but so far no man seems keen. Funny that . . .

5. *To the Brit abroad, small-town America holds a massive holiday appeal. We imagine loading up our Winnebago and touring the States for months on end, stopping in at roadside diners that really do sell homemade apple pie and capturing some real American life away from the bigger cosmopolitan cities. However, should you find yourself cruising through Maine and see a casual sign for either of the next two towns, just keep your eyes on the road and the wheels straight ahead . . .*

Castle Rock is a name that needs no introduction and should already be a place most horror fans have visited and revisited on occasion. On the surface, this is a typical small New England town, but as its founder is Stephen King, it comes as no surprise to discover that it's the home to several dark secrets. It first appeared in *The Dead Zone* and ended in the deliciously dark *Needful Things*.

Derry is another town which brings a nervous smile of familiarity to the faces of any ardent horror aficionado and is a place I just can't stop myself popping in on from time to time, but it isn't one for the faint-hearted. *Bad* things happen in Derry. *It* is the defining Derry novel, although *Insomnia* and *Bag of Bones* are also both (in some part) set there. If you do by accident turn off the interstate and find yourself there, avoid the following locations:

> *29 Neibolt Street* (Bad things can be found under the porch.)
>
> *Kitchener Ironworks* (It hangs out here a lot: When not killing kids, It hibernates here.)
>
> *The Standpipe* (Apparently destroyed, but I still don't trust it—too spooky to even talk about. I've got shivers . . .)

6. *Don't be fooled after reading this into thinking that big cities are safe. You would be wrong.*

Paris? Out of the question for the nervous traveller. There were murders in the rue Morgue, there are phantoms in the opera, and a hunchback in Notre Dame. And that's without even thinking about Anne Rice's elegant vampire population.

London? Equally out. Dr. Jekyll and Mr. Hyde battle for control in the night. Count Dracula pops out for quick pint or two when the sun goes down, but it isn't the local beer he's got a taste for. James Herbert's giant rats sneak in the sewers seeking out the weak and fleshy, and in Crouch End a gateway to another dimension threatens to suck you in.

Eastern Europe? Well that's a total no-go area for far too many reasons to go into in this list. Aside from the superstitions, the vampires, and the werewolves, the back-packing hostels leave a lot to be desired—like a route of escape from butchering psychopaths! And that aside, the plumbing is never good in the old Eastern bloc.

So, weary travellers, here's my advice to you when planning your next vacation: If you want to stay safe and warm, why not just lock the door, unplug the phone, and curl up on your sofa for a fortnight . . .

Perhaps with a pile of good books.

JOEL LANE'S TOP TEN WEIRD LANDSCAPES IN HORROR FICTION

Joel Lane is the author of two collections of horror stories, The Earth Wire *(1994) and* The Lost District *(2006), as well as two novels and two collections of poetry. His articles and essays on weird fiction have appeared in* Wormwood, All Hallows, Foundation, *and many other journals.*

1. **"The Willows," by Algernon Blackwood.** First published in *The Listener and Other Stories,* in 1907). The opening tells us that the river Danube passes through "a region of singular loneliness and desolation." This is a masterpiece: fatalistic, disorientating, and precisely observed.

2. **"The Bad Lands," by John Metcalfe.** First published in *The Smoking Leg,* in 1925. A stressed-out visitor to the Norfolk flatlands wanders into a decaying region that is not on the map. A quiet but unrelenting sense of despair pervades this story.

3. **"The Colour Out of Space," by H. P. Lovecraft.** First published in *Amazing Stories* in 1927. A farmer refuses to leave his land after a meteorite poisons the soil. This elegiac portrait of a ruined landscape leaves the reader shaken and worried.

4. **"And No Bird Sings," by E. F. Benson.** First published in *Spook Stories,* in 1928. A quiet English wood conceals a realm of darkness and corruption. Benson has no inhibitions about bringing you face to non-face with the underlying cause.

5. **"Mive," by Carl Jacobi.** First published in *Weird Tales,* in 1932. A stretch of marshland is devoid of animal life, apart from a black flapping thing that may be a giant butterfly. This brief mood piece creates a powerful sense of unease.

6. **"Genius Loci," by Clark Ashton Smith.** First published in *Weird Tales,* in 1933. An artist becomes obsessed with a meadow that has "the air of a vampire" and exerts a malign hold over people's minds. This vividly imagined rural horror story makes one wish that Smith had written more in this vein.

7. **"The Hill and the Hole," by Fritz Leiber.** First published in *Unknown Worlds*, in 1942. A surveyor finds a place that is either a hill or a pit, depending on how you approach it—though you might do better not to. An early example of Leiber's ability to mess with the reader's mind.

8. **"The Lonesome Place," by August Derleth.** First published in *Famous Fantastic Mysteries*, in 1948. Two small-town boys are afraid of a particular spot they sometimes walk through at night. In one of his best stories, Derleth evokes the loneliness of childhood.

9. **"Canavan's Back Yard," by Joseph Payne Brennan.** First published in *Nine Horrors and a Dream*, in 1958. An aging bookseller discovers that his back yard is truly a wilderness: a place where the call of the wild can be heard. This story is understated and terrifying—an authentic weird classic.

10. **"Camera Obscura," by Basil Copper.** First published in *Not After Nightfall*, in 1967. A ruthless businessman visits a debtor who owns an antique scale model of the town where they live. Never mind the dubious characterization, just read this for its surreal and nightmarish ending.

FIVE MEMORABLE HORROR WORKS SET IN VENICE

Venice, Italy, is often referred to as the most romantic and magical city in the world, yet its maze of canals and sinking buildings also provide a sinister backdrop that has inspired authors time and again to terrify us. A few Venetian shudders take place in the following tales.

1. **"Don't Look Now," by Daphne du Maurier:** In du Maurier's famous novella, a young couple goes to Venice to assuage their grief after the death of their young daughter. The pair attempt to repair their shattered hearts, and soon meet up with two strange, elderly British sisters, one blind and psychic. Subtle and terrifying evil is set in motion. As in other tales on this list, Venice itself becomes menacing, increasing the plight of the couple. The author strips away the Venice of tourism to show the dark heart of a decaying, sinking city steeped in tragedy. Nicolas Roeg directed the outstanding film version, which preserves the tale's legendary shocker of an ending.

2. **"Ganymede," by Daphne du Maurier:** A tale of purely psychological terror, this is an unsung tingler by the author of *Rebecca*. A bachelor travels alone to Venice, and becomes infatuated with a winsome waiter at a café in the Piazza San Marco. As he works his way further into the boy's life, true horror unfolds, leading to a harrowing ending. While it's not supernatural, "Ganymede" is as disturbing as the most ghostly piece of horror fiction. There is just a touch of grue, but, typically, du Maurier lets the reader's imagination do the awful work.

As described in Daphne du Maurier's short story "Ganymede": The Piazza san Marco in Venice, Italy. (Photograph by Sylvia Wallace, used by permission.)

3. **"Never Visit Venice," by Robert Aickman:** A lonely bachelor named Henry Fern visits Venice. Before he departs England, he is haunted by a dream of finding the magnificent woman he has always sought. During the first weeks of Fern's holiday, Aickman writes, "Much as the folk had pillaged the Roman villas, so Venice was being pillaged now; and Fern sensed that the very fact of the pillage being often called preservation, implied that total dissolution was in sight. Venice was rotted with the world's new littleness." Fern finally takes a supernatural gondola ride with— the woman of his dreams, or a bag of bones? Before they set out, she tells him, "Everyone is Venice is dead. It is a dead city. Do you need to be told?" And not long after she says, too late, "Never visit Venice." Aickman takes us far out to sea, away from the cozy shell that is the surface Venice, and the appealing niches of gondola paths and waterways, into the open sea of terror.

4. *Death in Venice,* **by Thomas Mann:** This great classic tells the story of Gustav von Aschenbach, an aging homosexual author who holidays in Venice and falls in love with a comely boy named Tadzio. When cholera sweeps the city, the besotted protagonist refuses to leave, setting in motion his ultimate doom. One of Mann's most famous novels, *Death in Venice* isn't a horror story in any conventional genre sense, yet its macabre and melancholy take on the question of whether it is more dangerous to visit Venice alone or with a partner earns it a place on this list. The novel was filmed to great effect by Luchino Visconti, starring Dirk Bogarde as von Aschenbach. The film changed his profession from writer to composer, allowing Gustav Mahler's Third and Fifth Symphonies to "play" the role of von Aschenbach's compositions.

5. *The Comfort of Strangers,* **by Ian McEwan:** Like "Don't Look Now," this is a shocker about a young English couple adrift in Venice. When they meet an older couple who offers to show them "the

real Venezia," the stage is set for an appalling climax, as sinister motives slowly become apparent. Paul Schrader directed an acclaimed film version from a screenplay adaptation by playwright Harold Pinter, which features pitch-perfect acting by Christopher Walken and Helen Mirren as the spooky older couple. Like all the tales on this list, *The Comfort of Strangers* rips apart the "Venice as cute holiday locale" cliché, displaying in its place a decadent swamp of perversity and evil.

—A.W.

"YOU CAN'T GET THERE FROM HERE": THIRTY MEMORABLE BUT NON-EXISTENT TOWNS AND CITIES IN HORROR AND HORRIFIC FICTION

1. Castle Rock, Maine—numerous works by Stephen King, including *Cujo*, *The Dead Zone*, *The Dark Half*, *Needful Things*, and others.
2. Millhaven, Illinois—Peter Straub's Blue Rose trilogy (*Koko*, *Mystery*, and *The Throat*) and several affiliated works.
3. Derry, Maine—several novels and short stories by Stephen King, including *It* and *Insomnia*.
4. McGuane, Arizona—*The Town*, by Bentley Little.
5. Point Pitt, California—several short stories by David J. Schow, including "Not from Around Here" and "Red Light."
6. Arkham, Massachusetts—numerous works by H. P. Lovecraft.
7. Dunwich, Massachusetts—"The Dunwich Horror," by H. P. Lovecraft.
8. Moonlight Cove, California—*Midnight,* by Dean Koontz.
9. Potter's Field, Wyoming—*The Totem,* by David Morrell.
10. Oxrun Station, Connecticut—numerous works by Charles L. Grant, including *The Hour of the Oxrun Dead* and *Black Carousel*.

11. Malcasa Point, California—Richard Laymon's Beast House trilogy (*The Cellar*, *The Beast House*, and *The Midnight Tour*).

12. Stovington, Vermont—*The Shining*, *The Stand*, and *Christine*, by Stephen King.

13. Hampden, Vermont—*The Secret History*, by Donna Tartt.

14. Gatlin, Nebraska—"Children of the Corn," by Stephen King.

15. Innsmouth, Massachusetts—"The Shadow Over Innsmouth," by H. P. Lovecraft.

16. El Rey, Mexico—*The Getaway*, by Jim Thompson.

17. Jerusalem's Lot, Maine—"Jerusalem's Lot," "One for the Road," and *'Salem's Lot* by Stephen King.

18. Piecliff, New York—*Heart-Shaped Box* and "Best New Horror" by Joe Hill.

19. Big Tuna, Texas—*Wild at Heart* by Barry Gifford.

20. Roundtree, Massachusetts—*Black Creek Crossing* by John Saul.

21. Pico Mundo, California—the *Odd Thomas* series by Dean Koontz.

22. Dead River, Maine—*Off Season* and *Offspring* by Jack Ketchum.

23. Snowfield, Colorado—*Phantoms* by Dean Koontz.

24. Stepford, Connecticut—*The Stepford Wives* by Ira Levin.

25. Gilead, New Jersey—*The Ceremonies* by T. E. D. Klein.

26. Corban, Utah—*The Association* by Bentley Little.

27. Fairvale, California—*Psycho* by Robert Bloch.

28. Greentown, Illinois—*Dandelion Wine* and *Something Wicked This Way Comes* by Ray Bradbury.

29. Cedar Hill, Ohio—numerous works by Gary A. Braunbeck.

30. Pequot Landing, Connecticut—*The Other* by Thomas Tryon.

—Compiled by S.B.

STEVE RASNIC TEM'S THIRTY MOST MEMORABLE HORROR SHORT-STORY READS

Steve Rasnic Tem's 300-plus stories have garnered him the World Fantasy, Bram Stoker, British Fantasy, and International Horror Guild awards. Some recent work has appeared (or will appear) in Cemetery Dance, Dark Discoveries, Albedo One, Blurred Vision, Matter, Exotic Gothic, *Ellen Datlow's* Poe: Tales Inspired by Edgar Allan Poe, *and in* That Mysterious Door, *an anthology of stories set in Maine. His latest novel, written in collaboration with his wife, Melanie Tem, is* The Man on the Ceiling *(Wizards of the Coast Discoveries), based on their award-winning novella of the same name.*

1. "A Country Doctor" by Franz Kafka
2. "The Lottery" by Shirley Jackson
3. "The Beckoning Fair One" by Oliver Onions
4. "Evening Primrose" by John Collier
5. "The Jar" by Ray Bradbury
6. "The Hospice" by Robert Aickman
7. "The Howling Man" by Charles Beaumont
8. "Sticks" by Karl Edward Wagner
9. "The Dark Country" by Dennis Etchison
10. "Mackintosh Willy" by Ramsey Campbell
11. "The Autopsy" by Michael Shea
12. "The Body" by Stephen King
13. "Stephen" by Elizabeth Massie
14. "Mr. Dark's Carnival" by Glen Hirshberg
15. "The Last Feast of Harlequin" by Thomas Ligotti
16. "William Wilson" by Edgar Allan Poe
17. "Pork Pie Hat" by Peter Straub
18. "The Night They Missed the Horror Show" by Joe Lansdale

19. "In the Hills, the Cities" by Clive Barker
20. "The White People" by Arthur Machen
21. "Child's Play" by Villy Sørensen
22. "Oh, Whistle, and I'll Come to You, My Lad" by M. R. James
23. "The New Mother" by Lucy Clifford
24. "The Willows" by Algernon Blackwood
25. "The Whimper of Whipped Dogs" by Harlan Ellison
26. "Feesters in the Lake" by Bob Leman
27. "The Sea Was Wet as Wet Can Be" by Gahan Wilson
28. "Confess the Seasons" by Charles L. Grant
29. "The Girl With the Hungry Eyes" by Fritz Leiber
30. "The Hell Screen" by Akutagawa Ryûnosuke

THE ORIGINAL TITLES OF TWENTY HORROR NOVELS

1. Original Title: *The Shine*
   Final Title: *The Shining* (1977)
   Author: Stephen King

2. Original Title: *Cancer*
   Final Title: *Dreamcatcher* (2001)
   Author: Stephen King

3. Original Title: *Butcher Boy*
   Final Title: *Play Dead* (2005)
   Author: Michael A. Arnzen

4. Original Title: *Knife Edge*
   Final Title: *The Face That Must Die* (1979)
   Author: Ramsey Campbell

5. Original Title: *The Morbidity of the Soul*
   Final Title: *Hannibal* (1999)
   Author: Thomas Harris

6. **Original Title:** *The Incarnations*
   Final Title: *Incarnate* (1983)
   Author: Ramsey Campbell

7. **Original Titles:** *Behind the Mask*
   The Lecter Variations
   Final Title: *Hannibal Rising* (2006)
   Author: Thomas Harris

8. **Original Title:** *Nightmare New York City*
   Final Title: *Dead Lines* (1989)
   Authors: John Skipp and Craig Spector

9. **Original Title:** *Skull & Crossbones*
   Final Title: *Ripper* (1994)
   Author: Michael Slade

10. **Original Title:** *Blind Dark*
    Final Title: *The Hungry Moon* (1986)
    Author: Ramsey Campbell

11. **Original Title:** *The Mantis Syndrome*
    Final Title: *Ladies' Night* (1998)
    Author: Jack Ketchum

12. **Original Title:** *Home to Mother*
    Final Title: *The Nameless* (1981)
    Author: Ramsey Campbell

13. **Original Titles:** *The Summer of the Shark*
    The Terror of the Monster
    The Jaws of the Leviathan
    Final Title: *Jaws* (1974)
    Author: Peter Benchley

14. **Original Title:** *For the Rest of Their Lives*
    Final Title: *Obsession* (1985)
    Author: Ramsey Campbell

15. **Original Title:** *We Love the Scream*
    Final Title: *The Scream* (1988)
    Authors: John Skipp and Craig Spector

16. **Original Title:** *Birdland*
    Final Title: *Drawing Blood* (1994)
    Author: Poppy Z. Brite

17. **Original Title:** *The Funhole*
    Final Title: *The Cipher* (1991)
    Author: Kathe Koja

18. **Original Title:** *The Huntress*
    Final Title: *She Wakes* (1989)
    Author: Jack Ketchum

19. **Original Titles:** *Second Coming*
    Jerusalem's Lot
    Final Title: *'Salem's Lot* (1975)
    Author: Stephen King

20. **Original Title:** *The Un-Dead*
    Final Title: *Dracula* (1897)
    Author: Bram Stoker

—Compiled by S.B.

GARY BRANDNER'S TEN FAVORITE HORROR NOVELS
(IN NO PARTICULAR ORDER)

Gary Brandner, born in the Midwest, followed such diverse career paths as bartender, surveyor, loan company investigator, and technical writer before turning to fiction. He is the author of The Howling, Cameron's Closet, Floater, Walkers, Doomstalker, Rot, *and numerous other horror novels. A hit movie version of* The Howling *was released in 1981. He has also contributed short fiction to many anthologies, including* Post Mortem *and* Dark Delicacies. *Brandner lives with his wife and cats in California's San Fernando Valley.*

1. *Dracula,* **by Bram Stoker:** There are slow patches, but you can't be a real horror fan if you haven't read it.
2. *The Shining,* **by Stephen King:** Some really shuddery scenes, from back when the King was doing real horror.
3. *The Exorcist,* **by William Peter Blatty:** Even scarier than the movie.
4. *The Amityville Horror,* **by Jay Anson:** Who cares if it's true or not? This will keep you awake nights.
5. *The Silence of the Lambs,* **by Thomas Harris:** The best of the Hannibal Lecter series.
6. *Rosemary's Baby,* **by Ira Levin:** Proves you don't need blood to be scary as hell.
7. *Something Wicked This Way Comes,* **by Ray Bradbury:** Poetic spooky atmosphere with a great carnival centerpiece.
8. *All Heads Turn as the Hunt Goes By,* **by John Farris:** For the cool title, if no other reason.
9. *'Salem's Lot,* **by Stephen King:** The best vampire novel ever.
10. *7 Footprints to Satan,* **by A. Merritt:** The first horror story I ever read. Satanic images that stick with me.

NINE HORROR WRITERS WHO HAVE WRITTEN
CHILDREN'S OR YOUNG ADULT BOOKS

1. Roald Dahl

Today Roald Dahl is better known for his children's books than his earlier excursions into the macabre. But it was with his tales of horror that he made his initial mark, publishing in periodicals such as *Playboy* and producing collections such as *Switch Bitch* and *Kiss Kiss*. However, with his skewed vision—and since many children's fantasies trade in revenge against grown-ups—Dahl quickly found an enormous audience with his first children's book, *James and the Giant Peach*. On the first page, the parents of young James are dispatched by "an angry rhinoceros that escaped from the London Zoo and ate them in full daylight." Soon our hero is entrusted to the "care" of two evil relatives, Aunt Spiker and Aunt Sponge, who meet their comeuppance when they are squashed by a giant peach. Dahl's other best-known children's work is *Charlie and the Chocolate Factory*, which became the basis for two hit films.

2. George R. R. Martin

A bestselling fantasy novelist and much-acclaimed horror writer, Martin also published the lovely children's fantasy novella *The Ice Dragon*. In this book, a young girl named Adara, born during the worst winter in the land, befriends a dragon made of ice. Martin packs enough plot and fine writing in his tale to satisfy adults as well as children; and, in typical horror fashion, there are touches of dark, macabre drama, and a melancholic rather than happy ending.

3. Algernon Blackwood

A highly prolific author known for classic chillers like "The Wendigo" and "The Willows," Blackwood penned several works for children as well. In one, *A Prisoner in Fairyland*, the protagonist passes through a "crack" between yesterday and tomorrow into a timeless fairy land. Another, *The Education of Paul*, reads like a children's book but proves to be a thoughtful exploration of a deep mystical experience.

4. Stephen King

The King of Horror published his fantasy work for children and adults, *The Eyes of the Dragon*, in 1987, saying that he wrote the book for his daughter Naomi, who wasn't a fan of her father's tales of terror. Although the book is far gentler than any of King's works to that date, it does have several interesting connections to other tales by the author, in particular, his *Dark Tower* series.

5. Clive Barker

Though his name is synonymous with some of the most extreme horror ever in fiction and film, Clive Barker has also written several works for younger readers, including the fable *The Thief of Always* and the internationally bestselling *Abarat* series. The multitalented author also provided original illustrations and paintings to accompany these works.

6. Whitley Strieber

The author of *The Wolfen*, *The Hunger*, and *Communion* produced the young adult novel *Wolf of Shadows* in 1985 as a sort of companion piece to his book about the aftermath of nuclear war, *War Day* (written with James Kunetka). The harrowing but poetic and intensely moving tale depicts a postnuclear world from the point of view of a wolf.

7. Kathe Koja

Known to horror readers for the acclaimed novels *Skin*, *Bad Brains*, and others, Koja in recent years has become an acclaimed author of young-adult fiction with such novels as *Buddha Boy*, *Kissing the Bee*, and *Talk*, which have earned raves from both adolescents and adults for their lyrical writing and insightful depiction of the teenage world.

8. Ian McEwan

The author of creepy novels such as *The Cement Garden* and *The Comfort of Strangers* (as well as acclaimed mainstream literary works, including *Atonement* and the Booker Prize–winner *Amsterdam*) has also authored a pair of books for children. *The Daydreamer* is about the rich fantasy life of a little boy, while *Rose Blanche* concerns a young German girl who secretly aids the prisoners in a concentration camp during World War II.

9. Joyce Carol Oates

The prolific Joyce Carol Oates is as well known for her mainstream literary works as she is for her horror fiction. But she's also written a number of young-adult and children's books, most recent, *Naughty Chérie*, about a kitten who learns the importance of not misbehaving.

—*A.W. and S.B.*

TIM LEBBON'S TOP TEN APOCALYPSES IN HORROR FICTION

Tim Lebbon is a bestselling novelist from South Wales. His books include Dusk, Dawn, 30 Days of Night, Berserk, The Everlasting, Hellboy: Unnatural Selection, Exorcising Angels *(with Simon Clark),* Dead Man's Hand, White and Other Tales of Ruin, *and* Desolation.

Future publications include two more fantasy novels and a series of contemporary fantasy novels in collaboration with Christopher Golden (all for Bantam Spectra), and a series of young-adult novels based on the adventures of Jack London (also in collaboration with Golden). He has won three British Fantasy Awards, a Bram Stoker Award, a Shocker, and a Tombstone Award. His novella *White* is soon to be a major Hollywood movie, and several more works are in development in the U.S. and UK. Find out more at his Web sites: www.timlebbon.net and www.noreela.com.

1. *The Day of the Triffids,* by John Wyndham: I've always been a sucker for end-of-the-world scenarios set in the UK, from *Survivors* to *The War of the Worlds* (see below), and this is one of the best. We all know the story, and I just love the originality. And for walking plants, ridiculous as the concept may be, the Triffids are bloody scary!

2. *The Mist,* by Stephen King: King has destroyed the world several times over, but for me this is his best, turning the end of life as we know it into a tense, claustrophobic siege story in which survivors are besieged from the inside as well as from without.

3. *The Death of Grass,* by John Christopher: This one sticks in my mind because it's just so plausible, not relying on zombies, biological warfare, or anything else, other than crop blight. Brutal, bleak, and quite unrelenting, it's a very British take on the apocalypse.

4. *The Body Snatchers,* by Jack Finney: One of the best and most imaginative takes on alien invasion, which spawned one of the scariest horror movies (the 1978 Kaufman version of *Invasion of the Body Snatchers*, for me, takes the biscuit). Maybe it is all about Cold War paranoia, and not knowing your enemy from your friend, but it's damn scary.

5. *I Am Legend,* by Richard Matheson: One of the best vampire novels ever. While Robert Neville agonizes over what has happened, his day-to-day survival in a world infected by vampirism is fascinating, and terrifying. This brilliant novel drags us, kicking and screaming, to one of the best climaxes in apocalyptic fiction.

6. *The War of the Worlds,* by H. G. Wells: Usually classed as science fiction, but for me it's a horror story. A sense of hopelessness pervades the book, and to the Martians, we humans are simply germs—which makes the ending even more ironic.

7. *Blood Crazy,* by Simon Clark: One of Clark's best, and a brutally realized, imaginative take on the end of the world. It's obvious that John Christopher and John Wyndham influence Clark's fiction in a very positive way. You won't look at your parents the same way again.

8. *The Rising,* by Brian Keene: Zombies have enjoyed a resurgence over the past few years, and Keene's take on them is interesting and refreshing. Zombies possessed by demons? You just know there are going to be problems.

9. *The Night Land,* by William Hope Hodgson: Dark, forbidding, mysterious, and almost endless, you need to spend a day in the sun after reading this one.

10. *Domain,* by James Herbert: A perfect end to the *Rats* trilogy. Herbert upped the ante on this one, throwing in a nuclear war on top of the rats for his heroes to tackle. And that ending . . . oh my!

A TRIFFID BY ANY OTHER NAME WILL STILL KILL YOU: TWELVE ALTERNATE NAMES FOR TRIFFIDS

In John Wyndham's horror/science fiction novel *The Day of the Triffids* (1951), when the walking, stalking, carnivorous plants with "that active, three-pronged root" are first discovered, nobody quite knows what to call them. Eventually, they come to be known as "triffids." But before that, according to the book, "what the newspapers and the public wanted was something easy on the tongue and not too heavy on the headlines for general use. If you could see the papers of that time you would find them referring to . . ."

1. Trichots
2. Tricusps
3. Trigenates
4. Trigons
5. Trilogs
6. Tridentates
7. Trinits
8. Tripedals
9. Tripeds
10. Triquets
11. Tripods
12. Trippets

—*S.B. (Source:* The Day of the Triffids *by John Wyndham)*

LISA TUTTLE'S TEN FAVORITE SCARY SHORT STORIES

The prolific and award-winning Lisa Tuttle was born in Houston, Texas, in 1952. She moved to London, where she spent twenty years of her life, and now resides in Scotland with her husband and their daughter. She has written science fiction, fantasy, erotica, and extremely upsetting horror. She began as a writer of short stories—a form for which she retains a strong attachment—but is also known for her nonfiction (The Encyclopedia of Feminism)*, anthologies* (Skin of the Soul)*, and novels (including* The Pillow Friend, The Mysteries, *and* The Silver Bough*).*

1. **"The Yellow Wallpaper," by Charlotte Perkins Gilman:** Totally creeped me out when I first read it as a kid. Years later, when I discovered the writer had written it about her own experience, it was even more horrifying.

2. **"The School Friend," by Robert Aickman:** The only story that ever made me scream out loud. It was the first of Aickman's strange stories I encountered, and I was so caught up in its spell that I thought I was alone, until my roommate spoke.

3. **"The Mezzotint," by M. R. James:** A deceptively mild and donnish little tale, chillingly unforgettable.

4. **"The Monkey's Paw," by W. W. Jacobs:** A powerfully mythic horror story.

5. **"Afterwards," by Edith Wharton:** The perfect ghost story.

6. **"The Victorian Chaise Longue," by Marghanita Laski:** Most time-slip fantasies are romantic, but this one is full of dread and terror.

7. **"The Demon Lover," by Elizabeth Bowen:** Works with beautiful ambiguity: supernatural or real-life horror?

8. **"Casting the Runes," by M. R. James:** Great story, good movie (*Night of the Demon*), and inspiration for the scariest party game I've ever played.

9. **"The White People," by Arthur Machen:** Brilliant evocation of a hidden world, secret knowledge, and the dark side of folklore.

10. **"The Pear-Shaped Man," by George R. R. Martin:** Okay, this is personal. I met a (*the?*) pear-shaped man and told George about the weird encounter, and he wrote it up as fiction. It's true, I tell you!

AMY WALLACE'S THIRTEEN MOST MEMORABLE MOMENTS READING HORROR FICTION

Amy Wallace is the co-author of The Book of Lists: Horror *and cocreator (with her father Irving Wallace and brother David Wallechinsky) of the Book of Lists series.*

1. **"The Veldt," by Ray Bradbury:** This was the first story that scared me as a child. I have only reread it once, and it held up. This story (and several other Bradbury classics of that era, like "The Next in Line") led to many disturbed nights and worry about what might be under the bed, even though it's not about things under the bed. Read and beware.

2. *Conjure Wife*, **by Fritz Leiber:** The only novel ever to scare me so silly that I read it until dawn, like a deer fixed to headlights or a tongue stuck to the freezer. I was twenty-one, and traveling in Paris with my parents and husband, and even my snoring better half beside me gave me *zero* solace. I'm afraid to read it again. Some similar themes are explored in Ira Levin's novels *The Stepford Wives* and *Rosemary's Baby*, both fantastic, but with all due respect, they didn't scar my psyche like *Conjure Wife* did. *Shudder.*

3. **"Lukundoo," by Edward Lucas White:** Oh, dear. A shattering, terrifying story about a fellow who's wronged a woman and his punishment is . . . to have excrescences growing out of his body. They . . . gibber. The end is a mysterious shocker, with a few unforgettable, haunting lines from our suffering protagonist. He is utterly doomed. Just as good with every read.

4. **"Petey," by T. E. D. Klein:** When it comes to Mr. Klein, it is difficult to choose. Another Klein story, "Nadelman's God," battled for a place on this list. But in the end, that story made me melancholy and disturbed, while I always get a frisson out of "Petey." I have a weakness for horror in suburban settings—the macabre in the midst of cocktail parties and the like. "Petey" is, in part, the tale of a housewarming thrown by a bourgeois couple, complete with an amateur tarot reading that leads to no good. It was this get-under-your-skin story that made me conquer my shyness and acquire Mr. Klein's telephone number, thus leading to what has been, to me, a most gratifying friendship by phone and mail. He does sound like Alfred Hitchcock on the phone, yet I'm not sure *how* scary he is. Probably very.

5. **"The Howling Man," by Charles Beaumont:** My relatively recent discovery of Charles Beaumont led to a long, obsessed binge. I believe "The Howling Man" to be the greatest of his stories. (Some of you may remember it from *The Twilight Zone*.) As I mentioned, I love suburban horror, and second place goes to Beaumont's spine-cracking "The New People," about a very unusual suburban tract neighborhood. To say more would be to risk spoiling.

6. **"The Pear-Shaped Man," by George R. R. Martin:** A writer now best known for his fantasy—which is utterly horrific—and previously known for his horrifying science fiction, I've always read

anything by Martin I could get my hands on. If you read "The Pear-Shaped Man" (see Lisa Tuttle's list for a surprise) you'll never be able to look at a cheese puff without trembling. Kudos, too, for the runner-up tale "The Monkey Treatment."

7. **"The Box," by Jack Ketchum:** This short, sour masterpiece deserved its Bram Stoker Award. It concerns a large man with a box. To say any more would be travesty. One of the most impressive very short stories I've ever read; a haiku of foreboding and terror.

8. **"Manskin/Womanskin," by Lisa Tuttle:** Discovering Tuttle led me on a long, still-continuing quest to read every word she's ever written, no matter if it be humor, horror, or sci-fi, or just that plain old thing we call literature. Like George R. R. Martin (with whom she collaborated on a novel), her writing defies categorization. She is my favorite writer about the dark, bleak side of "love" relationships. I could have picked any of fifty stories—sitting down to a Tuttle is like tucking in to a favorite meal. I chose this one because it is one of her quirkiest "love is strange" pieces. Tuttle is my favorite living female author. My favorite deceased is Edith Wharton (four stars to "Afterwards" by Wharton).

9. *Pet Sematary*, **by Stephen King:** While not a *favorite* book, this was a truly seminal horror read. It's rumored that King scared himself so much as he wrote it that he hid it a drawer. As the story goes, he had to deliver a book to get out of a contract, and is said to have slapped on an ending and whammo . . . bestseller! I can't tell where the tacked-on ending begins. Anyway, in 1986, I was recently divorced and feeling blue when my friend Ned Claflin, who had turned me on to much horror, called to say "How are ya?" I said I was depressed, to which he replied, "Wait right there! I'll be over!" He sped from San Francisco to where

I lived in Berkeley and we trolled crummy paperback shelves in that bookish town until we found *two* (I still didn't know what was going on) copies of the novel. Ned finally said: "A person cannot be scared shitless and depressed at the same time. This is the cure. We'll sit down and read the first 10 pages together, then I'm going home." Every day, Ned called leaving scary quotes from the book, such as "Injun stole my fish," on my answering machine. And guess what? Ned was right—you can't be that scared (and it was the height of summer at the beach!) and stay depressed. This is a dangerously scary book (unless you're depressed). Thank you, Ned.

10. **"The Wendigo," by Algernon Blackwood:** Thanks again, Ned. Again, it's hard to choose with Blackwood, but whenever I want to be truly "taken out of myself" and no martini is at hand, I read "The Wendigo," a deep country terror set in the wilds of Canada. The dialogue toward the end is among my favorite passages in all literature. The ending is one of my favorites in all of literature.

11. **"The Bushmaster," by Conrad Hill:** Leave it to Julian (brother of Andrew) Lloyd Webber to track down the *extremely* reclusive Mr. Hill and reprint this masterpiece in his anthology *Short Sharp Shocks*. Reading "The Bushmaster," I discovered that humor and horror really could go hand in hand, something I'd always been dubious about. Ngomo, a mysterious African businessman, sells a most unusual vacuum cleaner from his native land to a man with a neat-freak wife. Mayhem, awfulness, and hilarity ensue. I often read aloud to my boyfriend and coauthor Scott Bradley his favorite scene in the story, in which the henpecked hubby acquires the titular creature in Ngomo's deliciously mysterious shop, and watches it go to work for the first time.

12. **"In the Hills, the Cities," by Clive Barker:** Was there ever a more imaginative tale than this? No attempt to describe it—and nevermind a spoiler—could ever do it justice. As I began to read it, it was creepy; it proceeded to terrify me, and by the end I was astounded by the visionary heights Barker reached. I don't love all of Barker's work, but this story wins my Nobel Prize for weirdness and somehow stretches beyond horror into something unnamable. I can't imagine having a mind that could even conceive this tale. Read it and be awed.

13. **"Into the Wood," by Robert Aickman:** I've saved my all-time favorite story for last: "Into the Wood" is the insomniac's bible. Margaret Sawyer is an English housewife on a business trip with her husband in Sweden. Alienated, she decides to visit a forest "rest house" named the Kurhaus. No story has ever represented the interior of my mind and soul so perfectly. Reading it I felt, "You're not alone," even though the story is about loneliness. The "rest house" is an ironic name; it is a place for people who *never* sleep, who walk forest paths from dusk till dawn. The guests have nothing in common but their existential dilemma. When Margaret encounters a courtly colonel, he tells her why he and the guests walk at night. "They go," he said, "because they have reached their limit. For men and women there is to everything a limit beyond which further striving, further thought, leads only to regression . . . For those who do not set out, the limit varies from individual to individual, and cannot be foreseen. Few ever reach it. Those who do reach it are, I suspect, those who go off into the further forest." Before reading this, I could not have explained my own feelings, even to myself. Truly great horror fiction holds a mirror up to our secrets. When the colonel speaks of striving deep into "the further forest," Aickman expressed for me the true reason for continuing—with the regime of the path, one may someday break away into the unnamable, be it light or dark, both or neither.

EIGHT MEMORABLE QUOTES FROM HORROR AUTHORS

1. "I have the heart of a small boy. I keep it in a jar on my desk."

   —Robert Bloch

2. "I recognize terror as the finest emotion and so I will try to terrorize the reader. But if I find that I cannot terrify, I will try to horrify, and if I find that I cannot horrify, I'll go for the gross-out. I'm not proud."

   —Stephen King

3. "The oldest and strongest emotion of mankind is fear, and the oldest and strongest kind of fear is fear of the unknown."

   —H. P. Lovecraft

4. "The kind of horror I like drags things into the daylight and says, 'Right. Let's have a really good look. Does it still scare you? Does it maybe do something *different* to you now that you can see it more plainly—something that isn't quite like being scared?'"

   —Clive Barker

5. "Horror is not a genre, like the mystery or science fiction or the western. It is not a *kind* of fiction, meant to be confined to the ghetto of a special shelf in libraries and bookstores. Horror is an emotion. It can be found in all literature."

   —Douglas E. Winter

6. "The best horror stories are stories first and horror second, and however much they scare us, they do more than that as well. They have room in them for laughter as well as screams, for triumph and tenderness as well as tragedy."

   —George R. R. Martin

7. "Let's say it once and for all: Poe and Lovecraft—not to mention a Bruno Schulz or a Franz Kafka—were what the world at large would consider extremely disturbed individuals. And most people who are that disturbed are not able to create works of fiction. These and other names I could mention are people who are just on the cusp of total psychological derangement. Sometimes they cross over and fall into the province of 'outsider artists.' That's where the future development of horror fiction lies—in the next person who is almost too emotionally and psychologically damaged to live in the world but not too damaged to produce fiction."

   —Thomas Ligotti

8. "Horror fiction upsets apple carts, burns old buildings, and stampedes the horses; it questions and yearns for answers, and it takes nothing for granted. It's not safe, and it probably rots your teeth, too. Horror fiction can be a guide through a nightmare world, entered freely and by the reader's own will. And since horror can be many, many things, and go in many, many directions, that guided nightmare ride can shock, educate, illuminate, threaten, shriek, and whisper before it lets the readers loose."

   —Robert R. McCammon

—*Compiled by S.B. and A.W.*

THE HORROR WRITERS ASSOCIATION BRAM STOKER LIFETIME ACHIEVEMENT AWARDS, 1987–2007

2007—John Carpenter; Robert Weinberg

2006—Thomas Harris

2005—Peter Straub

2004—Michael Moorcock

2003—Anne Rice; Martin H. Greenberg

2002—Stephen King; J. N. Williamson

2001—John Farris

2000—Nigel Kneale

1999—Edward Gorey; Charles L. Grant

1998—Ramsey Campbell; Roger Corman

1997—William Peter Blatty; Jack Williamson

1996—Ira Levin; Forrest J. Ackerman

1995—Harlan Ellison

1994—Christopher Lee

1993—Joyce Carol Oates

1992—Ray Russell

1991—Gahan Wilson

1990—Hugh B. Cave; Richard Matheson

1989—Robert Bloch

1988—Ray Bradbury; Ronald Chetwynd-Hayes

1987—Fritz Leiber; Frank Belknap Long; Clifford D. Simak

—*Courtesy of the Horror Writers Association (www.horror.org)*

T. E. D. KLEIN'S TWENTY-FIVE MOST FAMILIAR
HORROR PLOTS

☠ *T. E. D. Klein is the author of the novel* The Ceremonies
(1984) and two collections, Dark Gods *(1985) and* Reassuring Tales *(2006). His fiction has appeared in such acclaimed*
anthologies as Dark Forces *and* 999. *He also cowrote the screenplay*
for Dario Argento's film Trauma. *He was the editor of the legendary*
Rod Serling's Twilight Zone Magazine *from 1981 to 1985 (which*
inspired the following list) and the editor of CrimeBeat *from 1991*
to 1992. The following list is excerpted from his nonfiction chap-
book, Raising Goosebumps for Fun and Profit.

1. **Hey, I'm Really Dead!**—The victim of a car crash or some other accident discovers, at the story's end, that he didn't survive after
   all. Often he can't under-
   stand why friends look right
   through him or scream when
   he approaches. Occasionally,
   he hitches a ride from a driver
   who turns out, at the end, to
   be Death. Final image: a funeral, or a corpse in a crum-
   pled car. Cf. *Twilight Zone*
   episode "The Hitch-Hiker,"
   Isaac Bashevis Singer's "A
   Wedding in Brownsville," and
   of course *The Sixth Sense*.

   Most Familiar Horror Plot
   #1, "Hey, I'm Really Dead!"
   (Illustration by Peter Kuper,
   used by permission)

2. I'm Really in Hell—The TV's on the fritz again, the wife or the job keeps growing more annoying (or merely more boring), and suddenly the hero realizes that he's actually died and gone to hell. A gloomy attempt to make sense of life's little miseries. Cf. ending of the *Twilight Zone* episode "A Nice Place to Visit," with that famous zinger: "Send me to the other place," begs the cad. Replies the angel (or demon): "This *is* the other place!"

3. They're All Against Me!—A paranoid fantasy turns out to be true. Cf. Robert Heinlein's "They," whose hero is the ruler of the world—if only They'd let him remember; Richard Matheson's

"Shipshape Home," whose subbasement turns out to be the engine room of a spaceship; and Gahan Wilson's cartoon shrink who asks the patient, "When did you first become aware of this supposed plot to get you?" while secretly beckoning to the dagger-wielding assassins who've just slipped into the room.

Most Familiar Horror Plot #3, "They're All Against Me!" (Illustration by Peter Kuper, used by permission)

4. I'll Show Them! (Version 1)—Parents don't believe their child's tale of an invisible playmate (or a monster in the closet, etc.), but in the end the "imaginary" figure turns out to be real, saving the child's life . . . or killing the child . . . or better still, killing Daddy. Famous examples: "Thus I Refute Beelzy," by John Collier, "The Thing in the Cellar," by David H. Keller, and "The Boogeyman," by Stephen King, complete with monster disguised as shrink (which also makes it an example of #3).

5. **I'll Show Them! (Version 2)**—A shy, misunderstood youngster is rejected by schoolmates for being "different," but is vindicated when he (although it's usually a she) turns out to be gifted with startling psychic powers. Frequently submitted by sensitive teenage girls, perhaps inspired by *Carrie*.

6. **The Magic Picture**—It draws one in. The hero or heroine—often an unhappy soul, as in #5—vanishes mysteriously and is later found depicted in an old painting, photo, tapestry, wallpaper pattern, etc. Usually, the unchanging world inside the picture is an improvement on real life, though in the *Night Gallery* episode "Escape Route," the ex-Nazi protagonist accidentally dooms himself by escaping into the wrong picture.

7. **The Magic Typewriter**—An author (or would-be author) acquires a supernatural typewriter which either transforms his writing style or churns out bestsellers all by itself. Sometimes—as in Gary Brandner's "The Loaner"—it's haunted by the ghost of its previous owner. A perennial writer's fantasy (for obvious reasons) ever since John Kendrick Bangs wrote *The Enchanted Typewriter* in 1899, right up to David Morrell's "The Typewriter" and Stephen King's 1982 variation, "The Word Processor."

8. **The Forgetful Vampire**—He fails to remember that it's daylight savings time and emerges from his coffin one sunny hour too soon.

9. **Not Just a Game (Version 1)**—A child gets so caught up in a fantasy role-playing game that he murders friends or family.

10. **Not Just a Game (Version 2)**—A video or computer game provides training for galactic combat; or sometimes the "game" itself is actually a real war. Plays on the wish that our most trivial pastimes have world-shaking consequences, that we're actually destined for something important, or that at least someone's watching us and is (we hope) impressed. Cf. films such as *WarGames, Tron, The Last Starfighter,* etc., and Philip K. Dick's novel *Time Out of Joint.*

11. **Make a Wish**—*The Twilight Zone* TV show's favorite plot, an illustration of Oscar Wilde's maxim about there being only two tragedies in this world: not getting what one wants . . . or getting it. The hero or heroine in this type of story is granted three wishes, or one wish, or some long-wished-for superhuman power—and soon learns to regret it, for it goes horribly awry, often because (out of malice or stupidity) the wish-granting genie, god, or benevolent alien has taken the wish too literally. It's a plot as old as King Midas, as old as the oldest fairy tale in which a hero was forced to use the third of three wishes to remedy the damage done by the previous two. Cf. the fisherman who wishes for the sausage, the wife who wishes it on his nose, and the third wish wasted in getting it off. Most celebrated example: "The Monkey's Paw." Classic variations: Wells's "The Man Who Could Work Miracles" and Hawthorne's "The Ambitious Guest." Moral: Don't rely on wishes; you've got to work for what you want. Alternate moral: Leave well enough alone, be content with what you've got, and don't try to rise above your station—the sort of defeatist belief that would have stopped human progress in its tracks.

12. **Ironic Retribution**—The classic EC (Entertaining Comics) plot. A murderer, haunted by his victim, is driven to suicide; a strangler is strangled; a war criminal is gassed; a man who blinded someone is blinded himself; a cat-killer is killed by a real (or ghostly) feline; hunted animals take revenge on a cruel hunter; machines get back at a cruel owner (as in the *Twilight Zone*'s "A Thing About Machines"), etc. Cf. Hans Christian Andersen's "Girl Who Trod on a Loaf," who pulled the wings off flies and was punished when they crawled over her frozen face.

13. **Meet the Myth**—The hero or heroine encounters a hitchhiker, a seductive woman at the beach, a new neighbor, a tramp, etc., etc., who turns out to be a centaur, a mermaid, Pan, Cthulhu, or Medusa.

14. **The Living House**—Yes, it's really alive, and it eats anyone foolish enough to enter. Or imprisons impertinent visitors. Or crashes on the head of an evil real estate developer.

15. **The Henpecked Hubby**—A milquetoast plans the intricate murder of his wife. Often ends with "Come in, dear, I have something to show you!" as the

Most Familiar Horror Plot #13, "Meet the Myth" (Illustration by Peter Kuper, used by permission)

husband sits waiting for her in a room full of giant carnivorous plants. Commonly submitted by men.

16. **You Can't Cheat Fate**—A prophecy proves true, usually in some irritating, ironic way. A man fated to die of "cancer" is murdered by an astrological Cancer; a future "plane crash" victim refuses to fly but is killed when a plane hits his home, etc. A plot as old as Oedipus, not forgetting *Macbeth*, *Moby-Dick*, and William Lindsay Gresham's *Nightmare Alley*.

17. **You Can't Cheat the Devil**—It's crazy to make a pact with the Devil—everyone *knows* the Devil always wins—but in story after story, people go ahead and do it anyway. Tedious variation on #16. Last really satisfying example: Christopher Marlowe's *Dr. Faustus* (1588). Two notable exceptions: William Hjortsberg's *Falling Angel* (from which, the film *Angel Heart*) and Stephen Vincent Benét's "The Devil and Daniel Webster," in which humanity triumphs at last.

18. **Cannibals**—Funeral ends with eating of the corpse, an isolated town barbecues unlucky strangers, an odd-tasting dinner turns out to be old Fred, etc. A cute variation that we ran at *Twilight Zone*, D. J. Pass's "Anniversary Dinner," had a couple of sweet senior citizens boiling a stoned-out-of-her-gourd young hippie in their hot tub.

19. **Yankee, Go Home!**—Modern-day urban paranoia. Visiting a sinister, isolated community—often, but not necessarily, a small Southern town—a traveler discovers that, despite the locals' sleepy rustic smiles, some terrible rite is about to be enacted. Sometimes this turns out to be a variation on #18 (as in Richard Matheson's "The Children of Noah," a nasty bit of sadism set in coastal Maine), but it can also be a satanic mass (as in Algernon Blackwood's "Ancient Sorceries," in which a charming French hamlet is populated by witches with a penchant for turning themselves into cats) or some sort of age-old pagan sac-

rifice (as in the film *The Wicker Man*, set on an isolated Scottish island). Grossest example: the exploitation film *Two Thousand Maniacs!*, in which, as a sort of gory centennial, a resurrected town in Dixie slaughters several Yankee tourists in vengeance for the Civil War.

20. **The Jaws of Sex**—Still more paranoia. The hero or heroine (sometimes with dishonorable intentions) meets an attractive stranger, perhaps in a bar, and anticipates a night of romance. The shock comes when they climb between the sheets: The stranger turns out to be a vampire, werewolf, alien, squid, giant spider, or gelatinous mass—all the things we've feared in a one-night stand. Most famous example: William Sansom's "A Woman Seldom Found," whose arm snakes out across the room and switches off the light. Niftiest example: "Honeymoon," by Joe R. Lansdale and Roy Fish, in which a murderer's intended prey announces before bedtime that she's going to "change into something more comfortable"—and reappears as a werewolf.

21. **Gotcha!**—Stories that end with "And then the great jaws opened," "And then it sprang," "And then it was upon him," or "He had time for one final scream." Cf. William Tenn's classic "The Human Angle": "Because her teeth were in his throat." Shirley Jackson's "The Lottery"—a memorable variation on type #19—ends just as bleakly: "'It isn't fair, it isn't right,' Mrs. Hutchinson screamed, and then they were upon her." Often the ending is a moral one: Mass murderer gets comeuppance when seemingly helpless victim turns out to be a monster (see #20, above).

22. **The Punch Line**—Beloved by Robert Bloch, this type of story carries a gruesome pun at the end. (The last line, as you might expect, is usually written first.) Examples: Bloch's "Catnip"

("Cat got your tongue?") and "The Night Before Christmas" ("Louise was decorating the Christmas tree"—with her organs festooned among the branches). Cf. lots of Fredric Brown short-shorts.

23. **It Was Only a Dream**—Believe it or not, this one wasn't retired with *Alice in Wonderland*. Variations are still being dreamed up. The most popular of them deserves a title of its own: I *Thought* It Was Only a Dream—But It Turned Out to Be All Too Real!

Most Familiar Horror Plot #22, "The Punch Line" (Illustration by Peter Kuper, used by permission)

24. **Trick or Treat!**—Costumed Halloween celebrants turn out to be monsters, aliens, ghouls, dead kids, etc. Sometimes they take revenge on a child-killer, the sort who'd hide razor blades in apples. Cf. variations by Ray Bradbury.

25. **Ho Ho Ho!**—A UFO sighted over the North Pole in late December is taken for a Russian sneak attack—but it turns out to be Guess Who. Commonly submitted in winter. Most frequent ending: "Merry Christmas to all, and to all a good night!"

—Originally appeared in a slightly different form in Raising Goosebumps for Fun and Profit (Footsteps Press, 1989), reprinted by permission of the author

1. "The hammering and the voices and the barking dog grew fainter, and 'Oh, god,' he thought, 'what a bloody silly way to die . . .' "

   —"Don't Look Now" by Daphne du Maurier

2. " 'You won't know till afterward,' she said. 'You won't know till long, long afterward.' "

   —"Afterward" by Edith Wharton

3. "Shiloh doesn't care."

   —*Red Dragon* by Thomas Harris

4. "I am legend."

   —*I Am Legend* by Richard Matheson

5. "Entertainment for the penguins."

   —*Flicker* by Theodore Roszak

6. "When Marge arrived tonight, she would watch over Dunlap while the one-armed man and the son in need of a father would ride out to check the steers, and in the meantime, Slaughter leaned back, smiling, as the setting sun cast an alpenglow on Lucas who rode straight and strong, and a colt veered from its mother, and they gamboled in the sun."

   —*The Totem* by David Morrell

7. "His unending fury."

   —*Christine* by Stephen King

8. "I have never, for one instant of her life, wished her harm."

   —*The Lizard's Tail* by Marc Brandel

9. " 'It isn't fair, it isn't right,' Mrs. Hutchinson screamed, and then they were upon her."

   —"The Lottery" by Shirley Jackson

10. " 'I'll let you know immediately I get out of the wood,' she promised. 'It's one of those things you have to live through until you emerge the other side.' "

    —"Into the Wood" by Robert Aickman

11. "Well—that paper wasn't a photograph of any background, after all. What it shewed was simply the monstrous being he was painting on that awful canvas. It was the model he was using—and its background was merely the wall of the cellar studio in minute detail. But by God, Eliot, *it was a photograph from life.*"

    —"Pickman's Model" by H. P. Lovecraft

12. "All of them had his face."

    —"Sandkings" by George R. R. Martin

13. "Roger tried to scream but his mouth and lungs were full of filth."

    —"The Bushmaster" by Conrad Hill

14. "God help me, it's the doorbell."

    —"But At My Back I Always Hear" by David Morrell

15. "Then the beautiful house was no longer quiet, for there rang a bright freezing scream of laughter, the perfect sound to accompany a passing anecdote of some obscure hell."

    —"The Frolic" by Thomas Ligotti

16. "And let God sort it out."

   —*The Scream* by John Skipp and Craig Spector

17. "It was not until they had examined the rings that they recognized who it was."

   —*The Picture of Dorian Gray* by Oscar Wilde

18. "It is no ordinary skeleton."

   —*The Phantom of the Opera* by Gaston Leroux

19. "I have no mouth. And I must scream."

   —"I Have No Mouth, and I Must Scream" by Harlan Ellison

20. "Someone has already taken out a Minolta cellular phone and called for a car, and then, when I'm not really listening, watching instead someone who looked remarkably like Marcus Halberstam paying a check, someone asks, simply, not in relation to anything, '*Why?*' and though I'm very proud that I have cold blood and that I can keep my nerve and do what I'm supposed to do, I catch something, then realize it: *Why?* and automatically answering, out of the blue, for no reason, just opening my mouth, words coming out, summarizing for the idiots: 'Well, though I know I should have done *that* instead of not doing it, I'm twenty-seven for Christ sakes and this is, uh, how life presents itself in a bar or in a club in New York, maybe *anywhere*, at the end of the century and how people, you know, *me*, behave, and this is what being *Pat*rick means to me, I guess, so, well, yup, uh . . .' and this is followed by a sigh, and above one of the doors covered by red velvet drapes in Harry's is a sign and on the sign in letters that match the drapes' color are the words THIS IS NOT AN EXIT."

   —*American Psycho* by Bret Easton Ellis

   —*Compiled by S.B. and A.W.*

CHAPTER 3

"They Did the Monster Mash . . ."

A LITTLE NIGHTMARE MUSIC

EIGHT HORROR NOTABLES WHO HAVE DIRECTED MUSIC VIDEOS

1. John Skipp (author of *The Long Last Call* and coauthor of *The Light at the End*)
   "The Disappearing Heart"—Also
2. E. Elias Merhige (director of *Begotten* and *Shadow of the Vampire*)
   "Anti-Christ Superstar"—Marilyn Manson
   "Cryptorchid"—Marilyn Manson
   "Serpentia"—Glenn Danzig
3. John Landis (director of *An American Werewolf in London*)
   "Thriller"—Michael Jackson
4. George A. Romero (director of *Night of the Living Dead* and *Martin*)
   "Kick It"—Peaches featuring Iggy Pop
5. Jim Van Bebber (director of *The Manson Family*)
   "They Dwell Beneath"—Necrophagia
6. Jörg Buttgereit (director of *Nekromantik* and *Schramm*)
   "Die Neue Zeit"—Mutter
   "Rise Up"—Die Krupps

7. **Richard Stanley (director of *Hardware* and *Dust Devil*)**
    - "The Body"—Public Image Ltd.
    - "Preacher Man"—Fields of the Nephilim
    - "Blue Water"—Fields of the Nephilim
8. **Donald Cammell (codirector of *Performance* and director of *White of the Eye*)**
    - "Pride (In the Name of Love)"—U2
    - "All You Zombies"—The Hooters

—Compiled by S.B.

DAVID T. WILBANKS'S TEN FAVORITE DARK WORKS OF CLASSICAL MUSIC

When he's not working his day job or listening to loads of music, David T. Wilbanks writes. He is the author of many nonfiction articles and short stories for various horror publications, has coedited the acclaimed small press anthology Damned Nation, *and is the co-author, with Mark Justice, of* Dead Earth: The Green Dawn, *a dark science fiction novella available from PS Publishing. Check out his Web site for more news at www.davidtwilbanks.com.*

1. **"Night on Bald Mountain," by Modest Mussorgsky:** A powerful tone poem depicting a witches' sabbath. The Disney film *Fantasia* is one place to make its acquaintance.
2. **"In the Hall of the Mountain King," from *Peer Gynt* by Edvard Grieg:** This music, written for the play, lives up to its title—complete with trolls.
3. **"Der Doppelganger," from the lieder cycle *Schwanengesang* by Franz Schubert:** A man sees his tormented self outside the house of a lost love. A tragic song.

4. *Dracula,* by Phillip Feeney: This is music to a ballet about Stoker's legendary creation. Put this on and enjoy the creepy atmosphere.

5. "The Isle of the Dead," by Sergei Rachmaninoff: Another tone poem, this one based on the bleak painting by Swiss artist Arnold Böcklin.

6. "Danse Macabre," by Camille Saint-Saëns: This famous work portrays dancing Halloween skeletons with Death itself playing a tune on the violin.

7. "Atmospheres," by György Ligeti: Used to great effect in the film *2001: A Space Odyssey.* If you like this, Ligeti has much more to offer for those with a taste for the bizarre.

8. Nocturne in F Minor, op. 55, no. 1, by Frédéric Chopin: A moonlit walk along a wet sidewalk with a bit of adventure along the way? Perhaps only in *my* mind. A haunting night piece by this sensitive composer.

9. "The Crusaders in Pskov," from the *Alexander Nevsky Cantata* by Sergei Prokofiev: We're not in *Peter and the Wolf* territory here. German invaders. Executions by fire. This is definitely not for the meek. The music was composed for the Sergei Eisenstein film.

10. The "Dies Irae" from Giuseppe Verdi's *Requiem*: A terrifying piece for when you're in the mood for something nearly overwhelming.

KIM NEWMAN'S TWENTY GREAT
HORROR MOVIE THEME SONGS

Kim Newman is a novelist, critic, and broadcaster. His fiction includes Anno Dracula, Life's Lottery, *and* The Man From the Diogenes Club. *His nonfiction includes* Nightmare Movies, Horror: 100 Best Books, *and* Horror: Another 100 Best Books *(both with*

Stephen Jones), and BFI Classics studies of Cat People *and* Doctor Who. *He is a contributing editor to* Sight & Sound *and* Empire. *Newman also wrote and directed the short film* Missing Girl *(available online at www.johnnyalucard.com/missinggirl.html), and has written radio and TV documentaries (BBC Radio 4's* Dicing With Dragons; Time Shift: A Study in Sherlock*). His radio work includes a play for BBC Online (*Mildew Manor*). His Web site is www .johnnyalucard.com.*

1. **"Attack of the Killer Tomatoes," written by John De Bello, performed by Lewis Lee for *Attack of the Killer Tomatoes* (1980).** An ominous march with strangled vocals, and even more strangled rhymes: "I know I'm going to miss her/a tomato ate my sister!"

2. **"Ben's Song," written by Walter Scharf and Don Black, performed by Michael Jackson for *Ben* (1972).** Not the least annoying aspect of the squeaky theme to this rat-movie sequel to *Willard* is that Jackson pronounces it "Bin." Horrible as it seems, it was a hit.

3. **"Black Leather Rock," written by James Bernard and Joseph Losey, for *The Damned* (1963).** Most obnoxious catchy chorus in pre-punk pop: "black leather black leather smash smash smash black leather black leather crash crash crash black leather black leather kill kill kill got that feeling black leather rock."

4. **"The Blob," written by Burt Bacharach and Hal David, performed by the Five Blobs (actually Bernie Nee) for *The Blob* (1958).** Probably the catchiest monster theme song, and an early work by authentic lounge geniuses. The semi-camp song must have been an afterthought, because the film itself is rather straight-faced.

5. **"Burke and Hare," written by Roger Webb and Norman Newell, performed by the Scaffold for *Burke and Hare* (1971).** The 1960s novelty

hit-makers ("Lily the Pink") applied their sleazily jolly Liverpudlian style to a narrative song about the body-snatching team. Cheery refrain: "Burke and 'Are, beware of 'em/Burke and 'Are, the pair of 'em."

6. "Carry on Screaming," written by Myles Rudge and Ted Dick, performed by Jim Dale (allegedly) for *Carry On Screaming* (1966).

7. "Ghostbusters," written and performed by Ray Parker Jr. for *Ghostbusters* (1984). The real justification for this record was to prevent "Ben's Song" from being the biggest chart hit on this list.

8. "Green Slime," written by Sherry Gaden, performed by the Green Slime for *The Green Slime* (1969). "People have looked into space with wonder/for thousands of years/wondering if life could be somewhere/and now it's here!" And now join in on the chorus, "Greeeeen Sliiimee, ooo-ooo-oooh, Green Slime!"

9. "Hush . . . Hush, Sweet Charlotte," written by Frank DeVol and Mack David, performed by Al Martino for *Hush . . . Hush, Sweet Charlotte* (1964).

10. "He's Back (The Man Behind the Mask)," written and performed by Alice Cooper for *Friday the 13th, Part VI: Jason Lives* (1987). If Wayne and Garth had heard this, they'd have greeted Alice with, "We're much worthier than you."

11. "Look for a Star," written by Mark Anthony and performed by Gary Miller during the high-wire act in *Circus of Horrors* (1960).

12. "Love Song for a Vampire (Theme from *Bram Stoker's Dracula*)," written and performed by Annie Lennox for *Bram Stoker's Dracula* (1992). Like most modern theme songs, this was playing over the special effects technician credits after you left the theatre.

13. "Paper Angel," sung by the Black Whole, in *Lemora: A Child's Tale of the Supernatural* (1973).

14. "Putting Out the Fire with Gasoline (Theme from *Cat People*)," written and performed by David Bowie for *Cat People* (1982).

15. "Save the Earth," written by Riichiro Manabe and Adryan Russ, for *Godzilla vs. the Smog Monster* (1971). An afterthought in the dubbing, this has the immortal verse "Save the Earth, save the Earth/There's one solution/Stop the pollution." Musically, a lot less pleasant than "Mosura-Yi," the *Mothra* theme written by Yuji Koseki and sung by the Peanuts.

16. "Scream and Scream Again," written by Dominic King and Tim Hayes, performed by the Amen Corner for *Scream and Scream Again* (1969). A rare use of a theme for scare purposes as the film cuts from Yutte Stensengaard about to be tortured to the Amen Corner belting out the screaming song in a club.

17. "Stay Forever My Love," presumably by Orville Stoeber, from *Let's Scare Jessica to Death* (1971). A genuinely creepy and oddly memorable ballad.

18. "Strange Love," written by Harry Robinson and Frank Godwin, performed by "Tracy" for *Lust for a Vampire* (1970). Excruciating. On the whole, I'd rather listen to that theme song from *The Lost Continent*.

19. "Yee-Hah, the South's Gonna Rise Again," written by H. G. Lewis, performed by the Pleasant Valley Boys for *Two Thousand Maniacs!* (1964). Well, it is the best thing about the film. Johnny Legend has cut a fun cover version.

20. "You've Got to Have Ee-ooo," written by Skip Redwine and Paul Dunlap, performed by John Ashley for *How to Make a Monster* (1958). Marginally more memorable than the songs from *I Was a Teenage Werewolf* ("Eenie Meenie Miney Moe"), *Eeegah!* ("Nobody Lives on the Brownsville Road"), and *Horror of Party Beach* ("The Zombie Stomp")—and let's not get into *Hillbillies in a Haunted House* and *The Incredibly Strange Creatures* ("the first monster musical!"), etc.

KARIM HUSSAIN'S TOP TEN HORROR MOVIE SOUNDTRACKS

Karim Hussain is the cowriter of Nacho Cerdá's The Abandoned *(2006), and the director of* Subconscious Cruelty *(2000). He wrote, directed, and photographed the art-house genre film* Ascension *(2003), which won the New Visions Award at the 2003 Sitges Film Festival in Spain. He also codirected, cowrote, and photographed the short film* La Deniére Voix *in 2002, which was nominated for a Jutra (Quebec Academy Award) for Best Short.* La Belle bête *(2006), his third feature as director/producer/cinematographer, premiered at Sitges and played numerous other film festivals, including Mar Del Plata, Fantasporto, and Austin Fantastic Fest. From 1997 to 2001, he was a programmer for the Fantasia Film Festival in Montreal.*

1. *Suspiria* (Goblin with Dario Argento)
2. *Angst* (Klaus Schulze)
3. *Prince of Darkness* (John Carpenter)
4. *Near Dark* (Tangerine Dream)
5. *Day of the Dead* (John Harrison)
6. *In a Glass Cage (Tras El Cristal)* (Javier Navarrete)

7. *The Beyond* (Fabio Frizzi)
8. *Dust Devil* (Simon Boswell)
9. *Full Circle* (Colin Towns)
10. *Tetsuo: The Iron Man* (Chu Ishikawa)

BRYAN SMITH'S TOP TEN HORROR-THEMED ROCK 'N' ROLL SONGS

Bryan Smith is the author of the horror novels House of Blood, Deathbringer, The Freakshow, *and* Queen of Blood *(all published by Leisure). He lives in Nashville with his wife, and likes loud rock 'n' roll and dark beer. More information can be found at his official Web site www.bryansmith.info.*

1. "TV Set" by the Cramps
2. "I Walked With a Zombie" by Wednesday 13
3. "Now I'm Feeling Zombified" by Alien Sex Fiend
4. "Braineaters" by the Misfits
5. "Release the Bats" by the Birthday Party
6. "I Love the Dead" by Alice Cooper
7. "I Eat the Living" by the Creeping Cruds
8. "Don't Shake Me Lucifer" by Roky Erickson and the Aliens
9. "Bela Lugosi's Dead" by Bauhaus
10. "The Ripper" by Judas Priest

CORALINA CATALDI-TASSONI'S TEN FAVORITE TRAGICALLY ROMANTIC HEROINE DEATHS IN OPERA

Coralina Cataldi-Tassoni made her first opera appearance at the age of 3 in Puccini's La Bohème. *She was born in Manhattan and sailed to Italy at age of 5 with her opera-stage-director father and mezzo-soprano mother. From there, she went on to work in opera houses around the world. Thanks to a bizarre set of circumstances, she encountered Dario Argento, becoming his murder muse in various films, and presented with Argento a popular Italian television series called* Giallo. *In her films with Argento, she was cut open with scissors as Giulia in* Opera, *strangled by her own intestines in* Mother of Tears, *and spared, just by chance, in* Phantom of the Opera. *Lamberto Bava blinded and impaled her as Sally in* Demons 2, *and she also appeared in movies directed by Pupi Avati, Luciano Odorisio, and many more. Coralina's love for the arts spreads to her mystical paintings and music. She recently released her debut CD,* Limbo Balloon, *and has had solo and group art exhibits in New York City, Chicago, and Rome.*

1. **Crushed to Death—*Salome* (Richard Strauss):** Salome lap-dances for the head of John the Baptist, then tongue-kisses the saint's decapitated head. Revolted, her stepfather Herod orders his soldiers to crush her under their shields.

2. **Dismembered by Mad Scientist—*Tales of Hoffman* (Jacques Offenbach):** At the height of her simulated passion, robot lover Olympia is destroyed by her vengeful creator Coppellius.

3. **Buried Alive—*Aïda* (Guiseppe Verdi):** Aïda sneaks into an Egyptian tomb to be buried alive with her lover Radamès.

4. **Guillotine Decapitation—*Dialogues of the Carmelites (Les Dialogues des Carmélites)* (Francis Poulenc):** Kill-crazed revolutionaries execute an entire convent full of nuns.

5. **Human Sacrifice—*Norma* (Vincenzo Bellini):** Druid priestess Norma and her Roman lover Pollione are burned alive when she violates her sacred vows of virginity.

6. **Suicide from High Balcony—*Tosca* (Giacomo Puccini):** Opera singer Tosca leaps to her death after killing the secret policeman who tortured and executed her lover.

7. **Strangulation—*Otello* (Guiseppe Verdi):** Tricked by scheming Iago, jealous Otello strangles his innocent wife Desdemona with her own hair.

8. **Death by Clown—*I Pagliacci* (Ruggiero Leoncavallo):** Snuff, opera-style. Tormented clown Pagliacci kills his unfaithful wife Nedda on stage, while the audience thinks it is part of the play.

9. **Accidental Assassination—*Rigoletto* (Guiseppe Verdi):** Hunchback court jester Rigoletto hires an assassin to kill the Duke who seduced his daughter Gilda, but the assassin accidentally kills Gilda instead.

   And finally, in true operatic style, anything worth doing is worth over-doing. . .

10. **You Only Die Twice—*L'Orfeo* (Claudio Monteverdi):** Eurydice gets to die twice in this opera! Once, when she is bitten by a poisonous snake on her wedding day, and again when her groom Orpheus fails to rescue her from Hades.

S. P. SOMTOW'S TOP TEN GRUESOME OPERATIC DEATHS

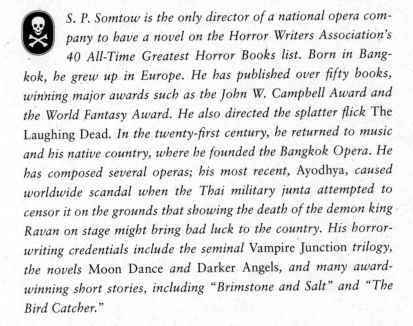

S. P. Somtow is the only director of a national opera company to have a novel on the Horror Writers Association's 40 All-Time Greatest Horror Books list. Born in Bangkok, he grew up in Europe. He has published over fifty books, winning major awards such as the John W. Campbell Award and the World Fantasy Award. He also directed the splatter flick The Laughing Dead. *In the twenty-first century, he returned to music and his native country, where he founded the Bangkok Opera. He has composed several operas; his most recent,* Ayodhya, *caused worldwide scandal when the Thai military junta attempted to censor it on the grounds that showing the death of the demon king Ravan on stage might bring bad luck to the country. His horror-writing credentials include the seminal* Vampire Junction *trilogy, the novels* Moon Dance *and* Darker Angels, *and many award-winning short stories, including "Brimstone and Salt" and "The Bird Catcher."*

1. In *Dialogues of the Carmelites (Les Dialogues des Carmélites)*, by Francis Poulenc, an entire convent of nuns is decapitated. They line up meekly for the guillotine and all go out soulfully singing. It's quite charming . . . a sort of macabre campfire girls outing.

2. In *Aïda*, by Giuseppe Verdi, the hero, Radamès, is walled up alive underneath the Temple of Ptah. His girlfriend, the beautiful slave-girl Aïda, somehow manages to have sneaked inside this living tomb as well—blame the poor security—and they sing a touching duet as the oxygen runs out.

3. In *Lulu*, by Alban Berg, the heroine is hacked up by celebrity serial killer Jack the Ripper while moonlighting as a prostitute in London. It's her comeuppance for having somehow caused all her previous husbands to die horribly. Her corpse is discovered by her lesbian sidekick, the Countess Geschwitz.

4. Well, you can't blame me for including this, but in my own opera *Mae Naak*, the heroine, Naak, who happens to be dead, takes revenge on the midwife whose negligence caused her death by reaching into her belly and pulling out her intestines (while singing an aria). Malpractice insurance could have solved this. (In another scene, she also rips off someone's head.)

5. In Richard Wagner's *Götterdämmerung*, our heroine, the Valkyrie Brünnhilde, sets herself and her horse on fire while singing an eighteen-minute aria. The fire gets out of hand and accidentally consumes the entire earth, as well as spreading up to the sky and burning up Valhalla and all the Gods. Luckily, the River Rhine overflows its banks and puts out the flames, but meanwhile, everyone on earth has perished. Only the three Rhinemaidens remain, presumably because they know how to breathe underwater.

6. In Meyerbeer's *Les Huguenots*, the entire cast, after five acts of emotionally wrenching love triangles, betrayals, religious conversions, and heroic displays of honor, are savagely butchered by a bunch of marauding soldiers.

7. In Hans Werner Henze's *Bassarids*, King Pentheus is talked into cross-dressing by the God Dionysus. He is then dismembered by a gang of crazed women, including his own mother. This Oedipal-cross-dressing-slasher theme puts our hero in the noble company of Norman Bates.

8. In Mozart's *Don Giovanni*, a statue doesn't just come to life—it comes to dinner. It doesn't eat much, but sings up a storm as it drags the unrepentant rake off to hell.

9. In Puccini's *Tosca*, the heroine leaps off the parapet of the Castel Sant'Angelo and is supposed to drown in the Tiber. This would not be so gruesome except that it has been scientifically computed, from the angle, distance of the walls from the river, terminal velocity, trajectory, and so on, that the correct sound effect should be *splat* rather than *splash*.

10. In *Bluebeard's Castle*, by Béla Bartók, the heroine's punishment for being too inquisitive about her new husband's past is to be locked into a room with all his former wives. The kicker is that they haven't been brutally murdered. They're all *alive* inside that room—*for all eternity*. I shouldn't include this as a gruesome operatic death, strictly speaking, but this fate actually *is* worse than death. Presumably, eventually, the ladies do die . . . of boredom.

CHAPTER 4

"And He Answered, 'Legion . . .' "

A MISCELLANY OF TERRORS

CHRISTOPHER GOLDEN'S TEN FAVORITE
SUPERNATURAL TV SERIES

Christopher Golden is the author of such novels as The Myth Hunt-ers, Wildwood Road, The Boys Are Back in Town, The Ferryman, *and* Of Saints and Shadows. *Golden cowrote the lavishly illustrated novel* Baltimore or, The Steadfast Tin Soldier and the Vampire *with Mike Mignola, which they are currently scripting as a feature film for New Regency. He has also written books for teens and young adults, including the thriller series* Body of Evidence, *honored by the New York Public Library and chosen as one of Young Adult Library Services Association's Best Books for Young Readers. With Thomas E. Sniegoski, he is the coauthor of the young readers' fantasy series* OutCast *and the comic-book miniseries* Talent, *both of which were recently acquired by Universal Pictures. Golden was born and raised in Massachusetts, where he still lives with his family. His work has been translated into more than a dozen languages around the world. Please visit him at www.christophergolden.com.*

1. *The Twilight Zone*: Rod Serling's classic anthology series combined the supernatural, science fiction, and social commentary in five seasons of one of the greatest television shows of all time. Many of its episodes are among the finest programs to ever grace the small screen. The 1980s update gets an honorable mention for a handful of stunning hours, some of which held up to the best of the originals.

2. *Kolchak—The Night Stalker*: Darren McGavin was utterly convincing as the curmudgeonly reporter who stumbled upon chilling supernatural mysteries week after week. Though it lasted only one season, the series was an inspiration to writers of novels, films, and television, including *The X-Files* creator Chris Carter.

3. *Buffy the Vampire Slayer*: Joss Whedon's landmark series brought a new wave of female empowerment to television, added a whole new cadence to American language, and became a worldwide phenomenon, despite being seen by only five or six million people per week in the U.S. It offered monsters that mirrored the troubles of teenage experience and characters whose relationships were the source of boundless passion on the part of the series' faithful.

4. *Twin Peaks*: David Lynch's ingenious series had one of the most wonderfully creepy first episodes in the history of television, and was layered with murder and magic. Its weirdness gave rise to one of the earliest Internet fan communities. Unfortunately, it fell apart in season two, spinning away into oblique surrealism.

5. *The X-Files*: Chris Carter promised us that the truth was out there, and that one day everything would be explained. Sadly, it turned out that the producers of the show had no more idea how it all fit together than the viewers did. When Mulder and Scully were on,

however, and particularly in the supernatural-based episodes, *The X-Files* was riveting.

6. *Bewitched*: This charming comedy about a hapless advertising executive married to a witch may be here simply because the nine-year-old in me will always be in love with Elizabeth Montgomery as Samantha. Or perhaps it really was as wonderful as I remember it.

7. *Angel*: Joss Whedon's *Buffy the Vampire Slayer* spin-off was a gem all its own, beginning as a hard-boiled detective series about a vampire attempting to redeem his soul, morphing into a show about a law firm whose clients are all monsters—human and otherwise, and finally becoming a show about a motley group of troubled people who are the only chance the world has against cosmic evil. Its final episode may have been its very best. There's nothing like going out on top.

8. *Miracles*: This short-lived series starred Skeet Ulrich as a Vatican expert on the supernatural, and lasted only half a dozen episodes (seven additional episodes are available on the DVD edition), but each one is a breathtaking masterpiece. Wonderful television series are canceled all the time, but few leave the kind of impression that *Miracles* did.

9. *Carnivale*: HBO's tale of a dustbowl-era conflict between good and evil—with a righteous minister becoming the tool of evil and a troubled carnival worker given a divine touch—was unsettling, terrifying, and beautifully crafted. It was also unique in the history of television.

10. *The Outer Limits, Boris Karloff's Thriller, Night Gallery*, and *Tales from the Darkside*: While none can compare to *The Twilight Zone*,

each of these wonderful anthology series produced some extraordinary supernatural television, episodes that were harrowing originals, as well as some adapted from the works of classic
horror, fantasy, and science fiction writers.

—*Originally appeared in* The New Book of Lists
by David Wallechinsky and Amy Wallace (2005)

SCOTT HEIM'S TEN CREEPIEST MADE-FOR-TV MOVIES (OR TV SERIES EPISODES)

Scott Heim is the author of the novels We Disappear, In Awe,
and Mysterious Skin *(which was made into an acclaimed 2005
film by Gregg Araki). Originally from Hutchinson, Kansas,
he now lives in Boston. His Web site and blog can be found at
www.scottheim.com.*

1. *Don't Be Afraid of the Dark* (directed by John Newland, 1973): Sally,
   played by Kim Darby, inherits a Victorian mansion. When she
   and her husband decide to open a sealed basement fireplace, a
   freaky tribe of tiny murmuring creatures with furrowed blue
   faces begins stalking her. The scene where they invade Sally's
   dinner party is truly terrifying.

2. *Bad Ronald* (directed by Buzz Kulik, 1974): A couple of years before
   he starred in *The Little Girl Who Lives Down the Lane,* the
   excellent Scott Jacoby played the title role in this film based on
   a now rare book by Jack Nance. When teenage Ronald accidentally kills a neighborhood girl, his ailing mother hides him
   behind the walls of the house. But soon, Mom dies, and a new

family moves in. Increasingly kooky Ronald begins to spy on the new family through the tiny peepholes he's drilled in the walls.

3. The "Screamer" episode of *Thriller* (directed by Shaun O'Riordan, 1974): "Screamer" was the most chilling episode from this British series that ran from 1973 to 1976 and was occasionally shown on late-night American TV. It starred scream queen Pamela Franklin (who also starred in *The Innocents* and *The Legend of Hell House*). An American girl, vacationing in the British countryside, is raped and nearly murdered. Later, she exacts revenge on her attacker—only to see his face in nearly every man she encounters.

4. *Trilogy of Terror* (directed by Dan Curtis, 1975): This is perhaps the obvious choice for this list; anyone who sees it won't forget it. Karen Black played the lead role in three connected stories, but it was only the final third, written by Richard Matheson, that packed the punch. In that segment, titled "Amelia," a crazed Zuni fetish doll with razor-sharp teeth comes to life and terrorizes poor Karen in her apartment.

5. *Vegetable Soup* (various episodes, various directors, 1975–1978): This wasn't a horror film; it was merely a PBS kids' series. But certain things about it were (unintentionally?) nightmarish. At the beginning of most episodes was a strange puppet fantasy sketch called "Outerscope One," wherein a group of children crash-land on various planets, including a frightening germ-free world called Sani-Land (which is ruled by the twitching, brush-bodied King Scrub and Queen Polish). Everything about this show—the misshapen, expressionless puppets with large, swiftly moving hands . . . the warped-sounding voices . . . the acid-trippy quality of the sets—produced much more childhood horror than entertainment.

6. *Force of Evil* (directed by Richard Lang, 1977): This film was originally shown as the Quinn Martin–produced *Tales of the Unexpected*. It was narrated with typical solemnity by William "Cannon" Conrad, and it starred Lloyd Bridges, Pat Crowley, and Eve Plumb (only a few years after she was Jan Brady). The plot was lifted from *Cape Fear*, but this version is much scarier, and it predated the "killer who won't stay dead" premises of *Halloween* and *Friday the 13th* by a few years.

7. *'Salem's Lot* (directed by Tobe Hooper, 1979): One of the best adaptations of a Stephen King novel was made for television. Tobe Hooper, five years after *The Texas Chainsaw Massacre*, directed this mini-series. It starred *Starsky & Hutch*'s David Soul and *James at 15*'s Lance Kerwin. The movie contains some truly unforgettable images, namely the grinning, floating, gray-faced child knock-knocking at the bedroom window, and bald, razor-fanged Reggie Nalder as the lead vampire.

8. *Dark Night of the Scarecrow* (directed by Frank De Felitta, 1981): Bubba, a mentally retarded man, is wrongly accused of attacking a girl. A town's vigilante mob (including Charles Durning) searches him out, ultimately finding him disguised as a scarecrow in a field. The vigilantes torture and kill the innocent Bubba. But soon after, one by one, they are terrorized by a scarecrow that mysteriously appears in their pastures and fields . . .

9. *Twin Peaks* (Season 2, Episode 7: "Lonely Souls," directed by David Lynch, 1990): *Twin Peaks* had many eerie or downright terrifying moments, especially in its first season. But the last seven minutes of this episode, wherein "Killer Bob" is finally revealed, are among the most horrifying and disturbing ever shown on prime-time TV. And Sheryl Lee screams better than anyone else.

10. *The X-Files* (Season 4, Episode 2: "Home," directed by Kim Manners, 1996): Agents Mulder and Scully investigate tiny Home, Pennsylvania, where the remains of a deformed infant have been found partially buried. They soon discover a very creepy house, an even creepier inbred family, and something unspeakable under the bed. Fox gave this episode a parental warning when it was aired, and looking back, it's easy to see why.

FIVE THINGS BANNED BY THE COMICS CODE AUTHORITY

The Comics Code Authority (CCA) was instituted by the Comics Magazine Association of America in 1954 due to public concern (fueled by Dr. Fredric Wertham's book Seduction of the Innocent*) about graphically violent and sexually suggestive material in comic books, particularly the popular EC horror comics of the day. Although the CCA had no legal authority over publishers, most distributors would not carry publications that did not come with the CCA seal of approval. The following are some of the restrictions initially imposed by the CCA on comic book publishers.*

1. The words "horror" and "terror" were not permitted in comic book titles.
2. No "scenes of horror, excessive bloodshed, gory or gruesome crimes, depravity, lust, sadism or masochism" were allowed.
3. Sympathy for criminals, "unique details" of a crime, or any treatment that tends to "create disrespect for established authority" were banned.
4. "Profanity, obscenity, smut, vulgarity, ridicule of racial or religious groups" were not allowed.

5. "All characters shall be depicted in dress reasonably acceptable to society, [with] females drawn realistically without exaggeration of any physical qualities."

—*S.B.* (*Source:* Time *magazine, November 8, 1954*)

NINE AMAZING HORROR BOARD GAMES

1. Ouija—"Mystifying Oracle" Talking Board Set

"Explore the mysteries of mental telepathy and the subconscious with this time tested favorite."

The granddaddy of spooky board games is said to date back to the late 1800s and was popularized by Parker Brothers. Its famous (and trademarked) 1901 William Fuld design has become iconic as has its elongated heart-shaped "message indicator" with its transparent dial through which numbers and letters are revealed. Users rest their fingertips lightly on the indicator which then moves from symbol to symbol spelling out words and answering "yes" or "no" to questions. The fact that the board proudly states it's been manufactured in Salem, Massachusetts (home of the infamous witch hunts), just adds to the creepiness. Regan McNeil communicates with Ol' Scratch, aka Captain Howdy, using the Ouija board in *The Exorcist*, and the talking board also inspired the underwhelming *Witchboard* films.

2. Green Ghost

"The exciting game of mystery that glows in the dark."

The first glow-in-the-dark game by Transogram Toys used both dice and a rotund ghost spinner, whose thumb pointed players (using game pieces of a cat, rat, bat, or vulture) the way around a board decorated with a plastic shipwreck, haunted house, and gnarled tree. The board rested on stilts so players' pieces could fall through traps. Keys to mysterious doors yielded prizes of bat feathers (huh?), bones, and snakes. Players also collected little baby ghosts. Awwww . . .

3. Voice of the Mummy

"Listen to my voice! Contains built in record player with changing messages that tell you your next move."

Milton Bradley's multitiered pyramid game board, elaborately decorated with Egyptian symbols around a fake-gold mummy, was a knockout of design. Playing pieces were male and female "Explorers" (archeologists, sporting pith helmets, of course) seeking to collect the most jewels and ultimately achieve a crown jewel without encountering the cobra shaped "spell." Though the game itself wasn't quite as interesting, the brittle voice emanating from a tiny record player was suitably creepy, with pronouncements such as, "The Sun God Ra stirs the wind into a sandstorm! Save yourself!" or "The unholy snakes of Amon reach from below. Move up one level."

4. Ka-bala

"The mysterious game that tells the future. Glows in the Dark. Fortune telling with tarot cards. Read what your astrological scope predicts. Ask Questions. The eye of Zohar has the answers."

In this glow-in-the-dark game from Transogram, after players rest their fingertips Ouija-style on the edge of the board, a huge glowing eyeball in the center of the luminous plastic game surface follows a black marble, rolled roulette style on a circular track, until the black orb stops on a "tarot" card, symbol, or astrological sign. The game's kitchen-sink hocus pocus made no sense, but the experience, particularly in the pitch-black closet under the staircase, was always a trip. It was, of course, impossible to read the cards drawn from the luminous board because they, alas, did not glow in the dark. The instructions were in the form of an EC-style comic strip!

5. Séance

"The Voice from the Great Beyond."

A Milton Bradley follow-up to "Voice of the Mummy" (though visually less impressive), this game substitutes a talking table (record player concealed within) and the 3-D setting of an old drawing room. Deceased Uncle Everett assigns possessions from beyond the grave to players (the greedy relatives named in the will) and once the goods are handed out, the record is flipped and value is assigned to the objects. The player with the most valuable total wins. There may be more skullduggery in Clue, but Colonel Mustard never had to deal with voices from beyond the grave!

6. Creature Features

"The Game of Horror. Starring the Greatest Movie Monsters in Film History."

Admittedly, this Athol Research Company game is a shameless rip-off of Monopoly, but if *Famous Monsters of Filmland* had ever designed a board game, this is probably what it would be like. Players roll and circle a board buying "Classic Movie Titles" ranging from actual classics like *King Kong* and *The Phantom of the Opera*, to disputable ones like *Willard, Dr. Phibes,* and *Dracula Has Risen from the Grave* (sadly, the black-and-white images rob us of seeing Christopher Lee's bloodshot red eyes). Houses and hotels are replaced by "Ghoul Star" thespian cards, adding value to productions. "Ghoul Agency," "Dead or Alive," and "Tombstone Award" help or hinder properties as players compete to be the ultimate Monster Movie producer. This mid-seventies game was made in a simpler time, when images and titles from studios were easier (and cheaper) to acquire. This game would probably cost a fortune to license these days!

7. Which Witch

"Who's going to be first to get through the haunted house and break the witch's spell?"

Milton Bradley repackaged this game as Ghost Castle and Haunted House, all using the 3-D, four-roomed board with variations on characters and design. The European versions were even more macabre, but the American version boasted rooms with names like the Bats Ballroom and Spell Cell. Players passing from room to room drew cards that turned the tide of the game. Wanda the Wicked would transform you into a mouse—freezing you on the spot. A Glenda the Good card could release you, and Ghoulish Gerty would signal a "whammy ball" dropped down the center of the game-board structure that could erupt into any room and cause damage. That was much more fun and less predictable that that silly steel ball in Mouse Trap.

8. 1313 Dead End Drive

"Can You Survive My Traps and Inherit My Millions?"

This Parker Brothers game plays like one of those *Night Gallery* episodes about greedy heirs trying to do each other in and become the surviving heir. Players conceal their identities and brave threats such as a loose boar's head, dangerous stairs, and a revolving fireplace as they try and eliminate each other in Aunt Agatha's mansion. Best of all is the suit of armor that can be toppled onto a competing player. The greedy character types hoping for a pay off include a maid, chef, doctor, tennis pro, lothario, and butler (of course). The game was repackaged as 13 Dead

End Drive, but no explanation for the mysterious dropping of the second "13" can be found.

9. Vampire Hunter

"The game that transforms right before your very eyes!! What you see in the day turns frightful at night!"

In this 2002 Milton Bradley game, male and female vampire hunter game pieces (looking more like Indiana Jones and Lara Croft than Van Helsing!) gather weapons before a ghost ship patterned after the ill-fated *Demeter* (from *Dracula*) reaches the "master's tower." When the lights are doused, the glowing vampire's tower illuminating the game board transforms playing pieces: numbers change on the dice, villagers turn into werewolves, traps are revealed, and vampires appear. It ain't Green Ghost, but these days, when it comes to glow-in-the-dark games, you takes what you can gets.

—*M.B.*

STEVE NILES'S TOP TWENTY
HORROR COMIC COVERS

Named by Fangoria *magazine as one of the "13 talents who promise to keep us terrified for the next 25 years," Steve Niles wrote the groundbreaking graphic novel* 30 Days of Night, *and cowrote the screenplay for the 2007 film version. He has written comic-book adaptations of works by Harlan Ellison, Clive Barker, and Richard Matheson, and his short fiction has appeared in many anthologies. He lives in Southern California.*

1. **Black Cat Mystery #50**—This cover really set the world on fire. This cover depicting a man's face being melted off by radium is one of the most memorable and graphic from the fifties. The art is by Lee Elias, who will make more than one appearance on this list.

Black Cat Mystery #50
(Lee Elias)

2. **Tales to Astonish #34**—An almost-perfect Jack Kirby monster looms outside a man's window lulling the man to confess "Heaven Help Me it's true! There IS a Monster at my window!" Yeah, like, duh. Love that one.

3. **Creepy #86**—Come on, a robot strangling Santa Claus?! What's not to love? Cover art by Ken Kelly.

4. **Horrific #3**—Known simply as the bullet-through-the-head cover, this jarring image was illustrated by Don Heck, who went on to become one of *Iron Man*'s greatest artists.

5. **Tales to Astonish #13**—This cover, featuring "GROOT, the LIVING ROOT" is one of my all-time faves, more for its humor than its horror, but if we can't laugh at our monsters, what can we laugh at? Art by Jack Kirby.

Tales to Astonish #13
(Jack Kirby)

6. *Creepy* **#32**–Frank Frazetta paints the perfect looming monster for this legendary issue. With one image, the monster looking down over an unsuspecting village, Frazetta tells an entire story, and a terrifying one at that.

7. *The Goon* **#16**–Of the modern horror artists, Eric Powell stands alone as one of the greats, and the cover for *Goon* #16, while not his most complex work, offers a simple poked, bleeding eye image that one will never forget.

8. *Creepy* **#1**–Jack Davis provided the first cover for the maga-zine/comic series and it's still one of the best. The art shows a

group of monsters crowded around the storyteller waiting to hear another creepy tale. Great, just great.

Creepy #1
(Jack Davis)

9. *Saga of the Swamp Thing* #28— With art by Stephen Bissette and John Totleben, both at the top of their game, this image of the Swamp Thing rising from the swamp with the bones of Alex Holland is one of the best.

10. *Chamber of Chills* #24—EC who? I always loved these pre-hero horror covers. This one is pure classic, with a dead hand rising from the ground. Lee Elias at it again!

11. *The Goon* #8—Modern horror master Eric Powell hits the list again with this classic vampire image, calling to mind Morticia and Vampira. Great stuff. It's also worth noting that Powell did a run of *Swamp Thing* covers that rank among the best ever for that series.

12. *Crime Suspenstories* #22—Rendered by Johnny Craig, this image of a man holding an axe and a woman's *head* not only gave readers a heart attack, it gave Dr. Fredrick Wertham ammunition in going after horror comics as offensive material. When will they learn? In horror, offensive can be a good thing!

13. *Tales of Terror*—Thomas Ott is just plain creepy. His art is dark and

moody in a way we rarely see in comics, and *Tales of Terror* is one of his creepiest. That face haunts my nightmares. Seriously.

14. *Tomb of Terror* #15—Lee Elias strikes again with this explosive cover. Too bad it's a dude's face that's exploding. In the fifties, readers found this image disturbing, and even today it holds its own as one of the best horror comic covers of all time.

15. *Skin Deep*—This list wouldn't be complete, in my mind, without an entry from Charles Burns. No artist makes your skin crawl like he does, with his thick ink lines and bizarre characters. *Skin Deep* features what can only be described as a heartbroken homunculus, drawn as only Burns can do it.

16. *Twisted Tales* #3—Richard Corben is one of the most twisted minds in comic art, and this cover from *Twisted Tales* proves it. Again we have an artist that can tell an entire story in a single image. In this one, a terrified night watchman walks in on a T. rex after his night-night meal. It's a bloody mess, and a great horror cover!

17. *Seduction of the Innocent* #1—Not usually associated with horror comics, artist Dave Stevens knocks this one out of the park with a simple and sexy image of a witch in front of a pile of evil jack-o'-lanterns.

Seduction of the Innocent #1
(Dave Stevens)

18. **Dracula Lives #3**—This classic image of Dracula holding a woman over the edge of a gargoyle-decorated ledge was an instant classic! It was illustrated by Neal Adams, who managed to give a sinister touch to everything he did, including an *amazing* run on *Batman*.

19. **Doomed #4**—Ashley Wood returned to his *Creepy* magazine roots and created this beautiful cover depicting a woman with a gun and knife standing at a grave. At once thought-provoking and horrifying, this cover deserves a place in horror comics history.

20. **Tales of the Zombie #2**—When not painting muscle-bound men and women, Boris Vallejo would occasionally take on a gig for one of the horror comic mags, and this cover for *Tales of the Zombie*, well, rocks. A beautiful woman lies unconscious on the ground of a cemetery while the zombie battles (presumably) the men who harmed her. Another story in a single image. Classic.

SIX WORKS OF FICTIONAL HORROR
THAT FOOLED THE AUDIENCE

1. **"The Bowmen" (1914 short story by Arthur Machen):** In 1914, British and German armies fought at Mons, Belgium; shortly after, Welsh author Arthur Machen wrote and published a short story titled "The Bowmen," in which ghostly archers from the Battle of Agincourt appeared at Mons to aid British troops. In the wake of its publication in London's *Evening News*—and despite the author's protestations that the story was only a product of his imagination—numerous people came to believe that "the Angels

of Mons" (as the phantoms were dubbed) had indeed participated in the battle on the side of the British. To this day, the Angels of Mons remain part of World War I's Fortean lore.

2. *The War of the Worlds* (1938 radio broadcast by Orson Welles): October 30, 1938, is now known as "the night that panicked America," thanks to a radio broadcast presented by *wunderkind* writer/director/producer Orson Welles (three years before his groundbreaking film *Citizen Kane*). His adaptation of the classic H. G. Wells novel, presented to the radio audience as a live news broadcast, launched a wave of hysterical panic throughout the U.S. as an entirely fictitious Martian invasion commenced in the small town of Grover's Mill, New Jersey.

3. *Snuff* (1976 film by Michael and Roberta Findlay): Promoted with the immortal tagline, "A film that could only be made in South America . . . where life is CHEAP," this grindhouse classic concludes with a scene featuring the simulated murder of a film crew member (added to the movie for shock value by the film's distributor, Alan Shackleton). Upon *Snuff*'s release, fake protesters were hired to picket theaters showing the movie; shortly after, the activist group Women Against Pornography began protesting for real, helping the film to fuel countless urban legends about the existence of actual "snuff" movies.

4. *Guinea Pig—The Flower of Flesh and Blood* (1985 film by Hideshi Hino): Japan's *Guinea Pig* series is one of the most notorious works in the underground horror scene, thanks to its realistic and unapologetic presentation of torture, mutilation, and murder. In the early nineties, when horror journalist Chas. Balun presented scenes from *The Flower of Flesh and Blood* to a friend as part of a gore compilation—and the footage found its way to actor Charlie Sheen—things got serious, as the civic-minded movie

star, convinced that he had seen an actual snuff film, called the Motion Picture Association of America, who in turn called the FBI. A thorough investigation found the footage to be top-notch special effects, not ghastly murder.

5. *Ghostwatch* **(1992 television broadcast directed by Lesley Manning and written by Stephen Volk):** Broadcast by BBC One on October 31, 1992, this is one of the most notorious television productions in history, even being cited by the *British Medical Journal* as the first TV program to cause post-traumatic stress disorder in children. An apparent "reality TV" investigation of a London haunted house, its verisimilitude was helped by the participation of several real-life British television personalities playing themselves. A postmodern "sequel" short story titled "31/10" was written by Stephen Volk, published in his collection *Dark Corners*, and nominated for the 2006 Bram Stoker Award for short fiction.

6. *The Blair Witch Project* **(1999 film by Daniel Myrick and Eduardo Sanchez):** Prior to the film's release, the three lead actors—Heather Donahue, Joshua Leonard, and Michael C. Williams—were listed on the Internet Movie Database as "missing, presumed dead"; the film itself was initially promoted by its producers via the movie's Web site as found footage, causing numerous rumors to circulate in cyberspace. It was only after the massive theatrical success of *The Blair Witch Project* (and lots of talk-show and magazine appearances by its cast) that many viewers finally realized the movie was fiction; a 2000 sequel, *Book of Shadows: Blair Witch 2*, was a pointed commentary on the entire *Blair Witch* phenomenon.

—S.B.

ARMAND CONSTANTINE'S FIVE SCARIEST
HORROR VIDEO GAMES

Armand Constantine is a writer of video games, horror, and fantasy fiction. His most recent game writing projects include work on Pandemic Studios' Saboteur and Ubisoft Montreal's Far Cry 2. For details on these and other projects, please visit www.armandconstantine.com.

1. *Silent Hill*
   Konami, PlayStation, 1999
   The setup: On the way to resort town Silent Hill, Harry has a car accident and wakes up to find his wife and baby missing. He sets out to find them in a seemingly deserted town enveloped by fog.
   Particularly badass: Great use of atmosphere. Fog and snow limit vision while audio effects heighten suspense.

2. *Silent Hill 2*
   Konami, PlayStation 2 and PC, 2001
   The setup: James Sutherland has received a letter from his long-dead wife claiming she's waiting for him in Silent Hill. He sets out to find her in a town that's every bit as terrifying as the one in the last *Silent Hill* installment.
   Particularly badass: More terrifying fog and audio. And I'm serious. It's terrifying.

3. *Fatal Frame*
   Tecmo, PlayStation 2 and Xbox, 2001
   The setup: Supposedly based on a true story, the game-play follows Miku Hinasaki, a college student searching for her missing little brother. He's gone missing in the Himuro Mansion, a place believed to be steeped in blood, curses, and worse.

Particularly badass: Perhaps one of the coolest (and scariest) game weapons ever used against ghosts: a camera.

4. *Clive Barker's Undying*

Electronic Arts/DreamWorks Interactive (Aspyr/Westlake Interactive: Macintosh), PC and Mac, 2001

The setup: World War I veteran and occult investigator Patrick Galloway receives an urgent plea for help from his friend Jeremiah Covenant. Galloway travels to the Covenant estate in Ireland to stop an occult plot that was set in motion long ago.

Particularly badass: Great use of cinematic horror techniques. You'll love the mirrors. And, of course, you'll love the signature Barkeresque alternate-world landscapes.

5. *Condemned: Criminal Origins*

Sega/Monolith Productions, Xbox 360 and PC, 2005

The setup: Ethan Thomas, an FBI forensics investigator falsely accused of murder, hunts a serial killer in the midst of a broken and violent city.

Particularly badass: Dear God, brace yourself when you start seeing the mannequins . . .

MICHAEL A. ARNZEN'S TOP FIVE HORROR COLLEGES

Michael A. Arnzen was born in Amityville, New York. He is the author of the novel Grave Markings *and the poetry collection* Freakcidents, *both of which won a Bram Stoker Award. He earned yet another Stoker for his e-mail newsletter, the Goreletter, which is "rich in strange microfiction, offbeat humor, horror poetry, surprises, and tiny oddities." Find out more at www.gorelets.com.*

1. **Brown University (Providence, RI):** Welcome to Miskatonic U—for real. Brown holds the collected writings of H. P. Lovecraft—letters, manuscripts, and more than a thousand books and magazines (like a ton of *Weird Tales*)—in a special collection lurking somewhere deep in its John Hay Library. But Cthulhu isn't the only version of hell on earth. I hear they've got a great Dante collection there, too . . . and even a library of books retrieved from Adolf Hitler's secret bunker! Web site: http://dl.lib.brown.edu/libweb/index.php.

2. **Douglas Education Center (Monesson, PA):** Tom Savini—grand master of horror film special effects—runs two programs in horror movie production at this trade school, which can actually get you an associate's degree in Specialized Business. The new Digital Film Production Program has you assist on the set in the making of independent movies, and you get a laptop and digital camera when you enroll. The Special Make-Up Effects Program will not only have you casting your own molds, but also participating in actual film productions and—my favorite—working in a live haunted attraction in the Pittsburgh area every Halloween. Web site: http://www.douglas-school.com/.

3. **University of Maine (Orono, ME):** The Stephen King archives are here in the Folgler Library's Special Collections. I can think of no better library for a horror student to hang out in. Plus, you're close to Bangor, where you will find all things King. Who knows? While you're there, you might even bump into other semi-local horror authors—like Joseph Citro, T. M. Gray, Mark Edward Hall—at a bookstore (try Betts Bookstore in Bangor . . . like the archives at UM, it is a Kingdom of King). Web site: http://library.umaine.edu/speccoll/FindingAids/Kingstep1.htm.

4. **University of California, Riverside (Riverside, CA):** Horror fans shouldn't only gather on the East Coast. Plenty lurks out West. At the University of California, Riverside campus, you'll find the Eaton Center—a vast collection of books in not only science fiction, but also horror, fantasy, and utopian literature. Its proximity to Hollywood guarantees more horrors to come. While there is a smattering of other great science fiction–oriented library collections like this one out there (like James Gunn's Center for the Study of Science Fiction at University of Kansas, or the Cushing Library at Texas A&M), a name like "Eaton" sounds scarier to me . . . like something you'd munch on. Web site: http://eaton-collection.ucr.edu/.

5. **Seton Hill University (Greensburg, PA):** I am a professor with tenure here, so I'm clearly biased . . . but the reason I chose to teach at SHU to begin with was because of their openness toward genre fiction. That might explain, too, why such horror luminaries as David Morrell, Tom Monteleone, Gary A. Braunbeck, Lawrence C. Connolly, Scott Johnson, and Tim Waggonner—among others—have also taught horror writing at SHU. At Seton Hill, you can get a master's degree in Writing Popular Fiction for penning a horror novel, when you're not otherwise hunting for revenants in the recesses of this Gothic Catholic campus. Not many graduate schools will accept horror writers, let alone help them write a novel-length horror thesis for publication; Seton Hill admits them regularly, producing numerous success stories. The undergraduate curriculum also features the occasional horror literature course, in addition to other related studies of pop culture, like science fiction and fantasy, the art of film, and more. I usually teach *The Exorcist* in my Literary Criticism course for English majors. Enough said. Web site: http://fiction.setonhill.edu.

THE TRUE TALES OF FIVE
LEGENDARY TV HORROR HOSTS

The TV horror host first appeared in the fifties, when it became apparent to TV affiliates that their showings of horror and science fiction flicks could get a ratings boost by featuring a local "ghost host" to introduce the films. The idea caught on even more when, in 1957, Universal Studios created the Shock *package of classic pre–1948 horror films for sale to TV stations. The ghost host was entirely different from nationally recognized hosts like Rod Serling (*The Twilight Zone*) or Alfred Hitchcock (*Alfred Hitchcock Presents*), who not only presented their shows but also produced and oversaw the creation of the content (half-hour or hour-long dramas rather than movies) for the big TV networks. By contrast, the local horror host was a hometown or regional celeb, often topping the films they showed as the primary attraction for viewers. While video and cable largely killed the concept, their legacy is far from forgotten. In that spirit, we offer a look at a few beloved examples of the TV horror host.*

1. **"Zacherley":** Considered by many to be *the* quintessential horror host of all time, Zacherley's real name was John Zacherle. He began in Philadelphia in 1957 at WCAU-TV with a character called Roland, hosting the station's airings of the *Shock* films. He proved so popular that he was offered a job by New York's WABC-TV, because their *Shock Theater* was experiencing low ratings. He started there in September of 1958, as Zacherley (aka "The Cool Ghoul" or just plain "Zach"). In 1960, he moved to WOR-TV, where he launched a "Zacherley for President" campaign (he lost to John F. Kennedy, although one can't help but wonder how Zacherley might have handled the Cuban Missile Crisis). Zacherley also recorded a top-ten novelty hit, "Dinner with Drac," in 1958, and later in his career appeared in director

Frank Henenlotter's cult movies *Brain Damage* and *Franken-hooker*. Zacherley continues a busy schedule of convention appearances, and has an official Web site at www.zacherley.com.

2. **"Vampira":** Vampira—a slinky, pale-skinned beauty of the Morticia Addams type—was the horror host for KABC-TV in Los Angeles from 1954 to 1955. She was played by Finnish actress and dancer Maila Nurmi, who was discovered for the role at (appropriately enough) a Halloween party. Notable as one of the horror hosts to appear on TV before the release of Universal's *Shock* package, Vampira is also famous for her appearance as "the Ghoul Woman" in Ed Wood's *Plan 9 from Outer Space*. In her personal life, Nurmi was known for her friendships with many Hollywood notables of the day (she even briefly dated Orson Welles), including James Dean, who said, "I have a fairly adequate knowledge of satanic forces, and I was interested to know if this girl was obsessed with such a force." In the eighties, Nurmi unsuccessfully sued Cassandra Peterson, claiming that Peterson's Elvira character was a rip-off of Vampira. In 2006, Nurmi/Vampira was the subject of a documentary film called *Vampira: The Movie*. She died on January 10, 2008, in Los Angeles.

3. **"Ghoulardi":** Cleveland, Ohio's great horror host was Ghoulardi, played by Ernie Anderson as part-ghoul and part-beatnik. A former disc jockey, Anderson started as Ghoulardi in 1962 at WJW-TV. Featuring a stuffed pet raven named Oxnard, and a variety of silly catchphrases (like "stay sick" and "turn blue"), Ghoulardi's anarchic spirit was a big hit among the kids in Cleveland. He also wasn't shy about commenting on the films he showed, routinely labeling lesser efforts "dogs" and "bombs." Anderson-as-Ghoulardi stayed at WJW until 1966. After that, he moved to Los Angeles and became a highly paid voice-over artist

(his voice can be heard, among other places, in Steven Spielberg's *Close Encounters of the Third Kind*). Anderson died in early 1997 of cancer. One of his four children is the acclaimed writer/director Paul Thomas Anderson (*Magnolia* and *There Will Be Blood*), who named his production company "Ghoulardi Film Company" and dedicated his film *Boogie Nights* to his father's memory.

4. **"Dr. Cadaverino"**: If you lived around Milwaukee, Wisconsin, between 1964 and 1977, the place to catch horror movies was *Nightmare Theater* on WITI-TV, hosted by Dr. Cadaverino. Starting as a disfigured creep and then evolving into a macabre hipster vampire, Dr. Cadaverino was played by local TV personality Jack Du Blon. Endlessly mocking the B movies he showed, and aided by a headless sidekick named (of course) Igor, Dr. Cadaverino made a huge impression on his viewership, including a young man named John Skipp, who grew up to become one of the founders of splatterpunk fiction with novels like *The Light at the End* and *The Bridge*. Skipp states: "Dr. Cadaverino introduced me to the horror movie as both art form and object of ridicule. Therefore, he is one of the most important and formative influences in my life."

5. **"The Host"**: Known to legions of youngsters in Wichita, Kansas, as Major Astro—the host of an afternoon cartoon show that was "broadcast" from either Cape Kennedy, the cockpit of a rocket, or his moon base—Tom Leahy would don greasepaint on Friday nights and portray the Host, assisted by hunchback Rodney. The Host, with his campy, somewhat befuddled attitude, would deliver the word "horror" as "horror-ror-ror-rorror. . . ." Rodney would be played by Lee Parsons, Jim Herring, or John Salem. The duo appeared on several different area stations from 1958 to the early nineties. In its 1970s incarnation,

called *Nightmare*, the Host's ghoulish shenanigans were pitted against another station's horror offering, *Friday Night Fright*, forcing pre-VCR horror fans to make agonizing choices between dueling terrors. The Host and Rodney's ghoulish re-working of "The Night Before Christmas" is remembered by many a fan who preferred the Host's "Ghoul-tide" celebration to competing local Christmas staple "Santa Claus and Kakeman." Now in his seventies, Leahy made a recent appearance as the Host promoting a Halloween haunted house contest in Wichita.

—*S.B. and M.B.*

GARY A. BRAUNBECK'S SEVEN
DISPARATELY HORRIFIC TRIPLE FEATURES

Gary A. Braunbeck is the author of ten novels, eleven short-story collections, one non-fiction book, and has served as coeditor on two anthologies. His work has been praised as being among the most emotionally hard-hitting being written today—Publishers Weekly said, "Braunbeck's fiction stirs the mind as it chills the marrow." He has received several awards, including the Bram Stoker Award for Superior Achievement in Short Fiction, in 2003 for "Duty," and again in 2005 for "We Now Pause for Station Identification"; that same year, his novella Kiss of the Mudman *was awarded the International Horror Guild Award for Long Fiction. In 2006, his collection* Destinations Unknown *was awarded the Stoker for Superior Achievement in Fiction Collection. He lives in Columbus, Ohio, with his wife, author Lucy Snyder, and five cats who permit him to take care of them. To learn more visit: www.garybraunbeck.com.*

So, you're in the mood for a little horror one night but don't quite feel like spending the entire evening watching movies or DVDs of classic television series. What's a jaded horror fan to do?

Simple: Instead of just floundering about, choose a particular theme for the evening's fright-fest, and explore that theme through different sources that, combined, will offer a fascinating parallax view on your chosen subject. In this case, I offer you the following triple features: the first being a movie, the second being a short story or novella, and the third being a piece of music.

1. Snipers

Movie: *Targets* (1968, directed by Peter Bogdanovich)

Boris Karloff (in a superb performance) stars as aging horror-movie star Byron Orlock, who agrees to make his last public appearance at a Los Angeles drive-in, where his newest schlock-fest is premiering. Tim O'Kelly plays your typical all-American boy, a Vietnam veteran and family man, who snaps and goes on a killing spree. The two storylines converge at the movie premiere in a nerve-wracking final sequence that remains one of Bogdanovich's finest directorial achievements.

Short Story: "Cain Rose Up," by Stephen King

A stunner, this one, its power derived from purposefully *not* telling you the motivations behind the killer's actions.

Song: "Sniper," by Harry Chapin

Yes, I know—*Harry Chapin and horror?* You'd better believe it. This 10-minute masterpiece from Chapin isn't so much a song as it is a mini-opera, following the sniper in question from the start of the day until his last moments. The echoing layers of "voices" that run underneath the music throughout are chilling, Chapin's vocal performance (he plays all of the characters) is both potent and nuanced, and the song builds to a finale that is both horrifying and strangely poignant.

2. War

Movie: *Deathwatch* (2002, written and directed by Michael J. Bassett)

It's 1917, World War I, the Western Front. A handful of British soldiers are separated from their company following a hellish battle and stumble upon a seemingly abandoned, labyrinthine German trench. Taking shelter there, they soon discover a lone German soldier, who begs them to leave because something evil dwells in the shadows of the trench. What follows is an eerie, claustrophobic, and genuinely frightening descent into madness and murder, as the evil force within the trench takes possession of the soldiers one by one, forcing them to torture and kill one another. Filled with some astounding imagery, filmed with great care, *Deathwatch* is an intelligent, well-acted, surrealistic nightmare.

Novella: *Iverson's Pits*, by Dan Simmons

A brilliant story-within-a-story about a young boy who, in the summer of 1913, on the fiftieth anniversary of the battle of Gettysburg, is assigned to chaperone one of the Civil War veterans who fought there. The soldier in question tells the boy an incredible story about an area of the battlefield that literally came alive during the fight, and the dark reasons behind it. Like all Simmons's work, this novella is painstakingly researched and executed, containing a horrifying revelation and a final line that will send a trickle of ice down your spine.

Song: "War Pigs," by Black Sabbath

In 1971, parents the world over heard a sound that convinced them the mouth of Hell had just opened and spewed out a river of Satan's own spit; that sound, of course, was the opening of Sabbath's "War Pigs," the first cut on the first side of their classic second album, *Paranoid*. Instead of singing about the Vietnam War, Tony, Ozzy, Geezer, and Bill roared a powerful warning about the nuclear arms race. The lyrics are filled with unforgettable imagery that remains just as disturbing today as it was thirty-six years ago.

3. Identity

Movie: *3 Women* (1977, directed by Robert Altman)

One of the tag lines used to describe this indescribable masterpiece read: "1 woman became 2; 2 women became 3; 3 women became 1," and while it's not exactly *wrong*, it grossly oversimplifies this story about loneliness, denial of the Self, and the ultimate fragility of a human being's individual identity. Shelley Duvall, Sissy Spacek, and the late Janice Rule give rich performances as the three women in question, all of whom meet at the same emotional and psychological crossroad: Duvall, as Millie, is heartbreaking as a woman who has embraced an identity that only she can see (while others mock her behind her back); Spacek, as Pinky, is an unstable lost soul in search of an identity, and soon becomes something of a chameleon, assuming the characteristics of whomever she feels closest to at the time; and Rule, as Willie, is an enigmatic artist who is pregnant and speaks not at all until near the film's end. The scene where Willie miscarries her baby is one of the most horrifying, heart-wrenching, and mesmerizing sequences to come out of American films during the seventies; and the final scene will leave you numbed and trembling.

Short Story: "The Yellow Wallpaper," by Charlotte Perkins Gilman

A nameless narrator, suffering from what is now called postpartum depression, is taken on vacation by her physician husband, who locks her in an upstairs room of a colonial mansion and refuses to let her leave. Sinking further into depression and delusion, the narrator comes to believe that she herself has become consumed by the yellow wallpaper in the room, and, separating even more from her grasp of individual identity, vows to "free" the woman trapped there. Considered by many to be the first piece of feminist fiction, "The Yellow Wallpaper" is also a devastating study of a mind and personality that chips away before the reader's eyes, until, in the end, it shatters.

Song: "Angie Baby," by Helen Reddy

A haunting story-song of loneliness and madness about a young, friendless girl named Angie who is shut off from the outside world, taking solace in the music from her radio and the fantasy lovers who come at night to dance with her. When Angie is left alone in the house one night, a neighbor boy breaks into the house to rape her, but never gets the chance; Angie's loneliness and fantasies have achieved sentience, and what happens next is worthy of Richard Matheson and Charles Beaumont. Reddy's lilting vocals provide a chilling contrast to the darkness at the core of the song, one that serves as a perfect bridge between *3 Women* and "The Yellow Wallpaper."

4. Music

Movie: *Fingers* (1978, written and directed by James Toback)

Harvey Keitel delivers a fine performance as Jimmy Fingers, a young virtuoso pianist who also happens to work as a strong-arm collector for his mob-connected loan-shark father. Torn between his loyalty to his father, his mentally ill mother, and his desire to rise above his station in life by pursuing his dream of becoming a concert pianist, Jimmy's love of music becomes his own personal demon as the film progresses, and every time Keitel looks at the fingers on his hands, the viewer begins to fear the horrible alternatives Jimmy might be considering. (Did I forget to mention that, during all of the *Sturm und Drang*, Jimmy is preparing for an audition that could launch his career on the concert circuit?) The overripe script teeters uncomfortably close to camp melodrama, but Keitel's commanding performance—and the shocking final ten minutes—keep this film from falling into a pit of *bathos*.

Novella: *The Unfinished Music*, by Christopher Conlon

"Dolly," a music history and critical theory professor who is writing a book on Mahler's uncompleted Tenth Symphony, accepts an invitation to visit with her sister Anne during a summer sabbatical. The sisters, who have never been close, circle one another with a painful caution, neither of them wanting to address the emotional abuse they suffered as children. Anne's husband, Ben—a professor of biology at the local university—serves as a buffer between Anne and Dolly. During her first night at her sister's house, Dolly discovers a small human fetus in a jar on the floor of her closet. As this astonishing novella progresses, Mahler's unfinished symphony becomes less of an abstract metaphor and more of a sentient force as Dolly's relationship with the fetus—which appears to be slowly coming back to life—deepens. On the surface, the story appears to be about familial bonds and how isolation can fragment an individual's psyche; but look deeper, and you'll find a frightening and poignant parable about the pain, fear, and madness that is necessary to bring anything—music, art, a human life, even the reclamation of one's sanity and self-worth—into existence, and just how fragile a thing that existence can be.

Music: *Bug* (Original Film Score), by Brian Tyler

A cross between King Crimson during their *Larks' Tongues in Aspic/Starless and Bible Black* period and the more melodic, less percussion-based music of Thomas Newman, the *Bug* soundtrack is a deliberately discordant yet simultaneously elegiac mini-symphony, both electronic and acoustic, that is not only perfectly suited to the great William Friedkin film for which it was written, but echoes in certain areas the variety of tones to be found in both *Fingers* and *The Unfinished Music*. Sometimes disturbing, sometimes achingly beautiful, but always compelling, Brian Tyler's score is a shattering experience.

5. The Safety of One's Children

Movie: *The Offence* (1973, directed by Sidney Lumet)

After twenty years on the British police force, Detective Sergeant Johnson (Sean Connery) has seen too much: murders, rapes, beatings, torture, and countless other unspeakable crimes. He has seen so much that the images of these horrible crimes are all he can think about, and as a result, he's a bomb waiting to explode—and explode he does: during a long and painful interrogation of a suspected child molester (Ian Bannen), Johnson realizes that he has become as much of a monster as those he's spent decades pursuing, and when the suspected child molester forces him to admit that ". . . nothing I've done is half as terrible as the thoughts in your head," Johnson beats him to death and must face an official inquiry. Written by the late John Hopkins (based on his stage play *This Story of Yours*) and told in a nonlinear fashion, *The Offence* is an emotional and intellectual powerhouse of a film, never daring to blink when illustrating the ugliest and most brutal layers of the human animal. Connery and Bannen are electrifying, the script is literate and pulls no punches, and Lumet's direction harkens back to *Fail-Safe* in its ability to keep your stomach in knots from start to finish.

Short Story: "Finding Amy," by Stewart O'Nan

Like *The Offence*, O'Nan's tour de force of a story unfolds in a nonlinear fashion, and challenges the reader to fill in what at first appear to be blanks but are, in fact, time-shifts in the chronology of events designed to distract the reader from the ugly truth that lies at the story's center: that the people surrounding little Amy, the missing child, are more concerned about how the events are going to affect *them*, than they are about finding Amy alive. Told in an almost clinically detached manner, "Finding Amy" is a harrowing experience, ending with a final paragraph that will both chill you and punch you right in the heart.

Song: "Daddy," by Emerson, Lake & Palmer

ELP return to the softer, more understated days of their debut album with this song that unfolds as a monologue delivered by a spirit-broken father whose little girl fails to come home from school at her regular time. A search turns up her socks and shoes, and she is never seen again, but her voice, pleading, "Daddy, come take me home," echoes in the father's mind day and night. The use of a children's choir—at first a single voice, and by the end of the song many voices—adds a discomforting note of utter hopelessness that makes this song difficult to confront for a second listening.

6. Serial Killers/Mass Murderers

Movie: *The Boston Strangler* (1968, directed by Richard Fleischer)

Tony Curtis delivers a stunning, multilayered performance as Albert DeSalvo who, in the 1960s, murdered 13 women in the Boston area. Told in the style of police procedural documentary, *The Boston Strangler* has a gritty, intense tone that reaches a fever pitch by the time DeSalvo is taken into custody. Henry Fonda plays a surprisingly dislikable police detective, who tracks down DeSalvo and then must coax a confession from him. The finale—a long, suspenseful interrogation scene between Fonda and Curtis that equals Fonda's call to the Kremlin in the original *Fail-Safe* for sheer mounting tension—is a dazzling showcase for both actors, ending with a long close-up of Curtis's face frozen in an expression of madness that you won't soon forget.

Novella: *The Escape Route*, by Rod Serling

Serling never received enough credit for his prose fiction, and this feverish, crackling, morally vindictive novella proves it. Later adapted for the television movie *Night Gallery*, the novella is a tighter, more intensely focused, and blisteringly angry piece of work, following SS *Gruppenfuehrer* Joseph Strobe, now a war criminal, hiding out in Argentina. Strobe's dreams are filled with nightmare images of his being caught and brought to justice for the crimes he committed against Jews in the concentration camp he oversaw. Still convinced that he's a victim of unjustified persecution—"We were just following orders"—Strobe finds his only solace in a painting at a local museum: a fisherman out in his small boat in the middle of a still, cool lake. Strobe slowly begins to convince himself that he can *will* himself into the painting, and eventually, for one second, achieves the goal before the museum's closing bell snaps him back to reality. Soon after, he is recognized by a former inmate of the camp, who Strobe kills—but not before the man has informed the newly arrived Israeli authorities where Strobe is. The Israelis chase Strobe back to the museum, where he meets an ironic and wholly appropriate form of justice. Arguably Serling's finest achievement as a short fiction writer.

Song: "Ticking," by Elton John

The last few hours in the life of a young man who, reaching the end of his psychological rope, snaps in a diner, kills a waiter, and takes the rest of the customers hostage. Melodically lovely and lyrically horrifying, "Ticking" nearly equals Chapin's "Sniper" for its portrayal of the inner agony of a man who finally breaks and takes several people with him.

7. Second Chances

Movie: *Seconds* (1966, directed by John Frankenheimer)

Harlan Ellison once called this film ". . . one of the greatest horror movies ever made in this dimension or any other . . ." and I couldn't agree more. Based on David Ely's novel of the same name, it tells the story of a middle-aged businessman (portrayed by the great John Randolph) who has grown weary and depressed about his life. He turns to a mysterious organization that promises its clients a fresh start, a new life, a new form. It begins with the company arranging his "death," using another body with the same physical characteristics but with all fingerprints, teeth, and other identifying pieces removed—in Randolph's case, he "dies" in a hotel fire. After signing the agreement with the company, Randolph undergoes the surgery, becoming a "Second," and—in the form of Rock Hudson—prepares to start his new life. But doubts and nagging guilt about the way he ruined his former life persist, and Hudson is drawn back to his now-widowed wife to see if he can figure out where he went wrong. A devastating study in how "you can't go home again," *Seconds* features surreal visuals, a tight, literate script, jaw-dropping photography by James Wong Howe, and Rock Hudson, delivering the finest performance of his career. *Seconds* also boasts a final three minutes that remain, for me, the single most terrifying closing sequence ever put on film.

Novella: *The Ballad of the Sad Café,* by Carson McCullers

A grotesquely poetic masterpiece, McCullers's novella tells the story of Miss Amelia and her café, and how it came to be a "dreary," boarded-up derelict of a building where, on occasion, a face can be spotted peeking out from behind one of the curtains. Miss Amelia runs the café, and though she treats her customers well, she has no friends to speak of, and has always been a little feared by the townspeople. Then her redemption arrives, in the form of a hunchbacked dwarf—her "Cousin Lymon," who brings Miss Amelia out of her shell and transforms her before everyone's eyes. Then Miss Amelia's exhusband, Marvin Macy, shows up, and Cousin Lymon—in a fashion worthy of Iago—sets about turning the two against one another. A story that almost makes Flannery O'Connor look cheerful, *The Ballad of the Sad Café* is arguably the first Southern Gothic horror story, an exquisite, disturbing cautionary tale about the dangers of redemption, hope, and loving another human being.

Song: "Bartender," by the Dave Matthews Band

A simple, long, bitter monologue delivered by a nameless narrator to an equally nameless bartender, filled with self-loathing and despair at the unspoken but strongly implied trail of lost second chances at redemption. By the end of the song, the narrator is no longer talking to the bartender, he's *praying* to him, because all he's got left is the bar, the drinking, and the man who serves the wine. Haunting and heartbreaking.

And that will do it for this baker's half-dozen of triple features. So the next time you want to enjoy a night of horror, remember: expand your definition of what constitutes the genre, as well as the methods used to explore the genre, and you might find that you'll come up with some pretty interesting triple features of your own.

FIVE SCARY TRADITIONAL HALLOWEEN STORIES

1. **"Cruachan" (ancient Celtic legend)**—On Samhain (the Celts' Halloween), a warrior named Nera first brings a corpse to life, then follows a fairy army into the underworld; a year later, he leads a raid on the underworld to steal an ancient crown, but winds up staying there forever.

2. **"Tamlane" (traditional Scottish ballad)**—Janet falls in love with Tamlane, a young man stolen by fairies; her only chance to rescue him is to pull him from his horse when he rides with the fairies on Halloween night. The malevolent fairies turn Tamlane into a snake, a toad, and a burning iron, but Janet hangs on throughout and is finally triumphant.

3. **"The Young Man in the Fairy Knoll" (Irish folktale)**—On Halloween, two young men are invited to join in a fairy dance. One young man sticks a needle in the doorway of the house, and escapes,

but his friend is trapped in the fairy underworld. When he's encountered a year later, he's pulled from the underworld, but dies instantly, having danced himself to skin and bones.

4. **"Red Mike's Rest" (Irish folktale)**—An Irish Halloween party turns sour when local bully "Red Mike" (so called because of his red hair) draws a bad lot in a fortune-telling game. Red Mike curses the partygoers, then flees into a nearby bog and is never seen again. Although a priest removes the curse, all travelers are warned to avoid "Red Mike's Rest."

5. **"November Eve" (Irish folktale)**—A late-night traveler stumbles on a great Halloween gathering, full of dancing and drinking. Although he recognizes some of those present as fairies, it takes a while before he realizes the rest of the revelers are the spirits of the dead. He escapes, but the next day his arms are covered with bruises from where the ghosts grabbed him, trying to pull him into their dances.

—*L.M.*

MELISSA MIA HALL'S TEN FAVORITE HORRIFYING ARTISTS

Melissa Mia Hall is an author and artist. A veteran book fiend, she contributes regularly to Publishers Weekly, sci-fi.com, *and other venues. Her literary essays on the ghost and the siren in pop culture are included in* Icons of the Supernatural, *edited by S. T. Joshi. Her short fiction has appeared in many publications and anthologies, including* Front Lines, *edited by Denise Little,* Cross Plains Universe, *edited by Scott Cupp and Joe Lansdale, and* Retro Pulp Tales, *edited by Joe Lansdale. She edited and contributed to the 1997 anthology* Wild Women, *and her short story "Psychofemmes" was reprinted in the 1998 edition of* The Year's 25 Finest Crime and Mystery Stories, *edited by Ed Gorman and Martin H. Greenberg.*

Images that terrify can sometimes be oh-so-inspiring. This informal list focuses on just a few fantastic classic artists. A few of them influenced what I perceive as the post-Picasso period that began the Modern Art movement. (I didn't include Picasso, but must also note that some of his work was pretty horrifying, including his impressive antiwar statement *Guernica* [1937].) Only four entries straddle my casual time-line cut-off: the surrealists Paul Delvaux (who died in 1994), René Magritte, Salvador Dalí, and Frida Kahlo. The artists are listed in no particular order, just as they popped into my head. Most of them also excelled in expressing lighter emotions and less terrifying subjects.

I am a writer and an artist. Great art and music influence my work far more than any film, TV show, book, or short story, unless they suggest lingering images in my brain. I wish I could insert little photos of these paintings alongside each title, but hopefully my list will inspire others to seek out the art available to be viewed on the Web. And maybe you'll feel a shiver just by reading about them here. And, of course, I have more than ten favorites. Other artists worth investigating include Leonardo da Vinci, James Ensor, Gustave Doré, Arthur Rackham, Dante Gabriel Rossetti, Elihu Vedder, Arnold Böcklin, Alphonse Mucha, Hugo Simberg, Paul Gauguin, and Franz von Stuck.

1. Paul Delvaux

Most horrifying work: *Le Village des Sirenes* (*The Village of the Sirens*) (1942)

In this surrealistic painting, a row of enigmatic blonde white women sit on chairs, waiting. They are meekly dressed in high-necked, long-sleeved blue gowns. Are they prostitutes, or would-be nuns? Are those cells or cribs behind each woman, their dark doorways open? Are they waiting for something to happen, something to end, someone to arrive, or someone to leave? Their blank faces suggest emotion beyond mute terror. Have they accepted some horrible fate, or are they just lonely beyond belief?

2. Hieronymus Bosch

Most horrifying work: *Tondal's Vision*

A vision of heaven or hell? Certainly of sin. The people trapped in this hell appear to be having a good time, until you look closely. An angel caressing a nude woman's rear? A game or a dinner inside the open mouth of a monster appears to have ended with one man spewing blood or wine? Another feeds another companion blood or wine? Frog legs squirm under a table? Odd happenings with various other humans suggest punishments. Must be hell. In the distance, a castle goes up in flame. No hope lives here. Just sin and depravity.

3. Edvard Munch

Most horrifying work: *The Scream* (1893)

This painting has become so well-known and even parodied so much, it's almost lost its ability to terrorize the viewer with its garish oranges, yellows, and turbulent blue-green sea. The screaming person is bald, yet could be male or female. Two shadowy figures approach on a bridge behind the screamer. It inspires uneasy laughter until you really think about it. Still, there are many more horrifying Munch masterpieces, including the chilling lithograph, *Attraction* (1896), in which two lovers stare into each other's black-hole eyes. Munch was a master of chilling imagery; other works include *The Vampire* (1893), featuring two young girls in a scary embrace, and *Madonna* (1895–1902), with a demonic little embryonic creature lurking in the corner. His many dark artworks are always good for a shriek or two.

4. Vincent van Gogh

Most horrifying work: *Wheat Field with Crows* (1890)

Like Munch's *The Scream*, this is an iconic painting that was completed during his last summer in Arles. Often thought to be his last painting, it was just one of several, but indicated the torment he was suffering. A murder of crows flies over a bright yellow field that's parted in the middle by an ominous road. Will the viewer choose that path or another?

5. John Everett Millais

Most horrifying work: *Ophelia* (1851–1852)

An unforgettable Pre-Raphaelite masterpiece that rarely fails to invoke chills, it was inspired by the scene in *Hamlet* in which an insane Ophelia drowns herself after her lover murders her father. It has another added horror factor: The model is Lizzie Siddal, the fragile wife of Dante Rossetti, addicted to laudanum after a miscarriage. She was to overdose several years later. Her husband, another celebrated Pre-Raphaelite painter and poet, exhumed her body years later to rescue some poetry he had failed to make copies of. Millais actually preferred more quiet, less upsetting themes, but this still rates as one of the most horrifying paintings I've ever seen.

6. Henri Rousseau

Most horrifying work: *War* (1894)

A demonic little girl with bright white teeth and wearing a ragged white gown brandishes a sword and a smoking firebrand as she runs barefoot alongside a black horse, jumping across corpses of naked civilians and one soldier still wearing his trousers. Carrion crows are already feasting on the bloody remains on this nightmarish battleground, backlit by a brilliant pink and blue sunset and enhanced by skeletal trees. Rousseau was also highly skilled in depicting savage but glorious jungle paintings, complete with animals devouring other creatures. His eerie masterpiece *The Snake Charmer* (1907) is also a bit unsettling. Will the summoned snake bite the charmer? Or will the jungle devour the listener?

7. Salvador Dalí

Most horrifying work: *The Three Sphinxes of Bikini* (1947)

The Persistence of Memory (1931), the one with the melting clock faces, certainly had a scary flavor, but the three heads in this painting create a more forbidding aspect. You can't see the face, only that the featureless backs of the heads were inspired by the bombs dropped on Nagasaki, Hiroshima, and experimentally on Bikini. The middle head is made of a tree split almost in half; the other two heads, one in the foreground and one in the background, are gray clouds of doom, a mute warning. A pioneer of the surrealist movement, Dalí completed paintings that haunt and disturb, especially those depicting his controlling but beloved wife, Gala.

8. René Magritte

Most horrifying work: Two versions of *The Rape* (1934) and (1948)

Depicting a woman's face, the mouth, eyes, and nose of which have been replaced by her sex organs, reducing a woman to her body parts, are two of Magritte's most scary works. This often playful surrealist is best known for puzzling but uplifting imagery, such as floating mountains, magical landscapes infused with exquisite clouds, skies and birds, hats, pipes, and lovely portraits of his wife. But even one of his whimsical paintings, *Golconde* (1953), turned nightmarish for me when the imagery became animated in one of my recent dreams. Businessmen descending from the sky like bowler-hatted raindrops or bullets? Several other pieces invoke a shiver or two as well, due to the sheer enigmatic emotions that charge his work with an electric tension, which endures long after you turn away from them.

9. Henry Fuseli

Most horrifying work: *The Nightmare* (1781)

The name of the artist might not be familiar, but the painting has been reproduced many times. A goblin sits on a female dreamer who appears to be falling from her bed, arms extended, hair a tumble of curls. Night demons have never been so exquisitely expressed. Has the goblin sucked her life force dry? Is she just sleeping?

10. Frida Kahlo

Most horrifying work: *Mi Nana y Yo* (*My Nanny and I*) (1937)

This outstanding Mexican surrealist was influenced by Diego Rivera, who she married and divorced. She painted many exquisite and exotic self-portraits. They read like graphic messages from her soul, charting an artistic journey that was unflinchingly honest if sometimes horrifying. Described as a "ribbon around a bomb" by surrealist André Breton, this self-portrait depicts Frida being nursed by a massive woman wearing a dark, enigmatic mask. Frida's adult head is attached to a tiny child's body clad in white gown similar to a First Communion dress. The breast she's sucking from is either poisoning or nourishing her. Frida was severely injured in a streetcar accident when she was only fifteen, and endured many futile operations. She tried but was unable to bear children, and this painting reflects her agony with excruciating intensity. Other outstanding works—among many—include *Roots* (1943) and *Self-Portrait with Thorn and Hummingbird* (1940).

JASON AARON'S SIX FAVORITE COMIC BOOK DEMONS AND DEVILS

Alabama-born Jason Aaron is the current writer of the ongoing Ghost Rider *series from Marvel Comics. His other comic-book writing credits include* Scalped *and* The Other Side *for Vertigo, and* Friday the 13th *for Wildstorm. He is also collaborating (with* The Book of Lists: Horror *coauthor Scott Bradley) on the literary biography of author Gustav Hasford. Jason lives near Kansas City, Missouri, with his wife and children.*

1. **Son of Satan (Marvel Comics):** His father is the Devil. His mother is an unsuspecting innocent. Meet Ira Levin's *Rosemary's Baby,* all grown up and with an attitude. He's half human, half fallen angel. The pompous and savage heir to Hell. Satan's only begotten son. But like a lot of other college-age youngsters, Daimon

Hellstrom (yes, that's Hellstrom, not *Hellstorm*, as he was later called) winds up defying his domineering dad, preferring instead to go his own way. In Daimon's case, that just happens to mean thwarting biblical prophecy by refusing to become the Antichrist. Instead, he sets up shop as an exorcist, opposing his father at every turn. Only problem: Daimon deeply despises humanity, seeing it as beneath him, and he usually threatens the life of any poor human who dares defy him. After first appearing in 1973's *Ghost Rider* #2, Daimon later headlined *Marvel Spotlight* under the title "The Son of Satan," before spinning off into his own short-lived series, the last issue of which shipped in 1977. In 1993, an updated version of Daimon starred in *Hellstorm: Prince of Lies*, but this recasting of Satan's son in a grim and gritty role only stripped away the last bits of mad flair and wild irreverence that had made the original character so memorable. For my money, Daimon was at his high point when written by Steve Gerber in the pages of *Marvel Spotlight*: red cape flowing, pentagram emblazoned on his bare chest, wielding a trident of "psycho-sensitive Netheranium," riding a fiery chariot pulled by flying demon-horses, spouting exclamations like "By the Seven Circles!" and "By the Hadean Chimes!" his cover blurbs promising "Exorcism! Excitement! In the eerie Marvel manner!"

2. *Ghost Rider* (Marvel Comics): The thoroughly lame Nicolas Cage flick aside, ol' flamehead is still *the* most badass supernatural superhero to ever straddle a chopper. As his origin goes, stunt cyclist Johnny Blaze made a deal with the devil to try and save a sickly loved one. To the surprise of no one but Johnny, the deal didn't work out as planned, and instead, he ended up possessed by a demonic spirit of vengeance, forced to ride the city streets by night, dishing out beat-downs to evildoers. Think Faust on a motorcycle, with a flaming skull for a head. Since his first appearance in 1972, Blaze has headlined several different titles, joined

the short-lived, Los Angeles–based superteam the Champions, and at one point wielded a shotgun that spewed hellfire, while playing second fiddle to his long-lost brother, Danny Ketch. These days Blaze is back in the driver's seat, and after kicking the devil's ass once again, he has his sights set on an all-new enemy: the renegade angel Zadkiel.

3. *The Demon* (DC Comics): When you got a name like Jason Blood, chances are your life's gonna be less than rosy. Created in 1972 by comics legend Jack Kirby during one of his most wildly imaginative periods, Jason Blood is a demonologist who's been permanently bonded with an honest-to-God demon. By reciting the words, "Gone, gone the form of man, rise the demon Etrigan," Blood goes all Jekyll and Hyde, transforming into a yellow-skinned demon who's pretty savage and cool, in spite of his cape and little red booties. It was some time after his first appearance that Etrigan began speaking all in rhymes, which has since become his trademark, and was eventually explained to be a requirement of his current ranking among the hierarchy of hell.

4. *Blue Devil* (DC Comics): Dan Cassidy is a stuntman playing the role of a blue-skinned, devil-horned monster, but when his film shoot accidentally unleashes the demon Nebiros, Cassidy gets zapped and fused to his costume, leaving him stuck as a real-life Blue Devil. Running for thirty issues in the late eighties, Cassidy's adventures in the pages of *Blue Devil* were high on laughs, including battles with bumbling aliens, second-rate supervillains, and even a cartoon goose. At one point, he even got his own teenage sidekick, dubbed Kid Devil. In the years after his series cancellation, Blue Devil returned as a member of the Justice League and today appears in the pages of *Shadowpact* alongside other offbeat supernatural characters.

5. *Hellboy* (Dark Horse Comics): He's a demon conjured by Nazis whose oversized fist, dubbed the "Right Hand of Doom," is supposed to bring about the apocalypse, but instead he keeps his horns filed off and works as a paranormal investigator for the U.S. government. As drawn by creator Mike Mignola, his tales are some of the most gorgeously rendered comics of the modern age.

6. *Lucifer* (Vertigo Comics): What does the devil do when he gets tired of ruling the underworld? He gives up the keys to hell and moves to Earth to open a piano bar. Or at least that's what happened in the pages of Neil Gaiman's landmark *Sandman* series, and later, the character spun off into his own title, which lasted seventy-five issues and was published by Vertigo, the mature-reader imprint of DC Comics. Think Milton's *Paradise Lost* starring David Bowie. Brooding and navel-gazing never seemed so hipster.

WARREN MARTENSE'S TEN THINGS H. P. LOVECRAFT NEVER ASKED FOR IN A BAR

Warren Martense is a leading figure in horror fiction's underground. He hails from the Catskill Mountains, where his complex love-hate relationship with his family inspired his controversial novel Stormy Monday.

1. A large bourbon.
2. A prawn sandwich.
3. The barmaid's phone number.
4. A bottle of Thunderbird.
5. The name of the sax player on the jukebox.

6. Kosher snacks.
7. A Budweiser from the fridge.
8. Directions to the local whorehouse.
9. Whatever Hemingway drank.
10. One more for the road.

TEN HORROR COCKTAILS
(AND HOW TO MAKE THEM)

1. BLOODY MARY

1½–2oz. vodka
3 oz. tomato juice
1 dash lemon juice
½ tsp. Worcestershire sauce
2–3 drops Tabasco sauce
salt and pepper to taste

Mix all ingredients, shake with ice, and strain into glass over ice cubes. A wedge of lime may be added.

(In his short story "The Chymist," author Thomas Ligotti offers up a disturbing variant called "the Sweet and Sour Bloody Mary," which consists of "high-test vodka, sugar, a lemon slice, and ketchup.")

—Source: *Mr. Boston Official Bartender's and Party Guide*

2. VAMPIRE

    1 oz. vodka
    1 oz. chambord
    1 oz. lime juice
    1 oz. cranberry juice

Fill a shaker half-full with ice cubes. Pour all ingredients into shaker and shake well. Strain drink into a cocktail glass.

—Source: www.whattodrink.com

3. ZOMBIE

    2 oz. light Puerto Rican rum
    1 oz. dark Jamaican rum
    ½ oz. 151-proof Demerara rum
    1 oz. curaçao
    1 tsp. Pernod or Herbsaint
    1 oz. lemon juice
    1 oz. orange juice
    1 oz. pineapple juice
    ½ oz. papaya or guava juice (optional)
    ¼ oz. grenadine
    ½ oz. orgeat syrup or sugar syrup to taste
    mint sprig (optional)
    pineapple stick

Mix all ingredients, except mint and pineapple stick, with cracked ice in a blender and pour into a tall, chilled collins glass. Garnish with mint sprig and pineapple stick. (Note: This is a re-creation of the original Zombie recipe by Don the Beachcomber.)

—Source: *The New American Bartender's Guide*

4. WEREWOLF

    1½ oz. Jack Daniel's
    1½ oz. Drambuie

Shake with ice and strain into a lowball glass.

—Source: www.nextrecipe.com

5. FRANKENSTEIN

    ½ oz. blackberry liqueur
    ½ oz. melon liqueur
    1 oz. pineapple juice

Pour all ingredients into a cocktail shaker with a few ice cubes.
Shake and strain into a 2 oz. shot glass, and serve.

—Source: www.idrink.com

6. EXORCIST

    1½ oz. Tequila
    ¾ oz. blue curaçao liqueur
    ¾ oz. lime juice

Shake all ingredients in a cocktail shaker half-filled with ice cubes.
Strain into a cocktail glass, and serve.

—Source: www.drinksmixer.com

7. MUMMY

    2 oz. vodka
    1 oz. orange liqueur

1 tbsp. lemon juice
1 tbsp. club soda

Mix vodka, orange liqueur, and lemon juice in an old-fashioned glass half-filled with ice. Top off with club soda. Stir.

—Source: www.1001cocktails.com

8. DEVIL'S TAIL

1½ oz. gold rum
½ oz. vodka
½ oz. apricot liqueur
½ oz. lime juice
½ tsp. grenadine
lime peel

Mix all ingredients except lime peel with cracked ice in a blender and pour into a chilled cocktail glass. Twist lime peel over drink and drop into glass.

—Source: *The New American Bartender's Guide*

9. THE HEMORRHAGING BRAIN

1 shot of peach schnapps
½ shot of Bailey's Irish Cream
grenadine

Pour schnapps into double shot glass. Add Bailey's, which congeals into a brain-like lump of fissures. Top with grenadine for the bloody hemorrhage.

—Source: www.droogle.ca

1½ oz. vodka
3 dashes bitters
ginger ale

Pour the vodka and bitters into a collins glass and add several ice cubes. Fill with ginger ale and stir. Decorate with a slice of orange.

—Source: *Mr. Boston Official Bartender's and Party Guide*

—*Compiled by S.B. and J.S.*

ELEVEN HORROR FOOD AND DRINK PRODUCTS

1–5. Count Chocula, Franken Berry, Boo Berry, Yummy Mummy, and Fruit Brute cereals: Arguably the best-known and most-beloved of all horror foods, this series of monster-themed breakfast cereals was manufactured by General Mills and debuted in 1971 with Count Chocula and Franken Berry. Each featured a different archetypal horror character as the name and logo for a different flavor: The vampire Count Chocula (chocolate), the Frankenstein's monster-like Franken Berry (strawberry), and the ghost Boo Berry (blueberry). Less successful entries in the line were Yummy Mummy (fruit-flavored) and the werewolf Fruit Brute (also fruit-flavored). In 1999, *The Onion* ran a spoof article which revealed Count Chocula's full name to be Vladimir Elysius von Chocula and reported on a press conference held by the Count at General Mills' headquarters "to restate his long-standing advocacy of the presweetened breakfast cereal that bears his name."

6. **Monster Munch Corn Snacks:** Chips (crisps) sold in the UK, manufactured by Walker, these also used the concept of different spokescreatures for each flavor: They were, to quote from the product's Wikipedia entry,

> Pink Monster (a tall, gangly creature who put in his main appearance on Roast Beef flavor), Orange Monster (who assumed various duties over the years, including both Pickled Onion and Bacon flavors), Blue Monster (a behatted, floppy-eared creature with four arms whose finest moment was his appearance on Salt and Vinegar), and Yellow Monster (a one-eyed, red-nosed creature found on Cheese and Cheese & Onion flavors). At some point there was also a Green Monster, although he may not have actually appeared on any packets. He is mentioned in the "monster munch munchers" club pack, most notably for his appearance in the story of the "monster's bounce," where he drank too much lemonade down the monster munch mine and had to be rescued by the other monsters.

The snacks themselves have been produced in two different shapes, a monster claw (which may also be a monster eye) and the shape of the Pink Monster. There have been no recent sightings of the Green Monster.

7. **Gremlins Cereal:** Produced by Ralston Foods from July 1984 to September 1985 as a tie-in with the blockbuster produced by Steven Spielberg and directed by Joe Dante (concerning sweet, furry creatures that transform into malevolent reptilian monstrosities if fed after midnight), many have noted the suspicious similarity to another Ralston cereal, Cap'n Crunch, in taste, texture, and color. While cuddly Mogwai Gizmo appeared on the box cover (and was the basis for the shape of the cereal pieces

themselves), stickers featuring Spike and other evil gremlins could be found inside as a prize.

8. **Night of the Living Bar-B-Q Sauce:** This potent number, from Kansas City's Cowtown BBQ Products, features a label illustrated by nationally syndicated cartoonist Charlie Podrebarac depicting zombie pigs and cows pursuing a terrified BBQ chef. The bottle's ad copy says: "Reanimate your taste buds with this killer hot sauce! Howling good when splattered on beef, pork, poultry or fish . . . repeat after me: 'It's only a Bar-B-Q sauce . . . it's only a Bar-B-Q sauce . . . it's only a Bar-B-Q sauce. . . .'" Night of the Living Bar-B-Q Sauce won first place in the hot sauce category (2002) and the People's Choice Award (2007) at the American Royal BBQ Competition. It's available on the web from www .cowtownbbq.com, and at Oklahoma Joe's Barbecue, which describes itself as "a BBQ restaurant in a gas station" because it is, in fact, situated inside the Shamrock gas station at Forty-seventh and Mission in Kansas City, Kansas.

Night of the Living Bar-B-Q Sauce (Illustration by Charlie Podrebarac, used by permission of Cowtown Barbeque Products LLC)

9. **Alien Fresh Jerky:** This Area 51–themed store sells many varieties of homemade jerky, stuffed olives, nuts, and dry fruits, all festooned with slightly sinister-looking aliens of the *Communion* variety (some of them decked out in cowboy gear!). Originally launched in Lincoln County, Nevada, Alien Fresh Jerky has since relocated to Baker, California, on Interstate 15 (the main route between Las Vegas and Los Angeles). Of the jerky varieties sampled by *The Book of Lists: Horror*, the hot flavor was the hands-down favorite. More information is available at www .alienfreshjerky.com.

10. **Monster Energy Drink:** Appearing in 2002 as a competitor to the massively successful Red Bull Energy Drink, this product's can features three claw-marks from, presumably, the eponymous monster as its logo. The can exhorts drinkers to "Unleash the Beast!" and says, "We went down to the lab and cooked up a double shot of killer energy brew. It's a wicked mega hit that delivers twice the buzz of a regular energy drink." Monster comes in a variety of flavors, including low-carb, and is available at most convenience and grocery stores.

11. **Screamin' Demon Pickled Sausage:** The whole concept of the liquor/convenience store staple that is the pickled sausage qualifies as a "horrifying" food for many, but this brand, manufactured by Jack Link, actually uses a horror motif—a green cartoon demon, seen on the wrapper munching on one of the sausages. According to the company's Web site, the Screamin' Demon is "300% hotter than our Hot Head Pickled Sausage." The label lists, among the ingredients, "mechanically separated chicken, pork, pork hearts." Leatherface would be proud!

—*S.B.*

AGUSTÍ VILLARONGA'S TOP FIVE WORKS OF HORROR

Spanish filmmaker Agustí Villaronga is the director of the infamous transgressive horror classic In a Glass Cage (Tras El Cristal). *Among his other works are* 99.9, *the Aleister Crowley–inspired* Moonchild, *and* The Sea (El Mar). *His films have screened at numerous international film festivals, including those at Cannes, Berlin, Chicago, Montreal, and Torino.*

1. Ron Mueck's Sculptures

Ron Mueck is an Australian living in England who began doing special effects in cinema. His hyper-realistic sculptures reproduce the human body in detail. However, he alters the human scale to the extent that it becomes something monstrous. The first of these sculptures, "Dead Man," reproduces his father's dead body, but reduced to two-thirds of its real size. It is made of silicon and other materials, but uses, nonetheless, his father's own hair. His next sculpture: "Boy" is five meters tall and is compressed inside a structure. Lastly, he has a newly born baby that is 15 meters long. A simple change in scale together with a most amazing realism ends up turning these human beings into monsters. The whole thing is, if not terrifying, at least quite disturbing.

2. The film *Who Can Kill a Child? (¿Quién puede matar a un niño?)* (1979)

Who Can Kill a Child? is a Spanish film directed by Narciso Ibáñez Serrador. This film shows to what extent evil can appear in the guise of innocence. The story begins with a young English couple who arrive on a small island off the coast of Spain for a vacation. The wife is pregnant with their child. Strangely enough, there are only children on this island. These children, who want to take revenge on all the evils that adults have inflicted upon them, have killed all the adults. It is very much in the spirit of *The Birds*, by Alfred Hitchcock. The couple is harassed to the point that they end up locked up in a room, guarded by the tribe of children, who clamour for their death. But when confronted with these innocent and virginal faces, and what they stand for, who can kill a child?

3. The Musical Composition *Threnody for the Victims of Hiroshima* by Krzysztof Penderecki

Music, abstract or otherwise, produces emotions, and even more so when it makes allusion, as in this case, to an event whose consequences are known to all of us. This piece was written in 1959 for fifty-two string instruments, which play continuous, loud, and dissonant notes without pause, creating a sensation both solemn and catastrophic. It was recently used by Alfonso Cuarón in the chaotic final sequence of his film *Children of Men* (2006). Penderecki remarked: "Let the *Threnody* express my firm belief that the sacrifice of Hiroshima will never be forgotten and lost."

4. The novel *Frisk*, by Dennis Cooper

Cooper's recurrent themes are violence, sex, youth culture, and the search for an object of desire. In *Frisk*, his second novel, the story is told through a series of letters the narrator sends from France and Holland to an old friend, explaining the crimes he is perpetuating. His fantasies almost always culminate in the murder and horrendous mutilation of young people who, at the moment he perpetuates the crime, are usually in a terrible state of confusion due to drugs, sickness, or agony. In his work, there are echoes of Bret Easton Ellis and even the Marquis de Sade, but Cooper goes so much farther that he has even received death threats from the gay community.

5. The book *The Trial of Gilles de Rais,* by Georges Bataille

Georges Bataille's book takes as a starting point the judicial records of the trial of Gilles de Rais (the Bluebeard of the legend), accused of killing more than four hundred children whom he sodomized and beheaded amidst satanic orgies. Gilles de Rais, a good Catholic, was a noble marshal who fought with Joan of Arc during the Hundred Years War. He never lost his faith, not even while perpetuating his most cruel and degenerate crimes. The account of the confession of his crimes during the trial, in front of several of his victims' mothers, is absolutely horrifying. Bataille says: "The crimes of Gilles de Rais are the crimes of the world he was living in." He warns us that even today there may be in every one of us a potential Bluebeard "subdued by the conventions of the community that we live in."

ANDY DIGGLE'S FIVE CREEPIEST MOMENTS FROM ALAN MOORE'S *SWAMP THING*

Andy Diggle is the current writer of Vertigo's flagship horror comic Hellblazer. *His past credits include* Swamp Thing, Silent Dragon, Green Arrow: Year One, *Guy Ritchie's* Gamekeeper, *and* The Losers, *the latter two of which are currently in feature film development at Warner Brothers.*

This was going to be a list of the creepiest moments in comics, but then I realized that most of them were from Alan Moore comics . . . and most of *them* were from his legendary run on DC Comics' *Swamp Thing.*

1. A Murder of Crows

The naïve punk Judith has made a terrible bargain with the *Brujeria*, a tribe of cave-dwelling sorcerers who have promised to change her into a bird. But this is no fairy-tale transformation. It seems almost a kindness to the reader that much of the scene is rendered in stark silhouette—except that what we picture in our imagination is infinitely worse. We hear only the awful gagging sounds she makes as she vomits her intestines into an earthenware bowl and, as her head comes away like an old tooth, crow talons scrabble and scrape their way out through the withered stump of her neck . . .

2. The Monkey King

"Whatever you're scared of, that's what it looks like . . ." Inadvertently summoned from Hell by an innocent Ouija game, the Monkey King has slipped into a home for mentally disturbed children to feed upon their deepest fears. Guilty little Roberta sees her baby brother reaching for her, his tiny hand cold and blue; hears the sound of polyethylene going in and out, very fast. Little Michael is terrified of cancer—but as nobody ever explained to him what cancer really is, his imagination fills in the rest, and fleshy tentacles swarm and flail above his bed. But worst of all is little Jessica, visited in the night by a leering, monstrously deformed simulacrum of her own father, its voice a slurred and mindless parody as it repeats over and over, *"Mommy needn't know . . ."*

3. The Bogeyman

Our narrator is a nameless serial killer who haunts the lonely byways of the Louisiana bayou. He asks you to think of a number, any number, between one and 165 so that he can describe, in vivid detail, the eyes of that particular victim. He believes himself to be the Bogeyman; his predecessor—and first victim—being the old janitor at his childhood school, who would grab him by the hair of his temples for running in the hallway. Confronting the vengeful, thorn-encrusted Swamp Thing, our narrator flees in terror—straight into the swamp. And as he sinks down through the ink-black water, he begins to hear voices. "Who are you?" he asks. "That depends," comes the reply. "Just think of a number . . ." *"And in the darkness, somebody takes hold of the short hair at my temple and begins to tug. I try to scream, but my lungs are filled with mud . . ."*

4. The *Invunche*

Elderly Catholic nun Sister Anne-Marie is taking the London tube home when she senses she's being followed. Stepping off the train, she realizes only as it pulls away that this Underground station is dark and empty, closed for renovation. And whatever is following her is locked in down here with her. Inhumanly strong, clothed only in a loincloth made of human skin, the *Invunche* is a creature of black magic, powered by the pain of its own creation. One arm is twisted behind its back, the hand sewn into the shoulder blade. And, bizarrely, its neck is twisted around to face backwards, mouth foaming, eyes mad with pain and hate. Steeling her courage, Sister Anne-Marie resolves to look her attacker in the face—only to find, in her final moments, that it doesn't seem to have one . . .

5. Still Waters

A group of boys bathing in a forest lake suddenly panic as they realize it's infested with leeches. All of them, that is, but fat, slow Nicky, who remains in the water, motionless, his features slack, the color gradually draining from his body. Because there are worse things in the water than leeches. Once there was an entire town down there, long ago submerged by the building of a dam. And down in the deep dark where the sunlight cannot penetrate, the *vampires* feed and breed . . .

THE REAL NAMES OF ELEVEN HORROR LEGENDS

You Know Them As . . .	But Their Real Name Is . . .
1. Boris Karloff (actor)	William Henry Pratt
2. Jack Ketchum (author)	Dallas Mayr
3. Marilyn Manson (musician/filmmaker)	Brian Hugh Warner
4. Charles Beaumont (author/screenwriter)	Charles Leroy Nutt
5. Rob Zombie (musician/filmmaker)	Robert Bartleh Cummings
6. Saki (author)	Hector Hugh Munro
7. Béla Lugosi (actor)	Béla Ferenc Dezsö Blaskó
8. Alice Cooper (musician)	Vincent Furnier
9. Michael Slade (author)	Jay Clarke and Rebecca Clarke
10. Lon Chaney, Sr. (actor)	Leonidas Frank Chaney
11. Ozzy Osbourne (musician)	John Michael Osbourne

—*Compiled by S.B. and A.W.*

BRIAN W. ALDISS'S EIGHT FAVORITE
WORKS OF HORROR

One of the legends of the science fiction genre, Brian W. Aldiss's numerous novels include Frankenstein Unbound, Dracula Unbound, Moreau's Other Island, Harm, *and the* Helliconia *trilogy. His short story "Supertoys Last All Summer Long" was a long-time dream project for director Stanley Kubrick, and was eventually filmed after Kubrick's death as* A. I.: Artificial Intelligence, *by Steven Spielberg. He resides in Oxford, England.*

I. Literature

1. Mary Shelley's *Frankenstein* or *The Modern Prometheus*
   Of course. The immortal horror story: poor creature without parents.
2. Bram Stoker's *Dracula*
   Read first as a boy by candlelight, when electricity had failed.
3. Oliver Onions's "Beckoning Fair One"
   To think that women could be so weird. . .

I'm not really into horror in book form—unless you include *Family Health*, a fat encyclopedia which tells you of a thousand things of which you could die.

II. Films

4. Again, *Frankenstein*, by James Whale
   With Boris Karloff as the Creature.
5. Stanley Kubrick's *Shining*
   Some scenes of outstanding ghastliness, almost too horrific too watch.

6. Roy Andersson's *Songs from the Second Floor*

My family did not find this Swedish film funny; I love its delicious sly wit and its depiction of worldwide mental breakdown. Surreal, unique.

7. Clouzot's *Les Diaboliques*

A rundown boarding school. Chief characters: the headmaster, his rich wife, and a female teacher who becomes his mistress. The interplay between these three characters is chilling and motivated by human cruelty. Full marks for a horrifying ending. Tremendously wily direction of a classic!

III. Television

8. Alan Ball's *Six Feet Under*

Probably brave HBO's masterpiece. Close-ups of entire family ghastliness. Never criticize U.S. television again after this shuddersome wonder!

CHAPTER 5

"I'm Your Biggest Fan."

SHRIEKS FROM THE GALLERY

We decided to end The Book of Lists: Horror *with a clawful of contenders we just couldn't resist, submitted by fans of the genre. They may not be famous, but they too brought the passion and enthusiasm that is the bloody heart and transcendent soul of horror.*

—Eds.

ZOË BRIAN'S TOP TEN CREEPY MOVIES FOR A SEVENTH-GRADE SLUMBER PARTY

Zoë Brian is twelve years old and goes to Indian Hills Middle School in Prairie Village, Kansas. She enjoys listening to music, watching movies, throwing parties, and playing with her pets. She has a dog named George and a hedgehog named Lucy.

1. *Sleepy Hollow* (starring Johnny Depp and Christina Ricci): My personal favorite, *Sleepy Hollow*, is about young Ichabod Crane, who finds himself solving the murderous crimes that are engulfing Sleepy Hollow. When everyone tells him the Headless Horseman is doing the killings, he is determined to find the *real* killer.

This movie is sure to have almost all the girls screaming in terror and at the edge of their seats! Rated R for blood and language.

2. *Little Shop of Horrors* (starring **Rick Moranis and Ellen Greene**): Seymour is a geeky guy who works (and lives) in a flower shop. One day when he is out buying exotic flowers, he finds a "strange and interesting" plant that brings his shop sudden success! But the Audrey Two, his plant, is not growing and he doesn't know what to feed it—until he cuts his finger and finds that the plant feeds off blood! This musical is a toe-tapping, sing-along, get-up-and-dance movie that everyone should love! Rated PG–13 for blood and language.

3. *Pan's Labyrinth* (starring **Ivana Baquero and Sergi López**): A village in 1944 Fascist Spain is ruled by the captain of a sadistic army. His new wife is pregnant with an heir and comes to live with him, but she brings something he wasn't expecting: a young girl named Ofelia. Ofelia is visited in the night by a fairy who leads her to the center of a labyrinth, where she meets an old faun, who tells her she is a princess and if she ever wants to see her real father, the king, she must perform three tasks. If she fails, the consequences could be dire. *Pan's Labyrinth* is a fairy tale with a twist that all (who have the patience to watch a subtitled movie) should see. Rated R for blood and language.

4. *Edward Scissorhands* (starring **Winona Ryder and Johnny Depp**): *Edward Scissorhands* is the tragic tale of a misunderstood creature with scissors for hands. When Peg Boggs, an Avon salesperson, finds Edward alone in the attic, she takes him home to care for him. There he falls in love with Peg's daughter, Kim. But everyone is afraid of Edward—until they find his gift. The suburbs he now lives in will never be the same, as the neighborhood learns that not all things different are bad. *Edward Scissorhands*

is an amazing story that will have everyone wanting to know what happens next and might even have a few tearing up! Rated PG–13 for language and suggestive material.

5. *Beetle Juice* **(starring Michael Keaton, Alec Baldwin, Geena Davis, and Winona Ryder):** Adam and Barbara are killed in a car crash and trapped as ghosts in their house. Soon, an annoying family named the Deetzes moves in. When Lydia Deetz, the daughter, discovers Adam and Barbara, she befriends them and tries to help in the ghosts' quest to get the family out of the house. With little luck, Adam and Barbara call on a demonic specialist of fright named Beetle Juice—but is he too much to handle? The special effects and crazy characters are sure to have everyone intrigued! Rated PG for language.

6. *Phantom of the Paradise* **(starring Paul Williams and William Finley):** This is *Phantom of the Opera* in rock 'n' roll form. Winslow Leach is a gifted musician who wants his music to be heard, but when it is stolen by a big record-label producer, Swan, he wants to destroy his company. When his revenge backfires, he is mangled in the record-making machinery. Swan cuts him a deal, promising to give him his voice back if he sells him his music and (without Leach knowing) his immortal soul! When Phoenix, Leach's secret love, gets together with Swan, he is torn apart and must destroy Swan—even if that means destroying himself. This film has great music and a scary story to tell. Guests will be shocked out of their wits when his mask is removed! Rated PG for language, suggestive material, and disturbing images.

7. *Heathers* **(starring Winona Ryder and Christian Slater):** Veronica Sawyer is part of the most fearsome clique in school. The three Heathers rule the school and have a reputation for being mean. When she meets a new kid named J. D., she falls for his rebel-

lious personality. But when he kills Heather Number One, J. D. talks Veronica into helping him write a suicide note to make it look like Heather killed herself. But the murders don't stop here. What will happen to the school when all the popular kids seem to be committing suicide? This movie is a tragedy with a comedic edge. Many girls will love this movie. Rated R for suggestive material and nudity, language, and blood.

8. *The Nightmare Before Christmas* (starring Chris Sarandon and Catherine O'Hara): Jack Skellington doesn't want to be king of Halloweentown anymore, and there is something missing inside of him. When he stumbles into Christmastown, he realizes Christmas is just what he needs, and decides to take matters into his own boney hands. But will the children appreciate what Jack is doing for them? And what does Sandy Claws think of this? This movie is a dark Disney musical with loveable characters. It actually scared me the first time I saw it (when I was 6)!

9. *Buffy the Vampire Slayer*—Season Four, Episode Ten—"Hush" (starring Sarah Michelle Gellar and Alyson Hannigan): Buffy is a teenage girl who is chosen to fight the forces of darkness and defend the world. In this episode, which is one of the creepiest, everyone in the town of Sunnydale loses their voices. People are being found with their hearts ripped out and nobody knows how this is happening—until Giles finds a fairytale about the Gentlemen. When you can't talk, or scream, how can you call for help? Rated TV–14 for language.

10. *Scary Movie 3* (starring Simon Rex and Anna Faris): Although this is a comedy, it is a perfect choice to watch at a slumber party. This movie is a takeoff of all the scary movies made around the year 2002 and back. Spoofing everything from *The Ring* to *8 Mile* (now *there's* a scary movie!), this movie is sure to have everybody

laughing . . . and a few others grossed out (especially when Kate's head falls off). It may not be creepy, but it sure is fun! Rated PG–13 for language and suggestive material.

LIAM VOLK'S TEN FAVORITE HORROR VENDETTAS

At the ripe old age of thirteen, Liam Volk is a life-long horror fan. He attends Pontypridd High School in South Wales and his uncle is Stephen Volk, whose list appears elsewhere in this volume. Liam grew up on Universal Classic monsters, but now prefers Doctor Who (and James Bond). He also likes The Simpsons.

1. Jaws vs. the Brody Family (*Jaws* films)
2. Dracula vs. Van Helsing (*Dracula* films)
3. Michael Myers vs. Jamie Lee Curtis (*Halloween* films)
4. Michael Douglas vs. Glenn Close (*Fatal Attraction*)
5. Robert De Niro vs. Nick Nolte (*Cape Fear*)
6. Cindy Campbell vs. cars (*Scary Movie*)
7. Freddy Krueger vs. the children of Elm Street (*Nightmare on Elm Street* series)
8. Aliens vs. Sigourney Weaver (*Alien* films)
9. Dr. Jekyll vs. Mr. Hyde (*Jekyll & Hyde* films)
10. Doctor Who vs. the Daleks (*Doctor Who*)

CHARLES BLACK'S FIVE FAVORITE
NIGHTMARE ON ELM STREET TIE-IN PRODUCTS

Charles Black has an unhealthy pop-culture obsession, which extends to cinema, television, literature, video games, and any other sort of media he can experience. A love-hate relationship with horror lasted throughout his teenage years (and yes, as much as it shames him, he had nightmares for two weeks after seeing The Gate*), but he was instantly converted the day he read his first Stephen King novel. These days, even the best horror movies don't scare him, but he still loves them. He is working on several horror-themed film projects, trying to establish himself among all the other great artists who cause people to sleep with their lights on.*

In the interest of full disclosure, I should note that I am a fan of the *Nightmare on Elm Street* series, in all of its incarnations. In fact, though I relentlessly mock the following items, I'll openly admit to having owned/watched/played/etc. *all* the damn things. My obsession began when I was about twelve, on vacation with my family on a houseboat in the middle of a lake, listening to my older cousin, Josh, recap the first three films of the series in loving and gruesome detail. I was both terrified and fascinated by such tidbits as . . .

". . . and then you see a little light come on in Kristen's dollhouse . . . and the movie ends!"

Well, I *had* to know what happened next. And a horror geek was born. Thanks, Josh.

1. Freddy's 1–900 Number

As a last-ditch effort to cash in on a decade—the eighties—defined by greed, the trend of celebrity 1–900 numbers was a hilarious yet utterly despicable way to manipulate young people into running up Mom and Dad's phone bill. For a nominal (ha!)

per-minute fee, you could listen to recorded messages from your favorite New Kid on the Block, your favorite steroid-ridden athlete, or even . . .

. . . *Freddy Krueger?*

Sure, it made sense to want to listen to the impersonal (and most likely scripted) ramblings of your favorite dreamy celebrity, but do you *really* want to get cozy on the phone with horrordom's most infamous child-molesting charcoal briquette?

Well, I sure did. And I'm sure a lot of other disturbed young ones did as well. God help us all.

2. *Freddy's Greatest Hits,* (previously) available on LP and cassette

A long time ago, future Biggest Movie Star on the Planet Earth Will Smith showed that you *could* create a pop song about Freddy Krueger with the smash hit single "Nightmare on My Street," a catchy tune with creepy lyrics that made you giggle.

Unfortunately, that song—and any originality or charm that it contained—was painfully absent from *Freddy's Greatest Hits,* RiC Records' 1987 attempt to cash in on the *Elm Street* franchise.

Naturally, *Freddy's Greatest Hits* was a collection of songs about dreaming and/or sleeping. The best-known song on the compilation was "Do the Freddy," a cover of the 1965 Freddie and the Dreamers (nice coincidence!) hit, recorded by a gathering of musicians known as the Elm Street Group.

Other tracks included additional covers like "In the Midnight Hour" and "All I Have to Do Is Dream," as well as original tracks like "Don't Sleep," "Down in the Boiler Room," and "Elm Street Dreams." Sadly, the only ones being tortured and maimed were the people who bought this crap.

3. *A Nightmare on Elm Street:* The Board Game (from Cardinal/Victory Games Inc.)

Talk about fun! Round up a few friends and try to figure out which one of your buddies is actually Freddy Krueger in this clever and scary whodunit!

Okay, sorry. This charmer is actually a demented rip-off of *Clue*, only with rules that are nearly impossible to figure out. Most of the game involves drawing cards and suspecting which of the other players is actually Freddy in disguise. If you're playing with only two people, the confrontation devolves into a rousing game of "Liar, Liar, Pants on Fire."

You really need anywhere from four to eight people to have an interesting game, but then the kind of person who would own this game would have to be the kind of person who had friends in the first place.

The best part of this insanity is that the game is for "Ages 8 and up," so don't miss your chance to gather up a bunch of impressionable youngsters and watch them get slaughtered one by one by a resurrected child killer. Yippee!

4. The *Freddy's Nightmares* TV series

The 1980s produced a bumper crop of occasionally cool TV horror anthology shows, including a new version of *The Twilight Zone, Tales from the Darkside, Monsters, Friday the 13th: The Series,* and others. Not wanting to be outdone (or miss a chance to cash in on New Line's resident cash cow), network executives spawned *Freddy's Nightmares*.

The show was originally intended to be a TV series that followed a similar plotline to the films, but that idea was jettisoned when the studio realized that having a regular cast of teenagers didn't make sense, as Freddy would most likely dispatch them rather quickly. They decided to make the show into a standard anthology series, with Freddy as the Crypt Keeper–like host, spouting grisly one-liners and puns.

Even though they managed to work Freddy into a couple of the actual plotlines, it grew tiresome to see him relegated to bit player, and the actual anthology shows offered nothing original. Ultimately, the show was cancelled after two seasons, but these *Nightmares* continue to haunt us on cable, where reruns can be easily found.

5. The *Nightmare on Elm Street* video game for the Nintendo Entertainment System

Back in the pre-Internet days of video gaming, kids weren't able to rely on Web sites with reviews to keep them away from utter trash. We had to get our feet wet and, just maybe, have our legs devoured by a swarm of bloodthirsty piranhas.

In that era, companies used movie licenses (such as *Back to the Future, Friday the 13th,* and *The Karate Kid*) as a familiar marketing tool to sell games to the unsuspecting public. Apparently, no one told them the games actually had to be *good*. One of the worst games of its kind was, of course, *Elm Street*.

The game had almost no resemblance to *any* of the movies, with the exception of Freddy himself. Your mission was to guide your hero into battle against snakes and bats (?) armed only with your fists (?!), all to recover Freddy's scattered bones (which were shaped like your standard dog biscuit) and get them safely placed in consecrated ground.

If only they had buried this game in a similar manner.

R. B. PAYNE'S TOP TEN BEST HORROR
PULP MAGAZINE COVERS

A member of the Dark Delicacies Writing Group, R. B. Payne recently sold his first horror tale, literally and figuratively. Frightened

at the prospect of never being published again, he continues to write. He has several other tales in the publishing pipeline and has completed his debut novel. He lives in Los Angeles.

Pulp magazines were adventure, romance, western, war, detective/crime, and horror tales published on cheap paper (wood "pulp" paper) and sold at corner newsstands, drugstores, gas stations, and wherever else anyone was willing to part with some hard-earned coinage. Pulp magazines are generally associated with the 1910s to the 1950s but their heyday was really the Great Depression, from 1929 to the early 1940s.

Magazines such as *Weird Tales, Terror Tales, Uncanny Tales* (yes, there were a lot of "Tales"!), *Phantom, Eerie Mysteries, Horror Stories*, and others gave a start to many legendary writers such as Robert Bloch, Ray Bradbury, Hugh B. Cave, August Derleth, Robert E. Howard, H. P. Lovecraft, A. Merritt, Talbot Mundy, and Seabury Quinn, just to mention a few.

Much pulp artwork is unattributed: We don't always know who created them. Often they were painted in only a few days and went out unsigned. Many famous pulp cover artists included Frank R. Paul, Virgil Finlay, Edd Cartier, Margaret Brundage, and Norman Saunders. Pulp covers were so important to the magazine's sales that often they would be painted first. The authors would then be shown the cover and contracted to write a story to match.

The general recipe for a pulp cover was a woman in distress plus whatever was the magazine theme. So a half-naked woman threatened by a demon made it horror, an enemy soldier made it war, a criminal made it a crime pulp, etc. The only requirement was that the woman was scantily-clothed and you could only save her by buying the magazine.

World War II started the demise of these magazines (even this cheap paper was needed elsewhere), and the final nails in the coffin were comics, paperback books, and, oooooohhhh, television.

Here are some of my favorite horror covers from back in the day. Many of these are available as reprints, as most pulps have fallen into the public domain and are now being rediscovered and reprinted by fans worldwide.

1. *Terror Tales* (January 1935)

Terror Tales, January 1935 (© 1935 by Popular Publications. Reprinted by permission of Argosy Communications Inc.)

A terrific cover with undead hands pulling an innocent woman into a pool of blood while Death watches. This cover has it all, the inevitability of pain, death, and the realization there is no escape . . . for any of us! If I had seen this on the newsstand as a kid, I would have bought it in a heartbeat! *Buh-bump. Buh-bump.* All that blood. Try not to scream, my dear! This will teach you NOT to fall in love with a stranger!

2. *Uncanny Tales* (Special Quarterly, 1942)

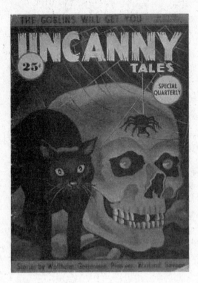

Uncanny Tales, Special Quarterly, 1942
(© 1942 by Manvis Publications, Inc.
Copyright not renewed, reprinted as public
domain.)

A spectacular cover that emphasizes
the deep fears explored by horror fans:
black cats, skulls, Death, the undead,
decay, and spiders and their webs.
And yes, THE GOBLINS WILL GET
YOU! Unfortunately, this was one of
the last issues of this wonderful magazine. It appears that the goblins *did*
get them, simply because goblins are
not known for their reading skills and
seldom subscribe to magazines.

3. *Weird Tales* (October 1933)

Weird Tales, October 1933
(© 1933 by Popular Fiction
Publishing Co. Reprinted by
permission of Weird Tales Ltd.)

I shouldn't really have to
explain why the thirteen-
year-old boy still inside
me would be drawn to
this cover. This woman is
frighteningly attractive. In
fact, this woman actually
looks *exactly* like someone

you could meet today (especially the leather!), at a Halloween bash anywhere on the Sunset Strip here in Los Angeles. When I see those alluring eyes and blood red lips I have to admit I would offer my neck . . . at a minimum! Please, please . . . bite me!

4. *Horror Stories* (October 1935)

Horror Stories, October 1935 (© 1935 by Popular Publications. Reprinted by permission of Argosy Communications Inc.)

Horror Stories magazine consistently had some of the scariest and gruesome covers ever to grace a newsstand. Some of these were purportedly so bone-chilling that women would be struck blind on the spot and men would go raving mad! (Young boys were hypnotized in an immediate purchase!) This particular cover pictures an unwilling woman being forced to marry a beast by a blindfolded priest with a noose around his neck and a gun at his back. Clearly the message is that the church can't protect you from a bad marriage. Only upon closer examination can we see her rescuer creeping down the stairs. Perhaps her virginity is safe after all!

5. *Sinister Stories* (February 1940)

Sinister Stories, February 1940 (© 1940 by Popular Publications. Reprinted by permission of Argosy Communications Inc.)

Here's another horrible marriage about to happen. Hmmm, I picked two of these in a row. Perhaps I have marriage issues, just ask any of my ex's—if you care to dig them up! What's great about this cover is that it shows that half-men can run complicated equipment like a buzz saw. The S&M aspect (I assume those are bridesmaids!), lightens the mood, and in this cover, there is no rescue! The overall concept begs the question though—what good is half a bride on a wedding night?

6. *Ghost Stories* (May 1931)

Ghost Stories, May 1931 (© 1931 by Good Story Magazine Company, Inc. Copyright not renewed, reprinted as public domain.)

Previous to the pulp magazines, mainstream horror had often focused on the ghost story or haunted house/ship/

castle tales. This was leftover from the "penny dreadfuls" of Victorian times. Although the pulps had been around for about ten years by 1931, the onset of the Great Depression dramatically accentuated the intensity of the covers as well as the drama. This copy of *Ghost Stories* is representative of the transition. The characters clearly look like the 1920s, but the style has become far more dramatic. Honey, he says, have I mentioned that my mother isn't entirely dead?

7. *New Detective* (October 1951)

New Detective, October 1951 (© 1951 by Popular Publications. Reprinted by permission of Argosy Communications Inc.)

By the early 1950s many horror, crime, and detective pulps followed the movie trend of "realistic" crime dramas. The pulps shifted away from "hero" magazines. *Doc Savage*, *The Shadow*, *The Phantom Detective*, *The Avenger*, and other crime fighters were "retired" and replaced by pseudo-true crime stories. Still, the gruesome covers depicted crazed murderers (like the ones that live next door?), serial killers (maybe your uncle from St. Louis?), and often a scantily clad victim. The bottom line: sex and blood sells. And there are those damn gloves. If they don't fit, you must acquit!

8. *Weird Tales* (September 1952)

This cover is the eeriest of the lot, the ghouls closing in to snatch your soul and consume your body. Appropriately this issue contained H. P. Lovecraft's poem "Hallowe'en in a Suburb," which accurately describes how I feel about suburban living. It's downright scary. Upon further research I discovered that these weren't really ghouls, just ordinary folks showing up for the monthly Homeowner's Association meeting in [name deleted], the deadest [expletive deleted] suburb I ever lived in. To quote Mr. Lovecraft, "For the village dead to the moon outspread, Never shone in the sunset's gleam."

9. *Phantom* (vol. 1, no. 5.)

I picked this one for two reasons: First, it is classic and the illustration captures the feel of the old monster films, and second, because it's how I visualize my wife and me if we were back in the 1930s. (That would be reincarnation, my friends; I am not that old!) As you can see, we have been admiring several of my bestsellers when we are haunted by . . . my ex-wife, or is it my old

writing partner? Gosh, where *did* all those great story ideas really come from? It doesn't matter; their bones are safely behind that wall!

Phantom, vol. 1, no. 5 (© 1957 by Dalrow Publications, Ltd. Copyright not renewed, reprinted as public domain.)

10. *Weird Tales* (July 1949)

Weird Tales, July 1949 (© 1949 by Weird Tales. Reprinted by permission of Weird Tales Ltd.)

Last, but not least, is this beauty. Two unearthly demons wrestle in a cave entrance filled with snakey-things, spidery-things, and reptilian-things. Not to mention the sexual nature of the embrace and the imminent vampirism. At first I thought what a great poster this could make for a wrestling federation: DON'T MISS! THE END OF THE WORLD MATCH FEATURING DOMINIC THE DEMON VS. THE GARGOYLE MONSTER. Then I realized this is just the L.A. rave scene and decided to let the dead rest. Well, at least until 2:00 A.M. when the after hours clubs open. See you there and bring your dancing shoes! And wear something low cut, please.

JIM GERLACH'S TOP TEN
UNINTENTIONALLY HORRIFYING FILMS

Jim Gerlach—think Harvey Pekar, minus the raw sexual magnetism . . . and talent. When not abusing his authority within the Missouri Department of Social Services, he can be found holed up in his apartment, spending less time than you might think wondering if androids do indeed dream of electric sheep. He is surprisingly single and curiously hairy.

1. *Kangaroo Jack* (2003): Jerry Bruckheimer—I hate you!
2. Anything featuring Madonna, with the possible exception of *Evita* (1996): She's a talented singer with reasonably attractive breasts, but she really should limit her exposure to the one digital cable/satellite channel that plays music videos.
3. *Psycho* (1998): Settle down . . . the original is an undisputed classic, and the sequels provide an enjoyable revisiting of the main character twenty-plus years later. Mr. Van Sant's remake, however, was unnecessary and unsettling because it diminished my enjoyment of the original.
4. *Grumpier Old Men* (1995), *Out to Sea* (1997), and *The Odd Couple II* (1998): I'll get hate letters for saying this, but the only positive aspect of the death of Jack Lemmon and Walter Matthau . . . is

that there will be no more horrific late-career screen pairings for these two screen legends.

5. *Caddyshack II* **(1988)**: We all have bills to pay, but committing bank fraud would have been preferable to making this film. I've showered countless times since last seeing this, and still don't feel clean.

6. *Battlefield Earth* **(2000)**: Clearly Xenu is a wrathful deity for inflicting this upon us. Repent, ye sinners, or a sequel be upon you!!!

7. Every *Police Academy* sequel: You may fault me for liking the first one, but as for the rest of those steaming piles of cinematic excrement . . . we are in total agreement.

8. *Feast* (2005) and the rest of the Project Greenlight films: I do admit to enjoying the television series, but the final products are quite unpleasant.

9. Anything post–1983 with the words "National Lampoon" in the title: Need I elaborate?

10. Every spoof of *The Blair Witch Project*: For the love of God, stop making these. I would imagine the film-going public would gladly give the aspiring directors who make these things cash money to just put the damn camcorder down.

DAVEY JOHNSON'S ACCOUNT OF THE INVOLUNTARY REACTIONS OF TEN DATES TO TEN HORROR MOVIE MOMENTS

Davey Johnson is an actor/comedian and astute film connoisseur. He writes and performs sketch comedy for the Steve Allen Theatre, Garage Comedy, and the Upright Citizens Brigade, and has sold his soul in numerous television commercials. He also performs in Frenetics, a rapid-fire sketch show. You can learn more at www .myspace.com/daveyjohnson. Davey and The Book of Lists: Horror *coauthor Scott Bradley are video bros, having both worked for a certain disreputable video rental shop in Los Angeles. Weeeeeeeeee!!!*

1. *The Ring* (2002): Thank you, Samara. On our glimpse of your first victim's twisty face, my date's hand shot right into mine, remaining there through the rest of your American rampage. It was almost enough to forgive the fact that studios saw fit to release an onslaught of PG–13 "horror" films inspired by your success.

2. *Deadly Friend* (1986): Sometimes Wes Craven directs bad films. This was one of them. A turd-fest about a sexy robot (Kristy Swanson) gone bad, this film failed to freak, until the nosy neighbor, played by Anne Ramsey, got her comeuppance: a basketball through the head. The slo-mo head explosion was so graphic and out of place, my date buried her face in my round tummy. Close enough. Ramsey fans would also note that she went on to have scissors stabbed through her skull in *Throw Momma from the Train* (1987), and to appear in *Meet the Hollowheads* (1989).

3. *Faces of Death III* (1985): Sometimes, a film's reputation is enough to create a jump moment. This film came to my small Nebraska town late, in the spring of 1997. My high school was abuzz—"It shows real deaths!!!" My question: How real can something be when it's narrated by a man called Dr. Francis B. Gross? Your answer: zero real. However, the theatre, in the grand William Castle tradition, passed out empty popcorn buckets before the show and told its patrons that more were available if we had more puke than it could hold. Then, instead of fading the lights before the film, they cut the circuit, leaving us in instant darkness.

The effect was so jarring, many panicked, including my date. She hugged me tight. Then the film started.

4. **The Passion of the Christ (2004):** This torture-porn paved the way for films ranging from *Hostel* (2005) to *Hostel: Part II* (2007). Also, it fooled many non-horror fans into witnessing some of the most brutal images caught on film. Thanks, Mel! When a cat-o-nine-tails digs into Jesus Christ's (James Caviezel) side, and rips away to reveal His ribs, my date winced and dug her teeth into my shoulder. This is . . . not a date movie.

5. **The Exorcist III (1990):** This is a great, underrated film, well worth viewing if only for the carp scene. Also, it features the most nerve-wracking single shot ever captured, with, perhaps, the best payoff. This will not do it justice, but: A nighttime nurse hears a noise, investigates it, and, because demons hate snoops, meets the beheading end of a pair of autopsy shears. Slow and quiet, this scene was so disturbing that I, Captain Stoic, turned away and hid my face in my date's bosom. The discerning reader may claim that this does not represent a jump moment for my date, but let's not forget that for every action there is an equal and opposite reaction. Newtonian 'til I die!

6. **The Exorcist: The Version You've Never Seen (1973, 2000):** I did not have a date for this movie. The girl I was courting claimed she had seen *The Exorcist* years earlier; clearly, she was not a big fan of reading titles. So, I'm alone, as is Chris MacNeil (Ellen Burstyn), who is in her kitchen, confused as to why the lights are flickering most mysteriously. She did not see the Kabuki-faced Captain Howdy flash his sinister visage. The audience did, and jumped. A girl sitting next to me, heretofore a complete stranger, squeezed my right arm, whispering, "I never saw *that* before!" I consider *that* a date.

7. *Zombie* (1979): This film has more alternate titles (including *Zombi 2* and *Zombie Flesh-Eaters*) than South Dakota has people . . . and at one point a zombie fights a shark. It was the latter fact that compelled me to see a midnight showing. Now, I realize that these newfangled fast zombies are becoming mainstay, but there's genuine terror in the slow approach of a helplessly impending demise. Regarding *Zombie*, when the damsel's eye was slowly pulled toward the jutting splinter, the known result was so gut-wrenching that my date actually crawled over her seat and curled up in my lap. No fast zombies ever got me that much nookie.

8. *Family Portraits: A Trilogy of America* (2004): You want to be an a-hole? Watch this on a date. If they return your calls, you should question why. It's masterfully disturbing. As soon as we saw a woman using steel wool to brush her lips right off her face, my date covered her mouth and ran away. I've given away nearly nothing. Happy viewing.

9. *The Brood* (1979): My college sweetheart made some extra clams as a babysitter for a few of her professors. Slick as I am, I decided one night to keep her company by bringing over a scary movie, David Cronenberg's *The Brood*. So, the kids are asleep, and my sweetie's ready for some tape-in-VCR action. I put it in after turning off the lights, which is how she liked it. Everything was tops, until we reached the scene where one of the Brood takes out Candice Carveth's (Cindy Hinds) babysitting grandmother by tenderizing her head. My gal quickly covered her own head with a quilt, and demanded I turn on the lights.

10. *The Sixth Sense* (1999): The first review I heard of this film came from a portly gentleman seated two rows behind me, just moments after the end credits began to roll. Said he, "It's a friggin'

chick flick!" I suppose that was the big twist. We'd been Shyama-laned! However, my chick found it terrifying at parts. Though we're all used to Mischa Barton's vomiting now, in 1999 we were not expecting her to show up in Cole Sear's (Haley Joel Osment) makeshift bedroom tent, upchuck on face. When she did, my date let out an *Eeeeep!* and socked my leg. Not so bad, though, as she spent the rest of the movie massaging it apologetically. Now, there's a twist I like.